THE NEW MIDDLE AGES

BONNIE WHEELER, *Series Editor*

The New Middle Ages is a series dedicated to transdisciplinary studies of medieval cultures, with particular emphasis on recuperating women's history and on feminist and gender analyses. This peer-reviewed series includes both scholarly monographs and essay collections.

PUBLISHED BY PALGRAVE:

Women in the Medieval Islamic World: Power, Patronage, and Piety
  edited by Gavin R. G. Hambly

The Ethics of Nature in the Middle Ages: On Boccaccio's Poetaphysics
  by Gregory B. Stone

Presence and Presentation: Women in the Chinese Literati Tradition
  edited by Sherry J. Mou

The Lost Love Letters of Heloise and Abelard: Perceptions of Dialogue in Twelfth-Century France
  by Constant J. Mews

Understanding Scholastic Thought with Foucault
  by Philipp W. Rosemann

For Her Good Estate: The Life of Elizabeth de Burgh
  by Frances A. Underhill

Constructions of Widowhood and Virginity in the Middle Ages
  edited by Cindy L. Carlson and Angela Jane Weisl

Motherhood and Mothering in Anglo-Saxon England
  by Mary Dockray-Miller

Listening to Heloise: The Voice of a Twelfth-Century Woman
  edited by Bonnie Wheeler

The Postcolonial Middle Ages
  edited by Jeffrey Jerome Cohen

Chaucer's Pardoner and Gender Theory: Bodies of Discourse
  by Robert S. Sturges

Crossing the Bridge: Comparative Essays on Medieval European and Heian Japanese Women Writers
  edited by Barbara Stevenson and Cynthia Ho

Engaging Words: The Culture of Reading in the Later Middle Ages
  by Laurel Amtower

Robes and Honor: The Medieval World of Investiture
  edited by Stewart Gordon

Representing Rape in Medieval and Early Modern Literature
  edited by Elizabeth Robertson and Christine M. Rose

Same Sex Love and Desire among Women in the Middle Ages
  edited by Francesca Canadé Sautman and Pamela Sheingorn

Sight and Embodiment in the Middle Ages: Ocular Desires
  by Suzannah Biernoff

Listen, Daughter: The Speculum Virginum *and the Formation of Religious Women in the Middle Ages*
  edited by Constant J. Mews

Science, the Singular, and the Question of Theology
  by Richard A. Lee, Jr.

Gender in Debate from the Early Middle Ages to the Renaissance
  edited by Thelma S. Fenster and Clare A. Lees

Malory's Morte D'Arthur: Remaking Arthurian Tradition
  by Catherine Batt

The Vernacular Spirit: Essays on Medieval Religious Literature
  edited by Renate Blumenfeld-Kosinski, Duncan Robertson, and Nancy Warren

Popular Piety and Art in the Late Middle Ages: Image Worship and Idolatry in England 1350–1500
  by Kathleen Kamerick

CHAUCER'S JOBS

David R. Carlson

palgrave
macmillan

CHAUCER'S JOBS
Copyright © David R. Carlson, 2004, 2008.

All rights reserved.

First published in hardcover in 2004 by
PALGRAVE MACMILLAN™
175 Fifth Avenue, New York, N.Y. 10010 and
Houndmills, Basingstoke, Hampshire, England RG21 6XS
Companies and representatives throughout the world

PALGRAVE MACMILLAN is the global academic imprint of the Palgrave
Macmillan division of St. Martin's Press, LLC and of Palgrave Macmillan Ltd.
Macmillan® is a registered trademark in the United States, United Kingdom
and other countries. Palgrave is a registered trademark in the European
Union and other countries.

ISBN-13: 978–0–230–60243–4

Library of Congress Cataloging-in-Publication Data

Carlson, David R. (David Richard), 1956–
    Chaucer's jobs / by David R. Carlson.
        p. cm.—(The new Middle Ages)
    Includes bibliographical references and index.
    ISBN 1–4039–6625–7 (alk. paper)
    ISBN-10: 0–230–60243–6 (pbk)
        1. Chaucer, Geoffrey, d. 1400. 2. Poets, English—Middle English,
1100–1500—Biography. 3. Customs administration—Great Britain—
History—To 1500. 4. Justices of the peace—Great Britain—History—To
1500. 5. Royal households—Great Britain—History—To 1500. 6. Public
works—Great Britain—History—To 1500. 7. Professions in literature. I.
Title. II. New Middle Ages (Palgrave Macmillan (Firm))

PR1905.C37 2004
821 '.1—dc22   2004044433

A catalogue record for this book is available from the British Library.

Design by Newgen Imaging Systems (P) Ltd., Chennai, India.

First PALGRAVE MACMILLAN paperback edition: June 2008

10 9 8 7 6 5 4 3 2 1

Printed in the United States of America.

Transferred to Digital Printing in 2008

For my children (and theirs)

Chaucer portrait (c. 1716), in Philadelphia, Rosenbach Library, Ms. 1083/30, fol. 72v. Reproduced by permission of the Rosenbach Museum & Library, Philadelphia.

CONTENTS

CHAPTER 1

WORK

Chaucer was the police, not in an attenuated or metaphoric sense: in the better part of his mature employments, he was an official of the repressive apparatus of state. Before that, he was a lackey, in domestic personal service. As a poet, he was both, police officer and domestic servant, in differing ratios, in differing poems, at differing times in his literary career. Still, his poetic work complemented and carried through to the realm of culture the other work he did, and this quality of his poetry, being a straightforwardly homologous reflection in the cultural sphere of his practical work in personal and state service, made his place in literary history. Chaucer's jobs determined his literary-historical role, in other words, his work in service and discipline shaping his work in literature, and it in its turn determining his reception. Chaucer was made "the father of English poetry" not because he was a good poet, though he was. There were other good poets. Chaucer was made the father of English poetry because he was servile, doing useful work serving dominant social interests, materially and ideologically, in both his poetic and other employments.

1. Domestic Service

Not to mention Chaucer's later literary prominence, the notably quick social elevation of the Chaucer family, accomplished mostly in the poet's lifetime—a trajectory that saw the family rise from a provincial to the metropolitan mercantile elite (in part by way of mortal street-brawling that yielded a considerable inheritance, including the surname Chaucer), and from there, by way of Geoffrey's career, to noble affiliations, in the personal and public career of his son Thomas, with any Chaucerian grandchildren related to the royal family—colors retrospectively his early documented employments.[1] It was something, that the vintner's son made his way into aristocratic service. The work may have imparted a certain relatively enhanced status (by association) to him,[2] and Geoffrey did well at it: he moved, from some lesser to greater domestic establishments. On the other hand, the numerous records of this early work are only obliquely articulate, and significantly so. During these years, Chaucer was strictly subjected, and, as a subject in this sense, from the perspective of the noble households in which he served, personally he did not matter. The aristocratic household system in which he was disciplined in his adolescent years was first of all a machine for asserting the status of those who paid for it. The machine had the secondary effect of schooling those placed within it in servility, iterating and reiterating their quasi-human or subhuman dependence and inconsequence.[3]

The earliest record (preserved as binder's waste, worked into the covers of a manuscript volume of Lydgate and Hoccleve—a nice summation of the way the Chaucerian tradition will both rely on and cover over its dependence on Chaucer's earliest servility) shows *Galfridus Chaucer Londinie* by 1357 serving in the household of Elizabeth de Burgh, countess of Ulster, that is, the wife (having a separate domestic apparatus) of Lionel the prince, the second surviving son of King Edward III, junior only to (the "Black Prince") Edward, prince of Wales, the heir.[4] The London boy Geoffrey later served Lionel himself, and by June 1367, he was in the household of King Edward, where he is called variously *esquier scutifer et serviens hospicii, esquier de meindre degree, scutifer camere regis, scutifer regis, vallectus in hospicio domini regis,* a person *de familia regis, servant,* and finally, nearer the end of his term of household service, by the king himself, *nostre ame esquier* and *dilectus armiger noster.*[5] Precise dates for Chaucer's movements into and out of these three noble households cannot be established, nor can the relations amongst the different terms used to describe his work: these were not matters of sufficient importance to rate documentary attention at the time.

In various cognate ways, all the documents to do with Chaucer's early domestic service treat him so badly. In 1360, for example, the king paid a ransom of £16 for Chaucer's release, after the valet had been captured by the enemy in France. This was a considerable sum, more than was paid to ransom a few though not many others captured during the same campaign: four smiths' boys were had back for a total of £4. On the other hand, the king paid more to replace single horses lost in the same fighting (£20 per horse, for example) than he did to ransom Chaucer.[6] Worth less than a horse: the commonest sorts of records of Chaucer's early household employments suggest he was subjected in other ways too to such routines of humiliation.

Since Chaucer was later employed diplomatically, on missions of moment, requiring his expertise and endowing him with some personal authority—though still always he was a subordinate, *armiger* to another's *miles*, no matter how long he had remained about such errands—the tendency is to imagine that other, earlier dispatches, about which less is known, were equally momentous, the silence of the records being taken to represent discretion. More likely, the records say less because there was less to say. The errands were insignificant. Chaucer was given them because he was insignificant. The exemplary instance, the model to be used for making sense of the other laconic dispatches, is the first, dating from October 1360, noting Chaucer's dispatch from Calais back to England, carrying documents home from Prince Lionel: "per preceptum domini eundo cum litteris in Angliam" [for going into England with letters by order of his liege].[7] As late as the period 1377–1381—when Chaucer was no longer quite the same kind of domestic servant he had been earlier—he was still being sent back and forth between England and France ("in obsequium" is the recurrent phrase characteristic of this series of documents) as a *nuncium*, carrying letters: "alant en son message."[8]

What other kinds of sources tell about such errands indicates that the conditions of the work were punitive. The errand mattered more than the errand-doer, who could consequently expect to be ill-treated. The *Pearl*-poet used messengership on behalf of one's lord as the paradigm of subjection, to sum up his poem's point about the virtue of patience ("Other gif my lege lorde lyst on lyve me to bidde, / Other to ryde other to renne to Rome in his ernde, / What graythed me the grychchyng bot grame more seche?"); in Langland's representation, message-carriers' state was so reduced, "their poverty practically ensured their safety as they traveled."[9] In Chaucer's case, the documents to do with his dispatches on errand often concern his efforts to recover his expenses afterwards. Subjection doubles: Chaucer was sent on humbling errands; when additionally he had had to pay himself, he had then also to work at getting his money back. During 1378–1380, a period of nearly two years Chaucer spent trying to recover £14 the crown owed him for travel to Lombardy, his king handed out gifts worth over £100 to others' message-carriers.[10]

The characteristic kind of record from the early period, when Chaucer was in domestic service, are those documenting his receipt of clothing and clothing allowances, especially for state and stately occasions. In these and other early documents, Chaucer's name always appears buried deep in long lists of other names, routinely well down such lists whenever there is a discernible prioritizing of them, amongst the "esquiers de meindre degree," for example, below even "esquiers de greindre estat"[11]—though all men always before any women, even male chattels before the queen.

Seeing these documents as they are represented in the *Chaucer Life-Records* or cited in biographies is disorienting. Chaucer has been singled out, a whiggish importance adhering to occurrences of the poet's name.

The originals are insignificant documentary materials, unprepossessingly made, which were buried deep in archival storage amongst masses of other similar insignificant documentary records or were thrown out. The analogue is not contemporary literary manuscript treasures, painstakingly made and transmitted, but the jumbles of discarded cuneiform records turned up periodically by excavation of rubbish tips and ruined buildings. Buried deep in the lists of names, the lists in turn buried deep in heaps of other bureaucratic detritus, from the perspective of the archive itself in its original form, Chaucer's significance is that he had no significance here.

The gifts of clothing that came to Chaucer (amongst numerous others) came at regular intervals, seasonally, different sorts of clothing requisite for different times of year, and these regular *dona*—gifts, not earnings—were augmented with special dispensations for special occasions such as state funerals: twenty shillings *pro roba sua estievali*, twenty shillings likewise *pro roba sua yemali*, and something special for the Christmas season (from 1368 survives a list "of the lords and other folk of the household who are ordained by right to be given clothing of the king our lord for the Christmas next to come"); and black cloth, or black cloth and fur, for state funerals.[12]

The documents can be careless when it comes to naming names (a "Philip" Chaucer appears at one point, for example, perhaps also instancing the confusion of Geoffrey with his evidently more arresting wife that occurs elsewhere too)[13] and careless as well when it comes to designating offices (as witness the various equivocations about Chaucer's). Individuals, endowed with personal names, even the official functions they discharged within the household, counted for little.

The records are never so careless about the stuff that was to be distributed on these occasions, tracking fine distinctions of quantity and quality with precision. The dispensations for mourning cloth are nicely calibrated, by amount of material, kind of material, and degree of fineness within differing kinds of material, to reflect nice distinctions of status within the household. The writ of allowance for the 1369 funeral of the queen distinguishes among cloth *de colour noir long fin, de colour noir long, de colour noir court, de colour noir de une aune en laeure*, and *de colour noir strott de une aune en laeure*, also in specified lengths ranging between sixteen ells and three. Amongst those—eighty-eight in number—who were to be given *troys aunes de drap de colour noir court*, of the total of 685 persons made allowance in this same document, was Chaucer.[14]

Such evocative gifts of clothing continued to come to Chaucer for the rest of his life, even after he left regular household service. The latest such of which record survives dates from 1395–96, when the future Henry IV is recorded as purchasing minever for decorating a scarlet robe for Chaucer ("pro furruracione unius goune de scarleta longa Galfrido Chaucer").[15]

It is possible to imagine Chaucer, with slightly paranoid solipsism, feeling pleased and even flattered by such gifts. They remained gifts, however, not earnings, the point of which was to flatter the giver. The gifts evoke and objectify the abjection of their recipients, dependent on the patron's munificence even for such basic requisites of life as food, shelter, and clothing. Such gifts symbolize: the power of the gift-giver, as well as the corollary dependence of the recipient, asserting it in ritual, perhaps inessential form and reminding of it in the case of a dependent like the mature Chaucer, no longer otherwise constantly reminded of the nature of his relation with his head-of-household.

Moreover, this giving of cloth and clothing—more so the irregular gifts for special occasions—in addition to bespeaking dependence, also reduced recipients to object-status, on a level with the furniture, rooms and buildings, animals, and other equipment that were also decorated for the same occasions. Persons like Chaucer were not persons from this perspective but things, decorative objects, the purpose of which was to make show of their patron's wealth and power. The quantities and qualities of the materials expended on such decorative purposes were tied to issues of status, not need: the greater the occasion, the greater the display of magnificence, but the gift-giving had not to do with any idiosyncratic or human nature about the decorated objects. This was the context in which Chaucer began to write poetry.

2. The Customs Work

In 1374, *Galfridus Chaucer Londinie* moved out of the royal household back into the urban, mercantile ethos from which he had come, and the documentary evidence of his employments begins to be more articulate. His part in affairs henceforth was to be more active, characterized by greater public prominence and personal responsibility, and the records show as much.

1374 was the year in which Chaucer took possession of apartments over the Aldgate in the city of London[16] and was made comptroller of certain customs for the port of London, a series of interrelated appointments he was to hold over a period of twelve years, longer than he held any other office, except as a domestic. On June 8, 1374 he was appointed comptroller of the wool custom, a nominally "ancient" export duty on wool, wool-fells, and leather, which in fact dated only from 1275; comptroller of the wool subsidy, a heavier duty on the same goods, allowed the king by parliamentary grant from time to time, though inevitably renewed during the reign of Richard II; and comptroller of the petty custom, a series of miscellaneous lesser duties on various other merchandise, not subject to either of the aforegoing, and including duties on the finished cloth that figured increasingly prominently in English exports at the time of Chaucer's tenure of office.[17] These 1374 changes of official occupation and residence are associated with changes in Chaucer's literary work, too: the shift from dependence on French models to other influences, especially Italian, and, more broadly, from entertaining to instructing.

The changes in his living and working arrangements may have seemed to Chaucer to be a defenestration, a setback or stall in his social ascent. In any event, he remained dependent on his aristocratic connections and continued to serve. In general, the mercantile element in the city did not form an independent class-like interest but, as an economic entity, remained almost entirely reliant for its existence on monarchic and noble spending, war-finance above all, though also the whole consumption of these nonproductive social elements, who were refining tastes for various luxuries and extravagance. The engine of the eventual social and economic changes associated with the transition to capitalism was a productive and acquisitive element of the peasantry, not this dependent merchantry.[18] Also, more specifically, throughout this period Chaucer remained subject to a royally run system for the distribution of rewards, an important by-product of which was to remind those implicated in it of their subjection.

The commonest, and again most characteristic and revealing sort of record from this period of Chaucer's life are those to do with collecting what was due him from the royal Exchequer. He had been granted (not in recompense for services in the first place, but "de nostre grace especiale," the point being patronal munificence again) a life-annuity of ten pounds by Edward III in 1367.[19] In 1374, Chaucer was granted a similar annuity by John of Gaunt, at the time of his departure from the royal household.[20] From the same time as his appointments in customs, when the city also gave him the Aldgate leasehold for nothing, Chaucer was also due the comptroller's wage and annual reward, payable by the Exchequer. Following the accession of Richard II in 1377, Chaucer had his ten-pound life-annuity continued by the new king, and the daily pitcher of wine that in 1374 Edward III had allotted him was converted to a second life-annuity of ten pounds, payable by the Exchequer.[21] In 1388, Chaucer transferred these annuities to someone else, in exchange for a lump-sum cash-payment;[22] though this someone else continued to collect them, in 1394 Chaucer was granted another Exchequer life-annuity by Richard II ("de gracia nostra speciali" again), who also allotted Chaucer an annual tun of wine (worth perhaps ten pounds) in 1397.[23] At the accession of Henry IV, the new king continued the twenty-pound annuity (as well as the wine-allowance) granted Chaucer most recently by Richard II, and added another Exchequer annuity of an additional twenty pounds.[24] This list does not include additional occasional gifts from the crown, likewise payable by the Exchequer.

Chaucer's comptroller's wage was often paid by assignment directly from the customs revenues and so (unlike his comptroller's annual reward) it would not have had to be collected from the Exchequer immediately, though the Exchequer would still have required a proper accounting. His wages later, as justice of the peace, parliamentarian, and clerk of the works, were similarly treated: sometimes assigned for payment elsewhere, but always accountable. Chaucer's annuity from John of Gaunt was payable by the treasury of the duchy of Lancaster rather than the royal Exchequer—different treasury, similar routines. For the rest, it was payable by the Exchequer, semiannually, on September 29 in Michaelmas term and on April 31 in Easter term.

Throughout the last twenty-five years of his life, Chaucer had to make his way into Westminster, to present himself at the proper place in Whitehall Palace to collect these various monies *per manus proprias*, from the Exchequer itself. In addition to collecting his annuities and wages there, Chaucer had also to go to the Exchequer to recover expenses he incurred doing errands for the crown, taking months and years in some cases; for the annual audit of his accounts as comptroller of customs, again a matter of weeks or months; and eventually for drawing money for the building-projects he supervised as clerk of the king's works, likewise subject to Exchequer audit.

Whitehall Palace had grown by accretion, and by this point the floor-plans resembled very late New Kingdom Egyptian temple precincts, where once regular outlines have been in-filled irregularly, discontinuous ad hoc improvisations made permanent over time, yielding a warren of irregular corridors connecting oddly sized, counterintuitively related rooms, like a maze only grown organically, without the rectilinear plotting usually put into maze construction.[25] Accounting procedures at the Exchequer within Whitehall Palace were at least equally disorienting.[26] The Exchequer was two departments, in fact, rather than just the one: upper and lower (though the terminology no longer had to do with their spatial relations inside the buildings), the lower doing the paying out of monies and the upper making sure that the paying out was done properly. Chaucer's monies, like the monies of numerous others, were payable semiannually, but, because of various transient exigencies at both ends of the transactions, the monies were never paid semiannually. For one reason or another, either the Exchequer paid late or Chaucer wanted the money early, the various resultant arrears (by the Exchequer) and prests (to Chaucer) then having to be carried forward from one semiannual accounting period into the next, and sometimes, more and less, into the next and the next and so on.

Prests made to Chaucer took two forms, namely: (a) True advances, made before any installment was due; (b) Payments of money due made in full or on account and without the necessary mandate, or occasionally made for part only of the money due and with the mandate. Payments originally made on account frequently became true advances by the payment of an install-ment in full, regardless of the sum already paid. Similarly, real advances were sometimes balanced by omissions of a later installment.[27]

In other words, not only were the monies never paid on the same dates, regularly, when they might have been expected; also, the amount of money that changed hands on these occasions was never the same twice. In addi-tion to juggling arrears and prests, in ways and for reasons that are not always immediately clear, clerks in the lower Exchequer seem occasionally to have resorted to still more extreme measures to make things look right for the upper Exchequer, with the troubling consequence that "the exact meaning of certain phrases used in [the financial] recitals" might on any occasion have been "immaterial to the Exchequer clerks."[28] The Exchequer also worked with a different calendar from the rest of the government and world, the so-called "Exchequer year."[29]

In this period, the Exchequer replaced the household as the quotidian mechanism for teaching Chaucer who he was and where he fit in the scheme of things. It put a mediating, bureaucratic layer between the crown and the subject still serving it, and the mediation may have brought with it for Chaucer a greater sense of autonomy. Having one's own house and respon-sibility for one's own clothing and food, more or less—as Chaucer did only after leaving the royal household in 1374—would also have contributed. But Chaucer was still always beholden to the crown, dependent on it for his well-being, in ways that the perverse ministrations of the Exchequer clerks would have reminded him. To know, by quarterly or monthly or constant experi-ence, covering a period of twenty-five years, this sort of inscrutable, implaca-ble system, of offices rather than the shifting personnel that filled them, where words might not mean what they said, even when written down and enrolled, would be to move about constantly in a disciplinary miasma, some-times more palpable, sometimes less, but never wholly lifting.

Chaucer's own work, during this lengthy period of his subjection to the disciplinary administrations of the Exchequer, diffuse and pervasive, was itself in cognate varieties of surveillance, first in surplus-extraction as a cus-toms officer, later in order-maintenance as Justice of the Peace and parlia-mentarian, and finally in ideologically driven revenue dispersal as clerk of works. Chaucer not only was subject to a disciplinary apparatus now, as he had been in his earlier servile household employments, but took an active part in making the state disciplinary apparatus work.

His employment in revenue extraction at the Wool Quay established the pattern. Import and export duties on wool and wool products—by far

England's chief trading commodities—made up the chief extraordinary revenue stream for the crown, at a time when such extraordinary revenue streams were of special importance to it, for funding its military undertakings, as well as the dissipation and profligacy of the Ricardian court, widely denounced in contemporary sources, documentary and literary.[30] Most famously, the chronicler-historian Thomas Walsingham castigated the degeneracy of the noble company Richard kept by him at court, in phrases repeated from contemporary poetry ("And nu ben theih liouns in halle, and hares in the feld"): "But these were knights rather more devoted to Venus than to Bellona, more potent in bed than on the battlefield, mightier of tongue than of lance, full of talk but then rather quiet when it came to actually doing anything war-like."[31] In the parliamentary "Record and Process" of King Richard's deposition in 1399, the first of the articles, charging him "for his evil government" in general, specifies, "namely, that he gave the goods and possessions of the crown to unworthy persons, and otherwise indiscreetly dissipated them, as a result of which he had to impose needlessly grievous and intolerable burdens upon the people;" and further, in the fifteenth article, that the king "not only gave away the greater part of his said patrimony to unworthy persons,. . .but he [also] dissipated it prodigiously upon the ostentation, pomp and vainglory of his own person."[32] The prodigious Ricardian "ostentation, pomp and vainglory" even attracted a quasi-official apologist, Roger Dymmok, who argued, *inter alia*, that the extravagance was a needful counter-revolutionary measure in present circumstance ("in fact it is obligatory for the kinds of lords whose job it is to rule peoples, in order that they might strike fear into their peoples, lest they rise up against their superiors too readily. For when peoples can see" their princes' "magnificence, they will regard their rulers as wealthy and competent, and they will regard overthrowing them as a thing so far impossible, to just that degree that their princes are seen to stand above their peoples").[33] "Unthyrft and wombes joyse / Steriles et luxuriosi [unproductive and luxuriant], / Gentyles, gromes, and boyse, / Socii sunt atque gulosi [are allies and ravenous]," a poet complained:

> The ryche maketh myry
>> Sed vulgus collacrematur [while the common folk lament];
> The pepulle ys wery,
>> Quia ferme depopulatur [for almost all is laid waste].[34]

Inasmuch as Chaucer contributed to such spectacle at court, by serving in it during his period of domestic employments about the royal household (and entertaining: "The ryche maketh myry"), the criticisms were already criticisms of him, individually. Thereafter, when working in customs,

Chaucer was additionally implicated by his oversight of the means by which the spectacle was financially sustained. Chaucer's contributions to the courtly scandals of the reign here, by raising the funds that made them possible, may have been less visibly direct than his earlier contributions, by the service he rendered at court, though it had been small service and insignificant. These later contributions were of greater consequence. The connection was recognized amongst Chaucer's contemporaries, the *Crowned King* poet, for example, warning the monarch against neglect of the welfare of those having care of the productive economic basis on which ruling-class ease and splendor rested ("Je voy en siecle qu'ore court gentes superbire, / De autre biens tenir grant court" [I see at the present time men giving themselves airs, living in great state on others' goods]: "Qui satis est dives non sic ex paupere vives" [Thou who art rich enough, live not thus on the poor man!]):

> The playnt of the pouere peple put thou not behynde,
> For they swope and swete and swynke for thy fode;
> Moche worship they wynne the in this worlde riche,
> Of thy gliteryng gold and of thy gay wedes,
> Thy proude pelure, and palle with preciouse stones,
> Grete castels and stronge, and styff walled townes.[35]

Furthermore, the contemporary *Richard the Redeless* poet asserted the particular causal nexus linking the Ricardian courtly excess to the Ricardian financial exactions, mentioning specifically "the custum of wullus" and "the custum of the clothe" for which Chaucer was made responsible in 1374:

> For where was euere ony cristen kynge that ye euere knewe,
> That helde swiche an household be the halfdelle
> As Richard in this rewme thoru myserule of other,
> That alle fynys for faughtis ne his fee-fermes. . .
> Ne alle the issues of court that to the kyng longid,
> Ne sellynge, that sowkid siluer with faste,
> Ne alle the prophete of the lond that the prince owed,
> Whane the countis were caste with the custum of wullus,
> Myghte not areche ne his rent nouther,
> To paie the pore peple that his puruyours toke,
> Withoute preiere at a parlement a poundage biside,
> And a fifteneth and a dyme eke,
> And with all the custum of the clothe that cometh to fayres?[36]

"That the pore is thus i-piled, and the riche forborn"—by consequence of which "The comonys love not the grete"—was Chaucer's doing.[37] For a

WORK   11

dozen years, Chaucer had a crucial role to play in managing this crucial business of wealth-transfer, his role being to police the process of revenue extraction on behalf of the crown.

The comptroller's job was to check the work of those responsible for collecting the revenues—the nominal collectors, who were normally absentees, and their deputies at the actual point of collection—to assure that the proper dues were being collected and (more to the point) that the dues collected were being properly accounted for: that they were not being pocketed or otherwise improperly diverted but that the surplus extracted went where it was supposed to go. The terms of Chaucer's appointment, specifying that the records had to be kept in his own hand, subject to annual Exchequer audit, meant that, though he did exercise a right to depute the record-keeping to someone else from time to time, when he had to absent himself on other royal business, Chaucer was otherwise present about the Wool Quay daily.[38]

The potential for abuse that characterizes this system was so great that the conflicts of interest built into it, structurally even, layer upon layer, come to seem, not accidental by-products, but necessary components, without which the system could not have been kept functioning. The customs system was corrupt by design. From the crown end, customs revenues could be regular and reliable, more or less, but were too slow to come in, especially when a military expedition needed funding. The chief outlays were punctual, at the front end, having to be paid at once, before the expedition could begin. The only way the crown could raise the large sums of ready money required was by borrowing, even on security of the crown jewels, and the chief current repository of such ready money was in the keeping of the merchant oligarchy of the city of London.[39]

For repaying its loans from the civic oligarchy, the crown regularly used the customs revenues, licensing its creditors to manage their own repayment directly out of the customs. The practice was to appoint to the collectorships of customs the great merchant capitalists of the city themselves, who had loaned the crown money in the first place, so that they could repay themselves—and their fellows, former and future collectors—directly by farms or by assignment on particular customs revenues. The crown could obtain ready money but without having to work directly at discharging the debts it incurred, economizing thereby.

Tax evasion of various sorts was a problem with this system, perhaps ultimately not a very great problem, though the natural paucity of direct evidence makes the problem difficult to see. There were cases, though known only when the evasion went wrong somehow. A comptroller was jailed for a time in 1389, in circumstances that suggest his collusion with a collector and a London importer to evade duties of about £65. In another case, a minor customs officer was fined for colluding in evasion with a cloth-exporter, afterwards attempting to bribe his collector and comptroller—who had both been excluded from the deal at the outset, it would seem—to continue to ignore the evasion. Chaucer himself, as comptroller in 1376, was granted wool worth over £70 that a London exporter had had to forfeit for evading duties on the same goods, in circumstances suggesting that the grant came to Chaucer by way of reward for having exposed the attempted evasion, an exposure more remunerative for him in the circumstance, apparently, than ignoring it would have been.[40]

Customs offices, including collectorships and comptrollerships, were desirable because officers made money holding them, one way and another. "For two yere a tresorier, twenty wyntre aftre / May lyue a lord-is life, as leued men tellen."[41] The evasion was kept to reasonable levels, however, by virtue of the interest the collectors had in making sure that customs duties were paid, as creditors of the crown seeing to their own repayment out of the duties they were able to collect. There were reasons why collectors (and comptrollers) would have been willing to collude in evasion: bribes. But evasion might impede loan-repayment, and the loans generally would have been worth more—hundreds and thousands of pounds—than any bribery a fiscally prudent importer–exporter would offer. If no duties were collected, there could be no loan repayment.

The greater problem than evasion was rapacity on the part of collectors—an excess of zeal about paying themselves back, or otherwise enriching themselves at the expense of the cash-hungry monarchy or import–export merchants. Here too the restraint was structural: less the surveillance of comptrollers like Chaucer than the fact that the collectors themselves were also the chiefest import–export merchants, on whose trade the customs dues were levied. As collectors, in other words, the same persons would have been stealing from themselves, as import–export merchants, if they became overzealous about duties-collection. The largest wool-exporter during Chaucer's comptrollership was also the collector of the wool-custom and the wool subsidy throughout the same period: Nicholas Brembre, also lord mayor of London, a major creditor of the crown, and a crony of the king, though only until his execution (for corruption, in part) by the "Merciless" parliament in 1388.[42] The merchant-oligarchs were loaning the crown money (at extortionate rates) and then repaying themselves (at favorable rates, not to mention the possibility of their allowing themselves the occasional bribe) by collecting customs duties (again at favorable rates) from themselves, on their own exports, to be marketed abroad (at a profit).

There was nevertheless scandal about this system, in the "Good" parliament of 1376, during Chaucer's comptrollership. The problem was that a small number of the infirm king's personal favorites were taking too much, to the exclusion of various eminent others, who would have felt they were due some greater share of the profits.[43] The person scapegoated was Richard Lyons—a bastard, consequently the more expendable from most perspectives, except that he had made himself very rich. His tomb effigy was to feature what the Elizabethan antiquary John Stow described as "a large pursse on his right side, hanging in a belt from his left shoulder,"[44] giving some evidence of the state of contemporary merchant self-consciousness. The man was a wallet.

In parliament in 1376, Lyons was found to have committed three varieties of excess.[45] Foremost, he was negotiating loans on behalf of the crown, to the crown from himself, at considerable rates of profit. The notable instance was a loan of £20,000, for which he paid himself a £10,000 premium—though this fifty per-cent margin appears to have been standard, as John of Gaunt testified to the "Good" parliament[46]—then repaying the loan to himself out of customs revenues. Lyons had owned a large share of the customs revenues since 1372, when he had been made collector of the petty custom and the petty subsidy for all English ports, excepting Great Yarmouth. Lyons was also found to have been buying royal debts from other creditors of the crown at discount and then paying himself the debts back at the full rate, out of the customs revenues. Finally, Lyons was also selling licenses allowing exporters to evade the Calais Staple: monies that otherwise staple-using exporters would have paid other participants in the staple-system, including the crown, were going directly to Lyons, at a discount, but still at personally remunerative levels.

The scandal reveals some of the potential for abuse within the system, but also that no one was much concerned. Few besides Lyons' competitive compeers in the merchant oligarchy were put out by what had been taking place. Lyons was removed from his customs farming offices, temporarily. His comptroller Chaucer—who had certified to the Exchequer at the end of 1374 and again in 1375 that all was well with the Lyons regime about the petty customs in the port of London—was untouched. After Lyons' removal, the crown and the other oligarchs continued as before, with new collectors, including Brembre, who were much the same as the old collector, only better bred, perhaps, and more circumspect. Early in the reign of Richard II, Lyons himself was reappointed, and he died still a rich man, in 1381, when he was one of the few people whom the revolutionaries troubled to execute in London.[47] Chaucer continued in his comptrollership as ever, until his promotion to higher office. The Latin tag in *Mum and the Sothsegger*, " '*qui tacet consentire videtur*,' " might be felt pertinent: "Who-so hath insight" "of shame or of shonde outher, / And luste not to lette it, but leteth hit forth passe," "He shal be demyd doer of the same deede."[48] But it is not. From the perspective of Chaucer and the others implicated, including the crown, evidently, there was no substantive wrong-doing, only excess, nor were substantive changes warranted. Fundamentally, the Lyons regime in customs was business as usual.

Policing the collector was what Chaucer did. The operating presumption was that the collector would try to cheat, and the comptroller would try to catch him at it; but at the same time, while the comptroller watched the collector, the Exchequer was watching the comptroller, who was evidently expected to try to cheat too. People did cheat. Some were caught, paid fines, went to jail, or were otherwise inconvenienced. Such failures of the system were extraordinary, however. For the most part, it functioned smoothly. It did not cost the crown much. All that was required was for the crown to leave the merchant oligarchy alone about its financial manipulations, in an expectation that, when there was need, money would be made available.

There was so little to the Chaucerian surveillance of customs revenues because of the community of interest between the monarch and the merchant-oligarchs, the aristocracy and the dependent urban elite. The relation was symbiotic, or parasitic. The merchants enriched themselves by supplying nobles with consumables and services, and then financed the same noble consumption by loaning money back to the nobility for further spending. As long as it continued to want to spend, the nobility needed the merchants, for goods and services as well as financing; more importantly, the merchants needed aristocratic spending, on which they were dependent. The nobility could have lived without merchants, though it did not want to. The merchants could not have lived without the nobility. Dependence provided the basic check.

As comptroller of customs, Chaucer was still a royal servant, as he had been in domestic employment, serving the king. His annual reward for the comptrollership was paid by the Exchequer, which was also dispensing his annuities. At the same time, Chaucer also shared much with the merchant-oligarchs whom he was also serving in a sense by this time. He was one of them, too, by virtue of familial circumstance (Lyons was a vintner, an associate of Chaucer's father, for example, and Brembre was married to an heiress of the pre-eminent oligarch, John Stodey, also a vintner, with whom Chaucer's father likewise had had dealings[49]), of daily familiarity at work (the names of Chaucer's collectors and their deputies recur again and again throughout the records of Chaucer's life, in contexts of all sorts), and of common financial interest, beyond bribes and profiteering: it was his collector, for example, who paid Chaucer his daily comptroller's wages. Of course Chaucer can be expected to have cooperated with the oligarchs, to have worked with them. Fundamentally, all were interested in preserving the well-being of the ruling class, Chaucer's only distinction as comptroller being that his particular part was to assure that the operation went smoothly on behalf of the crown rather than the oligarchs. Both the crown and the merchant-oligarchy wanted the same thing: more profit off others' production. Chaucer was amongst the "satellites" bringing it about that "Li riches a tort enrichiz sunt de autri aver" [The rich wrongfully get rich off others' belongings]:

> Ecce pravi pueri pauperes predantur,
> Ecce donis divites dolose ditantur,
> Omnes pene proceres mala machinantur,
> Insani satellites livore letantur.
>
> [Depraved boys, lo, they prey on the poor; rich men, lo, wrongfully get rich off their dues; all but all the nobles work at their wicked machinations; their servants, gone mad, take pleasure in spite.][50]

3. Justice of the Peace

As Justice of the Peace in Kent subsequently, Chaucer did similar work, albeit that the office put him on a different regional stage and more immediately at a point where the class conflict was open and direct, rather than at a point of intra-class fractional cooperation about exploiting the productive elements of the economy.[51] Chaucer worked in surveillance again, on behalf of the crown again, though in a way more directly to be associated with modern-day police-work. Chaucer became part of "the apparatus of state coercive power," in Antonio Gramsci's phrase, " 'legally' enforcing discipline on those groups who do not consent, either actively or passively," operating at a point of "crisis of command and direction, when spontaneous consent has failed," calling instead for "direct domination."[52] To this Chaucerian police-work there would also have been an immaterial, abstractly coercive dimension, of class-advertising or propaganda: "there is no such thing as a purely repressive apparatus," as Louis Althusser specified, since such apparatuses, thoroughly considered, can be seen to "function by ideology" as well, "both to ensure their own cohesion and reproduction, and in the 'values' they propound externally." Nonetheless, as a justice of the peace for Kent 1385–89, Chaucer was a part of the kind of repressive apparatus then functioning, "secondarily by ideology"—"since repression, e.g., administrative repression, may take non-physical forms"— but always "at least ultimately, predominantly and massively by repression, including physical repression," or, less abstractly, "by violence."[53]

No records of cases heard by the commissions on which Chaucer sat, as a lesser commissioner, have survived, so the kind of work he was doing has to be inferred from records of the work of other such commissions, the terms of his commission, and the historical circumstances in which he was working.[54] Kent was where the 1381 revolt began and grew, and where afterwards the work of repression was the more fierce. "In Kent this kare began, / Mox infestando potentes [late assaulting the powerful]," in the poet's account; "Nede they fre be most, / Vel nollent pacificari [nor would they be pacified]." The immediate ruling-class reaction was said to have been confused dismay:

> When the comuynes bigan to ryse,
>   Was non so gret lorde, as I gesse,
> That thei in herte bigon to gryse,
>   And leide heore jolyte in presse.[55]

A recovery of composure ensued, and then "Owre kyng hadde no rest" "Ne pateat sceleri via, sed mors inde futura" [Seeing to it that, for crime, there would be no way ahead, but only death to come of it]:

> Tandem post modicum, proceres simul arma resumunt,
> Pravos consumunt, vulgus capiunt inimicum.
> Horum pejores et conspirando priores,
> Ob pravos mores, detruncant ut proditores.
> Mactant signiferos, nec eis curant misereri,
> Ut doceant miseros proditoria tanta vereri.
>
> [Soon thereafter, the nobles took up arms again as one: the wicked they laid waste, and besieged the hated mob. The worst of them and the leaders of the conspiracy they cut down like traitors, on account of their depravity. They slaughtered the standard-bearers, nor cared they to show pity, in order to teach the wretched to dread betrayal on so great a scale again.][56]

As these verses imply, approvingly, there were massacres, with hundreds of victims, where armed men, including mounted knights-at-arms, on official business, rounded up or cornered revolutionaries and slaughtered them, at Sudbury and at Hatfield Peverel, where the boy-king is reported to have made his "Churls you were and churls you will remain" remarks:

> You will remain in bondage, not as before but incomparably harsher. For as long as we live and, by God's grace, rule over the realm, we will strive with mind, strength and goods to suppress you so that the rigor of your servitude will be an example to posterity. Both now and in the future people like yourselves will always have your misery as an example before their eyes; they will find you a subject for curses and will fear to do the sort of things you have done.[57]

And there were executions, too, notoriously under the "bloody assize" of Robert Tresilian—with whom Chaucer was to serve on his Kentish peace commission—who "spared no one," "causing great slaughter:"

> Whoever was accused before him on the grounds of rebellion, whether justly or out of hate, immediately suffered the sentence of death. He condemned (according to the nature of their crimes) some to beheading, some to hanging, some to drawing through the cities and then hanging in four parts of the cities and some to disemboweling, followed by the burning of their entrails before them while the victims were still alive, and then their execution and the division of their corpses into quarters to be hanged in four parts of the cities.[58]

The disembowelings, dismemberments, and other lurid methods used by Tresilian's assize and elsewhere would seem to have proved too inefficient. Generally, recourse was had to simpler beheadings and hangings. The gibbets made a ring around London, according to one chronicler, and lined the roadways between "the other cities and towns of the south county."[59]

The rebels of 1381 were violent carefully, chiefly not to persons but to things: contentious forms of property evidently to be regarded as oppressive and violent in their turn, so that to treat them with violence was just. The salient case was the Savoy Palace, destroyed but not looted, remarkably; the characteristic form was the holocaust of muniments.[60] The rebels also attacked three kinds of persons, all unequivocally agents of more or less direct order-enforcement: lawyers, tax-gatherers, and justices of the peace. The revolt "represented a spontaneous reaction against those"—"particularly those who acted as commissioners of the peace"—"who had for too long monopolized and abused royal government in the shires." It was

> not simply a rebellion against an inequitable tax but a protest against some twenty years of mismanagement, during which a small number of prominent landholders sitting on commissions of the peace had effectively taken over the administration of the shires and run it largely for their own benefit.[61]

That Chaucer may have beaten a friar in the street adjacent to one of the Inns of Court would probably not have been sufficient to qualify him as a lawyer, even in the fourteenth century.[62] With this possible exception, however, the persons whom the rebels attacked in 1381 were persons doing the same jobs as Chaucer. The peace commissions were "heavily involved in the general campaign of repression."[63] As a justice appointed to the Kent commission, Chaucer had a prominent public, official part in cleaning up after the revolt and seeing to it that there would be no repetition.

At the time of the rebellion in 1381, though Chaucer was still a resident of London, he did not meet the seditious riot in person. When the rebels entered the city by the Aldgate, over which the apartments in which Chaucer lived *per grace especiale* were located, he was away. But even without the rebel invasion, the Aldgate was already a public, visible location for direct expression of official control. Taxes were extracted there, on goods being brought into the city, and, because it was a vulnerable point, it was fortified and guarded from time to time. Chaucer would have seen the legal violence being applied at his doorstep openly and regularly. The gates did duty as places of incarceration, too: "some were used regularly as prisons, others as prisons temporarily."[64]

Though he was able to avoid the rebels in 1381, given his proximity to places and persons involved, memories and understanding of what the rebels had done in London would have colored Chaucer's subsequent work in "the apparatus of state coercive power," where he remained in association with persons like Brembre and William Walworth, who had had direct involvement in putting down the revolt in London at the time. It was Walworth, for example, who stabbed the peasant leader Wat Tyler to death in Smithfield (where Chaucer was to stage a tournament for the king), at the critical juncture June 15, later to be praised for doing so: "Regem transfodere ductor vulgi voluisset, / Ni Walword propere caput ejus praeripuisset [The mob's leader meant to run the king through, had not quick Walworth put the man's head off first]."[65] A clearer image of the merchant oligarchy's disposition to serve aristocratic need is not to be wished for.

By 1385, when Chaucer took up his appointment as a peace commissioner, the work of repression was ongoing in Kent, albeit in less spectacular forms, but still in ways that would have reminded of the continuity of his work with the fiercer effort of the cataclysmic, immediately postrevolutionary period. Chaucer resided in Kent after about 1386, and being a property-holding resident gave him an additional interest in order-maintenance there. By statute, commissioners of the peace were required to be magnates or gentry or legal professionals—persons whose stake in preserving order was already substantial, like Chaucer.[66] Moreover, Chaucer was appointed justice of the peace to replace a person—also a king's coroner and attorney of the king's bench—whose house had been invaded and burned by the revolutionaries in 1381, destroying all documentary records of his official functions.[67]

The commissions of the period of Chaucer's appointment had ordinary police jurisdictions, inquiring into and punishing disruptions of the peace of all or most sorts—most extortions excepted, which required to be referred to a different sort of court, extortion being the form of robbery practiced by persons with more power on persons with less, by violence or threat of it.[68] In 1386, when Chaucer was appointed, the commissions were under a general reform, whereby the separate commissions formerly charged with enforcing the ordinance and statutes of laborers were being eliminated—an administrative streamlining, which also had the benefit of hiding this salient of class-oppression under the rubric of maintaining peace—and their work was being brought altogether under the purview of the commissions of the peace, which had in any event already enjoyed such jurisdiction.[69]

In taking up his appointment from the king, "for hearing and determining diverse felonies and misdemeanors about the county of Kent, as well within as without its liberties,"[70] Chaucer swore the statutory oath "to serve the king, well and loyally, in the capacity of keeper of the peace and justice of laborers, weights and measures."[71] The statutes invoked in the oath extended to provision that "no servant or laborer, man or woman, may go out of the hundred, rape, or wapentake where he is staying before the end of his period of service there or go on a journey far off unless he bear a letter patent under seal showing the reason for his going and the time of his return."[72] Chaucer was also expressly charged with responsibility "over all who shall go or ride, or shall henceforth presume to go or to ride, in armed force, in conventicles, contrary to our peace and to the disturbance of our folk, and especially over such as shall lay in wait, or shall henceforth presume to lay in wait, for wreaking mayhem or doing injury amongst our folk."[73] Special provision was made for the commissions' safe record-keeping ("all records and documents of process rendered before you you are to keep under strong and secure guard"), especially important by light of the revolutionaries' attention to such material, and for scrutiny of the commissions' profits ("the proceeds of fines and amercements and other dues appertaining to the king you will cause to be rendered complete in written indentures"), for purposes of the familiar Exchequer audit again, to assure that the crown got its share of the proceeds.[74] As if again to ensure that they would discover actionable crime amongst those over whom they enjoyed jurisdiction, the commissioned justices paid themselves too out of the fines that their commissions imposed.[75]

The commissions so charged sat quarterly or more often, in three-day sessions, in different places within their districts. Out of session, single justices performed singly various cognate functions about keeping the peace. As Margaret Galway showed, "a resident justice" like Chaucer

> had to see to the enforcement of statutes concerning the regulation of wages, prices, labor and other matters, a task which often involved judicial as well as administrative business. He was also expected, among other things, to see that the inhabitants of his district did not go about armed, practice terrorism,

hold unlawful meetings, brawl at inns, or damage property not their own. He was empowered to arrest "suspects" and to take sureties from anyone who threatened injury to another. His jurisdiction covered "all manner of felonies and trespasses" short of treason. . . .The punishments justices could impose were loss of life or limb, imprisonment, fines, forfeiture of chattels to the crown and of lands to the lord.[76]

The work involved would have amounted to full-time employment.

We do not know that, in any particular instance, Chaucer was jailing people, overseeing executions, enforcing the pass-laws, or otherwise hounding seditious vandals, though he swore to do so and others positioned as he was did. The evidence does not permit such specificity. Still, Chaucer was employed at repressive (specifically, counterrevolutionary) police-work, on behalf of the crown, by appointment from the king. The commissions' geographical pervasion, the frequency and regularity of their public sessions, and the justices' out-of-session vigilance lent them at least this general disciplinary function, apart from any particular direct applications of violence they would have authorized, of making palpable the state's power to enforce, not justice necessarily, but order.

The innocuously named commission of walls and ditches to which Chaucer was royally appointed in 1390, after the end of his term as justice of the peace, worked similarly, at enforcement of class-discipline.[77] There had been a violent storm in March that made maintenance of waterways and works an acute problem, though the fundamental problem was of longer standing. The job of maintenance devolved, not directly on those whose property was affected, but on their tenants, who tended to resist additional impositions of uncompensated labor. Commissions of the sort to which Chaucer was appointed were to see to it that tenant-laborers did what the landlords wanted them to do—"by reason of our royal dignity, for overseeing the well-being of our kingdom," in the terms of the royal commission—by punishing those who would not.[78] Policing class distinction, prosecuting the class struggle on behalf of ruling interests by various legal forms of violence: this was Chaucer's job during the six-year period 1385–1390 of his employment as a royal commissioner.

From the perspective of this more important (though largely invisible) class-disciplinary work in which Chaucer and others like him were engaged during the postrevolutionary 1380s, parliament was a sideshow. Participation in it was restricted to "peeris and prelatis," with some admixture of dependant representatives, sitting as knights of the shire or burgesses, in commons, though commons participation was not strictly necessary and had only become unexceptional recently, in the reign of Edward III.[79] By consequence of its origin, in the king's peers' council, parliament did serve from time to time as a more or less public forum for factional infighting within the polity's ruling elite, between magnates and monarch, or amongst factions of the great, with mortal result sometimes, as in the case of Brembre. In practice, however, parliament was functioning chiefly as the institutional mechanism, traditionally sanctioned, by means of which the crown imposed taxes—there was no "right to grant or refuse taxation" in parliament, but only "a parliamentary obligation of consent which really meant no more than negotiation as to amount"[80]—which the un- and under-represented many then had to pay, or to evade.

That "Ceux que grauntent ne paient ren est male consititutum" [It is wrong to ordain that those who make a grant pay nothing] was recognized: "Nam concedentes nil dant regi, sed egentes" [Not one farthing do they give the king; it is the poor who pay] (44–45).[81] The alternative proposed by this contemporary witness was to make the rich pay ("Des grantz um le dust lever, Dei pro timore; / Le pueple plus esparnyer qui vivit in dolore" [The tax should have been levied on the great, for the fear of the Lord, more to spare the common folk, who live in affliction] [48–49]), since for them paying would not have posed the same problems ("Rien greve les grantz graunter regi sic tributum" [It does not hurt the great thus to make the king a grant] [41]):

> Depus que le roy vodera tam multum cepisse,
> Entre les riches si purra satis invenisse.
> E plus a ce que m'es avys et melius fecisse
> Des grantz partie aver pris et parvis pepercisse.
> Qui capit argentum sine causa peccat egentum.
>
> [Since the king wants to take such a huge amount, he will be able to find enough among the rich. And indeed in my opinion, he would have done both more and better to have taken something from the mighty, and to have spared the lowly. He who takes money from the needy without good cause commits sin.]
>
> (31–35)

From this perspective, parliament was a tool of extortionate theft: "A dire grosse veritee est quasi rapina: / Res inopum capita nisi gratis est quasi rapta" [To state the substance of the case it is like robbery: To take the goods of the poor against their will is as good as spoliation] (59–60). "Cest consail n'est mye bien, sed viciis pollutum" [This measure is in no wise good but tainted with vice]; moreover, it was predictable ("Je me doute s'ils ussent chief quod vellent levare" [Had they but a leader I doubt there might be a rising]) that people would act as if on such a perception, that it was "contra Dei nutum" [against the will of God] that "Les simples deyvent tot doner" [The lowly have to give all] (42, 64, and 43). The revolt in 1381 was touched off by widespread spontaneous evasion of the (regressive) third Ricardian poll tax of the same year, four pence a head for every lay person in the kingdom over fourteen years of age—following after other poll taxes in 1379 and 1377, subsidies, subsidies-and-a-half, and double subsidies (ten-, fifteen-, and twenty-percent levies, respectively, on moveable goods, i.e., not wealth in land) in 1380, 1379, 1374–75, and 1372–73, and the 1371 parish tax, all enjoying the legitimating sanction of enactment by the king and his peers in parliament.[82] Afterwards as before, the taxation continued, as did also the resistance and the complaints against it.

Chaucer was elected in 1386 as a knight of the shire, rather than a burgess. To have been chosen in this way may have been taken by him as an indication of royal favor, in recognition of the importance of the work he had taken on as a justice, perhaps. Knights of the shire were remunerated at twice the rate of the burgesses, the sum amounting in Chaucer's case to just more than £12.[83] From the perspective of the crown, however, Chaucer's election is more likely to have been an impersonal matter, of simple utility. There were twenty-four Ricardian parliaments. Chaucer sat only the one time. Kentish contemporaries of like substance were rotated into the same set of county seats, then out again, and, in some cases (not Chaucer's), back in yet again, in sequential parliaments, though generally not two parliaments in a row for any one sitter.[84] Such a relay-system would have broadcast the honors and pay more widely, so fostering obligation. By it, greater numbers of persons were implicated, the individuals changing from parliament to parliament. Differences otherwise amongst the elected subjects in parliament were of little functional account. Amongst crown, peers, these elect few (whose names changed), and the crown's other subjects, relations remained the same.

In the case of a knight of the shire like Chaucer, "election" denoted strictly that the individual had been nominated by a sheriff, the sheriffs in their turn being royal deputies.[85] Like the other elected members, in other words, Chaucer came to parliament on sufferance, by royal appointment, directly or at a remove. In either case, it was the king who paid him to sit. An allegorical-fictional "sherreve shoed al newe" carries "Mede" to Westminster in *Piers Plowman*. Fictional too appear to have been the mainpernors (witnessing guarantors, in effect) who gave legal, documentary surety for Chaucer's return by election.[86] The sheriff returning him was not made up, however: Arnold Savage, who had first been appointed sheriff of Kent immediately following the Great Revolt, at an unusually young age, in the autumn of 1381, and who was at the time of Chaucer's election to parliament in 1386 also serving as a justice of the peace for Kent on the same county commission to which Chaucer had been appointed about a year earlier.[87]

These processes could be regarded as unsatisfactory, or susceptible to corruption. The 1399 deposition articles, for example, charged Chaucer's king with buying and bullying parliamentary knights of the shire, expressly for purposes of manipulating the wool subsidy, for which Chaucer still had a responsibility while in parliament:

> Although according to both statute and the custom of the realm the people of each county ought to be free to elect and appoint knights of the shire to attend parliament, there to put forward their grievances and request remedies as seems expedient to them, yet the king, wishing to be free to impose his own arbitrary will upon his parliaments, frequently sent orders to his sheriffs telling them to send to parliament as knights of the shire men nominated by the king himself, whom he then often induced, sometimes by fear or by threats, sometimes with bribes, to agree to things prejudicial to the realm and burdensome to the people—in particular, the grant to the king of the wool subsidy.[88]

The most pertinent indictment of such parliamentary manipulations may come from the poem *Richard the Redeless*, whose author is thought possibly to have been a parliamentary clerk during Richard's reign.[89] The poet links the dissipation of the king and court, in "reot" and "reeuell," first to financial desperation again, and then to parliamentary manipulations "for proffitt of hem self." The crown bought sherrifs, who were buying knights of the shire, who could then be counted on to enact the royal will, "meved for mony more than for out ellis":

> And whanne the reot and the reeuell the rent thus passid,
> And no thing y-lafte but the bare baggis,
> Then felle it afforse to fille hem ayeyne,
> And feyned sum folie that failid hem neuere
> And cast it be colis with her conceill at euene,
> To have preuy parlement for proffitt of hem-self,
> And lete write writtis all in wex closid,
> For peeris and prelatis that thei apere shuld,
> And sent side sondis to schreuys aboughte,
> To chese swiche cheualleris as the charge wold,
> To schewe for the schire in company with the grete.[90]

Like the framers of the articles of deposition, the poet of *Mum and the Sothsegger* too had ideas about what "elected" knights of the shire ought to have been doing in parliament. "When knightz for the comune been come for that deede," their purpose was "forto shewe the sores of the royaume / And spare no speche, though thay spille shuld." In practice, however, it was proving, "The voiding of this vertue doeth venym forto growe."[91] "The pouer han al the grame," "So is trecherie a-bove, and treuthe is al tosquat":[92]

> For alle the perillous poyntz of prelatz and of other,
> As peres that haue pouaire to pulle and to leue,
> They wollen not parle of thoo poyntz for peril that might falle,
> But hiden alle the heuynes and halten echone,
> And maken Mum thaire messaigier thaire mote to determyne,
> And bringen home a bagge ful of boicches vn-y-curid,
> That nedis most by nature ennoye thaym there-after.
>
> That riot reyneth now in londe everiday more and more,
> The lordis beth wel a-paith therwith and lisneth to here lore,
> But of the pouer mannes harm, therof is now no speche.[93]

Finally, the *Richard the Redeless* poet has also an account of how such elected parliamentarians, knights of the shire like Chaucer, acted in the circumstance, constrained as they were by "fer of her maistris" or "the coyne that the kyng owed hem." "Comment fra houme bon espleit ex pauperum sudore / Que les riches esparnyer doit dono vel favore?" [How shall a man who, for gift or favour, is under pressure to spare the rich, bring forth good results out of the sweat of the poor?].[94]

> And somme slombrid and slepte and said but a lite;
> And somme mafflid with the mouth and nyst what they ment;
> And somme had hire and held ther-with euere,
> And wolde no forther affoot for fer of her maistris. . . .
> And some were acombrid with the conceill be-fore,
> And wiste well y-now how it sholde ende,
> Or some of the semble shulde repente.
> Some helde with the mo how it euere wente,
> And some dede rith so and wolld go no forther.
> Some parled as perte as prouyd well after,
> And clappid more for the coyne that the kyng owed hem
> Thanne for the comfforte of the comyne that her cost paied.

"Than satte summe as siphre doth in awgrym, / That noteth a place and no thing availeth," Chaucer amongst them, in some sense or other.[95] Nothing in evidence suggests that he took any part or even interest in the doings of the parliament in which he sat. He drew the standard four shillings a day pay for participation in fifty-nine days of sessional meetings and for two days' travel; meanwhile, he also transacted a good deal of non-parliamentary other, personal business in the city during the session. He settled various

debts and collected annuities from the Exchequer, and he testified on
behalf of the royal favorite Scrope in the notorious Court of Chivalry trial,
years of effort and reams of testimony to decide which of a pair of armiger-
ous claimants should have the right to bear the arms *azure a bend or*. Neither party was satisfied by the court's proposed compromise, that one of
them add a *bordure argent*.[96]

The 1386 Parliament in which Chaucer sat was similar to the Scrope-
Grosvenor trial in this respect. Their chief outcome predictable, having
been decided in advance—taxes would be imposed—it is hard to imagine
anyone caring about the parliamentary proceedings, with the exception of
the narrow elite most immediately implicated in the intra-class squabbling.
Such a view of the inconsequence of parliament was made articulate by
Chaucer himself in the *Parliament of Fowls*. Some attending the fictional
parliament there also find the interminable proceedings pointless, or worse:

> The noyse of foules for to ben delyvered
> So loude rong, "Have don, and lat us wende!"
> That wel wende I the wode hadde al to-shyvered.
> "Com of!" they criede, "allas, ye wol us shende!
> When shal youre cursede pleytynge have an ende?"

Perhaps only a goose would say such things: "Al this nys not worth a flye!"
Only a goose could rate a fly so highly. Implicit in Chaucer's attribution of
this view to this speaker, there must be criticism. And in any case, the *Parliament of Fowls* was written before Chaucer's participation in the actually
existing parliament of 1386.[97]

From the perspective of the ruling elite that Chaucer was elected and
paid to represent in the 1386 parliament, it may be that matters of some
moment were transacted there, though not immediately concluded. On the
occasion, in exchange for tax-monies, the king submitted to imposition of
conciliar management and impeachment of the royal favorite Michael de
la Pole. Pole was not greatly put out (he was back at Richard's court in
time for Christmas festivities that same season), and Richard was largely
able to circumvent the council's efforts to rule him.[98] Ruling-class business
continued as per normal, except that the rumblings in this so-called "Won-
derful" parliament (not the "Good" parliament) were the doing of an
inchoate noble faction that would become the Lords Appellant by 1388, in
the "Merciless" parliament, on whom Richard was revenged only in 1397,
in another parliament (the "Revenge" parliament), but whose heirs then
had their revenge in 1399, in parliament again, and so on. That Chaucer
was unaffected by these troubles within the ruling class—between the king
and his peers—confirms that his interests and obligation lay, not with any

individual or class-fraction, but with the ruling class generally, whose broad functioning too continued largely unperturbed despite the sporadic internecine and other troubles.

4. Clerk of the King's Works

The last, most briefly held of Chaucer's public offices, the appointment as clerk of the king's works that ran from 1389 to 1391, might be regarded as the most important of them, in two senses at least. The clerkship was the most responsible, most prestigious of the offices that Chaucer held, putting him at the head of the fourth greatest of the royally funded departments of state, after the household, the chamber, and the wardrobe.[99] Second, here if anywhere Chaucer may have been doing productive work—managerial if not industrial[100]—where his artistic creativity may also have been brought into play. As clerk, Chaucer would have been responsible for giving expression to royal power by immediate, concrete means. In addition to responsibility for maintenance of public utilities like roadways, drainage, and wharves, and for construction and repair about the archipelago of royal residences and other properties throughout the kingdom, whereby, moving from place to place, the monarchy gave its power palpable real presence, the clerk also had some responsibility for staging royal spectacles of one sort and another.[101]

Most suggestive are the records of the tournament in 1390 at Smithfield, the place where Richard II had had his decisive meeting with the rebels in 1381, when Wat Tyler was murdered by Chaucer's mercantile associate Walworth. On this later occasion, however, the king gave, not rural laborers, but recalcitrant city elements—especially city oligarchs, who were to approach outright insubordination in 1392 and to be thoroughly punished for it—an instruction about nobility. Sheila Lindenbaum argued that the event intended to foster "social integration," making a show of unity among king, nobles, and citizens, though in fact "the arrangements made by the king stressed not a thriving community united under his rule, but a demarcation between the nobility on the one hand and the merchant class of the city on the other."[102] The point of the tournament was ultimately international-diplomatic, intending to cement an anti-Valois alliance and to impress noble visitors from abroad with English royal magnificence.[103] The merchantry's role was subordinate, instructively so: to watch and to wonder at their rulers' big doings. Above all, their function was to supply, goods and services, as ever. The London merchants may have profited thereby, but no matter. The point about their dependent, ancillary place in the greater scheme of things was made. As clerk of works, Chaucer's function was similar, to supply the means whereby the royal glory might be made manifest. The records establish that Chaucer was responsible for construction of the scaffolding from which the spectacle was to be observed and otherwise preparing the grounds, though what if any other contribution he may have made is not clear; Lindenbaum calls him "a kind of assistant producer."[104]

Tempting as it may be to see Chaucer here putting his artistic-creative abilities into the royal service directly, by a kind of productive industry, the evidence indicates that here too, as clerk, Chaucer's job was again the kind of financial surveillance and managerial work he did elsewhere in the apparatus of state at other times. The laboring was done by various artisans hired for particular jobs; the artisans were supervised by various more or less permanent officials of the king's works: the master mason Henry Yevele, the master carpenter Richard Swift, the king's gardeners, and so on; these were supervised in turn by purveyors and other under-clerks of the works; and it was with this level of official that Chaucer dealt most often and directly.[105] He had extensive and serpentine dealings with the Exchequer again, both drawing official revenues from the Exchequer and accounting to the Exchequer, by annual audit, for his office's disbursements. Also, Chaucer had a comptroller, whom he had to pay to watch his financial doings, as he had been paid to watch those of others earlier.[106] "It is indeed chiefly as an accountant that the Clerk of the King's works figures in the surviving records;" "except as accountants, the activities of the Clerks of the King's works are not well known":[107] the evidence (howbeit partial) tends to indicate that Chaucer was a chief financial officer, or an executive vice-president with particular financial responsibilities, supervising largish construction projects, on behalf of the crown.

It was during his term as clerk of works that Chaucer was robbed by highwaymen. It is a curious, even mysterious episode in numerous particulars, and highly evocative, too, of Chaucer's place, individually, in the class struggle. Poverty, said Langland's Patience, "is a path of pees"—

> ye, thorough the paas of Aulton
> Poverte myghte passe withouten peril of robbyng!
> For there that Poverte passeth pees folweth after.
> And ever the lasse that he ledeth, the lighter he is of herte—
> *Cantabit paupertas coram latrone viator* [When poverty travels,
> even by thieves, she goes singingly]—
> And an hardy man of herte among an heep of theves;
> Forthi seith Seneca *Paupertas est absque sollicitudine semita* [The
> carefree path is poverty]
> (14.301–06)

In any event, for now, the evidentiary value of the episode is that it gives a view of what Chaucer did at work, in his capacity as clerk: not at home, in study, imagining cunning spectacles with which to delight and to instruct the king and court, but traveling a road, messenger-like again, in person, to deliver payroll to the royal palace at Eltham, where building-works his office supervised were in progress. His robbers saw an apt mark and acted.[108]

The second biggest job for which Chaucer had responsibility as clerk was renovation of the St. George chapel at Windsor palace. A better occasion for public gestures asserting the regime's magnificence could hardly have been chosen. Windsor was amongst the earliest founded of the royal fortresses and had been an object of special attentions from Richard's grandfather Edward III.[109] The particular chapel within it that Chaucer's office was to rebuild was the focal place of the Order of the Garter, to which its founder, Edward III again, had taken to electing distinguished exponents of English and international chivalry, as was still recalled, some generations later, by John Lydgate, writing to instruct a bourgeois audience, "of tharmorieres of London for thonour of theyre brotherhoode," with a verse life of the national saint, "this hooly martir, of knighthood loodsterre, / To Englisshe men boothe in pees and werre":

> In whos honnour sithen goon ful yoore
>   The thridde Edwarde of knighthoode moost entier
> In his tyme, bassent at Wyndesore
>   Founded thordre first and the gartier,
>   Of worthy knightes ay frome yeere to yeere
> Foure and twenty cladde in oo lyveree
> Upon his day kepte ther solempnytee.[110]

The order gave the English crown a measure of control over aristocratic honors, largely symbolic but a significant centralizing step nonetheless.[111] The chief function, however, would have been to sow confusion. The English king was not at one with the knightly members of the order, neither the locals nor those from abroad. Richard II was eventually removed from the throne by Garter knights whom he had chosen, and he was otherwise troubled by them in the meanwhile. Thomas Hoccleve's later paired ballads on the order—addressed to the king, "yow welle of honur and worthynesse," "And to yow, lordes of the garter, flour / Of chivalrie, as men yow clepe and calle"—were written in an effort to bring the king and Garter knights together, to stand against heterodox religions.[112] Nor, in larger perspective, were the interests of this aristocratic elite the same as those of the whole English polity ("Englisshe men boothe in pees and werre"), though pretending that the good of the Garter knights and their king was the same as the good of the English as a nation would have been expedient.

Little was achieved at Windsor during Chaucer's tenure of office, as likewise under his immediate successors in Richard's reign. The biggest business of Chaucer's clerkship, by far, was the rebuilding of the Tower Wharf in the port of London, on which Chaucer's works office spent over six times as much as it did on the construction at Windsor, and with better result.[113] This work would seem to have been of lesser gravity as a symbolic demonstration of the royal magnificence, for public consumption. There is no contemporary poetry in praise of the London dockyards (to my knowledge). Even John Gower's *paean* to Lady Wool ("O Leine, dame de noblesce/ Tu es des marchantz la duesse" [O Wool, dame of nobility, who are the merchants' very god] and so forth), in the *Speculum meditantis*, omits mention.[114] Nevertheless, the Tower Wharf construction was of greater consequence in real terms, and so it is more instructive about the substance of the Ricardian regime. It tells something about the crown's priorities, that the better part of its financial resources was invested here, improving infrastructure at this crucial location in its revenue extraction apparatus: fundamentally, what had to matter to the late Plantagenet regime was getting more. The crown's interest in improving physical plant in the port of London would also have signified, for the merchant oligarchy, a stabilization of the wool-trade. Predictability—maintaining the status quo—is always a good thing for business. Improving the Tower Wharf would have articulated concretely a royal intention to leave off its abrogations of the staple system and its periodic favorings of other ports, like Southampton or Hull, over the London port.[115] The investment in wharf-building may also explain Chaucer's qualification for the clerkship at the moment he took on the job: in addition to his long demonstrated managerial capacity, especially with accountancy, he had unparalleled intimate knowledge of wharvish business. No one had ever been as long in the London comptrollerships, serving the royal interest.

The longest single document in the surviving Chaucer life-records is the account he gave "of receipts and expenses about the king's works, at the palace of Westminster, the Tower of London, and the several other manors and residences appertaining to the king"; the longest section of this longest document is the list of dead stock—the stuff, to be transferred intact from one clerk to the next.[116] The length results from its enumeration of everything in the crown's possession—down to the "xxᵗⁱ grossi clavi cum capitibus stannatis" and the "i howe" and "i vanga pro operibus gardini" at Eltham palace[117]—for the keeping of which Chaucer was held responsible as clerk of the king's works. That instruments of war (from "C petre rotunde vocate engynstones" to great "machine" of war and "tribugetti") appear so often in this list may remind of the ultimate violence to the disciplinary work Chaucer was engaged in here as well.[118]

In the oath he took as clerk, Chaucer swore "to arrest or to lay hands on, and to give over into the keeping of our jails, all such as are found for his part to be contumacious or seditious," repeating this provision period-ically during his tenure.[119] Again, the records are not detailed enough to show which or how many subversives Chaucer may have had to arrest and hold on the king's behalf in this period. Most likely, the actual police-work would have been delegated, like the gardening. Nonetheless, the disciplinary nature of Chaucer's work in surveillance here too, howbeit on a more abstract level, perhaps, is clear enough already from the nature of the list of the dead stock. Chaucer's job as clerk of works was to keep track of the king's stuff. If any of it went missing, Chaucer had to explain. In fact, he spent nearly as long under Exchequer audit, his accountancy under official scrutiny, after he had left the clerkship, as he had spent discharging the office.[120]

The lengthy Exchequer audit established that what Chaucer contributed as clerk of the king's works, above all, was his own money: sums of sixty-six and nearly twenty-one pounds—five times what his life had cost to ransom in 1360—which he was owed by the Exchequer when he left office. Chaucer loaned the crown this much money, in other words, and had to leave the debt outstanding, without interest or other considerations for his costs, for a con-siderable period. King Richard had a record of using debts of this sort to fos-ter obligation, to cultivate a perverse sort of loyalty. Chaucer would have seen how this worked in customs. As long as the king owed the collectors money, which he licensed them to take from the customs revenues directly, he could expect the indebtedness to preclude substantive opposition to his interests from the oligarchs: attack the king, write off the debt. Richard used the same technique on a still grander scale with the corporation of the city of London in 1392: the city's reward for its submission was that it was permitted to loan the king a fabulous sum, as a sort of hostage to fate, guaranteeing the city's future tractability to the royal will. The very late Ricardian "blank charters," of 1397–1399, are only the egregious example.[121]

On a smaller scale, Chaucer was involved in the same sort of transaction with the crown during and after his tenure of office as clerk of the king's works. The loan enforced a bond of common economic interest between Chaucer and the king, of a sort that had not existed between them before. On this basic level, as a financial entity, Chaucer was here wholly absorbed by an interest in the crown's continuing well-being. Chaucer's subjection to the crown is most complete at this point. When his money was the crown's money, or vice versa, the two were one. The loan can be seen as the culmination of Chaucer's lifelong career in service, when his service was perfect, even to the point of his incorporation into the crown. Also, by way of recompense, the loan represented public warrant for the social standing Chaucer had achieved by service, the same sort of standing, though not on quite the same level, as was enjoyed, uneasily, by the others to whom the king was also in debt.

Once the Exchequer audit of the clerkship was finished, Chaucer's career in service was finished too. This was the point at which, for the first time, instead of going on to some greater, more responsible office, Chaucer stopped. There are records, indeed numerous records, from these last eight years or so of Chaucer's life, recording the continuation of old business, however, rather than any assumption of new. In order of weight and number, roughly, the records are of: continued dealings with the Exchequer, to do with the clerkship and to do with the assignment and collection of his various annuities and guerdons (worth about £50 per annum by his last year);[122] debt contraction and collection, both Chaucer's to others and theirs to him; the legal process against those who had robbed him during his clerkship (those who could be caught were killed); his possible appointment to a substitutionary forestership of the forest of North Petherton, an office his son Thomas may have held after him too; and his lease of a tenement in the Westminster Abbey precincts.

The lease on the tenement—an emolument, evidently, like Aldgate apartments earlier, given to others before and after Chaucer who, like him, had served the crown—was for forty-three years. Shorter leases were used, so the term suggests that Chaucer expected to be around.[123] Chaucer's other late activities give the same indication, of life-work as usual. His financial dealings featured Gilbert Maghfeld, on whose unsavory financial backing even bishops and the lord mayor of London had occasionally to depend, though Maghfeld seems never to have left off extending the smaller loans to humbler folk on which his fortune had been founded. One of the transactions in which Chaucer was involved, supplying what (perhaps negligible) coercive weight he disposed, was extortion: he witnessed a double charter registering the transfer of a property to a royal favorite courtier-friend of his, and then later the parties from whom the property was transferred swore in court "that the release [of the property] had been secured from them by threats" and "that they dared not take their case into the law courts for fear of death." Chaucer's forestership, highly dubious in any case, would have been a sinecure, not necessitating direct participation in seeing to it that ill-fed locals did not disrupt the hunt by poaching game.[124]

Then Chaucer died, unexpectedly perhaps, at a not very advanced age, perhaps in his early sixties. He was buried, where he belonged, at the entrance to the St. Benedict Chapel in the royal church, Westminster Abbey, "which had but recently become a burial place for courtiers and royal officials, at the instance of Richard II."[125]

CHAPTER 2

WRITING

The same submersion in the interests of power also characterizes Chaucer's other work, in poetry. Though the records omit to mention his writing, connection remains. Chaucer's writing did the same kind of work in the cultural sphere as he had contributed by his other employments to the concrete, less mediated work of social management. The homology of Chaucer's literary products to his social and industrial work is unusually straightforward. As a poet, Chaucer was doing the same thing he also did as domestic servant, tax-gatherer, justice of the peace, and so on: serve and protect. He did the same jobs, serving the same purposes, in both spheres, only using the technically different means that were available and appropriate.[1] Broadly speaking, the early poetry serves decoratively, by flattery, mythologizing the ideal of the aristocratic good life—beautiful ladies, courteous gentle men, and elegance, rendering invisible the exploitation and coercion that made the illusion at all tenable. Again broadly speaking, the later unfinished work on the *Canterbury Tales* serves by more actively disciplining what the writing represents as unruly, disruptive, recalcitrant social elements. *Troilus and Criseyde* is a middle term: though it has monitory, critical subtexts, standing against certain antisocial tendencies of the aristocracy, and settles in the end on an antisocial philosophical otherworldliness of its own, it too is an apology for the noble good life of erotic preoccupation.

1. The Complaints

The point of Chaucer's "Complaints" is to depict a world without work, for an audience that wanted to live in one but did not.[2] Chaucer wrote a half-a-dozen or so poems that have the term in the titles attached to them—"The Complaint unto Pity," "A Complaint to His Lady," and so on—generally brief, stylistically and substantively undistinguished pieces, about the authorship of which doubts will linger, and the chronology of which remains uncertain, though in the main they are to be taken as early products. The independent complaints are affiliated with other longer poems, undoubtedly of Chaucer's writing and datable to the earlier part of his career, in which complaint-like lyric passages are inset in narrative frames: the *Anelida and Arcite*, the *Complaint of Mars*, and the *Book of the Duchess* being chief examples, though there are others.[3]

With a significant exception, what the complaints have in common is that no one in them has anything to do, except lament unhappiness in love or pine for the imagined joys of romantic satisfaction, these being full-time occupations and more. The lover can afford to lay awake all night thinking of love and spend all day as well, "from the morwe forth til hit be eve," on the same private obsession, without impediment. No family, no job, no public obligations interfere with the lover's *otium*. Anelida, for example, "That pyneth day be day in langwisshinge," dreams even of her false lover, when she can sleep; all night long, "this wonder sight I drye," and all day long "for thilke afray I dye." The only *negotia* mentioned in the complaints, other than weeping and complaining, are singing, dancing, and going hungry at banquets.[4]

The persistent suggestion in them is that love-service is lifelong and all-encompassing ("While I lyve I wol ever do so": "serve and love yow and no mo"). "Ye been to me my ginning and myn ende," maintains one complainer: "To that day that I be laid in grave / A trewer servaunt shulle ye never have"; "Ever have I been, and shal, how-so I wende, / Outher to live or dye, your humble trewe." "Yeer by yere," romance comprises "worldes joye," "heven hool," and all else in between: "al my sufficaunce" and "al my plesaunce." In the "Complaint unto Pity," the lover's claim is that he has passed his entire adult life, "ful of besy peyne," only seeking pity in romance: "For I have sought hir ever ful besely / Sith first I hadde wit or mannes mynde."[5]

According to the complaints, love's worth is greater, "an hundred thousand deel, / Than al this worldes richesse or creature," "More then myself an hundred thousand sithe." Nothing compares, and the corollary of this exorbitant value attached to romance is that death is preferable to life without it. Absent satisfaction in love, there is nothing, at all: "The world is lore; there is no more to seyne." To be lovelorn is to be exiled, cast up on a "spitous yle"; all that remains is to long for death. Since lover belongs to beloved, for ever and in all, love's loss leaves only "dedly adversyte." "For either mot I have yow in my cheyne / Or with the deth ye mote departe us tweyne; / Ther ben non other mene weyes newe": there can be no compromise in the complaints' world: everything or nothing, either love or death.[6]

"But these are all lies: men have died from time to time, and worms have eaten them, but not for love."[7] The complaints themselves only rarely offer this sort of purchase, however—a vantage point from which a world outside them comes into view—for their exclusions, consistent and thorough, are not accidental.[8] All the wrangling in the poems, about what love is, how lovers ought to behave, and so on, obscures the fundamental point, that the concentration on love as it is depicted herein serves to distract, to shift attention away from other concerns. The complaints obliterate political economy, the world of work and social relations.

The *Book of the Duchess*, albeit an early poem, may yet be the extremest instance of this strategy of exclusionary distraction in Chaucer's writing. In it, even mock-industrial noble occupation at hunting is by allegory made into another version of the erotic obsession ("so at the laste / This hert rused and staal away" [380–81]). That the pining "man in blak" (445), whose complaint forms the center around which the various narrative frames are built, is John of Gaunt—his name is called out in the poem, *allegorice*, in the description of the final riding homeward to "A long castel. . ./ Be Seynt Johan, on a ryche hil" (1318–19)—makes Chaucer's exclusions the more audacious. This John, duke of Lancaster, earl of Richmond, was not someone to ignore politics and social business, even when it came to his *amours*. Chaucer's representation of him as the standard amatory complainant ("For y am sorwe and sorwe ys y" [597]), wholly occupied with *eros* ("For youres is alle that ever ther ys / For evermore, myn herte swete" [1232–33]), is a memorial tribute to the qualities of the dead "White" queen whom the "man in blak" has lost.[9] Nevertheless, this once in Chaucer's writing where he comes as near as ever he does to saying something about current events shows how the avoidance of the immediately political makes possible the constant ideological confabulation of his writing. It is possible for him always to be ideological because he is never political in so direct a way.[10] John of Gaunt did not die for love of the woman whose marriage brought him the Lancastrian inheritance. He was already making another profitable match for himself, of international state-diplomatic moment, with another heiress, and he may also already have been having sex with Chaucer's sister-in-law too, by the time Chaucer wrote the *Book of the Duchess*.[11] The point of the eulogy is to pretend—to propagate the fictional notion—that Lancaster might have died for love, as if erotics might matter more than state-building or the accumulation of wealth or otherwise exercising power—as if there could be an erotic world without work for Chaucer's patron.

The Chaucerian complaint-poems concentrate on the private, personal, amatory sphere that they call up, to the exclusion of the economic, social and political occupations characteristic of a public sphere; and it was in this exclusion that rested their appeal for Chaucer's original audiences. In domesticating literature of this sort to England late in the fourteenth century, Chaucer leading, English poets were responding to contemporary, local conditions—especially troubling conditions in the public sphere that would have made amatory complaint an especially useful and appealing literary type.

The determining feature of the period was the demographic catastrophe of the plague, striking first and most forcefully in 1349 and precipitating England's well-known disciplinary crisis—a "crisis of order," as it has been called.[12] The plague's coming must be regarded as the most extreme of the "disarticulating uneven developments" of the English Middle Ages. Pre-plague relations of production in the political sphere remained in place, unaltered; meanwhile, disposable forces of production were suddenly, radically changed, and for the worse, atypically, by way of diminution and regression.[13] By 1385, after repeated outbreaks, the plague had taken about half of England's pre-plague population, including a disproportionately great number of the productively laborious. The deaths were so numerous that the balance of relations between land-owners and land-workers shifted. After the plague, land was more plentiful than hands to work it. Landowners needed laborers more than laborers needed landowners, for it was from labor chiefly that they extracted the revenues out of which they maintained themselves, by way of regular, customary rents and dues, judicially imposed fines, and extraordinary taxes. Land-workers, on the other hand, who could have managed without the land-owning class at any time, made rarer by the death and so less able to meet land-owners' more pressing need for revenue, now became still less beholden to them for land to work.[14]

For the ruling class, the effects of diminishing incomes were exacerbated by a contemporary rise in spending. At a time when they were getting less, the landed needed more. Conspicuous consumption increased in the years after the plague's coming, this being a period of noteworthy bought magnificence, in art and architecture, as well as personal luxuries. The "consumption patterns" of this local landed aristocracy were characterized by a "hunger for luxuries," on the one hand, "as well as for the instruments of 'extra-economic' coercion, especially military goods, on which their economic power depended," more importantly.[15] By far the greatest drain on incomes was war: prosecution of the Hundred Years' War against France, occupying England's kings and nobles for the better part of the fourteenth century and beyond. The program of taxation and the disbursement mechanisms evolved to pay for so much were an extensive income redistribution scheme, as Lee Patterson put it, from poor to rich, designed

> to transfer wealth from the most productive sectors of society—the ecclesiastical manors, the wool and cloth producers, the urban merchants, and, above all, the steadily developing small commodity producers among the

peasantry—into the least productive sector, a spend-thrift aristocracy obsessed with buying the luxury goods necessary to ratify a life-style, and a social superiority, that was becoming progressively more difficult to justify.[16]

This confluence of forces—fiscal crisis for the rulers, arising out of falling revenue and increased expenditure, and growing independence for the ruled, though they had to bear higher per capita levels of taxation—created the manifold disciplinary troubles pervading England late in the fourteenth century and for the better part of the fifteenth: the struggles of monarch against magnates, leading to the deposition of Richard II in 1399, of magnates against one another, in the Wars of the Roses that followed, and of the ruled against the ruling class generally.

The Great Revolt of 1381 is only a salient product of the situational conjuncture. It was in fact one in a long series of numerous class-conscious, sometimes self-consciously revolutionary efforts of resistance, comprising a greater social movement among the ruled in the late fourteenth century and after.[17] These continuing efforts of resistance threatened the established order. In some instances, they had as their articulate aim the destruction of hierarchy and the overthrow of noble and royal privilege.[18] A generation later, recalling what had happened "in the time of the commons' insurrection," the Abbot of St. Albans (where John Ball's execution had taken place) remembered anarchy: in that time, "all sought to throw off the yoke of monarchy altogether and to live by laws of their own devising."

Sic regnum, olim prosperum,
Triste fuit et exterum
  Et pronum exterminio.[19]

[Consequently, the kingdom, late prosperous, was woebegone and ground down, like to be snuffed out.]

Threatened thus with extermination, the rulers' response was correspondingly serious: there were mounted pervasive efforts to maintain order, measures ranging from the concrete to the abstract, from more thorough policing to more effective class advertising at the level of ideas.

The Statute of Laborers of 1351 (basing itself on the assertion that "Servants, having no regard to the ordinance, but to their ease and singular covetousness, do withdraw themselves from serving great men and others, unless they have livery and wages double or treble what they were wont to take, . . .to the great damage of the great men and impoverishment of all the commonalty")[20] and the apparatus of peace elaborated to enforce the statute and maintain order—to the which work Chaucer contributed—responded

to the crisis directly, attempting by legislative and judicial means to impose
servile conditions of living on women and men only tenuously free in
practical terms anyway:

> Thin fadere was a bond man.
> Thin moder curtesye non can.
> Every beste that levyth now
> Is of more fredam than thow.[21]

The statutes obligated laborers to work where and when the landowners
wanted them to, at rates to be set by the landowners. The subsidies, double-
subsidies, poll taxes, and so on, levied almost annually during the thirteen-
seventies ("Ore court en Engletere de anno in annum / Le quinzyme dener,
pur fere sic commune dampnum" [Now the fifteenth runs in England year
after year, thus doing harm to all]), meant that more of whatever surplus that
fewer laborers generated was being transferred directly to the crown and
from the crown to the nobility; the taxation bound laborers to spend a
greater proportion of their time working for the benefit of their rulers.[22]

Social mobility too was a disciplinary reaction to the crisis, having the
effect, not of effacing class distinction, but of reinforcing it as a concept of
social organization. Mobility is a matter of exchanging class identities,
lower for upper or vice versa, rather than a matter of eliminating them.
With mobility, individuals and families may move from one class to
another; although the names of those composing the classes may change
from time to time, the structure does not alter. In fact, mobility "sharpened
the sense of status."[23] By engendering insecurity in families hoping to
maintain standing and ambition in families hoping to move up, mobility
gave both an increased stake in maintaining the basic distinction between
upper and lower.

Disciplinary measures are also in evidence at the more abstract level of
ideas and symbols of order. For example, the combination of new sumptu-
ary law, proscribing certain foods and styles of dress for some groups, with
new, more ostentatious forms of fashion and entertainment among the
rich, made it easier to see class distinction in publicly displayed symbols of
it.[24] The Smithfield tournament of 1390, in the mounting of which
Chaucer had a hand, is another example: the elaborate spectacle served to
draw class boundaries more sharply, making clearer "a demarcation
between the nobility on the one hand and the merchant class of the city
on the other."[25] And the re-emergence of literature in English in the late
fourteenth century is likewise a response to the disciplinary crisis, one way
and another, in the cultural sphere. No plague, no Statute of Laborers and
no trouble in 1381; also, no plague and no trouble, no Langland or Gower

or Chaucer. The great quantity of reformist English literature of the late fourteenth century, occupied with improving the functioning of particular estates while maintaining the social order basically as it was—covering much in both Langland and John Gower, from the late sections of the *Mirrour de l'homme* to the *Confessio amantis* prologue, with the pre-*Visio Angliae Vox clamantis* between—responds to the crisis of order directly.[26] So too, however, do the *Knight's Tale* and the quitting of the Knight by the Miller in the *Canterbury Tales*, albeit more obliquely. And so too does such ostentatiously apolitical writing as the Chaucerian complaints, albeit that their response is still more oblique.

Chaucer had a personal interest in preserving distinctions of class, at least to the extent that he had an interest in continuing the upward mobility of his own family—from the provinces to the capital, from merchantry to noble service, and then to distinction in the person of Thomas Chaucer. Of greater immediate consequence, however, is the fact that Geoffrey Chaucer's daily employments—what he did at work, day by day—kept him in the front lines of the crisis of order, working in the various capacities he did to maintain order on behalf of the ruling class. Clerk of the works, justice of the peace, revenue manager, household servant carrying messages: serving and keeping the dominant order is what Chaucer did.

As a poet, he served the same class interest, and the complaints have a special twofold historical importance as evidence on this point. First, amongst his contemporaries and his immediate successors in English literature, the complaints were the most often imitated of Chaucer's writings. Second, they were so often imitated in the short term in some measure because they established what kind of ideological service a poet might do.

Although the complaints do so obliquely—their obliqueness is essential to their success—they still do an important ideological job of class myth making. They propagate a particular point of view, as natural and inevitable, which might otherwise appear arguable or wrong—what Roland Barthes in the nineteen-fifties called "myth," and what was once called ideology, simply: bad-faith propagandizing for false consciousness.[27] For those who could afford to use Chaucer's complaints—persons of leisure and taste, with access to literacy—they propagated an ideal of the noble good life: leisurely, work-free, and untroubled by social conflict—by conflicts of any sort, except those of private erotic distraction. The complaints' response to the crisis of order was to pretend that there was no crisis. The pretense had the force of an assertion, paradoxically the more emphatic because implicit. So far from there being any crisis that might need addressing, in the complaints the aristocratic good life is shown to be going ahead worry-free. It was a flattering illusion for a poet to conjure up, and the poetry would have been useful enough on these terms alone, as enjoyable entertainment, offering respite in troubled times, distraction. Still, "court poetry, after all, is not merely a kind of writing but also a social practice, and one laden with ideological value."[28] The poetry had also always another, greater extrinsic usefulness as propaganda: contrary to the material reality of the conflicted contemporary aristocratic social and political situation, the poetry propagates myths of carefree noble *otium*. Tendentiously it asserts that the mythic aristocratic good life was: a good life.

The trouble lingering about Chaucer's complaints is that late fourteenth-century England was not untroubled. There was no world without work, even for the rich people. Wishing the world were without work—without even the work of exploiting others' industry or managing the exploitation in good order—could not make it so. Even when the wish was powerful enough to make it seem so, partially or briefly perhaps, and only in the mediated cultural sphere of verse-making and -using, the world of work would persist and intrude.

In the complaints, successful as they are, the intrusion takes varying forms. One is the transfer of a vocabulary of service ("Ne truly, for my deth, I shal not lette / To ben her truest servaunt and her knyght": "Love hath me taught no more of his art / But serve alwey and stinte for no wo") from the political to the private realm of amatory relations, importing an attenuated reminder of the public world outside. The same is true of the vocabulary transferred from religious devotion ("My righte lady, my sava-cyoun," "Myn heven hool"), *mutatis mutandis*; it too can recall larger concerns, transcendent concerns even, though not often does it do so to distraction.[29] "My spirit shal never dissevere / Fro youre servise" conflates the two registers, as does the "man in blak" in the *Book of the Duchess*: "I besette hyt / To love her in my beste wyse, / To do his worship and the servise / That I koude thoo"; but no matter how precise this vocabulary becomes, the transferred matter's subordination to erotics remains:

> Dredeles, I have ever yit
> Be tributarye and yive rente
> To Love, hooly with good entente,
> And through plesaunce become his thral
> With good wille, body, hert, and al.
> Al this I putte in his servage,
> As to my lord, and did homage;
> And ful devoutly I prayed hym to.[30]

The Parliament of Fowls does most with such extra-erotic references: with the transcendent, quasi-religious dimension in its figure of "goddesse Nature" ("the vicaire of the almyghty Lord / That hot, cold, hevy, lyght, moyst, and dreye / Hath knyt by evene noumbres of acord" [303 and 379–81]); and with a feudal quasi-political dimension in the concluding parliament itself. What "Nature" does, however, is facilitate aristocratic erotic preoccupation, as if it were natural for nobility, and so inevitable; what the lower-order fowls contribute finally—notwithstanding their intermittent, risible, wrongful disruptions of what is "natural"—is their acquiescence in the order of things that puts aristocratic erotics first. The disruptions reflect only impatience with order's slow workings, not with Nature's order itself; in the end, all rest content with the established authority. " 'Kek kek! kokkow! quek quek!' " (499): belittled and so easily dismissed, the dissent is hard to take seriously on the terms in which it is put forward. It is only seed-fowl, worm-eaters and such like complaining anyway. Adduction of these other extra-erotic perspectives on noble love-making in the *Parliament of Fowls* comes, not to criticizing, but to glorifying it further.

Of greater impact, then, than the vocabularies appropriated from religion or political relations, is the basic contradiction pervading the complaints. The job of entertaining the leisured was a job. Summoning the illusion of a world without work was itself work.

In the first place, there was the work of importing traditions of French culture into the English ambit—cultural cartage, literary import–export. French was the dominant culture internationally, throughout Europe, and had in England the additional historical weight of being the native culture of the conquerors who had continued to rule since the eleventh century, all but exclusively in French up to the time of the fourteenth-century plagues. French was so wound around noble power in England as to be its double; the conquerors' ascendance in material social relations was inseparable from the cultural hegemony of French language and literary-cultural produce. So inevitable during the 1350s and 1360s would have been the equation of culture with French culture that Chaucer would have started out as a French-language poet. Anything else could scarcely have been conceivable in his domestic situation, in aristocratic household service, and the recently published "poems of Ch." evidence all but certainly confirms the predictions of Rossell Hope Robbins.[31]

That when Chaucer began to write poetry in English he did so in strict emulation of French products may likewise seem inevitable; Chaucer's choice was nonetheless meaningful. The effects on linguistic and literary behavior of inequitable distributions of power in bi- and multilingual polities like Chaucer's England are well understood.[32] To ape the conquerors' language and culture acknowledges the social reality of dominance; at the same time, acknowledging the social dominance by translating it into culture also extends the dominance and strengthens it, by repeating it and embedding it in culture too. There was an alternative for someone like Chaucer, in the long-domesticated alliterative tradition forged before the conquest and persistent after it in certain quarters.[33] In rejecting this practically indigenous, nativist possibility in favor of French forms—"the total exoticism of form in Chaucer," Derek Pearsall called it[34]—Chaucer acted in subordination to power and in its support. To the degree that this *translatio* of French culture is the substance of Chaucer's contribution to founding subsequent English literary traditions, what he contributed was the literature's subordination to dominant order in this respect too.

Bringing French into English was work for Chaucer. It required study and practice. The difficulty of the labor is evident in part in the elaborate formal struggles of the Chaucerian complaints. In English, alliterations are easy and rhymes are hard—"Syth rym in Englissh hath such skarsete"[35]—the opposite of the condition of French. By comparison with Chaucer's other writings, the complaints are strikingly worked compositions, in elaborate and unconventional stanza forms, with repetitious, symmetrical, and mirroring rhyme-schemes, refrains and concatenated refrains. The other complaints have such features in less profusion, and even the *Book of the Duchess* and the *Parliament of Fowls* are polymetrous, by virtue of the metrically distinct lyric insets in them; however, the extreme case is Anelida's complaint, embedded in the *Anelida and Arcite*:

> After an introductory stanza (211–19) rhyming *a a b a a b b a b* (the *a*-rhymes of which are matched in the *b*-rhymes of a metrically similar concluding stanza, 342–50), the Complaint is divided into two matched halves of six stanzas each (220–80; 281–316), described by Skeat as the Strophe and Antistrophe. The first four stanzas of each part (220–55; 281–316) retain the *a a b a a b b a b* rhyme scheme in pentameters, while the matching fifth stanzas, elaborating on this basic measure in a way almost to resemble a virelay, introduce a scheme of *a a a b a a a b* and its reverse, *b b b a b b b a*, with the *a*-lines of the basic pattern reduced to four stresses while they are increased in number, and then continued in reverse rhyme. Then the matching sixth stanzas return to the basic metrical pattern, but include two internal rhymes in each of their lines. Although Chaucer infrequently repeats actual rhyming words in the Complaint, the repetition of rhyme-syllables artfully connects stanzas throughout. The third stanza of the Antistrophe (299–307) shows especial technical accomplishment, as it balances the two rhymes of the third stanza of the Strophe (238–46, regular pattern) with nine rhymes in *-ede*, apparently observing in the rhyme scheme the distinction of open and closed *e*'s. *Rime riche* is especially heavy.[36]

The world of work also intrudes into the complaints in these persistent, insistent formal reminders of the amount of literary labor put into the poems' fabrication. The formal elaborations refer to the fact that, even to evoke a world without work, it was work making complaints.

In Chaucer's "Complaint to his Purse"—the exceptional complaint, also written late in his life, in 1399–1400—this repressed, unpleasant reality returns. The poem uses features of the complaint-genre for talking about things the other complaints avoid: work and money—what persons dependent on the nobility, as Chaucer was, needed and what they had to do for it. In the other complaints, preoccupied as they are with propagating myths of an untroubled good life, this matter, of the quantity of work invested by poets in the job of summoning myths, is present chiefly in the formal super-text, by virtue of the poems' loud artificiality. The "Complaint to his Purse" moves the matter of poetic labor to front and center: the poet wants money, and literary labor is for getting it.

The "Complaint to his Purse" puts the poet's purse in the place otherwise occupied by a human love-object: "To yow, my purse, and to noon other wight / Complayne I, for ye be my lady dere" (1–2). The purse is to the poet "my lyves lyght / and saveour as doun in this world here" (15–16), and he cries out to it for "mercy" (6) and "curtesye" (20)—"Ye be my lyf, ye be myn hertes stere, / Quene of comfort and of good companye" (12–13). But the purse is "lyght"—a term that makes a pun of the purse's emptiness and the fickleness that can characterize the beloved in the other complaints. "Beth hevy ageyn," the poet asks, "or elles mot I dye" (7).

The poet worships and serves the purse, even though the purse does not reciprocate the poet's affection. In fact it cannot, and here the analogy the poem is based on—never a very exact one anyway—comes apart. It is not properly in the purse's power to satisfy its worshipper or to withhold satisfaction, as a lover can, for what the poet loves is not the purse but the coin the purse sometimes contains. The derivative complaint, by Thomas Hoccleve, to Lady Money—"of the world goddesse," "that lordes grete obeien"—is an improvement in this respect.[37] In Chaucer's case, a third party, the new king Henry IV, who could fill the purse up, has been remiss about doing so; for the poem's envoy, the analogy is dropped, and the poet addresses this third party directly, putting plainly the request for payment that the poem treats with artful indirection before:

O conquerour of Brutes Albyon,
Which that by lyne and free eleccion
Been verray kyng, this song to yow I sende,
And ye, that mowen alle oure harmes amende,
Have mynde upon my supplicacion.
(22–26)

This poem sheds light on Chaucer's sense of what poetry was for. The "Complaint to his Purse" treats poetry as trading: the poet trades the products of his literary labors for money. Chaucer's complaint is that his returns for the work he did were inadequate, not that poetry-making was work. The evidence is precisely that Chaucer subscribed to the notion that poetry-making was a job, an exchange of labor for rewards, though he may not have been dependent on the rewards his writing could bring and though those rewards need not have been cash. The corollary of this conception of poetic work is the *proskynesis* of the complaint's envoy—by turns hair-raising and risible—the gesture of self-abasing pronation to a divinized material power that a few among Alexander's Macedonian commanders finally felt was going too far. Chaucer's supine gesture of worship ("my supplicacion") makes a simple sort of brute physical force ("O conquerour of Brutes Albyon") into a deity, omnipotent ("that mowen alle oure harmes amende"). As it was for Polyperchon and others, the *proskynesis* is comical— the silliness of Chaucer's terrified effort to obliterate common humanness— but there were sometimes penalties for laughing; in any event, part of being the kind of employee that Chaucer represents himself to be in the "Complaint to his Purse" is making show of knowing who the boss is.[38]

These are the foundations on which rest the Chaucerian tradition, and indeed the whole later English literary tradition, to the degree that Chaucer is the father: writing as alienable labor, producing literary commodities to be traded for reward, and writing as subordinate, social-apologetic service. The complaints establish what would prove to be a widely transferable characterization for each component in a secular reified literary exchange, writer–writing–reader. The reader–consumer is almighty; the writer–producer, while still in possession of the requisite means of production, becomes a virtual wage-slave; and the alienable writing-product can only be flattery and propaganda, always at least implicitly encomiastic apologies for the dominance: bastard-feudalist realism.[39]

2. *Troilus and Criseyde*

Troilus and Criseyde is not different from the Chaucerian complaints and related early poems like the *Book of the Duchess*. It is bigger, anatomizing more thoroughly the possibilities and problems of the aristocratic, erotic world without work, making more extraordinary claims for erotic distraction, and founding its claims on philosophy. It is still a poem asserting the worth of human romance as an occupation, to the exclusion of work. Even when love fails him, the poem's protagonist Troilus persists in devoting his life to its service. Finally, he dies for it, belying even Shakespeare's Rosalind's assertion that such a thing should never happen. Meanwhile, the poem's basic postulate—as in the complaints and earliest dream-visions, love is all that matters—organizes all else.[40]

Troilus and Criseyde's beginning is the omnipotence of eroticism, a force so (implausibly) powerful that it carries all before it. Love improves Troilus, the narrative stresses at the outset; still more basically, it is only love that makes Troilus a thing of any interest to the poem. His extra-erotic involvements— in parent–child relations, broader ties to familial, gender, and other social groups in Troy, the antagonism of Trojans and Greeks, his religion—matter here only in relation to the eroticism that vivifies him.

The poem's central moment—toward which the rest builds, from which the rest subsides—makes of the sexual union of two persons, souls "in hevene ybrought" (3.1599), a thing of great wonder and utter value:

> Of hire delit or joies oon the leeste
> Were impossible to my wit to seye;
> But juggeth ye that han ben at the feste
> Of swiche gladnesse, if that hem liste pleye!
> I kan namore, but thus thise ilke tweye
> That nyght, bitwixen drede and sikernesse,
> Felten in love the grete worthynesse.
>
> O blisful nyght, of hem so longe isought,
> How blithe unto hem bothe two thow weere!
> Why nad I swich oon with my soule ybought,
> Ye, or the leeste joie that was theere?
> Awey, thow foule daunger and thow feere,
> And lat hem in this hevene blisse dwelle,
> That is so heigh that al ne kan I telle.
>
> (3.1310–23)

The larger scene's humor and even dangers—its refusal to exaggerate further by trying to obviate human imperfection—has the effect of strengthening the force of the passage, which has no like in contemporary English. Despite everything—the lovers' incompetence, their intermediary's perverse interest and consequent deceits, the social impossibility of the relationship—flesh fuses, obliteratingly, transcendently ("where his spirit was, for joie he nyste" [1351]), in unspeakable ecstasy.

"Thus sondry peynes bryngen folk in hevene" (3.1204), "For out of wo in blisse now they flete" (1221). "Thus in this hevene"—explicitly of flesh: "Hire armes smale, hire streghte bak and softe, / Hire sydes longe, flesshly smothe, and white. . ./ Hire snowissh throte, hire brestes rounde and lite" (1247–1248 and 1250)—"he gan hym to delite" (1251). "Flesshly," "he gan to stroke" (1248–1249). Then Troilus ejaculates his brief address ("O Love, O Charite!" [1254]) to "Benigne Love" (1261), the numerically central line (1271: "so heigh a place") of the numerically central stanza of the central book of the whole construction held inside his prayer. "They were oon" then (1405), *erastês* and *erômenê*:

> And for thow me, that koude leest disserve
> Of hem that nombred ben unto thi grace,
> Hast holpen, ther I likly was to sterve,
> And me bistowed in so heigh a place,
> That thilke boundes may no blisse pace,
> I kan namore; but laude and reverence
> Be to thy bounte and thyn excellence.
>
>   (1268–74)

Nor is so much achieved between them only the once: "And many a nyght they wroughte in this manere" (3.1713), "For if it erst was wel, tho was it bet" (1683), "As muche joie as herte may comprende" (1687), albeit not perfectly, prolongedly or permanently: still, "This passeth al that herte may bythynke" (1694). More of "this hevene blisse"—worth as much as "soule" itself—it "Were impossible to my wit to seye," the narrator professes. The god had spoken through, nonetheless:

> For either sex is filled with procreative force; and, in that conjunction of the two sexes, or, to speak more truly, that fusion of them into one, which may properly be termed *Eros*, or *Aphrodite*, or both at once, there is a deeper meaning than humans can comprehend. It is a truth to be accepted as sure and evident above all other truths, that by god, the master of all generation, has been devised and bestowed upon all creatures this sacrament of eternal procreation, with all the affection, all the joy and gladness, all the desire and heavenly love that are inherent in it. And there were need that I should tell of the compelling force with which this sacrament binds man and woman together, were it not that each one of us, if he directs his thought upon himself, can learn as much from his inmost feeling. For if you note that supreme moment when, through intercourse, we come at last to this, that either sex infuses itself into the other, the one giving forth its issue and the other taking hold on it and laying it up within, you will find that, at that moment, through the intermingling of the two natures, female acquires masculine vigor and male relaxes in feminine languor. And so this sacramental act, sweet as it is, and a thing that must needs be done, is done in secret, lest, were it done openly, the ignorant should mock, and thereby the deity manifested in either sex through the mingling of female and male should be made to blush.
>
> The soul sees god suddenly appearing within it, because there is nothing in between. They are no longer two but one; as long as this presence lasts, they cannot be distinguished. Lovers [*erastai*] and their beloveds [*erômenoi*] are an imitation of this when they desire to be one flesh.[41]

The tradition of erotic mysticism that these remarks in the *Corpus Hermeticum* and Plotinus represent was etiolated in western and northern Europe by Chaucer's day, never having been very strong.[42] Certainly, it does not figure in Chaucer's Boccaccian source, where sex is regularly rendered animal, rather than in terms of the supernatural ecstatic effacement of difference and physical-spiritual interpenetration that *Troilus and Criseyde* evokes, where the Chaucerian *erastai/erômenoi* too

> Alternant animas, laqueataque corpus in unum
>   Corpora spiritibus pervia corda parant.
> Corpora spirituum transfusio languida reddit,
>   Dumque sibi moritur vivit uterque pari.[43]

> [exchange souls, and, intermingled as into a single body, their bodies render their hearts permeable, for spirits too. Interchange of spirits leaves bodies quiet; yet, while each dies to itself, in its other each too comes alive.]

There is a passage in the contemporary English poem *Cleanness*, in which the deity—*propria persona*, in direct speech, Hermes Trismegistus-like—insists on the sheer enjoyable pleasure of sex, the deity's own considerate invention, his boon to humankind, graciously:

> I compast hem a kynde crafte and kende hit hem derne,
> And amed hit in Myn ordenaunce oddely dere,
> And dyght drwry therinne, doole alther-swettest,
> And the play of paramorez I portrayed myseluen,
> And made therto a maner myriest of other:
> When two true togeder had tyghed hemseluen,
> Bytwene a male and his make such merthe schulde conne,
> Welnyghe pure paradys moght preue no better.[44]

Though, by God here, "In love the grete worthynesse" is equated too, Chaucer-like, to "pure paradys," the only close contemporary analogue to the central passage of *Troilus and Criseyde* may be the correspondent section of Chaucer's own *Complaint of Mars*—where *erastês* "lappeth" "the flour of feyrnesse" of *erômenê*—written at about the same time as *Troilus and Criseyde* (in part in the same stanza), possibly as a preparatory exercise for it, which is yet much less precise and dilatory:

> The grete joye that was betwix hem two
> When they be mette ther may no tunge telle.
> Ther is no more but unto bed thei go,
> And thus in joy and blysse I lete hem duelle.

This worthi Mars, that is of knyghthod welle,
The flour of feyrnesse lappeth in his armes,
And Venus kysseth Mars, the god of armes.

(*Mars* 71–77)

Absence of parallels in Chaucer's contemporaries confirms how extraordinary, even troublesome, the central section of *Troilus and Criseyde* may be. In *Cleanness*, God's encomium of human erotics still subordinates it—the "merthe" of this "pure paradys" ("Wel nyghe")—to the exigencies of an argument in favor of the orthodox Christian doctrine, for which sex could only be a prophylaxis against adultery (and other putative sins) and a *techné* of procreation, both within sacrimentalized marriage. "The orthodox teaching on the sacrament of Christian marriage" involved strict segregation—a "disastrous separation," in David Aers's analysis—"of love from sex and marriage." "Orthodox Christian tradition consistently separated love from both sexuality and the primary purposes of marriage," making of "sexual intercourse. . .something only tolerable as a pleasureless and instrumental act for begetting children to serve God or for preventing adultery."[45]

At its center, Chaucer's *Troilus and Criseyde* evokes something else, and different—something utopian, or revolutionary even, in the terms of Ernst Bloch's aesthetics, or Herbert Marcuse's, whose assertion is that " 'authentic' or 'great' art," by its nature, "subverts the dominant consciousness":

A work of art can be called revolutionary if, by virtue of the aesthetic transformation, it represents, in the exemplary fate of individuals, the prevailing unfreedom and the rebelling forces, thus breaking through the mystified (and petrified) social reality, and opening the horizon of change (liberation).[46]

From the perspective of Christian orthodoxy, Chaucer's erotics—in *Troilus and Criseyde* chiefly, though elsewhere as well—might be seen as such an imaginary breakthrough. At central points in *Troilus and Criseyde*, Chaucer evokes an enjoyable human *eros* beyond the dominant Christian doctrine of strictly prophylactic or procreative sexual activity, so "opening the horizon of change" and making way for a possibility of "liberation." That, barely articulately perhaps, Chaucer does so much here only transiently, on his way to something else, may be beside the point. By any or most criteria, *Troilus and Criseyde* is or has "great art" in it.

The accomplishment of Chaucer's poem in this "aesthetic dimension"— its representation in art, "in the exemplary fate" of the fictional individuals it depicts, of an over-coming of the contemporary realities reflected in the poem—is different from, though related to, the social work in the world that the poem also does. Walter Benjamin distinguished between reflection and implication in writing, between "the *attitude* of a work to the relations of production," on the one hand—the literary work's simple passive reflecting, or its active apologizing, or its critical over-coming of prevailing conditions, still within its own literary-fictional representations[47]—and, on the other hand, a work's "*position* in" relations of production—the fact that writing is always itself a form of production, raising, Benjamin says, the question of "the function the work has within the literary relations of production of its time."[48] The literary work is "the product of a certain labor, and hence of an art. But not all art is artificial: it is the work of a laborer, and not of a conjurer or a showman," in Pierre Macherey's view:

> Art is not man's creation, it is a product (and the producer is not a subject centered in his creation, he is an element in a situation or a system). . . .Before disposing of these works—which can only be called theirs by an elaborate evasion—men have to *produce* them, not by magic, but by a real labor of production. If man creates man, the artist produces works, *in determinate conditions.*[49]

As such, in this perspective of Benjamin, writing is a way of working in and on the world, so taking part in the class struggle, contributing to it, as productive labor, one way or another. Marcuse's assertion, that the work of art—at least, the " 'authentic' or 'great' " work of art—strictly by means of its ambitions in the "aesthetic dimension," always necessarily exceeds what is, so "opening the horizon of change," is primarily a matter of reflection within the literary work, what Benjamin characterizes as "the *attitude*" of the literary work "to the relations of production," without yet or also addressing the work's "*position* in" relations of production: the effects that the attitudinal representations can have in literary production and consumption within determinate historical circumstance. Whatever Chaucer's aesthetic accomplishments in *Troilus and Criseyde*—be they viewed in Marcusean perspective or some other—there remains this additional (though related) sociological matter of what work in the world, in production, the poem and by it its writer were doing.

The elevated secular erotics represented in *Troilus and Criseyde* remains personal, private, and unproductive in any social sense. In addition to reaching beyond Christian doctrine, Chaucer's erotics is beyond social engagement, too, and so ultimately has the same antisocial, aristocratic, secular-apologetic character as do the Chaucerian erotic complaints generally. In *Troilus and Criseyde*, the powerfully transcendental, mystical eroticism evoked is also implicated in other conceptions of love, including broader, more encompassing ones, and more orthodox.

Troilus and Criseyde solves the problem inherent in such elevated accomplishments of human eroticism as those it depicts—namely, that it is still always imperfect because transient, a mystical rose, perhaps, but that still must pass—by incorporating it in a broader Empedoclean *philotês*, pervading all and manifesting itself variously. Human eroticism is imperfect in *Troilus and Criseyde*, but it is still implicated in a comprehensive "amor che move il sole e l'altre stelle" [Love that moves the sun and other stars], in the Dantean phrase.[50] Chaucer cannot use Dante's strictly constructed amorous literalism—by which Dante's love for Beatrice is literally propaedeutic: she who makes blessed leads him to God—in his tale of pre-Christian lovers. Chaucer's vocabulary for describing pervasive, comprehensive love comes chiefly instead from the Boethian *Philosophiae consolatio. Troilus and Criseyde* translates Boethius's crucial meter, cataloguing the influence of *regens et imperitans Amor* ("Hanc rerum seriem ligat / Terras ac pelagus regens / Et caelo imperitans Amor" [This great concatenation of all things is held together by Love: guiding earth and ocean, and ruling all in the heavens])[51] twice, once from Boccaccio's version in the *Filostrato* and again directly from Boethius, in the inset, intercalated lyric "*Canticus Troili*" of the central Book Three:

> Love, that of erthe and se hath governaunce,
> Love, that his hestes hath in hevene hye,
> Love, that with an holsom alliaunce
> Halt peples joyned, as hym lest hem gye,
> Love, that knetteth lawe of compaignie,
> And couples doth in vertu for to dwelle,
> Bynd this acord, that I have told and telle.

> That, that the world with feith which that is stable
> Diverseth so his stowndes concordynge,
> That elementz that ben so discordable
> Holden a bond perpetuely durynge,
> That Phebus mote his rosy day forth brynge,
> And that the mone hath lordshipe over the nyghtes:
> Al this doth Love, ay heried be his myghtes!

> That, that the se, that gredy is to flowen,
> Constreyneth to a certeyn ende so
> His flodes that so fiersly they ne growen
> To drenchen erthe and al for evere mo;
> And if that Love aught lete his bridel go,
> Al that now loveth asondre sholde lepe,
> And lost were al that Love halt now to-hepe.

So wolde God, that auctour is of kynde,
That with his bond Love of his vertu liste
To cerclen hertes alle and faste bynde,
That from his bond no wight the wey out wiste;
And hertes colde, hem wolde I that he twiste
To make hem love, and that hem liste ay rewe
On hertes sore, and kepe hem that ben trewe!

(3.1744–71)

A more thoroughgoing exploration of this conception might eventually have come to matters of social justice. *Troilus and Criseyde* does not. At its conclusion, the narrator adjusts the poem's representation of human eroticism to align it with a late medieval tradition of monastic theology (born out of the twelfth century's new monastic orders and their more direct implication in secular society) to be associated with Hugh of St Victor, for example, or the Cistercian Fathers, maintaining that once the possibilities of imperfect human love have been exhausted, by experience of its limits and its failures and reflection on them, the soul must turn to divine love for fulfillment, as the soul of Troilus does at the end of Chaucer's poem, after the protagonist's death.[52] Chaucer's friend John Clanvowe made the basic point repeatedly, in his devotional tract *The Two Ways*, that divine love "shal not passe as worldly love dooth, but it shal laste evere with outen ende,"[53] as does Chaucer himself too again, by implication, in the *Complaint of Mars* (not to mention the *Book of the Duchess*: "To lytel while oure blysse lasteth!" [211]):

To what fyn made the God, that sit so hye,
Benethen him love other companye
And streyneth folk to love, malgre her hed?
And then her joy, for oght I can espye,
Ne lasteth not the twynkelyng of an ye,
And somme han never joy til they be ded.
What meneth this? What is this mystihed?
Wherto constreyneth he his folke so faste
Thing to desyre, but hit shulde laste?

(*Mars* 218–26)

Translated "up to the holughnesse of the eighthe spere" and there "herkenyng armonye / With sownes ful of hevenyssh melodie" (5.1809, 5.1812–13), Troilus apprehends this difference between human romance and divine love, that the one is transitory, while the other need not be. For Troilus, following his bitter experience of the imperfection of human romance, with this apprehension of the heavenly harmony—the divine love that pervades the cosmos—he "fully gan despise

This wrecched world, and held al vanite
To respect of the pleyn felicite
That is in hevene above. . .
And dampned al oure werk that foloweth so,
The blynde lust, the which that may nat laste,
And sholden al oure herte on heven caste.
                                        (5.1816–19, 1823–25)

The analogue in Lucan has the transported soul look back and laugh too,
though not with the same contempt and rejection. In the *Pharsalia*, after
laughing ("uidit quanta sub nocte iaceret / nostra dies risitque" [it saw the
depth of night beneath which lies our day and laughed]), the soul returns
to earth, inspiring others to continue the work of virtue there, as if mor-
tals' labors were still worthwhile: Pompey's great *manes* "ac sparsas uolitauit
in aequore classes, / et scelerum uindex in sancto pectore Bruti / sedit et
inuicti posuit se mente Catonis" [then flew among the fleets dispersed
upon the sea, and, avenging wickedness, it settled in the sacred breast of
Brutus and stationed itself in the mind of invincible Cato].[54] At the end of
Troilus and Criseyde, by contrast, Chaucer enjoins the "yonge, fresshe folkes"
in his audience, "Repeyreth hom fro worldly vanyte"—as if, in this world,
pilgrimage-like, "Her is non hoom" (*Truth* 17)—"and thynketh al nys but
a faire, / This world that passeth soone as floures faire" (5.1837, 1840–41).
Christ, on the other hand—"For he nyl falsen no wight, dar I seye, / That
wol his herte al holly on hym leye"—by contrast with a human lover like
Criseyde, can be constant, and so mortal *eros* is all put away:

And syn he best to love is, and most meke,
What nedeth feynede loves for to seke?
                                        (5.1845–48)

It may be possible to see in such an element of *Troilus and Criseyde* an
inchoate critique of aristocracy, or of the noble concentration on *eros*, as if
Troilus and Criseyde is the return of the Chaucerian repressed sometimes,
wherein the disaffection he must at times have felt finds a little voice. Troilus
is "small Troy" (Chaucer's London was "New Troy"), and the social macro-
cosm that Chaucer's protagonist represents was about to be destroyed, finally
and utterly, having been thoroughly deformed in the process, because of
misguided *eros*: Paris's fatal rape and the Trojan ruling caste's myopic commitment to perpetuating it. *Troilus and Criseyde* may contain (i.e., both
incorporate and control) a portrait of an inequitable aristocratic society of
the sort Chaucer always served effectively bent on its own destruction, distracted from attending even to class self-preservation by preoccupation with

the powers of eroticism and pleasure. Chaucer's long poem may also be connected once to English history, by the Trojan parliament that sells Criseyde to the Greeks. To the degree that the Trojans' forensic deliberations are analogous to contemporary English magnate debates, some taken up in the English parliament, or that the deformations of Trojan society by noble self-indulgence are analogous to contemporary English deformations, the poem anatomizes contemporary social troubles.[55]

However, as Patterson has shown, *Troilus and Criseyde*'s implications in historical social process, relatively slight in any case, work to obviate the importance of such process. This kind of history does not matter to the poem, except as invoked to be excluded, sharpening the anti-historical, antisocial concentration on the erotic. "The drama of love creates an essentially anti-social force," to quote Stephen Knight;[56] or, in Patterson's own terms,

> In this poem, the private stands wholly apart from and seeks to efface the public, just as, at the level of genre, romance, a story focused on the fate of a single individual, seeks to preempt tragedy, a story about (in the definition of Isidore of Seville) *res publicas et regum historias*. And at a still further level of complexity, the reader is so entangled in the inward world of eroticism and delicate feeling that. . .the experience should be one not of moral superiority but rather complicity. For the characters, their narrator go-between, and the poem's audience all come to share the desire to suppress the historical consciousness.[57]

The strategy is the familiar (liberal and Chaucerian) one, of containment and co-option: critical elements neutralized by an acknowledgment that incorporates them into the myth-making, in a way that works to strengthen the myth, which is shown to be able to face its own contradictions and yet persist. Chaucer does most with this strategy of containment in the *Canterbury Tales*; already, however, in the *Parliament of Fowls*'s representation of lower-order disaffection, for example, Chaucer worked with it, giving there too "an ultimate civic reassurance: socially based disagreements can be aired in forms that are adequate to containing difference."[58]

The *House of Fame*—possibly unfinished, with its scattershot indictments of honors-systems, set in Ciceronian perspective—may be the better place to look for articulate Chaucerian unease.[59] *Troilus and Criseyde*, meanwhile, rests content to make its case for the importance of human romance, as the central, vital human involvement, to the exclusion of other kinds of relationships, except possibly the still more antisocial *contemptus mundi* advocated at the very end, by a narrator willing to betray the poet's best work—Chaucer's "radical rejection of his own achievement"[60]—for the sake of Christian rectitude, in the conclusion's unreflected Christian moralizing, trying (but failing?) to obliterate the enjoyable worth of human love that the poem elsewhere and more thoroughly celebrates. The poem's concluding lines are "diversionary," Aers put it; "they seek to divert readers' attention. . .from the quite extraordinary and idiosyncratic achievements of the great poem we have been reading."[61] Despite the diversionary ending, *Troilus and Criseyde*'s central, crucial erotic mysticism invests the greatest value—transcendent, absolute value even—in human romantic preoccupation, to the exclusion of all else.

The extent of the poetic labor (ostentatiously) put into finishing the poem, which is the only substantive piece of writing Chaucer ever completed—Chaucer's complex *translatio* of contemporary Italian matter into English, his handling of the numerous other sources and authorities used and advertised in the poem, the careful bookish symmetries that mark its composition, the subtleties of its explorations of the central figures and relations of the narrative, informed by his concurrent Boethian studies, and finally the simple quantity of carefully measured words invested in the poem—all assert the worth of the erotic subject matter. *Troilus and Criseyde* is Chaucer's last, best devotion to the possibilities of an eroticized world without work, where everything beyond romance—production and the reproduction of the means of production is the summary phrase—is taken care of by utterly efficient, transparent others, effortlessly, without friction.

3. The *Canterbury Tales*

There are no such others, and there is always friction: the *Canterbury Tales* is an incipient disciplinary machine. As in his industrial and managerial service there came a point, in 1374, when Chaucer took on, less passive service to the hegemony, a more active part in maintaining it and extending it, so too in his writing his turn to the *Canterbury Tales* makes a homologous shift. The chronology of the shift in Chaucer's poetic work is inscrutable—nothing in it bespeaks even *post hoc ergo propter hoc* causality—and is further complicated by the fact that the new work consisted in some measure of *compilatio*—reassembling pieces written earlier for other purposes, like the "Palamon and Arcite" and "the lyf also of Seynt Cecile" that were rewritten as the *Knight's Tale* and *Second Nun's Tale*.[62] Likewise, the imperfection of the *Canterbury Tales*—extending even to such basics as the shape of the framing journey, as a romance-like riding out and return or a one-way penitential *processus* from sin to salvation, about which Chaucer's thinking changed while working—renders meaningless many remarks about it as a whole work.[63] Chaucer did not finish the *Canterbury Tales*. Consequently, it saw no authorial publication. Some evidence may be taken to indicate that parts of the unfinished work, conceived exclusively as parts of the unfinished work (in this unlike the "Palamon and Arcite," for example), may have leaked into a limited circulation amongst familiars while Chaucer still lived.[64] It was not released by its author into general uncontrolled circulation, however, for use by strangers, in the way *Troilus and Criseyde* evidently was and other earlier finished poems. That the *Canterbury Tales* did not begin to be published until some point or points in the decades 1400–1420 explains too the work's striking absence of influence in the critical earliest phase of Chaucer's reception-history. Even as thoroughgoing an early Chaucerian as Thomas Hoccleve does not appear to have known anything of the *Canterbury Tales* until 1420 or so, when the better part of his Chaucerian work had already been done.[65] Immediately, Chaucer for others could only be the erotic poet of the shorter early poems and *Troilus and Criseyde*.

Finishing the *Canterbury Tales* and causing it to be known as such was not Chaucer's doing, but that of others later. What social work in the world the *Tales* might have done or might have been meant to do by Chaucer himself, had he finished and published, cannot be known. Strictly, the work remained imperfect at the time of his death. Nevertheless, hypotheses about what the work is and does can still be formulated and tested on the basis of what survives. Chaucer finished some parts more than he did others, arguably. Chaucer's work in the *Canterbury Tales*, howbeit imperfect, addresses social relations in direct ways that the erotic apologias avoid, adumbrating thereby schemes of relations that carry active admonitory force. Imperfectly, still the *Canterbury Tales* teaches about certain kinds of social order and orderliness, arguing on their behalf.[66]

As a disciplinary implement, the *Canterbury Tales* works in large part by exclusion again, though the exclusions differ. The work advocates a polity where again class conflict is all but invisible, as if it did not exist. What conflict occurs is attenuated, restricted to talk, and is resolved without resort to force, in deference to tacit consensual standards. By means of such strategic occlusions, the *Canterbury Tales* obviates the real intermittent revolutionary violence associated with contemporary peasants, on the one hand, with their fire and farming tools and other preindustrial weapons, frightful but pathetic; more importantly, it also glosses over the greater actual quotidian violence of exploitation and class rule.[67]

The *Canterbury Tales* leaves out the refractory social extremes, most often and most publicly in open violent conflict. Neither the titular aristocracy nor the peasantry is represented on Chaucer's pilgrimage. There is a plowman amongst the pilgrims (1.529–41); that he is an equestrian, on pilgrimage, simply though well dressed, already indicates something of his peculiarity, that he is a prosperous, successful plowman, especially

arrestingly so by contrast with the other sorts of plowman described elsewhere in the contemporary literature:

> And as I wente be the waie, wepynge for sorowe,
> And seigh a sely man me by, opon the plow hongen.
> His cote was of a cloute that cary was ycalled,
> His hod was full of holes, and his heer oute,
> With his knopped schon clouted full thykke.
> His ton toteden out as he the londe treddede,
> His hosen overhongen his hokschynes on everiche a side,
> Al beslombred in fen as he the plow folwede.
> Twey myteynes, as mete, maad all of cloutes;
> The fyngers weren forwerd and ful of fen honged.
> This whit waselede in the fen almost to the ancle,
> Foure rotheren hym byforn that feble were worthen.
> Men myghte reken ich a ryb, so reufull they weren.
> His wijf walked him with, with a longe gode,
> In a cutted cote, cutted full heyghe,
> Wrapped in a wynwe schete to weren hire fro weders,
> Barfote on the bare ijs, that the blode folwede.
> And at the londes ende laye a litell crom-bolle,
> And theron lay a litell childe lapped in cloutes,
> And tweyne of tweie yeres olde opon another syde,
> And alle they songen o songe, that sorwe was to heren;
> They crieden alle o cry, a carefull note.
> The sely man sighede sore and seide, "Children, beth stille!"[68]

This plowman is the social system's dangerous victim, bodying forth the
personal cost of the exploitation on which the ease of Chaucer's pilgrims
rests. His children are starving.[69] By contrast, Chaucer's plowman represents
the same servitude positively, as beneficial, paying dividends. He embodies
the possibility that quiet hard work within prevailing relations of
production—specifically, "the relative weakness" of English landlords'
"access to 'extra-economic' means of exploitation by direct coercion" and
an answering "cost-effective and competitive production, specialization,
accumulation and innovation" on laborers' part—might engender greater
material ease and independence: the possibility on which the capitalist
order would in time be founded.[70] Chaucer hides the one and shows the
other, obfuscating the damage while lionizing the exploitation's potential
for benefit. About his plowman, Chaucer tells three things: he pays taxes
"ful faire and wel" (1.539–40), pointedly unlike the rebels of 1381; he
would work "withouten hire, if it lay in his myght" (536–38), again unlike
the laborers disciplined by means of the statutes Chaucer enforced as a justice, whose demands for "hire" were precisely the problem; and he was

"a trewe swynkere and a good," specifically, "lyvynge in pees and parfit charitee" (531–32), unlike the pained or angry plowmen of other literature. Chaucer's Plowman knows his place and cherishes it, evidently. His place is to be still, in all senses. This plowman speaks no word and tells no tale but only goes along: the very definition of "a trewe swynkere and a good."[71]

By means of this quiet, grateful Plowman and his still quieter counterpart, the invisible exploiting feudal landlord, having obviated the possibility of some 1381-like violence occurring amongst his pilgrims, the *Canterbury Tales* misrepresents. It leaves out the preponderant demographic— that proportion of the population preoccupied with the labor of production—and it leaves out the economically preponderant group as well—the tiny fraction that yet owned and disposed all the socially accumulated wealth.[72] The notion that the *Canterbury Tales* encompasses the whole of medieval English society, or its corollary, the Robertsonian fantasy that "the medieval world was innocent of" such matters "as class struggles," is mistaken.[73] Chaucer's exclusions are ideological aggression, a bad-faith strategy for propounding a tendentious, class-interested idea of contemporary social relations. Moreover, "Chaucer's work itself becomes a social agent in the constructive possibilities it imagines."[74] By means of its exclusions, the *Canterbury Tales* could pretend that there was no real or significant class conflict, and by pretending contributed something towards making it so.

The exclusions also left Chaucer free to concentrate on the more tractable interstitial or middle social strata. The concentration has the effect of encouraging an equation of this peculiar middle part with the social whole, rendering the part normative and in practice all encompassing. Chaucer's community of penitents, "evene-Cristene" everyone, without extremists, stands in metonymically for a complete society; and so it might be argued that, here again, by equating middle strata with the social whole, Chaucer was doing something "utopian."[75] Already in the *Canterbury Tales*, before the material conditions were in place that would make its realization possible, comes an imaginary evocation of a post-feudal, predominantly bourgeois order, making the whole world over into an image of itself.[76] Similarly, the dissent given voice at various points in the *Canterbury Tales* may evoke even possibilities for the Marcusean "liberation" to come, again before real conditions were in place.[77] The *Canterbury Tales* was not finished. Nonetheless, whatever possibilities for the inchoate bourgeois-capitalist hegemony or personal, individual dissent within it are discernible in Chaucer's writing still always ultimately serve there for bolstering feudal discipline.

In representing (utopian) relations among the middle strata standing in for the social whole on his pilgrimage, Chaucer does the disciplinary labor of delineating an idealized liberal polity, acting towards one another in idealizedly liberal ways, within a particular system of social relations. The society is in fact (and narrowly) orthodoxly Christian, European, feudal, patriarchal, and heteronormative, capable of containing and co-opting whatever dissent or deviance it acknowledges by means of a liberal good will that coerces normalcy by ignoring difference and systemic contradictions. Racial others—Jews and Saracens—and national differences are acknowledged only in passing, and comparatively illiberally, racial and national identities remaining beyond discussion, with Norman- and Anglo-Saxon-derived Englishness the tacit norm, evidently requiring no more defense than the exclusion of others.[78] More characteristically, the *Canterbury Tales* corrects the dissidents to whom it gives voices—the chief figures being the Miller, the Wife of Bath, and the Pardoner—through more and less thorough airings of the difficult issues of class, gender, and orientation that they raise, the discussions concluding with right order restored. "No blood is shed," Paul Strohm wrote. No one is killed or shackled or cast out. The *Tales* conveys this as its "reassuring message": the pilgrimage goes ahead.[79] The only pilgrims silenced are those who mock aristocracy: Chaucer himself and the Squire, whose incompetent performances in the *Sir Thopas* and the *Squire's Tale* still make ridiculous the self-important pretensions of aristocratic literary romance, and the Monk, who makes the single point again and again, that the great fall to ruin—"in se magna ruunt," in Lucan's curter expression—until the Knight stops him.[80] None of these is a potentially dangerous figure, unlike the churl, the woman, or the queer. The Chaucerian maker, the squire, and the monk: each of these enjoys a socially allotted right as such to some place in the dominant order, each serving its preservation, and each is content to be quiet when told to be quiet. The mockery makes nobility seem the stronger, by light of its demonstrated capacity (somewhat) to tolerate ridicule.

The same strategy of "repressive tolerance"[81] also characterizes such debates as do occur amongst Chaucer's pilgrims: the incipient discussion of gentle–churl relations in the early sequence of *Knight's Tale*, *Miller's Tale*, *Reeve's Tale*, *Cook's Tale*, and the still more loosely structured discussion of gender relations in the so-called "Marriage Group." Each discussion begins with a figure of authority articulating the dominance. The Knight fashions an apology for aristocratic power: despite forces that threaten disruption—chiefly accidents of erotic and violent excess, the Venus–Mars pair mediated by Diana in the spectacular theatre of order that Theseus builds, "like God creating the world by reducing chaos to order"[82]—power sustains order, as need arises by force (as with the Amazons) or by philosophy (as with Theseus's "Fair cheyne of love" speech in the end [1.2987–3065]).[83] Subsequently, an apology for male dominance ("Wommen are born to thraldom / And to been under mannes governance" [2.286–87]) is offered by a similar figure of authority, the Man of Law, the lawyer's job being the same as the knight's, order-maintenance for the apparatus of social discipline, albeit that the lawyer uses the comparatively more abstract means of ideas of legality, in addition to the simple physical violence and the threat of it that a knight embodies. In the *Man of Law's Tale*, despite forces threatening to disrupt male dominance—female assertion, in the figure of the Sultan's mother, for example, and ill-managed, excessive male violence, in the attempted rapes—the good woman, Constance, remains constant in her obedience to male figures of authority (God, father, husband), and the male authorities reward her. "To Chaucer's courtly patrons, employers, and friends," Sheila Delany wrote, such a tale would "have been a welcome reaffirmation of hierarchical values."[84]

Such acknowledgments of the troubles of the dominant order as are allowed in the Knight's and Man of Law's apologetics are not left to stand by themselves, and each discussion continues with a dissenting voice. In the first case, the Miller "quites" the Knight by telling a tale that is the same as the Knight's—the same plot, with the same array of characters, the resolution depending on a fall—only inverted: not romance but fabliau, not long ago and far away but here and now, not gentles but churls, not an ethereal love-object for the men to fight over but an animalistic, objectified one, and so on. The point of the Miller's performance is clearest at its conclusion, where chaos prevails, not order. Things looked one way in the Knight's tale—despite accidents, order can still be imposed—and the opposite in the Miller's—despite efforts to impose order, accident triumphs. Similarly, albeit that explicit linkage is out in this second case, the Wife of Bath's performance inverts the *Man of Law's Tale*. Her self-representation in her prologue and the tale she tells show women, not "born to be under man's governance" and constant, but outside governance or exercising governance over men. As a secular childless widow, with her own business interests and property, the Wife is unusually free financially; concomitantly, her attitude towards the usual array of male figures of authority—her husbands and absent father, and the patriarchal authority of the church, as represented by scripture and the individual clerics with whom she must deal—is un-Constance-like and bad.

In both cases, the product of dissent is near chaos, evidence that the story-telling might disintegrate altogether into a non-functioning cacophony of conflicting voices, shouting and speaking over one another rather than taking turns. The Miller is this chaos impersonate. Drunkenly, angrily disregarding the host's authority to elect the Monk to follow the Knight, the most elevated of those who pray to follow the most elevated of those who fight, the Miller insists that his churlish voice should have precedence. "The Miller's revolt is socially based," Strohm has said, effectively "a literary Peasants' Rebellion."[85] Even before he begins his tale proper, he so

offends, not only the gentles, but also the Reeve that the Reeve insists on
following the Miller, and already the Host's order of telling is lost. Authority is overthrown. The Reeve's vindictive, *ad hominem* reply to the Miller
pleases no one but the diseased Cook, whose oozing flesh, resembling his
blancmange, represents a churlish cancer threatening to poison the whole
order, but on which the Cook's masters must still feed. The Cook too disputes the Host's authority, going so far as to attack him directly. The Cook's
tale degrading him disintegrates in dissolution (riot and the "wyf" who
"swyved for hir sustenaunce" [1.4421–22]) before the subversive job it is
promised to do has been done, but not before its oblique, exemplary point
about the consequences of subverting authority has been made: from
Miller to Reeve to Cook, such subversion induces to chaos.[86]

The subversion of right order begun by the Miller yields greater disor-
der, by way of the Reeve's rejoinder leading on to the Cook's fragment.
The dissolution ensuing must look more frightening than the coercive,
abusive authority with which the sequence began; however disagreeable
the Knight and his surrogate Theseus may be to elements amongst the pilgrims, demonstrably they are not worse than the churlish alternative on
offer. The relatively thorough airing that the churlish alternative is given in
this sequence of tales works in this way ultimately to strengthen authority,
establishing at once that, no matter how objectionable authority may be,
the alternative to it is worse, and also that authority is strong enough to
absorb criticism, even to be corroborated by it. The Knight may leave
authority looking intermittently horrific ("Myn is the prison in the derke
cote; / Myn is the stranglyng and hangyng by the throte" and so on
[2457–58]), but the alternative, as bodied forth in the churls' performance,
is the end of the world.

The destructive propensities of criticism are also made clear through the
performance of the Wife of Bath, though in the end the subversion of
gender-roles that she represents calls for more explicit, thorough disciplinary
rectification than did the incompetent rumblings of the churls. Like the
Miller's, the Wife's dissidence invites others to intervene, to interpose their
idiosyncratic agendas, at odds with the order the host would impose. First,
the Pardoner interjects his perverse question about marriage (3.163–92).
That the pilgrim apparently least likely to marry traditionally should be the
one to point out that the Wife's implicit underminings of marital canons in
her remarks can lead to further questionings of marriage repeats the pattern
established in the previous group of tales, with subversions of order provoking further subversions of order, leading on to chaos. The Wife subverts male
dominance, overturning the "natural" superiority of male over female; given
the problems he poses the other pilgrims ("I trowe he were a geldyng
or a mare," the narrator puts it [1.691]), the Pardoner's interruption

must raise the further subversive possibility of undoing the dominant gender-categories with which even the Wife works: not male sovereign over female, nor yet female sovereign over male, but not even a functioning distinction between male and female. The disruptive implications of the Pardoner's interjection are left dangling. Subsequently, the Friar interrupts the Wife too, implying that her speech has violated the womanly ideal of silence (3.829–56). To her defense comes the Summoner, whose relations with the Pardoner are suggested to be close (in the General Prologue, "This Somonour bar to hym a stif burdoun" [673]). So, after the Wife is finished, the Friar and the Summoner take their turn trading tales on their own initiative, for purposes at odds with the order of the tale-telling contest. Churls work with churls, implicitly, upsetting right order at the outset; here, misfits of other sorts—the Wife, the Pardoner, and the Summoner—work together differently though with the same chaotic result for the host's order. Dissent invites dissolution; questioning established order unleashes anarchy.

However, here a threat of anarchy has not enough disciplinary weight by itself, evidently. After the interruption of the Friar and the Summoner, various pilgrims take on the job of rectifying what the Wife has done, more and less explicitly, in the "Marriage Group." In his "paean to 'obseisaunce,' to the subordination an inferior owes to a superior,"[87] the Clerk repeats the Man of Law's idealization of womanly subservience in a still more extreme form, arguing, with explicit reference to the Wife of Bath and "al hire secte" (1171), that, even when male authority's demands are unreasonable, rewards still come to the constantly submissive woman. The Merchant shows the consequences of the kind of subversion the Wife championed, in his own and his protagonist's humiliation in submission to unnaturally sovereign wives ("This Januarie, who is glad but he? / He kisseth hire and clippeth hire ful ofte, / And on hire wombe he stroketh hire ful softe" [4.2412–14]).[88] And the Franklin's final compromise—"one of the most thorough pieces of conservative secular ideology in the whole Tales," it has been called[89]—ostensibly solving the Marriage Group problem, depends again on womanly submission, on a wife's willingness to submit to non-consensual sex when told to do so by her husband ("Trouthe is the hyeste thyng that man may kepe" [5.1479]).

The Canterbury Tales gives voice to some dissidence, in the Miller, the Wife, and the Pardoner. This is liberal. This is "fre." The dissidence is also disciplined, the threat of anarchy supplying one sort of sanction, the more explicit responses to the Wife supplying another; and the dissenters are welcomed back, more or less, into the fellowship. The Host's kiss, at the end of the Pardoner's performance, prompted by the Knight's violent intervention, is the model (6.960–68), though neither the Miller nor the Wife gets one.[90] This too is characteristically liberal: a capacity to tolerate a certain amount of dissent, within limits, provided that dissent, having been heard, is willing to capitulate or can be coerced. Dissent submitted to discipline makes rectitude look stronger than a less tolerant alternative could; thereby rectitude is proven to be capacious enough to hear dissent, and to absorb it even, still without fundamental disruption.

Historically, religious dissent was to prove less tractable, and the *Canterbury Tales*'s response to it is correspondingly the more profound. The criticism of pardons made through the Pardoner and his performance is reactionary, unlike Langland's. Piers Plowman pulls the pardon that comes to him in twain;[91] in Chaucer, the pardon's integrity is spared. Despite the manifold corruptions to which the institution was prey—corruptions already made clear in the *General Prologue* and then confirmed by the Pardoner himself in his confessional oratory—within the church's penitential-disciplinary program, pardons still worked. A thoroughly, cynically corrupt Pardoner can tell a morally efficacious tale, feeding his own greed while also preaching persuasively that "*Radix malorum est Cupiditas*" (6.334). By the same token, fraudulent pardons, forgeries even, if used in good faith, still had a power to contribute to souls' salvation. Within the church, no matter the imperfections of the persons who served it, all was well; outside it, nothing would work.[92]

The *Canterbury Tales* answers religious deviance back most forcefully by the framework of orthodox religious observance it invokes and uses, howbeit imperfectly: pilgrimage. Pilgrimage was already matter for struggle by the time Chaucer began writing about it in the 1380s or 1390s. Again, a contrast with Langland may be instructive. His intermittent critical remarks culminate in an all but outright rejection of pilgrimage in the sixth passus of the B-text, where its place is taken by the plowing of Piers's half-acre— the ordinary, active Christian good life of work in the world being by itself a preferable *via in Deum*.[93] As William Thorpe was to put it later,

> I clepe hem trewe pilgrymes travelynge toward the blis of hevene whiche, in the staat, degree or ordre that God clepith hem to, bisien hem feithfulli for to occupie alle her wittis, bodili and goostli, to knowe treweli and to kepe feithfulli the heestis of God, hatynge evere and fleynge alle the sevene dedli synnes and every braunche of hem. . . .Of these pilgrymes I seide, whatever good thought that thei ony tyme thenken, what vertues worde that thei speken, and what fructuouse werk that thei worchen, every such thought, word, and werke is a stap noumbrid of God toward him into hevene.[94]

The lollard attack on pilgrimage included specific criticisms—of the disruptions that reveling pilgrims brought in their wake, the wasteful spending on hospitality that the practice entailed, and so on, again described by Thorpe[95]—but pilgrimage also provided a visible, public focus for lollardy's most general source of disaffection: the church's interposition of hierarchy between God and Christians, the hierarchy serving neither God nor Christians but itself, exploiting its position of spiritual authority for worldly gain. Pilgrimage was revenue-extraction from this perspective, with the added benefit of binding Christian laity the more securely to the hierarchy's imposed scheme of penitential discipline. Again, in Thorpe's words,

> Siche madde peple wasten blamfulli Goddis goodis in her veyne pilgry-mageyng, spendynge these goodis upon vicious hosteleris and upon tapsters, whiche ben ofte unclene wymmen of her bodies, and at the laste tho goodis, of the whiche thei schulden do werkis of mercy aftir Goddis heeste to pore nedi men and wymmen, these pore men goodis and her lyflode these renners aboute offren to riche preestis whiche have moche moore lyfelode than thei neden. And thus tho goodis thei wasten wilfulli and spenden hem uniustli agens Goddis heeste upon strangeris, with the whiche thei schulden helpe and releeven aftir Goddis wille her pore and nedi neighebores at home.[96]

This lollard dissent is kept out of the *Canterbury Tales*, or made little, where lollardy is mentioned by name only in a brief joke at the expense of the most devout of the tale-tellers, the Parson, to do with a more peripheral lollard criticism, of oath-swearing, in a passage probably meant for cancellation appearing at the end of most of the manuscripts' *Man of Law's Tale* (2.1170–77).[97] Here again, by leaving out the most contentious element from the discussion, Chaucer renders the orthodox unarguable. He treats what was in fact controversial as if it were natural, as if it were a something that could go without saying. Chaucer's choice of pilgrimage for framing the *Canterbury Tales*, with his affirmations of its virtues in the *Parson's Tale*—"Chaucer's most elaborate tribute to the hegemony of penance," in David Lawton's phrase[98]—and intermittently *passim*, is tendentious. The purpose was discipline. When Alison "swoor her ooth, by Seint Thomas of Kent" to have sex later with "hende Nicholas" (who holds her "by the queynte"), it comes as a reminder of the pervasive religious-disciplinary purpose, at a moment in the tale-telling contest when that purpose might otherwise have seemed forgone.[99] In the end, Chaucer's Parson (the perfect disciplinarian because unrecognizable as such, unlike the Knight or Man of Law, and self-disciplining: "wonder diligent," the narrator points out, "but in his techyng discreet and benygne," "That first he wroghte, and afterward he taughte") is allotted the (surviving) last word, which he uses for spelling out the basic doctrinal point: life is pilgimage, and pilgrimage is life, a penitential-disciplinary process that is the only efficient *via in Deum*—"the righte wey of Jerusalem celestial," "a ful noble wey and a ful convenable, whiche may nat fayle to man ne to womman"—the "parfit glorious pilgrymage" guaranteed capable of delivering to salvation. To gain it, no way is allowed other than submitting to the discipline of penance. "The *Parson's Tale* seeks full submission to church authority as embodied in its injunctions and sacraments," Strohm put it; in the end, "the principle of hierarchy is firmly reinstated, with each person situated within a vertical *ordo* or scheme of subjection."[100]

A thread woven through the whole of Chaucer's literary production is this kind of police-work: enforcement of the established order by literary-cultural means. Writing was for him another job, alienable labor undertaken for reward. The rewards may have been ill-defined, and the connection between work and recompense tenuous. Nothing in the documentary records of Chaucer's doings matches the kinds of receipts that turn up in the Lydgate life-records.[101] Still, it is difficult to conceive that the *Book of the Duchess*—which would not have been written if it had not been written for John of Gaunt—yielded Chaucer nothing. Unlike John Gower, the nearest Chaucer comes to representing writer–patron relations directly is the (idealized, possibly ironized) account in the prologue to the *Legend of Good Women*: for fear as much as anything else, the writer does what the patron tells him to, though the order need not always be as explicit as it is there;[102] and in any event, the "Complaint to his Purse" confirms a self-consciousness on Chaucer's part of what literary work was for. Certainly writing was work for him, as confirmed by the formal elaborations—his cartage / *translatio* of various materials from elsewhere (French verse forms, Italian narrative matter, ancient philosophy), and the managerial work of *compilatio* that went into the *Canterbury Tales*.

The end product of Chaucer's literary labors—what Chaucer brought into the market-place for sale, to speak somewhat anachronistically—was the articulation of hegemony. Not open polemic on its behalf nor criticism of it for the sake of its repair, though both figure intermittently in Chaucer's *oeuvre*, but instead a kind of myth-making, serving and protecting hegemony by representing as natural and inevitable—as if the antisocial world without work, or noble erotic preoccupation, or a "fre" middling polity, purged of religious variety, the class-struggle rendered invisible, and so on, though not without compliant individual dissidence within it, might be taken for granted—states of affairs that were not.

CHAPTER 3

RECEPTION

The Horatian dictum *poeta nascitur non fit* wants to be reversed in the case of Chaucer. He was not a born poet, but a fabricated one, whose literary-historical place as the father of English poetry resulted less from talent or vision or any intrinsic merits of his verse born of either, but of his particular social location, doing his particular jobs at the time and place, this social location investing his verse with perspectives and attitudes and values that made the verse amenable to bearing the historical weight it has had and retains.[1] Chaucer has been a useful poet, rather than a good one, because he could serve. Immediately, the writings themselves served the same interests Chaucer worked for in his household and state bureaucratic employments; Chaucer's writings also served other writers, contemporaries and after-comers, as a useful model for what poetry and poetic success might be.

The motive force was class-conflict, again in the particular local forms resulting from the demographic catastrophe of the mid-century plague and its literary-cultural sublimate: the trouble with English. The trouble with English was William Langland. Langland was there already, in advance of any Chaucerian alternative. But as a father for English literature, Langland would not do: *engagé*, visionary, broadly political more than literary, and, in any event, manifestly unruly. *Piers Plowman* was amongst the causes of the Great Revolt of 1381. The leaders of those who came streaming into London by the Aldgate, where Chaucer's residence was, had given themselves Langlandian *nommes de guerre*, personification-like, nor is this the only evidence that the rebels' textbook was *Piers Plowman*.[2]

No matter that the 1381 revolution was fought over relations of production and the political arrangements sustaining them, nor that Wycliffite affinities amongst the revolutionaries were tenuous, the official explanation soon propagated was that it had been a lollard manifestation, driven by deviant religion.[3] Sedition and lollardy were equated, and the equation was widely put about. Because lollardy was "the English heresy," as Anne Hudson wrote, in the sense that realization of its practical and dogmatic religious program depended on broadening English usage and enfranchising the Anglophone population, the crackdown on lollardy in the generations between 1377, the first London trial of John Wyclif, and the Oldcastle rebellion of 1414, had palpable literary effects, both in determining what could be written and for the reception of what had been written.[4] Self-censorship disfigured the work of the *Mum and the Sothsegger* poet perhaps already in the fourteenth century; after the promulgation of the *De heretico comburendo* in 1401 and the Arundel Constitutions in 1407, it was illegal for certain sorts of persons to own or to use copies of *Piers Plowman*.[5]

English could not be obliterated, any more than labor, however. Just as from the perspective of authority labor had to be managed and controlled, for the sake of maintaining the dominance, so too English had to be co-opted into the job of maintaining the dominance instead of attacking or subverting it. The Chaucerian tradition is the literary-cultural complement to the antilabor legislation of the same period in the sphere of direct class discipline: an English literature which nevertheless still knew its place, which was to serve and to protect (not to subvert) the dominance of the ruling class. In the circumstance, had Chaucer not existed, it would have been exigent to invent him.

It might be felt that John Gower's work, representing another non-Langlandian alternative, might have served as well as Chaucer's for founding a complacent English literature. Ultimately, however, the problem with Gower was the same as the problem with Langland: Gower too was too political. Chaucer ignored the events of 1381, for example, except briefly to mock the peasant-revolutionaries, long afterwards, in the unpublished *Nun's Priest's Tale*; as Paul Strohm said, "Chaucer's usual tendency is deliberately to efface any demonstrable connections between contemporary politics and the meaning of his text."[6] Gower's implication in these same events was immediate and direct: the detailed, sanguinary *Visio Angliae* (later incorporated into the *Vox clamantis*) that he wrote to justify the campaigns of repression taking place throughout the late summer and fall of 1381. Gower's writings—including relatively later English ones like the prologue of the *Confessio amantis* ("For alle resoun wolde this, / That unto him which heved is, / The membres buxom scholden bowe") or the still later Lancastrian "In Praise of Peace" (addressing Henry IV, "In whome the glade fortune is befalle / The poeple to governe upon this erthe": "God hath the chose")—consistently incorporate direct apologies for class rule and hierarchy, arguing in their favor.[7] Not to mention the linguistic peculiarities of his output—first French, then Latin, finally English—nor his prosodic malfeasance—the fact that Gower never tried the sort of formal sophistications that characterize even Chaucer's earliest verse, but especially

Gower's persistence with the rude tetrameters for which Shakespeare ridiculed him personally still in the early seventeenth century—Gower's writing was as *engagé* as Langland's, albeit conservatively or reactionarily, and so too was insufficiently free for the kind of ideological confabulation that emerges as Chaucer's distinctive contribution.

The more tantalizing alternative might be the *Pearl*-poet: a Middle English writer of genius by any aesthetic measure, unparalledly skilled about his work with "lel letteres loken."[8] The religious matter in the four (fairly) securely attributable poems, especially *Cleanness* and *Patience*, though also *Pearl* and *Gawain*, is at once orthodox and also non-clerical or open in address, in the vernacular.[9] Openly, accessibly appealing but never anticlerical in religious matters, the poems are also without direct political comment or engagement in current affairs. *St Erkenwald* might connect the poet with metropolitan ecclesiastical politics, howbeit obliquely, but *St Erkenwald* might not be the same poet's work.[10] Such immediate problems about these poems, of dating and even of attribution, may raise the more generally consequential difficulty: the writing failed to find an audience. This failure may have been an accident of dialect and the pre-eminence that metropolitan English was already coming to enjoy by the time the *Pearl*-poet set to work. In any case, this was apparently a provincial poet, locally secure, whose work did not travel well or at all, from region to region or over time.[11]

Evidently, creative genius or aesthetic accomplishment cannot have been the only factors. Otherwise, the *Pearl*-poet might have been made the "father of English poetry," and he was not. Such canvassing of hypothetical alternatives—other possibilities besides Langland, Gower, or the *Pearl*-poet might yet be considered—may shed some light on what was distinctive about Chaucer's work, by contrast with what contemporaries of his were doing, possibly making Chaucer's work apt for the election that did fall on it, quickly. The fact is that, whatever the causes and no matter the conceivable alternatives, only Chaucer has had this peculiar preeminence in English literary history. His election to this preeminence can be seen as it was occurring, in the ways his contemporaries and immediate successors reacted to him and his writings.

Chaucer's *apocolocyntosis*, by means of which he was metamorphosed from an upper managerial financial officer to the official state poet, the canonical founder of English literature—this process of inventing a Chaucer who could be a father for English literature, servile and polite—was underway already while Chaucer lived, before he stopped writing, evidently even before he began to write the *Canterbury Tales*. It is tempting to imagine that Chaucer was himself mindful of what might be and connived at making it come about. The unusual concern he showed over his own literary corpus and its transmission—witness the several lists of his own writings that he made—is suggestive of a wish on his part deliberately to shape his own literary legacy as such.[12]

The *Canterbury Tales* is inconsequential for this process of transformation. There is no mention of the *Canterbury Tales*, nor any reference to something that must be a part of the *Canterbury Tales*, until 1420–22, when John Lydgate wrote the prologue for his *Siege of Thebes*.[13] There is some evidence suggesting that Chaucer made available some part of the unfinished *Canterbury Tales* to friends of his, while he was still alive and writing. This evidence is restricted to a remark by Chaucer himself, in a brief verse epistle to an intimate, about the Wife of Bath.[14] There are also references to a piece probably related to the surviving *Knight's Tale* though not identical with it: Chaucer himself refers to his having made something of "al the love of Palamon and Arcite" in the *Legend of Good Women*, and John Clanvowe quotes from such a work before 1391.[15] But the *Canterbury Tales*, left unfinished by Chaucer at the time of his death, seems not to have come into circulation—into being, even—until somewhat later. The earliest surviving copies date from about 1410, possibly slightly earlier, and it is conceivable that there were other now lost copies in earlier circulation, though the textual nature of the earliest surviving copies bespeaks fundamental editorial invention of the *Canterbury Tales* as we know the work still occurring as the earliest copies were being fabricated.[16] In any event, by choice or by default, those who made Chaucer a figure of literary authority did so largely or exclusively on the basis of his earlier, published erotic writings.[17]

The properties of a Chaucer who would serve as a father of English literature had already been articulated during the fourteenth century, largely or exclusively on the basis of his erotic writings, other than the *Canterbury Tales*. Chaucer could serve in this capacity because what he wrote (not excluding the *Canterbury Tales*) corroborated ruling class dominance. English literature in his practice was not only no threat to the dominance; it was also the most effective literary prop for the dominance that might have been fashioned: a literature confirming that the social status quo was optimal by obviating even the need to argue as much. This fundamental political-apologetic reaction of the literary production that characterizes Chaucer's own writing and the Chaucerian literary tradition following after it was already evident to those of his contemporaries and near-contemporaries who knew him while living and responded earliest to his writings. Eustache Deschamps, Thomas Usk, Gower himself, Jean Froissart, and John Clanvowe, already before 1400, articulate the properties that Chaucer had and would retain in his assumed role as the father of English literature; the slightly later work of Henry Scogan, in brief, and Thomas Hoccleve, at greater length, shows the incipient Chaucerianism of the fourteenth century already codified before the death of Henry IV in

1413: Chaucer distracted, unlike Langland or Gower pretending there was no trouble, and so Chaucer served. The establishment of literature as such for English—as a distinctive branch of writing—rests here: non-industrial distraction, *ars gratia artis*.[18]

1. Eustache Deschamps

The evidence is that already while Chaucer lived his writings were perceived by others (as perhaps he would have intended) as providing a safe alternative to seditious or overtly political English writing. Probably the earliest reference to Chaucer's literary work occurs in a poem by Eustache Deschamps, headed "Autre balade" in the unique surviving copy: another ballad.[19] It refers clearly only to Chaucer's English verse translation of the *Roman de la rose*, probably written by about 1380;[20] absence of reference to anything later in Deschamps' ballad suggests an early date for it, though the quality and extent of Deschamps' knowledge of Chaucer's literary work are dubious. William Calin makes the fundamental point about Deschamps' poem, that it (like much of the subsequent tradition of Chaucerian criticism and allusion) need not have had to do with any thorough knowledge of specific or peculiar qualities of Chaucer's writing:

> Deschamps would have had no occasion to learn English and, given the mind-set of the age, no reason to do so either. The famous 'Balade to Chaucer' is fulsome, conventional rhetoric that recalls earlier texts by a number of figures including Deschamps himself. It indicates no more than that Sir Lewis Clifford, an eminent habitué of French and English court circles, must have spoken to Deschamps on Chaucer's behalf, and Deschamps (1) was flattered and (2) wanted to please Clifford.[21]

No matter Deschamps' ignorance, his ballad can still delineate already at the beginning of the tradition the characteristics of Chaucerian poetry that were to determine its historical importance and utility for others. What mattered to Deschamps was Chaucer's social location–the fact that Chaucer was a king's person and enjoyed some more intimate link with Lewis Clifford—combined with Chaucer's espousal of a particular canon of taste in his literary work: the poetry is erotic, private not public, ostensibly personal rather than of corporate social concern. Despite the eventual preeminence of the *Canterbury Tales*—in the final analysis doing the same disciplinary job albeit by more direct means—it was the Chaucerian erotic writings, from the complaints to *Troilus and Criseyde*, that defined Chaucerianism for contemporaries and the immediately ensuing literary generations. Slight in content, though formally elaborate, the distinction of such Chaucerian writing was to reproduce within itself and to propagate subordination to dominance, celebrating an antisocial contemporary aristocratic culture of willful *otium*.

The organizing topic of Deschamps' ballad is a variety of *translatio studii*: from Greco-roman antiquity to France to England, a definite kind of polite cultural labor has migrated. The agent said herein to bring this migration to completion is Geoffrey Chaucer, whom the ballad's refrain represents as *grand translateur*. From this perspective, Chaucer is an instrument of cultural imperialism. Although Francophone political hegemony in England had dissipated, French dominance (albeit without hegemony) in culture still persists, by virtue of the colonized intellectual's work as a *translateur*, carrying over into the English context, not just the *ipsissima verba* of something like the *Roman de la rose*, but a whole broad system of values deriving from the French high culture.[22] Putting Chaucer and the English he represents in this position of cultural subordination entails ignoring distinctively English achievements—alliterative verse, for example—that did not reproduce French canons of taste. It also involves Deschamps in occasional oblique denigration of England, a brutish island of giants, big but slow, first conquered by the Trojan Brutus: "L'isle aux Geans, ceuls de Bruth" [the Isle of Giants, they of Brutus] (7). Deschamps uses even an antique backhanded compliment: albeit that the locals are physically prepossessing, angelic even, in the Gregorian pun, "en la terre angelique" [in the angelic land] (12) they are ignorant, their exterior beauty requiring extensive interior remediation, by others better formed than they are, for their own good.

To some incalculable degree, however, the subordinating implications of this topic are undone in the ballad's third stanza and envoy, where Deschamps suggests that, like other French cultural workers, he might learn from Chaucer too, rather than only vice versa:

A toy pour ce de la fontaine Helye
Requier avoir un buvraige autentique,
Dont la doys est du tout en ta baillie,
Pour rafrener d'elle ma soif ethique,
Qui en Gaule seray paralitique
Jusques a ce que tu m'abuveras.
Eustaces sui, qui de mon plant aras:
Mais pran en gré les euvres d'escolier
Que par Clifford de moy avoir pourras,
Grand translateur, noble Gieffroy Chaucier.

L'ENVOY
Poete hault, loënge d'escuîrie,

En ton jardin ne seroie qu'ortie:
Considère ce que j'ay dit premier—
Ton noble plant, ta douce melodie;
Mais, pour sçavoir, de rescripre te prie,
Grant translateur, noble Geffroy Chaucier.

[Wherefore I ask that I may have from thee a genuine draught from the spring of Hippocrene, whose rill is altogether in thy possession, so that I may check my feverish thirst for it: here in Gaul I shall be as a paralytic until thou shalt make me drink. A Eustace am I, thou shalt have some of my plants; but look with favor upon the schoolboy productions which thou mayst receive from me through Clifford, O great translator, noble Geoffrey Chaucer. High poet, (the) glory of squirehood, in thy garden I should be only a nettle: bethink thee of what I have described above, thy noble plants, thy sweet music! Nevertheless, that I may not be left in doubt, I beg thee to return me an official opinion, O great translator, noble Geoffrey Chaucer.]

(21–36)

This sort of self-cancellation, or suspension of the principle of noncontradiction, occurs often enough in Deschamps' ballad to be characteristic of it, beginning strikingly in the poem's opening invocation, addressing Chaucer:

O Socratès plains de philosophie,
Seneque en meurs, Anglius en pratique,
Ovides grans en ta poëterie.
[O Socrates full of wisdom, a Seneca in uprightness of life, an Aulus Gellius in practical affairs, an Ovid great in thy poetic lore.]

(1–3)

Grandness or grandeur is not perhaps the first quality to come to mind when considering the poetry of Ovid, including the *Metamorphoses*, where Ovid still shows regularly a spooky flair for turning even moments of potentially great pathos into low comedy (the burst sewer-main image, e.g., for Pyramus's mortal effusion), Chaucer-like perhaps.[23] Similarly, Aulus Gellius does transmit a great deal of rare information, some of which may have been of some utility; still, the *Noctes Atticae* may be the least practically useful thing ever composed: utterly diffuse, from which useful information can be gleaned only by hours and hours of leisured circumambulant reading. Seneca was a moralist, whose moralizing produced Nero and the Boudiccan revolt in Britain, while the philosophy of Socrates—the corrupter of youth, who had to be killed, for bringing in strange gods—was to have no philosophy, only questions.[24]

Chaucer was not another Socrates, no matter what Deschamps might say. The point is that, even leaving Chaucer out, what Deschamps has to say about Socrates is already incomprehensible. Deschamps' poem is characterized throughout by this sort of straining after effect, rhetorical and otherwise, even at the expense of sense. The formal elaboration of the ballad does not match the excess that characterizes others of Deschamps' production, nor that of such Chaucerian pieces as the complaint of the *Anelida and Arcite*: here, three ten-line stanzas with the same rhyme-pattern (*a b a b b c c d c d*) and the same four rhymes (*-ie*, *-ique*, *-as*, and *-ier*), the first and last of them (*-ie* and *-ier*) recurring also in the six-line envoy (rhyming *a a d a a d*), with a refrain repeated four times, concluding each of the sections. The vocabulary of Deschamps' poem is ostentatiously Greek—including *ethimologique* (15) as well as the more predictable *philosophie, theorique*, and so forth—the recurrence of such terms as rhyme-words—for example, the rhyme *ethique* and *paralitique* (24–25)—lending their appearance still greater emphasis. The syntax is tortuous—the verb ("tu edifias" [thou hast been constructing] [19]) for the object "un vergier" [a fruit-garden] (17) is three lines postponed, for example, and the dependent phrase "de la Rose" (12), of the book-title, is not completed until "le Livre" (16) comes up four lines further on, both the Gregorian anecdote and Deschamps' curiously personal etymology for "England" ("d'Angela saxonne" [from the Saxon lady Angela] [13]) separating them—and Deschamps' vocabulary too comes under stress: *ethique*, for example, in the phrase "ma soif ethique" (24). On the basis of such considerations, the poem has justifiably been characterized as "intensely artificial and rather difficult," written in "a style forced and *tormenté* to a degree unusual even for Deschamps."[25] But Deschamps does not even care always to make sense. No one has been able to divine what the term *pandras* (9) might mean.[26] Sense is not requisite.

Less rhetorically prominent than the *translatio studii* topic in the poem, though still pervasive, is a series of quasi-agricultural metaphors: the notion that Chaucer "as / Semé les fleurs et planté le rosier" [hast sown flowers and planted the rose tree] (7–8) and has for long been making "un vergier" (17) and a "jardin" (32), for which Deschamps (and others) offer *plants* (17, 27, and 34), though Deschamps fears "en ton jardin ne seroie qu'ortie" [in thy garden I should be only a nettle] (32). In this recurrent choice of metaphor, there may be an allusion to material production, the world of work that the Chaucerian erotic poetry wants to occlude but cannot obliterate—here, the fundamental agricultural variety of production. Specifically, though, Deschamps' metaphors refer directly only to gardening, the non-industrial, strictly decorative end of agriculture, as if England were no more than a garden, its maintenance no more fraught or conflicted a matter than ornamental recreation.

Deschamps uses this recurrent figure as an image for characterizing Chaucer's poetic work: Chaucer is praiseworthy as a poet because this is the sort of thing he does too, in Deschamps' company. The good poet's job is to produce (agricultural-laborer-like). But what the good poet produces (gardener-like) is strictly decorative and ornamental, not useful. Otherwise, the poetry is too troubling and not much good. This is the perspective from which nonsense can be desirable in a poem. As gardening is to productive agriculture, so formally elaborate, contentually vacuous poetry is to writing in general: pretty, and the more so the more pointless it is. Too much meaning is too much work, too connected as sense is by reference to extra-poetic reality. Nonsense is good decoratively because it has no such weighty obligations.

The kind of care-free decorative nonsense and semi-contingent sense that Deschamps produces and characterizes Chaucer as producing as well is suited to the context of class need, for sustaining the desirable illusion that a care-free aristocratic life is a good and possible life. Deschamps praises Chaucer for doing what Deschamps himself does in this same poem: cultivate a capacity for saying little or nothing, elegantly, for the sake of establishing a claim that nothing need be said. The claim is that this is a cultural milieu from which necessity has disappeared, non-industrial unproductive recreational diversion only remaining: a void culture, of formal elaboration, content-free or -thin, intending "to prove that crude practical considerations have been dispensed with, to prove, in particular, that one can spend one's time on the useless in order to improve one's position in the social hierarchy, increase one's social honor, and, finally, strengthen one's power over others. Culture turns against utility for the sake of a mediated utility."[27] Such a claim is best put obliquely, for stating it directly is to make it a matter for argument, where the point is conflict-suppression—conflict-management by conflict-avoidance: evasion.

Despite his likely and inevitable ignorances of much about Chaucer's writings, Deschamps is right about Chaucer in historically crucial ways. Though his ballad would not have circulated widely and so may not have had a causal agency in shaping the tradition of reception, still it sums up what mattered about Chaucer. Chaucer was an erotic poet: "Tu es d'amours mondains dieux en Albie" [Thou art a mundane God of Love in Albia] (11). Though there may be some difficulty about the adjective, the point was that Chaucer's writing was like Deschamps' ballad: if not strictly erotic then certainly not social or political or ethical or practical in some other way—possibilities that English literature might have fulfilled, had the example of Langland or Gower been taken as seriously as only the example of Chaucer was. The Chaucerian writing, by contrast, was of personal, individual fulfillment, in a private sphere, to the point of being antisocial;

moreover, in Deschamps' representation, it was also servile. The Chaucerian writing served cultural imperialism—the French cultural dominance without political hegemony that the *translatio studii* describes. Above all, it served to sustain an aristocratic culture of vacuity, to prop up the illusion, as much as possible without adverting to its illusory nature, for doing so would be to invite criticism. Erotic Chaucer was servile and antisocial too, as would also be the Chaucerian tradition developing from his example. In Deschamps' phrase, "noble" Chaucer, the "poete hault," is also always equally the "loënge d'escuîrie," the glory of servile station.

2. Thomas Usk's *Testament of Love*

Deschamps was perceptive about Chaucer's literary work—accidentally perceptive, as the result of shared similarities of situation and ambition rather than any particular knowledge or study on Deschamps's part: Chaucer had written little yet, and Deschamps had no English. The job of making an English literary tradition out of Chaucer's example—the Chaucer whose chief literary contribution, servile erotic distraction, was articulated already by Deschamps, though not necessarily with immediate consequence following from Deschamps' intervention—fell to writers working in Chaucer's own English circumstance, placed more or less as Chaucer was or had been in the peculiar local scheme of things: literate servants with cognate ambitions. Within a generation of the production of Deschamps' ballad, such locals would appear to have become numerous: Usk, Scogan, Hoccleve, and so on, all sharing a Deschamps-like perception of what Chaucer's literary accomplishment had been, a capacity to do similar things in writing, and a will to advertise their dependence on Chaucer's example.

The earliest of these self-conscious local emulants of Chaucer was Thomas Usk, who, probably during late 1384 and early 1385, wrote something he named *The Testament of Love*.[28] Though in its prose form and philosophical reach the *Testament* may appear to fasten on irregular facets of the Chaucerian corpus, its grasp of the Chaucerian basics is sound. It is insightful as Deschamps had been on the subject of what matters about Chaucer. Moreover, Usk used Chaucer's literary example, in ways that Deschamps could not or would not, and Usk's *Testament* makes a point of advertising its dependence, praising Chaucer for what he was accomplishing in the same field. Usk's *Testament* is explicitly antipolitical, arguing against activist engagement in social process and in favor of apolitical private enjoyment. Chaucer's early erotic work—the object of Deschamps' prior concentration too—made the same argument, albeit implicitly, the purpose being, more generally, to prop up the aristocratic good life, the job Chaucer did also in his later disciplinary writings like the *Canterbury Tales* by more direct means. By making explicit this socially conservative function of Chaucerian writing, on which the Chaucerian tradition was founded, with the *Testament* Usk carried forward the propagation of the relation of servile writer to beneficent power that Chaucer had started. Both for his literary manner and substance and for his writing's servility and his perception of his servile writing's potential to yield rewards—for form and content as well as for the social-productive functions of his writing—Usk was altogether dependent on Chaucer's example, and his work promoted it.

Usk belonged to a nascent social group of "textworkers," in Anne Middleton's formulation: persons "for whom documentary and bibliographic high literacy is a means and a medium of service," "men *of letters*" literally, "scriveners as well as versifiers, ecclesiastical and legal odd-job and regular-service men of several sorts."[29] Though his life took more dramatic turns than those of most employed as he was, being a scrivener by trade, Usk had this kind of craft-literacy in common with Chaucer already, in other words, in addition to their common involvement in secular politics and social engineering by their employments.

Before belatedly and briefly turning to Chaucerian writing, Usk had been a political agitator. By October 1381 and possibly as early as July 1376, Usk involved himself with the party of John Northampton, a guildsman and eventual militant populist mayor of London. Northampton employed Usk nominally as bill-writer; in fact, Usk was active—more active than published records indicate—as Northampton's "press agent and propagandist," especially in organizing and spreading the sedition that Northampton encouraged when he failed to win re-election as mayor in October 1383.[30] Usk was wholly occupied with political agitation on Northampton's behalf from October 1383 to about mid-February 1384 when the new mayor, Chaucer's customs colleague Nicholas Brembre, moved decisively to suppress his opposition, and Usk's name disappeared from the records for a time. He may have been among those who fled London following riots in February. In any event, Usk was arrested and imprisoned for his role in the sedition on about July 20, 1384. By the end of the month, however, when Brembre put a petition to the king for process of law against Northampton and several of his supporters, including Usk, Usk had turned against Northampton and his party. What enabled Brembre to move against Northampton at this point, most likely, was Usk's *Appeal*: a detailed account of conspiracy and subversion, written by an insider, which was introduced as evidence at a trial that began before the king at Reading on August 15, 1384. On the basis of Usk's *Appeal*, with the corroboration of other testimony, Northampton and other movement leaders were condemned; but on September 26, 1384, their sentences were commuted to banishment from London. On behalf of the other, temporarily ascendant party of Brembre, the king pardoned Usk at the same time; and from the summer of 1385, Usk received a series of royal preferments, including eventually appointment as a Sergeant-at-Arms to the king by May 1386, and appointment as Undersheriff for Middlesex in September 1387.

Evidently, it was in the interim between his September 1384 pardon and his preferment in mid-1385 that Usk finished the *Testament*, though he would have begun work on it earlier, probably following his arrest in the summer of 1384. During this period of writing, Usk would have felt that he had not yet received what was due him for his contribution to resolving the city troubles, though he might still be open to charges of opportunism or worse; and so on both counts he needed to put his actions in favorable light. In the circumstance, the *Testament* was made Usk's *apologia pro vita*.

In it, Usk denounces his former political activism, albeit somewhat indirectly, while also exculpating himself as best he could. The *Testament* takes the form of an allegorized dialogue, between Usk and a quasi-divinized personification, the lady Love. It served Usk's self-exoneration to model the dialogue as closely as he did on Boethius' *Philosophiae consolatio*, in which too an unjustly persecuted man is visited, consoled, and so compensated by a sapiential woman.[31] Allegory also made it possible for Usk to elide some particulars, such as the personal names of Northampton and other principals, and to forward some unsustainable claims on his own behalf.[32] Though by consequence of the allegory the talk about the London troubles of the Fall of 1383 is occasionally obscure, the crucial apologetic points are made plain. "In my youth," the interlocutor explains to lady Love,

> I was drawe to ben assentaunt and in my mightes helpyng to certain conjuracions and other great maters of ruling of cytezins. And thilke thynges ben my drawers in and exitours to tho maters werne so paynted and coloured, that (at the *prime face*) me semed them noble and glorious to al the people.
> (1.6.46–51)

By the time of Brembre's disputed 1383 election, however—when "thylke governour" whom Usk had served, evidently Northampton, "shope to have letted thilke electyon, and have made anewe himselfe to have ben chosen" (1.6.131–33)—the nature of what he had involved himself in had become clear. By Northampton and the other leaders had been drawn "the feoble-wytted people that have none insyght of gubernatyfe prudence to clamure and to crye on maters that they styred" (1.6.106–08). There were citizens who deserved "execucion that shal be doone for extorcions by hem committed" (1.6.120–21), the leaders told the "shepy people" of the city (1.6.144); unless such malefactors were put down, oppressyon of these olde hyndrers shal agayne surmounten and putten you to such subjection, that in endelesse wo ye shul complayne. The governe-mentes, quod they, of your cyte lefte in the handes of torcencious cytezyns, shal bringe in pestylence and distruction.

(1.6.113–16)

In fact, Usk discovered, the end in view was "malyce and yvel meanynge, . . .of tyrannye purposed" (1.6.60–61), creating civic discord of the worst sort:

> By whiche cause the peace, that most in comunaltie shulde be desyred, was in poynte to be broken and adnulled, also the cytie of London, that is to me so dere and swete, in whiche I was forthe growen and more kyndely love have I to that place than to any other in erthe, as every kyndely creature hath ful appetyte to that place of his kyndly engendrure and wylne reste and peace in that stede to abyde. Thylke peace shulde thus there have ben bro-ken and of al wyse it is commended and desyred.

(1.6.84–91)

Usk had already told this same story in his *Appeal*: "under colour of wordes of comun profit," he wrote there, by drawing "to hem many craftes and mochel smale poeple that konne non skyl of governance ne of gode conseyl," the leaders of the Northampton faction "so fer forth wolden deprave the worthy men of towne that the people was, and ys, the more embolded to rebel a-yeins thair governours, that bien now, and that shul bien in tyme komyng, . . .so that ys in poynt to truble al the realme, and the cite hath stonde in grete doute and yet doth" (204–05, 215–18, 224–26). A difference between the legal document and the allegorized literary fiction is that the *Testament* condemns Usk's political activity the more emphati-cally. The dialogue makes manifest that, though Usk may have meant well, his political engagement was misdirected, an "out-waye goynge" leading only to "sorowe and anguysshe" (1.8.12–13): "thilke service was an enpris-onment," lady Love teaches, "and alway bad and naughty in no maner to be desyred" (2.11.4–5).

From this distance, it is tempting to view the struggle over the London mayoralty in which Usk was involved as occurring fairly narrowly, within more or less indistinguishable oligarchic strata of the city's population, as if Northampton and Brembre were equal factionalists, with little or nothing for someone like Usk to chose between them. On the other hand, though both Northampton and Brembre represented powerful elements in city politics, they represented different elements, Northampton the productive non-victualling guilds, comprising chiefly artisanal labor within the city, and Brembre the non-productive victualling guilds, of merchant-capitalists, engaging in trade rather than production, making nothing but getting rich, by importing goods produced by others into the city and reselling them at a profit. Rodney Hilton has described the issues generally:

> The manipulation involved in buying the product cheap from the artisan and selling dear on the market was not strictly analogous to the exercises of non-economic coercion by the landowner to extract feudal rent from the peasant, but it created similar antagonisms. Social conflict in medieval towns often seems to be no more than factional struggle within oligarchies, but it often involved the mobilization of the resentment of the middle stratum of master craftsmen against town governments run by merchant capitalists.[33]

Northampton evidently understood matters in such terms and exploited the contradiction. Though Usk's *Appeal* tries to impute to Northampton and the other leaders self-interested aggrandizement—their "ful purpos. . .was to have had the town in thair governaile, and have rulid it be thair avys" (54–56)—and pure spite ("only for malice" [116]), as does also the *Testament of Love*, the evidence of specific programs and actions described in the *Appeal* suggests a class-conscious understanding of relations of production and exchange in the city economy and a will to alter them by legal political action. The leadership essayed legislation "for to chastise usurers," though in Usk's view thereby "shulde have be broght a-boute mocel of the evel menyng, to have undo the worthy membres of the town," leading to "the destruxion of the town with-inne a litel proces of tyme" (105, 113–14, 123–24). Northampton and the others are also said to have undertaken a popular re-education campaign, in which Usk was active: there was

> ever-more an excitation to the pore poeple to make hem be the more fervent and rebel a-yeins the grete men of the town, and ayeins the officers ek, and yt was seide thus to the poeple that ever the grete men wolden have the poeple be oppression in lowe degre, be whiche wordes, and be thair meigtenance, the dissension ys arrise betwene the worthy persones and the smale people of the town.
>
> (66–72)

The net result of the Northampton mayoralty was a less docile London populace, empowered by new knowledge, even of specific courses of action, that something might be done about oppressive mercantile manipulation.[34] Chaucer's associations with the opposing merchant-capitalist element in this class-derived political struggle were long-standing, of course, and personal: his wine-merchant father had been one of them (whereas Cecily Champaign's father, a baker, would have been of the other, productive sort), and Chaucer had worked closely with the merchant-oligarchs,

Brembre prominent among them, at the Wool Quay since the mid-thirteen-seventies. Chaucer's friend the "philosophical" Ralph Strode lost his job by consequence of Northampton's election.[35] That Richard II's support for the mercantile faction—costly as it later would come to seem—was as direct and unequivocal as it was at the time only underscores the close economic interdependence that always characterized relations between the crown and the metropolis's goods-traffickers late in the fourteenth century.

Chaucer's implication in the reticula of royal-mercantile relations, in other words, had also to be a matter of economic and political interest, beyond personal factors. Likewise, Usk's decision to abandon Northampton for Brembre had also to be a political choice, between competing, conflicting class fractions, and it was a fraught and consequential choice on this level, rather than a simply personal matter, relatively of social indifference. Given such a conflictual circumstance, Usk might be expected, not only to have denounced the Northampton faction and the class-interests it stood for, as he did in the *Testament*, but also to have advocated support for the interests represented by Brembre: merchant capital and the crown. He did not, however, except perhaps by choosing to emulate Chaucer. What he did in the *Testament of Love* instead was argue, not for the better political engagement, but for no political engagement at all.

In lieu of political activity, Usk put *eros*—capaciously conceived, after the fashion of Chaucer's *Troilus and Criseyde*.[36] In place of the misdirected agitation that had previously occupied him, the *Testament* proposes for Usk a life in service to the lady Love, devoted to loving a Margarite-pearl—represented at once as an actual woman and as a disembodied principle—leading eventually to Usk's attainment to a mystical erotic *summum bonum*: "my soule is yet in parfyte blysse," the interlocutor ejaculates at one point, "in thynkyng of that knotte" of erotic oneness (3.5.150), an "endelesse blysse in joy ever to onbyde" (3.5.5–6).

Usk's Love's idea of herself is that "al thynges by me shulden of right ben governed" (2.2.68). Usk's ultimate source Boethius expounds the same concept in the *Philosophiae consolatio*, especially in the eighth meter of the second book that Chaucer translated twice in *Troilus and Criseyde*.[37] Usk's Love's Latin song at the beginning of the second book of the *Testament*, in which she articulates this capacious conception of herself, recalls in addition the Boethian meter "Felix nimium prior aetas" (2.m.5), in that it is Love's lament for "the clyps of me, that shulde be his [sc. man's] shynande sonne" (2.2.13), and the "O qui perpetua mundum ratione gubernas" (3.m.9), in that the song is a catalogue of the things that Love is responsible for, as the *mobile* of much or all of universal order.

From amongst the varieties that she represents, Love singles out two of her responsibilities, for divine and for romantic love, to suggest that they are the highest. Love speaks of "a melodye in heven whiche clerkes clepen armony, but that is not in brekynge of voyce, but it is a maner swete thing of kyndely werchyng, that causeth joyes out of nombre to recken" (2.9.7–9); "al sugre and hony, al mynstralsy and melody ben but soote and galle in comparison by no maner proporcion to reken in respecte of this blysful joye" (2.9.34–36). This harmony exists in only two kinds of relationship, Love says: the relationship among the elements of the cosmos, and the relationship between men and women in romance: "This armony, this melody, this perdurable joye may nat be in doinge, but betwene hevens and elementes, or twey kyndly hertes, ful knyt in trouth of naturel understondyng, withouten wenynge and disceit" (2.9.36–38). Apprehension of the cosmic harmony is the greatest experience to which a person can aspire: "More soveraine desyre hath every wight in lytel sterynge of hevenly connynge, than of mokel materyal purposes in erthe"; and to this, the ambition of Love's servants is comparable: "Right so it is in propertie of my servauntes, that they ben more affyched in sterynge of lytel thynge in his desyre, than of mokel other mater lasse in his conscience" (2.9.22–26). The ineffable "armony" that she speaks of here is "what hath caused any wight to don any good dede" and a source of "endelesse joye" (2.9.63, 89). "No tonge may telle, ne herte may thinke the leest point of this blisse," (2.9.93–94) Love claims, recalling Chaucer's description of the erotic bliss of his protagonists in *Troilus and Criseyde*: of his lovers' "delit or joies oon the leeste/ Were impossible to my wit to seye," for they dwell in a "hevene blisse. . ./ That is so heigh that al ne kan I telle" (3.1310–11, 1322–23).

The interlocutor of Usk's *Testament* hopes for a better end to his love than that which comes to Troilus's. The object of Usk's affection has qualities beyond those of Criseyde. It seems clear enough from various remarks that "Margarite" in the *Testament* is the proper name of an actual woman— "a womanly woman in her kynde, in whome. . .of answerynge shappe of lymmes and fetures so wel in al poyntes acordyng nothynge fayleth" (2.12.101–03), with arms and so on; imprisoned as he represents himself to be, the interlocutor longs for her physical embrace: "Thus from my comforte I gynne to spylle, syth she that shulde me solace is ferre fro my presence," he says; "blysse of joye, that ofte me murthed, is turned into galle to thynke on thyng that may not, at my wyl, in armes me hent" (1.1.7–11). However, "Margarite" is also something more than a woman, too. In the course of this same initial complaint, Usk points out that "one vertue of a Margarite precious is, amonges many other, the sorouful to comforte" (1.1.22–23). The assimilation nascent at this point—of Usk's "womanly woman," named Margarite, to the "Margarite" proper, or pearl—is used later in the *Testament* to attribute to her various supernatural powers: as the jewel, she is "so good and so vertuous, that her better shulde I never fynde, al sought I therafter to the worldes ende" (1.3.70–71); she is "mother of al vertues," "endelesse vertue and everlastyng joy," and a "ful vessel of grace" (2.12.55–61); and she enjoys "knowyng of devynly and manly thinges joyned with studye of good lyvyng" (3.1.49–50). "Margarite a woman betokeneth grace, lernyng, or wisdom of God, or els holy church" (3.9.91–92), Usk says in the end; she must be both physically a real woman and such abstract qualities as the interlocutor would impute to her.

The end of the love-service Usk proposes to pursue in the *Testament*—in devotion to his capacious deity the lady Love, in loving his womanly woman, the divinized Margarite—is attainment of perdurable bliss, undistracted:

> Contynuaunce in thy good servyce, by longe processe of tyme in ful hope abydyng, without any chaunge to wylne in thyne herte: this is the spire, whiche if it be wel kept and governed, shal so hugely springe tyl the fruite of grace is plentuously out sprongen. For althoughe thy wyl be good, yet may not therfore thilk blysse desyred hastely on thee discenden; it must abyde his sesonable tyme.
>
> (3.6.5–10)

Boethius' work ends summarily, with *Philosophia*'s brief injunction to have faith in the *summum bonum* and to live the good life (5.pr.6); in the *Testament of Love*, the same end is actually achieved, in more celebratory and metaphorically more satisfying (if not rhetorically more effective) terms: Love enters and inhabits Usk (3.7.142–45), and he can now finish her analysis of predestination for her (3.8–3.9). Her inhabitation also gives him indelible summary knowledge of her teachings:

> Tho founde I fully al these maters parfytely there written: howe mysse-rule by fayned love bothe realmes and cyties hath governed a great throwe; howe lightly me might the fautes espye; howe rules in love shulde ben used; howe somtyme with fayned love foule I was begyled; howe I shulde love have knowe; and howe I shal in love with my servyce procede.
>
> (3.8.6–11)

Usk's *Testament* is thoroughgoingly Chaucerian, on various levels. In place of the pervasively available Latin original, Usk preferred to use Chaucer's *Boece* as his guide, even for verbal details. Where Usk departs from the model of Chaucer's *Boece*, in his Book Three, following instead the discussion of free will and foreordination in Anselm's *De concordia praescientiae Dei cum libero arbitrio*, he probably did so mindful of the Chaucerian precedent here too.[38] Chaucer had translated philosophy from Latin into English prose; Usk's *Testament* is a first attempt to follow Chaucer's accomplishments with such writings as the *Boece* and the *Melibee* in English

Kunstprosa. Also, more substantively, for the conception of love central to the *Testament*, Usk relied on Chaucer's *Troilus and Criseyde*. Usk's chief debt to Chaucer, however, was for the conception of literary work's social function embodied in the *Testament*. The *Testament* spells out the literary program of the erotic poetry of Love's "owne trewe servaunt, the noble philosophical poete in Englissh speche, "who" evermore hym besyeth and travayleth right sore. . .to encrese" Love's name, as Usk's Love calls Chaucer: if not some other harmless or safe literary distraction, mystical devotion, for example, espouse eroticism ("in love with. . .servyce procede"), but above all avoid implication in any variety of "mysse-rule" that might affront socially dominant authority.

By the time he wrote the *Testament*, however, it was apparently already too late for Usk to follow his own Chaucerian prescription, and he suffered again later for his political engagement. Having been pardoned by the king, Usk was subsequently preferred by him, after 1385, when the troubles about the London mayoralty had been resolved. Then the same "Merciless" parliament of 1388, by which the appellants effectively disbarred Richard II from exercise of power on his own behalf, also executed Usk, for treason, along with other more prominent royal adherents, including Brembre.

Usk wrote no more in the Chaucerian vein after finishing the *Testament*. Nor is it clear that the *Testament* itself had much circulation beyond the single handsome fair copy of it that Usk seems to have prepared himself, or to have had prepared for him; the only surviving textual witness is an early sixteenth-century printed edition apparently typeset from the authorial fair copy or something much like it.[39] Knowledge of the lineaments of Chaucerianism cannot have been spread far or wide by Usk, in other words; he had little or no influence. Moreover, as far as it could have been known indirectly, by repute, Usk's experience as a writer is unlikely to have been taken as establishing the benefits of advertising an adherence to Chaucerian canons of literary production.

3. Gower, Clanvowe, and Scogan

Usk did advertise his Chaucerianism, momentously for the immediate invention of the literary tradition. Usk's *Testament* shows a knowledge of other English-language writings, most likely something of *Piers Plowman*, but Usk lionized only Chaucer, in a section of the *Testament* where the interlocutor raises with Love a question of responsibility for evil, given divine foreordination of events.[40] To his inquiry, Love replies:

> I shal tel thee, this lesson to lerne: myne owne trewe servaunt, the noble philosophical poete in Englissh speche, evermore hym besyeth and travayleth

right sore my name to encrease. Wherfore, al that wyllen me good owe to do him worshyp and reverence bothe; trewly, his better ne his pere in schole of my rules coude I never fynde. He, quod she, in a treatise that he made of my servant Troylus, hath this mater touched, and at the ful this questyon assoyled. Certaynly his noble sayenges can I not amende; in goodnes of gentyl man-lyche speche, without any maner of nycite of storieres ymagynacion, in wytte and in good reason of sentence he passeth al other makers. In the *Boke of Troylus*, the answere to thy questyon mayste thou lerne.

(3.4.230–40)

Eustache Deschamps had already used Chaucer's name, in the ballad by means of which he meant to ingratiate himself with Lewis Clifford and, through Clifford, with the royal household or court more generally, which Chaucer served. For such a purpose, an acquaintance with Chaucer, even if only with Chaucer's name, had exchange-value, deriving in the first instance from Chaucer's place within the king's affinity, and secondarily from what literary accomplishment or repute that Chaucer yet had. Deschamps felt he could trade acquaintance with Chaucer for a benefit he wanted, namely, some still fairly vague aggrandizement of his own stature in England.

The same is true of the only other *in vita* record of Chaucer's literary activity. By contrast with the life-records of Chaucer's other work, these notices of his literary production are few, there being only the three: Deschamps's, Usk's, and John Gower's so-called "Chaucer greeting," in an early recension of the *Confessio Amantis*, deleted from the later versions in circulation by about 1395. Like Deschamps and Usk, Gower too represents Chaucer as an erotic poet exclusively, in this passage near the end of the *Confessio*, in which Venus's leave-taking from Amans incorporates a message:

And gret wel Chaucer whan ye met,
As mi disciple and mi poete:
For in the floures of his youthe
In sondri wise, as he wel couthe,
Of Ditees and of songes glade,
The whiche he for mi sake made,
The lond fulfild is overal:
Wherof to him in special
Above alle othre I am most holde.
For thi now in hise daies olde
Thow schalt him telle this message,
That he upon his latere age,
To sette an ende of alle his werk,
As he which is myn owne clerk,
Do make his testament of love,

As thou hast do thi schrifte above,
So that mi Court it mai recorde.[41]

Unlike those between Deschamps and Chaucer, relations between Gower
and Chaucer were direct, moreover eventually manifold and complex.[42]
There may have been friendship between them, in some substantial, meaningful sense, or admiration. Also, inevitably perhaps, there would have been
literary influence, possibly rivalrous emulation, especially when, relatively
later in their respective literary careers, Chaucer after Gower, both took to
working at narrative in English verse. What evidence there is, however, tends
to suggest that such effects went in one direction, from Gower to Chaucer,
but not much or at all in the other. Chaucer may have been preoccupied at
times with defining his own accomplishments in narrative by their relation—
even in some Bloomian agonistic relation—to what the senior English poet
had achieved.[43] The opposite seems not to have occurred. To "moral Gower"
(with "philosophical Strode" in second place), Chaucer directed his one finished grand-scale narrative poem, *Troilus and Criseyde* (5.1856–57). The brief,
corrective notice of Chaucer in the first *Confessio amantis* epilogue—later
expunged—is all there is of Chaucer in Gower's writings. Substantively,
Gower's massive trilingual sociocritical *opus*—described by Gardiner Stillwell
as a "tepid, sticky vastness" of "Titanic critical ambitions"[44]—is purely, strictly
Gowerian: pre-Chaucerian, as if Chaucer had not yet written.
   Neither by this remark in the *Confessio amantis* nor by the French ballad
do either Gower or Deschamps evince any ambition to write like Chaucer,
to be Chaucerian in the way that Usk was to be. Gower and Deschamps
each may share something with Chaucer, each in his own way, but by consequence of independent invention. Each goes his own way as a writer, not
depending substantively on Chaucer, in formal or contental matters, nor
deriving any understanding of their writing's social function from an
acquaintance with Chaucer's example. Each had already established himself
as a writer by the time Chaucer had done anything in the same way. Like
Deschamps, Gower was using only Chaucer's name, for whatever social
credit may have attached to it, accruing by virtue of Chaucer's long and
successful labors in royal service, chiefly by his ordinary employments
though also possibly his early erotic writings. Chaucer's name was valuable,
more than his writings, to Gower as to Deschamps, chiefly, if not exclusively, because of Chaucer's social place.
   The opposite case is also known to have obtained during Chaucer's life:
instances in which writers, omitting to use Chaucer's name, instead
borrowed substantively (more or less) from his writings. The one instance
involves Jean Froissart, who was intimate already with English aristocrats,

though he was no aristocrat, being instead in service to aristocracy, like Chaucer in this respect. Froissart was also intimate with socially elevate English culture, for he contributed to it: differing from Chaucer in this respect, his service to aristocracy was predominantly literary already. Froissart's *Dit dou bleu chevalier* and Chaucer's *Book of the Duchess* are so alike in a series of passages that an hypothesis of dependence is ineluctable. The chronologies are uncertain; what evidence there is tends to suggest that the Froissart poem was written after the Chaucer and so derives from it, rather than vice versa.[45] Neither Froissart nor Chaucer acknowledges any debt, however. Chaucer used French erotic poetry extensively for making the *Book of the Duchess*, including other pieces of Froissart's work, but never credits any of the contemporary French poets from whom he borrowed.[46] It may be that, in the case of Froissart's *Dit dou bleu chevalier*, the same has been done: the French poet found a substantive use for Chaucer's writing but no value yet in using Chaucer's name.

The clearer instance is the English poem known as *The Book of Cupid*, though it has also been known as *The Cuckoo and the Nightingale*, now generally understood to be the work of Chaucer's somewhat grander friend, the chamber knight John Clanvowe, who, among other evidences of acquaintance with Chaucer, witnessed on his behalf the quitclaim of Cecily Champaign in 1380.[47] Clanvowe made a noble death in 1391, crusading in easterly regions, so the borrowing took place during Chaucer's life, while he was still socially and culturally productive, if in fact the poem is Clanvowe's work.[48] Also—though again only if the poem is Clanvowe's writing—it probably witnesses the pre–*Canterbury Tales* state of what became the *Knight's Tale*, as Chaucer himself does in the *Legend of Good Women*, for the *Book of Cupid* begins by quoting and amplifying Chaucer:

The god of love, a! benedicite,
How myghty and how grete a lorde is he!
For he can make of lowe hertys hie,
And highe lowe and like for to die,
And herde hertis he can make fre.

And he can make, within a lytel stounde,
Of seke folke ful freshe, hool, and sounde,
And of hoole he can make seke;
He can bynde and unbynde eke
What he wole have bounde and unbounde.

To telle his myght my wit may not suffice,
For he may do al that he can devyse;
For he can make of wise folke ful nyse,

And in lyther folke dystroye vise,
And proude hertys he can make agryse.

Shortely, al that evere he wol he may:
Ayenst him ther dar no wight say nay,
For he can glade and greve whom he lyketh,
And who that he wol he laugheth or he siketh,
And most his myght he sheweth ever in May.

                                                    (1–20)

That this passage derives substantively from Chaucer's writing seems
unequivocal—early but not singularly, it illustrates the capacity of Chaucer's
verse to generate more verse, verse after verse ("Shortely" makes a parody
of it already)—though whether the derivation occurred during Chaucer's
life or later depends on the poem's date, and the attribution to Clanvowe
is not as certain as could be wished. In any case, it did happen, not only that
writers traded on the social value of Chaucer's name but not the substance
of his literary work, as in the cases of Deschamps and Gower, but also that
writers used Chaucer's writings but not his name, as may have happened
(or not) during Chaucer's life in these cases of the Froissart poem and the
English *Book of Cupid*. These latter cases impute no exchange-value yet to
Chaucer's name, though they find and exploit use-value in what Chaucer
had written.[49]

It was Thomas Usk, in the *Testament of Love*, who, still during Chaucer's
life, conjoined these two jobs that Chaucer could do for other writers: produce useful literary forms and topics, out of which such others could build
more writing, as did Froissart or Clanvowe; and lend, in the form of his name,
exchangeable social credit, by virtue of his social location, near power—the
product, in other words, above all of Chaucer's servile and disciplinary
employments in household and state apparatuses, though possibly also, to an
incalculable degree, of his literary accomplishments—on which others could
trade to improve their own status, as did Deschamps and Gower.

The invention of Chaucerianism taking place here was not a disem-
bodiedly cultural or literary event, born of the strictly artistic merits of the
Chaucerian writing. As John Burrow put it, the "rapid spread of Chaucer's
reputation cannot be ascribed simply to the force of his genius."[50] The
invention in the first instance was the product of specific material-historical
determinants and the particular, idiosyncratic subjective agency of Thomas
Usk in response. Placed as he was in the London troubles of 1383–84—the
troubles in turn produced by the contradictions of current forces and relations of production within the political economy of the city—Usk had to
look to persons like Nicholas Brembre and Richard II for support. Usk's
survival depended on their good will. Chaucer was one of them, by virtue

of his class location and implications. Usk, for fashioning the sort of literary apology he did, again needing to look after his rehabilitation during 1384–85, used such writings as were available, Chaucer's foremost. By virtue of their production by someone whose name also had value for Usk, he saw fit to publicize his use of them. There were no alternative precedents with the same array of literary and social qualities—use-value and exchange-value—on which Usk might have drawn at the time.

Reacting reasonably to a particular determinant historical conjunction of circumstance, Thomas Usk invented Chaucerianism—again: socially servile English literature, serving perpetuation of the dominance, made the more socially creditable by its associations with Chaucer's valuable name— in about 1385. Chaucer himself might equally well be credited with the invention—his own work has these already as its salient features—except for the semantic awkwardness of imputing discipleship to the master. In any event, Usk did less well out of the invention than had Chaucer and than would others later. Repetitions of the invention and its propagation, soon, within a generation of Usk's death, were made to work successfully, though again only in response to specific local circumstance.

An instructively thoroughgoing repetition of this Chaucerianism that Thomas Usk was already working with by 1385 occurs in brief compass in the so-called "Moral Ballad" of Henry Scogan, dating from the period 1400–07.[51] Scogan worked as an *esquier* of the royal household, as had Chaucer (he also borrowed money from Gilbert Maghfeld in the early 1390s, again like Chaucer), and he continued to serve in the royal household after Chaucer had gone on to greater, more independent (though still royal) employment, as can be inferred from the envoy of the Chaucerian "Lenvoy de Chaucer a Scogan," where Chaucer makes address (meanly, perhaps) to

> Scogan, that knelest at the stremes hed
> Of grace, of alle honour and worthynesse,
> In th'ende of which strem I am as dul as ded,
> Forgete in solytarie wildernesse.
>
> (43–46)

Scogan evidently also took on some responsibility for raising up the Lancastrian princes, still within the royal household, at some point after the 1399 coup. He died (after Chaucer) in 1407.

The "Moral Ballad" makes a good deal of Scogan's acquaintance with Chaucer—"my mayster Chaucer" (65, 98, 104), Scogan calls him repeatedly, "this noble poete of Bretayne" (126), the poem representing him as deceased: "god his soule have!" (65)—as it does also of Scogan's knowledge of Chaucer's writings. Scogan found Chaucer's name useful, in other words, as had Deschamps, Gower, and Usk earlier; and again, Usk-like (or Clanvowe-like or possibly Froissart-like), though with a difference, Scogan also found substantive use for Chaucer's writings. The "Moral Ballad" is in eight-line rhyming stanzas, of pentameter lines—a variant of Chaucer's *Troilus* stanza—though it has a metrically distinct lyric inset in it. The "Moral Ballad" also quotes Chaucer verbatim, as does *The Book of Cupid*, at least three times,[52] but it also, unlike *The Book of Cupid*, attributes its quotations sometimes to Chaucer by name, including its quotation in full (more or less) of the whole Chaucerian ballad now known as "Gentilesse," in three seven-line stanzas, though it here lacks the proper envoy that it would be expected to have had in independent circulation. The text and attribution of this ballad "Gentilesse" to Chaucer rest in part on what Scogan does with it here: incorporate it wholesale into his own poem while insisting that the inset is, not his own, but Chaucer's writing.[53] What Scogan does in the "Moral Ballad" is build a Chaucerian frame for representation of Chaucer's authoritative own wordings, accessible only by Scogan's offices, the frame also making a point of advertising the Chaucerian affiliation. As Usk had already done, in other words, Scogan's "Moral Ballad" too combines both using the substance of Chaucer's writings, even the Chaucerian *ipsissima verba*, and trading on what value had accrued to Chaucer's name.

Though Scogan can be believed to have been amongst the intimates who knew something about the incipient *Canterbury Tales* even before Chaucer's death, the "Moral Ballad" makes no explicit mention of such a work or any part thereof. Nor does the "Moral Ballad" use the most simply erotic of Chaucer's early writings. Instead, Scogan's election fell on work of the relatively more "noble philosophical poete," as Usk had described the Chaucer of *Troilus and Criseyde*. The Chaucerian "Gentilesse" that Scogan uses most thoroughly is in the same Boethian vein, and Scogan uses it in his "Moral Ballad" expressly for disciplinary purposes: to teach.

The "Moral Ballad" has as its stated purpose the instruction of the princely sons of Henry IV. "My lordes dere, why I this complaint wryte" "Is for to warne you" (33–35): "Your youthe in vertue shapeth to dispende" (40), and so "Passeth wysly this perilous pilgrimage" (46). Historically, Prince Hal ("I know you all, and will awhile uphold / The unyok'd humour of your idleness") came to be regarded as having succeeded well enough by doing the opposite of what Scogan advises, salving "The long-grown wounds of my intemperance" by eventual discovery of his real character ("I know thee not, old man"), to make himself, most famously, in "small time," "This star of England." "The courses of his youth promis'd it not," and Scogan says such a thing should never happen.[54] Scogan may represent himself as "a lay clerk preaching good meritocratic doctrine from a text by Chaucer;"[55] Scogan's lesson is otherwise similarly arguable, however. He enjoins, "Thinketh how, betwixe vertue and estat / There is a parfit blessed mariage" (81–82), such that "vertue bringeth unto greet degree / Eche wight that list to do him entendaunce" (172–73) and that "ay the vicious, by aventure, / Is overthrowe" (61–62); whereas Langland's Dame Study, for example, makes the opposite assertion, "That wikked men, thei welden the welthe of this worlde, / And that thei ben lordes of ech a lond, that out of lawe libbeth": "Thilke that God moost gyveth, leest good thei deleth."[56]

Finally, the other consequential repetition of Usk's Chaucerianism that Scogan's "Moral Ballad" makes, illuminatingly, is that the writing of it was undertaken for payment. The evidence is that it was commissioned for performance, before the Lancastrian princes, "at a souper of feorthe merchande in the Vyntre in London, at the hous of Lowys Johan"—that is, at a quarterly guild-meeting (mostly likely) of Chaucer's father's vintners, where the merchant-oligarchy re-performed in ritual its characteristic dependent subjection to nobility. Though the evidence is belated and not altogether clear, its particularity tends to persuade. At least, someone thought the story sufficiently creditable to invent it. Now, in any event, in Seth Lerer's phrase, Chaucer is a commodity, used and exchanged.[57]

4. Thomas Hoccleve

Chaucer was not a professional writer. The "Father of English Poetry" was occupied most of the time with jobs other than literary paternity, in circumstances in which writing had to be a spare-time activity for him, to be imagined in the terms his windy Eagle uses for addressing "Geffrey" in the *House of Fame*.[58] Chaucer could sit at his books only after his accounts were complete and all his other labors were done:

> For when thy labour doon al ys,
> And hast mad alle thy rekenynges,
> In stede of reste and newe thynges
> Thou goost hom to thy hous anoon,
> And, also domb as any stoon,
> Thou sittest at another book
> Tyl fully daswed ys thy look.
>   (652–58)

Although in the Chaucer life-records the divorce between the crown servant and the poet appears absolute, Chaucer's two occupations were not separate: his official employments, in domestic and state service, were continuous with his literary work, having also particular effects on the sort of thing he chose to write and on the way in which he chose to write. Likewise, it is difficult to imagine that Chaucer's poetry-writing was of no account for the material successes he enjoyed, though again the life-records fail to inform. On no occasion is it recorded that Chaucer was paid for writing or that his accomplishment as a writer figured in attracting to him the gifts and payments he did receive. Nevertheless, it seems plausible to suppose that writings like *An ABC*—if it was written for Blanche, duchess of Lancaster, as Speght said it was—or the *Book of the Duchess*—eulogizing the same Blanche, which would not have been written if it had not been written for John of Gaunt—must have yielded Chaucer something.[59] Chaucer's official situation and relations with Lancaster informed the conception and execution of these writings, even if Chaucer was not commissioned or directed to write them; and even though Chaucer may not have been paid outright for the *Book of the Duchess*, as for piece-work, writing it should have improved his stock with John of Gaunt, lending justification to Lancastrian preferment after the fact, or anticipating that Chaucer might in future do such literary jobs.[60]

Although none of the life-records makes any reference to poetry, direct or indirect, and although Chaucer can only be thought of as a part-time poet, it seems safe to make this inference, that writing brought Chaucer benefits, more and less immediately, of one sort or another, if not by way of direct payment, patronal gifts outright, or annuities, then, as seems more likely, by way of an increased esteem that could later be transvalued into payment or paid office. Whether or not this inference is a good one, however, Chaucer's immediate successors in English writing seem generally to have made it. By the early fifteenth century, and possibly in Chaucer's lifetime, the beliefs were apparently current: first, that writing had profited Chaucer; second, that if writing had profited Chaucer, it should be able to profit others as well; and third, that the likelihood of poetry being profitable was tied to the poetry being Chaucerian, one way or another.

The problem of making writing pay was only finally worked out in practice in England by humanist men-of-letters and vernacular writers-for-print late in the fifteenth and early in the sixteenth centuries—Stefano Surigone, Pietro Carmeliano, and Bernard André, for example, or Alexander Barclay, with John Skelton between the two camps. At which point, a properly amateur, aristocratic writing also began to be invented as such—flourishing in the work of Henry Howard, earl of Surrey, and Thomas Wyatt, in the reign of the *littérateur* King Henry VIII—as would in fact only have become possible once a properly, thoroughly professionalized alternative was in place.[61]

The possibility of professional writing had already approached realization in the career of John Lydgate earlier, "the nearest thing late medieval

England came to producing a professional poet," in Richard Firth Green's phrase.[62] From an early age, Lydgate enjoyed the material security that came of a monastic vocation. Of peasant class origin, moreover, Lydgate seems to have had no familial interest to pursue or to promote, nor any discernible ambition to play a part in the councils of church or state. It is difficult to imagine why Lydgate did what he did as writer. Nonetheless, what he did is clear: Lydgate wrote for money. Records of direct payments to him for particular pieces survive (£5 for his dual life of Saints Alban and Amphibal, for example); in other instances where there are no records (the "Mumming for the Mercers of London," "ordeyned ryallych by the worthy merciers, citeseyns of London"), it still seems clear that payment must have been made. His own remarks attest his interest in attracting material subvention by addressing writing to rich people ("O welle of fredam," "Onli be support to fynde me my dispence").[63]

This possibility of writing for pay is incipient too in Usk's *Testament*. In the longer term, things did not go according to plan for Usk. In the interim, however, he did attract preferment after his *Appeal* and the *Testament*, conceivably in some part because he wrote the *Testament*, though it seems unlikely to have done much for Usk directly. In any case, Usk apparently intended it to work this way: either by virtue of its qualities as literature or by virtue of the substance of its apology for Usk's political malfeasance, the *Testament of Love* was something Usk hoped he might exchange for benefit. It happened that no one much wanted Usk or the *Testament*—except possibly Nicholas Brembre during the brief period between July and December 1384, or Richard II again briefly between mid-1385 and late 1387—but no matter: Usk tried. Chaucer too had recognized the exchange-value of the writing he produced. All his writings embody such knowledge, though it only finds direct expression in something like the "Complaint to his Purse," where the writer's work is explicitly characterized as fungible.

Thomas Hoccleve made a career out of his writing's exchange-value. His literary production is Chaucerian in manifold (overdetermined) ways.[64] Verbally and stylistically he was indebted to Chaucer's example, as he was also substantively, in the kinds of things he wrote and the social functions his productions had. His work is Chaucerian most fundamentally in his continuation of the apologetic-propagandistic service to secular authority that Chaucer had founded for English literature. Hoccleve produced precisely the same two sorts of servile writing that Chaucer had as well: erotic myth-mongering and disciplinary admonition. Likewise, the hinge on which these two parts of Hoccleve's literary production swing is also in some sense Chaucerian, in that the change in Hoccleve's writing, from myth-making to discipline, appears to have depended on a change in his professional situation and his relation to the state apparatus, like Chaucer's 1374 move from the court back into the city. What happened to Hoccleve is that literary production became his job, quasi-officially and professionally. Hoccleve was not quite as Chaucer had been, an officer of the state disciplinary apparatus who extended his contribution into the literary sphere; Hoccleve became an officer of the state disciplinary apparatus working in the literary sphere exclusively or predominantly, for reward. Finally, it was in some part advertisement of his Chaucerianism that made this shift possible for Hoccleve.

Like Usk and Chaucer before him, Hoccleve too was a text-worker, employed throughout his adult life as a bill-writing Chancery clerk—a bureaucratic scrivener, like Usk though more securely employed and within the apparatus of state, and like Chaucer though not at the same level of elevation or responsibility.[65] Also, Hoccleve was never as successful or well rewarded as Chaucer. In any event, after a time, Hoccleve came to act as "an acknowledged quasi-official writer of verse on political occasions" on behalf of the state.[66] There is not documentary or literary evidence explaining how this change came about; still, it appears to have happened: once only a text-worker in the state bureaucracy with some subordinate literary ambition, Hoccleve became subsequently a state writer, producing literature from within its bureaucracy, on its behalf.

The point at which this change can be observed taking place is in Hoccleve's major writing, *The Regiment of Princes*, produced in about 1411.[67] Before the *Regiment*, Hoccleve had written only or chiefly erotic verse, advertising the aristocratic world without work after the fashion of Chaucer, basing himself on French models too, the best known piece being the exquisite *Letter of Cupid*.[68] After the *Regiment*, Hoccleve wrote disciplinary propaganda, as for example his poem on the 1414 Oldcastle rebellion ("And but yee do god, I byseeche a bone, / That in the fyr yee feele may the sore!"), justifying state murder and advocating more.[69] In the *Regiment*, Hoccleve makes the Chaucerian offer, to serve and to protect the wealthy and powerful, by whatever literary means might be devised, and he makes explicit the Chaucerian condition for doing so. Hoccleve can do Chaucerian literary service—erotics or discipline, indifferently as might be required—in exchange for rewards. Apparently, the offer he made was taken up.

The *Regiment of Princes* is about money. Hoccleve wants it. His idea is that, in exchange for literary labor, Prince Henry, the future King Henry V, should give it to him. In the work's lengthy prologue, Hoccleve voices various particular grievances—the physical damage his twenty years' service and more in the Office of the Privy Seal has caused him (988–1029; cf. 801–05);[70] his failure to gain a benefice from his service (1401–02, 1447–53, 1485–91); having been constantly cheated of his fees (1492–50);

the negligence of lords he has served (1793–95); and so on—but the prologue is chiefly a lamentation of his poverty, focused on two kinds of problems, repeatedly averred. His present income is inadequate, Hoccleve asserts, because the six marks (equivalent to £4) he has beyond his annuity is too little (932–35, 974–75, 1214–18, 1224–25) and his annuity of twenty marks (i.e., £13.6.8) is paid him too irregularly (820–31). Second, his future seems to him likely to be even more impoverished, because of an increased difficulty about collecting his dues that he expects will come once he is compelled by age to retire from court to his "pore cote" (831–40, 948–53). Hoccleve's interlocutor, a sapient Old Man he chances to meet after a night of sleepless agonizing over his financial situation, summarizes for him these salient points of worry:

> In short, this is of thy greef enchesoun:
> Of thyn annuitee the paiement,
> Which for thy long service is thy guerdoun,
> Thow dreddist, whan thow art from court absent,
> Shal be restreyned, syn thow now present
> Unnethes maist it gete, it is so streit—
> Thus undirstood I, sone, thy conceit,
> For of thy lyflode is it the substance.
>
> (1779–86)

Hoccleve is uncommonly frank about his work's motives, finding himself faced with such circumstance; he would even bribe the Old Man, in exchange for a solution to his problems: "Wisseth me how to gete a golden salve / And what I have I wole it with yow halve" (1245–46). The Old Man proposes that Hoccleve petition his prince, simply and straightforwardly, for the "golden salve" he needs: "now, syn thow me toldist

> My lord, the Prince, is good lord thee to,
> No maistrie is it for thee, if thow woldist
> To be releeved. Woost thow what to do?
> Wryte to him a goodly tale or two,
> On which he may desporten him by nyght,
> And his free grace shal upon thee lyght"
>
> (1898–04)

Adjacent passages amplifying the Old Man's proposal disambiguate the flatteringly nebulous "free grace" of this one: Prince Henry, whom Hoccleve claims "is my good gracious lord" (1836), "may be salve unto thyn indigence," says the Old Man (1834); "To him pursue and thy releef purchace" (1848):

> "Conpleyne unto his excellent noblesse,
> As I have herd thee unto me compleyne,
> And but he qwenche thy greet hevynesse,
> My tonge take and slitte in peces tweyne!"
>
> (1849–52)

By its prologue, the *Regiment of Princes* represents itself to its immediate audience Prince Henry as the execution of this plan for Hoccleve's material betterment. The *Regiment* proper—fifteen ostensibly admonitory chapters of advice to the prince—instantiates the literary service Hoccleve might do.

Hoccleve's advice is often self-servingly venal, continuing the petitions of the prologue. The tenth through the thirteenth of the *Regiment's* didactic sections, comprising various injunctions against parsimony and suasions to "largesse," recall Hoccleve's particular needs constantly, by means of generalities about annuities, for example, as well as by means of direct reference (e.g., 4173–79, 4383–89, 4789–95). For the rest, the advice Hoccleve ventures is anodyne—avoid gluttony, for example, and lechery; be kind to widows and orphans; and so forth—and when Hoccleve ventures out on to more controverted terrain, it is to offer safe comment, enjoining Henry to do what Henry was already doing anyway and would continue to do (this despite Hoccleve's numerous injunctions against listening to flatterers [e.g., 2939–45, 3039–66, 4439–52, 4915–21, 5253–85]): through strength make peace with the French—"The policy advocated in the final section of the *Regiment*—peace with France cemented with a royal marriage (5391–5404) is. . .exactly the policy that Henry V claimed to be following throughout his French campaigns and put into practice after the conquest of Normandy"[71]—and enforce adherence to the official doctrinal line of the established church, especially by spectacular means: show-trials, torture, and killings.[72] Often enough, Hoccleve just sounds confused in this way. The prince is to take counsel from the young (4880–82), but then again the prince is not under any circumstance to take counsel from the young ("Waar of yong conseil, it is perillous!" [4947]). No lords of the English are faithless oath-breakers—"no lord in al this lond / Is gilty of that inconvenience"—Hoccleve asserts (2241–45), though in an adjacent passage he complains that an English lord who is not faithless is nowhere to be found, "Men list nat so ferfoorth to trouthe hem bynde" (2287–89). "So been richesses to soules feedynge / Holsum" (4161–62), except that founding "felicitee" "on richesse and moneye" has destructive consequence (4019–21). Riot abroad in the realm is the doing of the poor ("Why suffrest thow so many an assemblee / Of armed folk?" [2791–92]):

> For they that naght ne han, with knyf ydrawe
> Wole on hem that of good be mighty renne,
> And hurte hem and hir houses fyre and brenne,
> And robbe and slee and do al swich folie.
>
> (2782–85)

Except that the unpeace "susteened is nat by persones lowe, / But cobbes grete this riot susteene" (2805–06).

This kind of self-canceling and contradictory advice in the *Regiment* is its best advice, nevertheless, in the sense that it makes most effectively the point Hoccleve most needs make. Hoccleve's point is that Henry is a great prince. He is so great a prince that someone like Hoccleve—anyone—could not possibly advise him. If the prince needed counsel, he could not take it, for the unwise prince (needing counsel) listens only to flattery, not wisdom. The wise prince would take counsel, though counsel is of no need, because already the prince is wise. The only counsel that can properly be proffered is that no counsel can be proffered. Otherwise, the work is, not laudatory, but an attack, socially critical, something in which the good prince could not recognize himself. Criticism measures the prince against an ideal from which he deviates; a *Fürstenspiegel* can only show the prince what already he looks like.[73] Hoccleve's advice has to be senseless. Otherwise, it would be derogatory, implying some fault or shortcoming in Henry, and Hoccleve's job is his magnification: propaganda in exchange for reward. This is what David Lawton has described as "the pose of dullness" in the fifteenth-century Chaucerians generally.[74] The stupider Hoccleve looks trying this job of advising his prince, the greater Henry appears to be.

In the end, this is what the *Fürstenspiegel* makes it possible for Hoccleve to do: magnify his prince. By advising him to do what he was already doing or would do anyway, by evincing confusion or resorting to mutually can-celing platitudes, Hoccleve magnifies his prince's praises. Henry would take advice, unlike Richard II; but Henry needs no advice. The encomiastic use-value made the exchange-value of Hoccleve's writing: propaganda was worth something. The evidence of Hoccleve's later work is that his offer was understood and accepted.

Hoccleve bases some of his claim for this exchange-value of his writing on his writing being Chaucerian. In the most fundamental ways possible, Hoccleve's writing was already unmistakably Chaucerian. It is propaganda, serving and protecting the interests of the wealthy and powerful. This pos-sibility for English literature was Chaucer's invention. In addition to being Chaucerian, however, Hoccleve also goes to considerable trouble to advertise the fact that he is being Chaucerian, as Usk had done in the *Testament*, only more emphatically, and as Scogan had done, only at greater length. Hoccleve repeatedly avers that Chaucer had been his "master" in matters poetical. The claim is not only that a knowledge of Chaucer's work informed his own writing, though this point too Hoccleve establishes, by the broadly Chaucerian qualities of his verse and by the appreciations of Chaucer's particular excellences built into the poem's three substantial eulogies of the dead poet (1958–74, 2077–07, 4978–5012): Hoccleve perceives in Chaucer a "flour of eloquence," a "mirour of fructuous entendement" "universel. . .in science," and "excellent prudence" (1962–65); Tully in "swetnesse of rethorik," Aristotle "in philosophie," and Vergil "in poesie" (2084–89)—each of these three (especially the oleaginous Stagirite) being a better informed choice than any of Dechamps'; "the firste fyndere of our fair langage" (4978); and so on.

Most to the point, Hoccleve also claims that he had known Chaucer; and, furthermore, he suggests that Chaucer had personally taken in hand his instruction in writing, in ambiguous passages that could be and probably were intended to be taken in this peculiar sense. A remark of the Old Man implies that Hoccleve already enjoys a reputation for Chaucer's familiarity: hearing Hoccleve's name, he responds, "Sone, I have herd or this men speke of thee; / Thow were aqweyntid with Chaucer, pardee" (1866–67). Hoccleve will admit, as if apologetically, that "I wont was han conseil and reed" of "the honour of Englissh tonge" (1959–60):

My deere maistir, God his soule qwyte,
And fadir, Chaucer, fayn wolde han me taght,
But I was dul and lerned lyte or naght.
(2077–79)

The Hoccleve portrait of Chaucer (frontispiece—figure 1) is put forward in this context, of Hoccleve's efforts to insinuate intimacy with Chaucer, as part of his effort to elicit benefaction. Near the end of the *Regiment* occurs a stanza with which Hoccleve confirmed his intimacy with Chaucer by promising to provide a verisimilar likeness of him. The authorized copies of the *Regiment* that Hoccleve had made for circulation included a painting of Chaucer at this point, adjacent to the stanza:

Althogh his lyf be qweynt, the resemblance
Of him hath in me so fressh lyflynesse
That to putte othir men in remembrance
Of his persone, I have heere his liknesse
Do make, to this ende, in soothfastnesse,
That they that han of him lost thoght and mynde
By this peynture may ageyn him fynde.
(4992–98)[75]

The claim that the image and these words make together—that the lines' author knew what Chaucer looked like—confirms Hoccleve's Chaucerianism, so intimate was he with Chaucer and the literary legacy. Hoccleve was petitioning for patronage, in some measure on the basis of the quality of the poetic service he had provided and could provide; he sought to base his claim for the quality of his poetic service in some measure on the claim that his work was Chaucerian; this claim that his poetry was Chaucerian was in turn based in some measure on his claim to have known Chaucer, not only through his writing but also personally; and he bases his claim to have known Chaucer personally in some measure on a claim to know what Chaucer had looked like.

In such an advertisement of affiliation, Chaucer's ultimate literary-historical job was already done: helping others prosper by doing as he had, namely, producing literary products that served to protect ruling-class dominance, in the historically appropriate forms of erotic myth-mongering and disciplinary admonition, in exchange for rewards.

Others later, in other historical circumstance, were to put this same Chaucer—both the corpus of useful writing and the vendible name, a quasi-brand name—to other particular literary-historical uses. The Lancastrian Chaucerianism, of Hoccleve's later work, after the *Regiment*, but especially John Lydgate's extensive post-1420 *opera*, is the early case.[76] Later in the same century and early in the next, another, different early Tudor Chaucerianism took shape, again for differing specific purposes in the differing historical circumstance.[77] And so on: the locally particular Chaucerianisms have been various. Meanwhile, the basic constellation of Chaucerian values—the use-value that the erotic and disciplinary writings themselves could have for serving dominance, and the exchange-value of fungible authority accruing to Chaucer's name—was fixed in place early: certainly by about 1411, when Hoccleve had written the *Regiment of Princes*, or by 1407, when Scogan had performed the "Moral Ballad," or as early as 1385, when Usk finished the *Testament of Love*.

In Deschamps's early ballad is articulated and linked to Chaucer's name already the possibility of a servile vernacular literature, serving the interests of the local *kaloi kai agathoi*, rather than criticizing or provoking. As Deschamps recognized, in Chaucer's own writings this possibility was already a commitment. Chaucer wrote nothing that did not already put such servility into vernacular literary practice. Others may have been doing the same, though none with the persistence of Chaucer and the prominence that his persistence had lent his practice already by ca. 1380, when Deschamps intervened.

Usk made the promise of Chaucerian writing clearer: vernacular text-work avowedly foregoing disruptive political engagements for other occupation, in the case of Usk's *Testament* specifically erotic occupation, ostentatiously apolitical though still serving the political agenda of the wealthy and powerful by its pretense that disengagement was desirable and possible. Again, in Chaucer's own writing the erotic preoccupation was pre-eminent—pre-eminent as well in Deschamps' preliminary reading of the Chaucerian *oeuvre*—and eventually paradigmatic: the exemplary instance of the broad, fundamental Chaucerian commitment to serve dominance by whatever literary means might be or become exigent, including relatively directly disciplinary writing like the *Canterbury Tales*.

With Scogan, Hoccleve made the same promise in the form of an explicit bargain, finding that it paid: in exchange for servile literary production—that is, literary production modeled on Chaucer's work, which had already defined what appropriately servile literary production could look like—the suitably servile vernacular text-worker was to be rewarded by those whose interests he promoted. In this enterprise, Hoccleve was doing only what Usk had tried earlier, and Scogan: use Chaucer's writings and advertise the use for exchange. Hoccleve's greater success was an accidental by-product of historical conjuncture. The altered political circumstance post-1399, his state-official position, demonized dissident religion, a better established Chaucer-figure: Hoccleve survived. He continued writing, and his work circulated. It is not clear, by contrast, that earlier Usk had been rewarded for writing the *Testament*, and, in any event, he failed to deliver on the basic Chaucerian promise—possibly for reasons beyond his control—to disengage from political activities that did not clearly promote ruling-class interests. But the bargain had already been struck, between Chaucer and those whom he had served by his writings—the "Complaint to his Purse," if nothing else, makes clear that for Chaucer writing had exchange-value: it was for sale—and, though the records are inexplicit, the bargain had already paid off for Chaucer too. He was well rewarded. He had done the job, both at his quotidian occupations and at his nocturnal literary employment.

This is the Chaucerian literary legacy, the foundation of English literature as such, among those who founded it at the time: immediately, Chaucer, and then those persons who knew (or knew of), praised, and emulated Chaucer's writings already during his life and before the passing of the generation after his death: Deschamps, Usk, and Hoccleve may have been chief agents, though others also contributed: Froissart, Gower, Clanvowe, Scogan, and so on. The legacy is the possibility, promise, and routine of servile literary production. Chaucer created it—though not altogether by himself—and others built it, using his name and example—though again the circumambient social totality determined its peculiar pathology.

At the same time, Chaucer's job of founding English literature was also done, when the servility to dominant interests that characterizes Chaucer's own writing throughout was become routine in the writings of others. The incipiently institutionalized Chaucerianism is only the subsequently preeminent mainstream of English literature, however, this hegemonic part coming to stand for the whole, in such versions of English literary history as make Chaucer the father. There were and have been alternative English literatures in fact, differing from the Chaucerian mainstream, characterized fundamentally by a different relation to authority. Meanwhile, by comparison with the alternatives, what made the Chaucerian tradition apt for the election it received was its collaborative subordination. It served.

NOTES

Chapter 1   Work

1. For the brawl, see Lister M. Matheson, "Chaucer's Ancestry: Historical and Philological Re-Assessments," *Chaucer Review* 25 (1991): esp. 179–81. Other information on Chaucer's ancestry is collected in *Chaucer Life-Records*, ed. Martin M. Crow and Clair C. Olson (Oxford: Clarendon, 1966)—henceforth, abbreviated *CLR*—pp. 1–8, and on his children, pp. 541–46. On the career of the especially distinguished Thomas, see additionally Martin B. Ruud, *Thomas Chaucer* (Minneapolis: University of Minnesota Press, 1926), and the supplementary information in A. C. Baugh, "Kirk's Life Records of Thomas Chaucer," *PMLA* 47 (1932): 461–515.

2. Paul Strohm, *Social Chaucer* (Cambridge: Harvard University Press, 1989), pp. 10–13 and 21–23.

3. The reference is to the work of Michel Foucault, specifically, here (as elsewhere), to *Discipline and Punish: The Birth of Prison*, trans. Alan Sheridan (1977; repr. New York: Vintage, 1995), esp. the "Panopticism" chapter, pp. 195–228, though also, more generally, to the operations of "power" in the technical sense of the term that Foucault worked with frequently and developed in his historical writings, most concisely explained in a few pages of a brief chapter in one of the *History of Sexuality* volumes (the chapter "Method," in *The History of Sexuality Volume 1: An Introduction*, trans. Robert Hurley [1978; repr. New York: Vintage, 1990], pp. 92–102), e.g., pp. 92–93:

   > By power, I do not mean "Power" as a group of institutions and mechanisms that ensure the subservience of the citizens of a given state. By power, I do not mean, either, a mode of subjugation which, in contrast to violence, has the form of the rule. Finally, I do not have in mind a general system of domination exerted by one group over another, a system whose effects, through successive derivations, pervade the entire social body. The analysis, made in terms of power, must not assume that the sovereignty of the state, the form of the law, or the over-all unity of a domination are given at the outset; rather, these are only the terminal forms power takes. It seems to me that power must be understood in the first instance as the multiplicity of force relations immanent in the sphere in which they operate and which

constitute their own organization; as the process which, through ceaseless struggles and confrontations, transforms, strengthens, or reverses them; as the support which these force relations find in one another, thus forming a chain or a system, or on the contrary, the disjunctions and contradictions which isolate them from one another; and lastly, as the strategies in which they take effect, whose general design or institutional crystallization is embodied in the state apparatus, in the formulation of the law, in the various social hegemonies.

Because the term "power" is acquiring this idiosyncratic, particular meaning in historical writing, by virtue of Foucault's influence, I have tried to avoid using it in the old-fashioned vulgar sense that Foucault criticized, of a hypostatized or reified something that, for example, having an identifiable location, in persons or institutions, might be struggled against. It has mostly been possible to use a more specific term instead—class, state, dominance, hegemony, ideology, repression, and so on, as called for—though not altogether: when convenient, I do sometimes use the term to mean "a general system of domination exerted by one group over another," including but not restricted to violence, "a system whose effects, through successive derivations, pervade the entire social body." Foucault himself devoted extensive writing to problems of such distributions of "power" in institutions of state—the "terminal forms" and "institutional crystallizations" that "power" takes—for example, in the papers "Governmentality" (1978) and " '*Omnes et Singulatim*': Toward a Critique of Political Reason" (1979), both in *The Essential Works of Foucault 1954–1984*, ed. Paul Rabinow, trans. Robert Hurley and others, 3 vols. (New York: The New Press, 1997–2000), 3: 201–22 and 298–325. Foucault's own answer to the question "is revolution possible?" was, persistently, "yes:" see, for example, "Useless to Revolt?" (1979), in *Essential Works of Foucault*, 3: 449–53.

4. Crow and Olson, *CLR*, pp. 13–18. The manuscript is in the British Library, London, Addit. 18632; on it, see M. C. Seymour, "The Manuscripts of Hoccleve's *Regiment of Princes*," *Edinburgh Bibliographical Society Transactions* 4 (1974): 275–76.

5. For Chaucer's service to Lionel, see *CLR*, pp. 19–22, and to Edward III, *CLR*, pp. 23–28 and 94–122. Contemporary royal household organization, including the more intimate chamber within it, to which Chaucer ("*scutifer camere regis*," e.g.) evidently had some intermittent responsibilities, is reviewed compendiously in D. A. L. Morgan, "The House of Policy: The Political Role of the Late Plantagenet Household, 1422–1485," in *The English Court: From the Wars of the Roses to the Civil War*, ed. David Starkey (London: Longman, 1987), pp. 26–34. In the main, however, I have relied on Richard Firth Green, *Poets and Princepleasers: Literature and the English Court in the Late Middle Ages* (Toronto: University of Toronto Press, 1980), pp. 5–7 and 13–70, who uses a noteworthily full range of evidence. The same writer's "Arcite at Court," *English Language Notes* 18 (1981): 251–57, has additional useful contemporary information on the status of household servants, warning, for example, that even brief recourse to the evidence has as its consequence that

"we must quickly disabuse ourselves of any romantic notion we may have harbored" of such household servants "as sprightly young gentlemen with neat tunics and bobbed haircuts" (253).

6. *CLR*, pp. 23–25.

7. *CLR*, p. 19. Crow and Olson, *CLR*, pp. 65–66, comment on Chaucer's inevitable subordination on such errands.

8. *CLR*, p. 47; for the errands of 1377–1381, see *CLR*, pp. 44–53.

9. *Patience* 51–53, and John Scattergood, " 'Patience' and Authority," in *Essays on Ricardian Literature in Honour of J. A. Burrow*, ed. A. J. Minnis, Charlotte C. Morse, and Thorlac Turville-Petre (Oxford: Clarendon, 1997), p. 300.

10. *CLR*, pp. 55–61, and, for explanation of the disparity, see Richard Firth Green, *Poets and Princepleasers*, p. 25. Alfred Larson, "The Payment of Fourteenth-Century English Envoys," *English Historical Review* 54 (1939): 403–14, details the steps involved in the process of collecting such dues (409–14), and shows (409–10) that two years was to be expected, though in the sample with which he worked, of ninety-five cases dating between 1327 and 1336, he found delays of two, three, six, eight, and forty years.

11. *CLR*, p. 99.

12. *CLR*, pp. 97, 100–02, and 94: "des seignurs et autres gentz del hostell qi sount ordenez destre as robes du roi nosseignur contre la Nowell proscheine avenir." There is comment on the social implications of this last document in Strohm, "Chaucer's Audience," *Literature & History* 5 (1977): 27–28.

13. *CLR*, p. 236.

14. *CLR*, pp. 98–100; cf. 103–05.

15. *CLR*, p. 275; cf. Strohm, *Social Chaucer*, p. 34.

16. The documents are collected in *CLR*, pp. 144–47; for discussion, see also Samuel Moore, "Studies in the Life-Records of Chaucer," *Anglia* 37 (1918): 10–13, and E. P. Kuhl, "Chaucer and Aldgate," *PMLA* 39 (1924): 101–22.

17. The documentary evidence for Chaucer's appointments is collected in *CLR*, pp. 148–270; see also Moore, "Studies in the Life-Records of Chaucer," 14–19, and "New Life-Records of Chaucer," *Modern Philology* 16 (1918): 49–52; and J. M. Manly, "Chaucer as Controller," *Modern Philology* 25 (1927): 123. For the nature of the work, I rely also on Olive Coleman, "The Collectors of Customs in London under Richard II," in *Studies in London History Presented to Philip Edmund Jones*, ed. A. E. J. Hollaender and William Kellaway (London: Hodder and Stoughton, 1969), pp. 181–94, and Eileen Power, *The Wool Trade in English Medieval History* (Oxford: Oxford University Press, 1941), esp. pp. 63–85. On the increasing trade in finished cloth, see E. M. Carus-Wilson, "Trends in the Export of English Woolens in the Fourteenth Century," *Economic History Review*, 2nd ser., 3 (1950): 162–79.

18. The fundamental work is in the three papers of Robert Brenner: "Agrarian Class Structure and Economic Development in Pre-Industrial Europe," *Past & Present* 70 (1976): 30–75; "The Origins of Capitalist Development: A Critique of Neo-Smithian Marxism," *New Left Review* 104 (1977): 25–92; and "Agrarian Class Structure and Economic Development in Pre-Industrial Europe: The Agrarian Roots of European Capitalism," *Past & Present*

97 (1982): 16–113. There is a brief summary in Brenner's more recent *Merchants and Revolution: Commercial Change, Political Conflict, and London's Overseas Traders, 1550–1653* (Princeton: Princeton University Press, 1993), pp. 649–51, and the issues are usefully reviewed in Ellen Meiksins Wood, "Capitalism, Merchants and Bourgeois Revolution: Reflections on the Brenner Debate and its Sequel," *International Review of Social History* 41 (1996): 210–15 and 225–32.

19. *CLR*, pp. 123–25.
20. *CLR*, pp. 271–74.
21. *CLR*, pp. 303–07.
22. *CLR*, pp. 336–39. For parallels to the transaction, see Moore, "Studies in the Life-Records of Chaucer," 19–25; and for a contrary suggestion, that Chaucer's resignation was extraordinary, in anticipation of trouble following from the "Merciless" parliament, see S. Sanderlin, "Chaucer and Ricardian Politics," *Chaucer Review* 22 (1988): 172–75, or Strohm, *Social Chaucer*, pp. 36–41 and 65–66, or Derek Albert Pearsall, *The Life of Geoffrey Chaucer* (Oxford: Blackwell, 1992), p. 208.
23. *CLR*, pp. 514–15.
24. *CLR*, pp. 525–27.
25. For the physical arrangements of the Exchequer offices, see R. Allen Brown, H. M. Colvin, and A. J. Taylor, *The History of the King's Works: The Middle Ages* (London: HMSO, 1963), 1: 538–43. For the Egyptian analogue, see, e.g., Barry J. Kemp, *Ancient Egypt: Anatomy of a Civilization* (London: Routledge, 1989), pp. 145–48.
26. The remarks that follow depend largely on Crow and Olson, *CLR*, pp. 133–43.
27. Crow and Olson, *CLR*, p. 142.
28. Crow and Olson, *CLR*, p. 143. There are good pages in Anthony Steel, *The Receipt of the Exchequer, 1377–1485* (Cambridge: Cambridge University Press, 1954), pp. 2–34, esp. on the "fictitious loans" problem, discussed also in Michael Mann, "State and Society, 1130–1815: An Analysis of English State Finances," *Political Power and Social Theory* 1 (1980): 169–70.
29. Crow and Olson, *CLR*, p. 137. There may well have been other costs to Chaucer's dealings with the Exchequer: the Latin verse satires of ca. 1398–1410 on the Exchequer routines—in M. Dorothy George, "Verses on the Exchequer in the Fifteenth Century," *English Historical Review* 36 (1921): 58–67—in addition to their contemporary witness to the complexities and difficulties of collection procedures from the perspective of a payee like Chaucer, also suggest that, at every step of the process, bribe-paying was requisite. The analysis of the often parallel case of Thomas Hoccleve, in Malcolm Richardson, "Hoccleve in his Social Context," *Chaucer Review* 20 (1986): 313–22, is highly instructive.
30. On the revenue, see Coleman, "Collectors of Customs," esp. 182–84. Figures are essayed in Mann, "State and Society, 1130–1815," 178–79, showing the crown's customs revenues exceeding its revenues both from hereditary dues (chiefly "rents from crown lands and the profits of justice") and from

all other forms of taxation (i.e., parliamentarily imposed subsidies and other taxes) in the reign of Richard II. On the Ricardian extravagance and criticism of it, see esp. Patricia J. Eberle, "The Politics of Courtly Style at the Court of Richard II," in *The Spirit of the Court*, ed. Glyn S. Burgess and Robert A. Taylor (Cambridge: Brewer, 1985), pp. 168–78; also John M. Bowers, "*Pearl* in its Royal Setting: Ricardian Poetry Revisited," *Studies in the Age of Chaucer* 17 (1995): 111–55.

31. The quotations are *The Simonie* 252, ed. James Dean, *Medieval English Political Writings*, METS (Kalamazoo: Medieval Institute Publications, 1996), pp. 193–212, and Thomas Walsingham, *Chronicon Angliae*, ed. Edward Maunde Thompson, Rolls Series 64 (London: Longman, 1874), pp. 375–76: "Et hi nimirum milites plus erant Veneris quam Bellonae, plus potentes in thalamo quam in campo, plus lingua quam lancea viguerunt, ad dicendum vigiles, ad faciendum acta martia somnolenti." Though *The Simonie* probably dates from the 1320s in its earliest form, John Finlayson, "*The Simonie*: Two Authors?," *Archiv für das Studium der neueren Sprachen und Literaturen* 226 (1989): 39–51, argues that it was rewritten for recirculation in the late fourteenth century; and Elizabeth Salter, "*Piers Plowman* and 'The Simonie,'" *Archiv für das Studium der neueren Sprachen und Literaturen* 203 (1967): 241–54, demonstrates its persistent currency in the 1370s, when it was used by Langland.

32. Trans. Chris Given-Wilson, *Chronicles of the Revolution 1397–1400: The Reign of Richard II* (Manchester: Manchester University Press, 1993), pp. 172–73 and 177.

33. Trans. in *Richard Maidstone: Concordia (The Reconciliation of Richard II with London)*, ed. Carlson, trans. A. G. Rigg, METS (Kalamazoo: Medieval Institute Publications, 2003), p. 109. On Dymmok, see H. S. Cronin, ed., *Rogeri Dymmok Liber contra xii errores et hereses lollardorum* (London: Wyclif Society, 1922), pp. xi–xv.

34. "On the Times" (*IMEV* 3113), 57–60 and 41–44, ed. Dean, *Medieval English Political Writings*, pp. 140–46; on this poem, see Richard Firth Green, "Jack Philipot, John of Gaunt, and a Poem of 1380," *Speculum* 66 (1991): 330–41.

35. "Against the King's Taxes" 51–52 and 50, ed. Isabel S. T. Aspin, *Anglo-Norman Political Songs* (Oxford: Blackwell, 1953), pp. 105–15; and *The Crowned King* 65–70, ed. Helen Barr, *The Piers Plowman Tradition* (London: Dent, 1993), pp. 205–10.

36. *Richard the Redeless* 4. 1–4 and 8–16, ed. Barr, *The Piers Plowman Tradition*, pp. 101–33. It was established by Dan Embree, " 'Richard the Redeless' and 'Mum and the Sothsegger:' A Case of Mistaken Identity," *Notes & Queries* 220 (1975): 4–12, that *Richard the Redeless* and *Mum and the Sothsegger* were, not parts of the same piece of writing, but separate poems; it has been argued more recently, by Barr, "The Relationship of *Richard the Redeless* and *Mum and the Sothsegger*: Some New Evidence," *Yearbook of Langland Studies* 4 (1990): 105–33, that, though the two are separate poems, they might be the work of the same writer.

37. The quotations are *The Simonie* 312 and "The Bisson Leads the Blind (1456)" (*IMEV* 884) 66, ed. Rossell Hope Robbins, *Historical Poems of the XIVth and XVth Centuries* (New York: Columbia University Press, 1959), pp. 127–30.

38. Cf. Crow and Olson, *CLR*, p. 169.
39. J. W. Sherborne, "The Costs of English Warfare with France in the Late Fourteenth Century," *Bulletin of the Institute of Historical Research* 50 (1977): esp. 143–45; also, W. M. Ormrod, "The English Crown and the Customs, 1349–63," *Economic History Review*, 2nd ser., 40 (1987): 27–40. Mann, "State and Society, 1130–1815," 182, remarks on the benefits to the crown of this method of financing war; his statistical analysis also shows that "the financial size of the English state reaches a peak in the fourteenth century and does not grow substantially thereafter until the late seventeenth century" (175) and that "every increase in the real financial size of the state up to 1688 is occasioned by two interrelated factors, the onset of war and changing military technology, and the bulk of state expenditure goes to meet these needs" (168). The social and economic distortions of late-medieval war-finance in general, in broader European context, are discussed in Richard W. Kaeuper, *War, Justice, and Public Order: England and France in the Later Middle Ages* (Oxford: Clarendon, 1988), pp. 77–117.
40. On these three cases, see, respectively, *CLR*, pp. 189–90, 185–86, and 269–70.
41. *Mum and the Sothsegger* 11–12, ed. Barr, *The Piers Plowman Tradition*, pp. 137–202.
42. For Brembre's pre-eminence as a wool-exporter, see Pamela Nightingale, "Capitalists, Crafts and Constitutional Change in Late Fourteenth-Century London," *Past & Present* 124 (1989): 13, or "Knights and Merchants: Trade, Politics and the Gentry in Late Medieval England." *Past & Present* 169 (2000): 52. The extent of the crown's indebtedness to Brembre at the same time is put in perspective in Steel, "English Government Finance, 1377–1413," *English Historical Review* 51 (1936): esp. 590–91.
43. Cf. George Holmes, *The Good Parliament* (Oxford: Clarendon, 1975), p. 181: "The attack in the parliament on the fiscal and commercial policies of the court had also been a dispute between groups of London merchants (Lyons, Pecche, and Bury on one side, Walworth, Francis, and their friends on the other), rivals for enjoyment of the financial advantages which resulted from political influence."
44. Quoted in Crow and Olson, *CLR*, p. 11. A contemporary, iconographically cognate portrait-image of John Philipot and his money, in the "St Albans Donors Book" (London, British Library, Cotton Nero D.v), is reproduced in Roger Sherman Loomis, *A Mirror of Chaucer's World* (Princeton: Princeton University Press, 1965), no. 23.
45. For Lyons's career, I rely chiefly on A. R. Myers, "The Wealth of Richard Lyons," in *Essays in Medieval History Presented to Bertie Wilkinson*, ed. T. A. Sandquist and M. R. Powicke (Toronto: University of Toronto Press, 1969), pp. 301–29, and, for the parliamentary attack on him, Holmes, *The Good Parliament*, pp. 69–90 and 100–18. In perhaps his most surreal piece of writing, "Chaucer the Patriot," *Philological Quarterly* 25 (1946): 278, Kuhl put something about relations between Chaucer and "that arch-embezzler" Lyons.

46. Given-Wilson, "Wealth and Credit, Public and Private: The Earls of Arundel 1306–1397," *English Historical Review* 106 (1991): 11–14. Cf. also G. L. Harriss, "Aids, Loans and Benevolences," *Historical Journal* 6 (1963): 1–2.
47. Myers, "The Wealth of Richard Lyons," p. 304.
48. *Mum and the Sothsegger* 145–50. For the broader currency of such a notion of official responsibility at the time, see Andrew Wawn, "Truth-Telling and the Tradition of *Mum and the Sothsegger*," *Yearbook of English Studies* 13 (1983): 270–87. Chaucer himself articulated a case (of a kind) in favour of self-interested "Mum"—"Dissimule as thou were deef" (347)—in the *Manciple's Tale*, especially in the Manciple's lengthy report of his Dame's admonitions at the tale's conclusion (318–62): "My sone, ful ofte, for to muche speche/ Hath many a man been spilt, as clerkes teche,/ But for litel speche avysely/ Is no man shent, to speke generally." There is remarkably insightful (though occasionally enigmatic) discussion of the general import of this aspect of the *Manciple's Tale* in Louise Fradenburg, "The Manciple's Servant Tongue: Politics and Poetry in *The Canterbury Tales*," *ELH* 52 (1985): 85–118. Fradenburg argues that "*The Manciple's Tale* signifies the ideological limitations which pressure both the *Tales* and Chaucer's own career from their inception, but which the design of the *Tales*, as pluralized discourse, seeks to transcend. *The Manciple's Tale* gives us the full measure of Chaucer's understanding of writing under the demand; gives us the full measure of his understanding of the mirages and captivations of the demand as well as of its real origins in courtly experience. *The Manciple's Tale*, as the last poem in *The Canterbury Tales*, precedes the abdication of Harry Bailey in favor of the parson, precedes the recovery of pluralized carnival by penitential prose. Its positioning thereby marks for us the ideological limitations of *The Canterbury Tales* as a whole, but also Chaucer's awareness—on what level we need not speculate—of those ideological limitations" (111): "To what extent does the carnival world of poetic rebellion against the laws of public language, of female rebellion against the bodily constraints of patriarchy, end by reminding us only that freedom has never, in fact, been the order of the day? *The Manciple's Tale* asks a similar question" (93).
49. Crow and Olson, *CLR*, pp. 5 and 11 n4.
50. "Vulneratur Karitas" 46 and 41–44, ed. Aspin, *Anglo-Norman Political Songs*, pp. 149–56.
51. It has been regretted that the manuscript of the third volume of *Capital* terminates within a few sentences of Marx having posed the question, "What constitutes a class?" The answer begins to be "the identity of revenues and sources of revenue," but then this is dismissed. Georg Lukács, for example, took this Marxian breaking-off as the setting out point for his 1920 paper "Class Consciousness," in *History and Class Consciousness*, trans. Rodney Livingstone, 1967 edn. (Cambridge: MIT Press, 1971), p. 46. On the other hand, Marx said a good deal elsewhere, coherently enough: e.g., "In so far as millions of families live under economic conditions of existence that separate their mode of life, their interests and their culture from those of the other classes, and put them in hostile opposition to the latter, they form

a class" ("The Eighteenth Brumaire of Louis Bonaparte," in *Selected Works*, 1:479). A consequence of the division of labor is conflict between classes, and "so the history of all hitherto existing society is the history of class struggles" ("Communist Manifesto," in *Selected Works*, 1:108). By the same token, the occurrence of struggle and conflict (evidence of people living "in hostile opposition") is fundamental to defining classes and class-relations in historical societies. Cf. Louis Althusser, "Ideology and Ideological State Apparatuses (Notes Towards an Investigation)," in *Lenin and Philosophy and Other Essays*, trans. Ben Brewster (New York: Monthly Review Press, 1971), p. 184: "Whoever says class struggle of the ruling class says resistance, revolt and class struggle of the ruled class:" "there is no class struggle without antagonistic classes." In the analysis herein, I have meant to follow the example of such particular, close-grained historical analysis as Marx himself made, most famously perhaps, in "The Eighteenth Brumaire" (in *Selected Works*, 1:398–487), or in "The Class Struggles in France, 1848–1850" (in *Selected Works*, 1: 205–99), though perhaps it should be noted in this connection that, in the same 1877 letter (in *Selected Works*, 3: 480) in which Marx seems to have coined the phrase "personality cult" in order to profess his "aversion to any," he also denounces "everything tending to encourage superstitious belief in authority," his own particularly.

52. Antonio Gramsci, *Selections from the Prison Notebooks*, ed. and trans. Quintin Hoare and Geoffrey Norton-Smith (London: Wishart, 1971), pp. 12 and 350.

53. Althusser, "Ideology and Ideological State Apparatuses," pp. 143–45.

54. For such information, I rely on Bertha Haven Putnam, *Proceedings before the Justices of the Peace in the Fourteenth and Fifteenth Centuries Edward III to Richard III* (London: Spottiswoode, 1938), esp. pp. xix–xxxv and lxxvi–cxxviii (the volume also prints and analyzes the records of contemporary commissions that do survive); and on Putnam, "The Transformation of the Keepers of the Peace into the Justices of the Peace 1327–1380," *Transactions of the Royal Historical Society*, 4th ser., 12 (1929): 19–48, and Rosamond Sillem, "Commissions of the Peace, 1380–1485," *Bulletin of the Institute of Historical Research* 10 (1932): 81–104. Additionally, some pertinent statutes of Edward III are printed in C. G. Crump and C. Johnson, "The Powers of Justices of the Peace," *English Historical Review* 27 (1912): 226–38.

55. The quotations are "Tax Has Tenet Us" (*IMEV* 3260) 9–10 and 27–28, ed. Dean, *Medieval English Political Writings*, pp. 147–49, and "The Insurrection and Earthquake (1382)" (*IMEV* 4268) 17–20, ed. Robbins, *Historical Poems of the XIVth and XVth Centuries*, pp. 57–60. Richard Firth Green, "Jack Philipot, John of Gaunt, and a Poem of 1380," 341, suggests that the "Tax Has Tenet Us" (*IMEV* 3260), cited here, may be the work of the same poet who wrote "On the Times" (*IMEV* 3113), cited above, n33.

56. The quotations are "Tax Has Tenet Us" 61, and the "Versus de tempore Johannis Straw" (unlineated), ed. Thomas Wright, *Political Poems and Songs Relating to English History Composed During the Period from the Accession of EDW. III. to that of RIC. III.*, Rolls Series 14, 2 vols. (London: Longman, 1859–1861), 1: 228–29.

57. Thomas Walsingham, *Historia anglicana*, in R. B. Dobson, *The Peasants' Revolt of 1381* (London: MacMillan, 1970), pp. 311–12. On the suppression, "mounted more or less like a military campaign," see Ormrod, "The Peasants' Revolt and the Government of England," *Journal of British Studies* 29 (1990): 20–22. Generally, I rely on Rodney Hilton, *Bond Men Made Free: Medieval Peasant Movements and the English Rising of 1381* (1973; repr. London: Routledge, 1988).

58. Henry Knighton, *Chronicon*, in Dobson, *The Peasants' Revolt*, pp. 313–14.

59. *Anonimalle Chronicle*, in Dobson, *The Peasants' Revolt*, p. 306.

60. Susan Crane, "The Writing Lesson of 1381," in *Chaucer's England: Literature in Historical Context*, ed. Barbara A. Hanawalt (Minneapolis: University of Minnesota Press, 1992), esp. pp. 204–07; and, on the Savoy incident, Steven Justice, *Writing and Rebellion: England in 1381* (Berkeley: University of California Press, 1994), pp. 90–94. Cf. also Ormrod, "The Peasants' Revolt," esp. 2–8.

61. Ormrod, "The Peasants' Revolt," 14.

62. The assault is mentioned only in a footnote, and only as pertaining to the question of Chaucer's education, in Crow and Olson, *CLR*, p. 12 n5. The evidence is presented in Edith Rickert, "Was Chaucer a Student at the Inner Temple?," in *The Manly Anniversary Studies in Language and Literature* (Chicago: University of Chicago Press, 1923), pp. 20–31; and there is further discussion in Joseph Allen Hornsby, "Was Chaucer Educated at the Inns of Court?," *Chaucer Review* 22 (1988): 255–68, or *Chaucer and the Law* (Norman: Pilgrim Books, 1988), pp. 8–15.

63. Ormrod, "The Peasants' Revolt," 26.

64. Kuhl, "Chaucer and Aldgate," *PMLA* 39 (1924): 102; cf. 105 and 106, and Moore, "Studies in the Life-Records of Chaucer," 11.

65. The quotation is from the "Versus de tempore Johannis Straw" (unlineated), ed. Wright, *Political Poems and Songs*, 1:228; cf. John Gower, *Vox clamantis* 1.1859–1862: "Unus erat maior Guillelmus, quem probitatis / Spiritus in mente cordis ad alta movet; / Iste tenens gladium quo graculus ille superbus / Corruit, ex et eo pacificavit opus." Translations of the other contemporary accounts of the killing are collected in Dobson, *The Peasants' Revolt*, pp. 166, 178, 186, 196, 203, 207, and 211; and cf. David Wallace, *Chaucerian Polity* (Stanford: Stanford University Press, 1997), p. 163.

66. Crow and Olson, *CLR*, pp. 512–13, summarize evidence for Chaucer's associations with Kent; for the date, see Pearsall, *The Life of Geoffrey Chaucer*, p. 225. On appointments to the peace commissions, see Putnam, *The Enforcement of the Statutes of Labourers During the First Decade After the Black Death* (New York: Columbia University Press, 1908), pp. 49–56, or *Proceedings before the Justices of the Peace*, pp. lxxvi–xcv. Thirteenth-century developments about the commissions are described in Alan Harding, "The Origins and Early History of the Keeper of the Peace," *Transactions of the Royal Historical Society*, 5th ser., 10 (1960), 85–109.

67. Crow and Olson, *CLR*, p. 349; cf. Ormrod, "The Peasants' Revolt," 11–13.

68. *CLR*, pp. 350 and 353. The evolutions of the commissions are delineated briefly in Putnam, *Proceedings before the Justices of the Peace*, pp. xix–xxxv; on

the problem of the commissions' jurisdictions in cases of extortion, see Sillem, "Commissions of the Peace," 88 and 96–97.

69. Putnam, "The Justices of Labourers in the Fourteenth Century," *English Historical Review* 21 (1906): 526–27, and cf. *Enforcement of the Statutes of Labourers*, pp. 10–19.

70. *CLR*, p. 348: "ad diversas felonias et transgressiones in comitatu Kancie tam infra libertates quam extra audiendas et terminandas."

71. *CLR*, p. 350: "qe bien et loialment servirez le roy en loffice de gardien de la paix et de justicierie des artificers, laborers, pois et mesure." For the oaths, see also Putnam, *Enforcement of the Statutes of Labourers*, pp. 40–43.

72. Quoted by Crow and Olson, *CLR*, p. 359.

73. *CLR*, p. 352: "de omnibus illis qui in conventiculis contra pacem nostram [sc. regalem] et in perturbacionem populi nostri seu vi armata ierint vel equitaverint seu exnunc ire vel equitare presumpserint; et eciam de hiis qui in insidiis ad gentem nostram mahemiandam vel interficiendam jacuerint vel exnunc jacere presumpserint."

74. *CLR*, p. 350: "touz les recordz et process qe serront faitz devant vous ferrez mettre en bone et seure garde" and "les extretes des fins et amerciementz et dautres profitz ent au roi appurtenantz ferrez entierement mettre en escript endentee."

75. Putnam, "Justices of Labourers," 536, and *Enforcement of the Statutes of Labourers*, pp. 111–13 and 133–35.

76. Margaret Galway, "Geoffrey Chaucer, J. P. and M. P.," *Modern Language Review* 36 (1941): 4; cf. Putnam, *Proceedings before the Justices of the Peace*, pp. xcv–cxii.

77. *CLR*, pp. 490–93.

78. *CLR*, p. 490: "racione dignitatis nostre regie ad providendum salvacioni regni nostri."

79. For English parliamentary history, I rely chiefly on the work of H. G. Richardson and G. O. Sayles, the fundamental contributions being Richardson, "The Origins of Parliament," *Transactions of the Royal Historical Society*, 4th ser., 11 (1928): 137–83, and "The Commons and Medieval Politics," *Transactions of the Royal Historical Society*, 4th ser., 28 (1946): 21–45; Richardson and Sayles, *The Governance of Mediaeval England* (Edinburgh: Edinburgh University Press, 1963); and Sayles, *The Functions of the Medieval Parliament of England* (London: Hambledon, 1988), chiefly a documentary collection. The work is summarized in Richardson and Sayles, *Parliaments and Great Councils in Medieval England* (London: Stevens, 1961), very briefly, and in Sayles, *The King's Parliament of England* (New York: Norton, 1974). A useful compendious overview of terms of meeting, membership, procedures, and so on, during the period of Chaucer's participation, is given by A. L. Brown, "Parliament, ca. 1377–1422," in *The English Parliament in the Middle Ages*, ed. R. G. Davies and J. H. Denton (Philadelphia: University of Pennsylvania Press, 1981), pp. 109–40. Florence R. Scott, "Chaucer and the Parliament of 1386," *Speculum* 18 (1943): 80–86, is not instructive.

80. Robert S. Hoyt, "Royal Taxation and the Growth of the Realm in Mediaeval England," *Speculum* 25 (1950): 45–46, continuing: "This was simply a

propaganda program of exalting the monarchy combined with a propaganda program designed to convince the already established communities of cities and boroughs, of the shires, and of the royal demesnes, that they were effective and interested parts of a larger community of the realm; that they were vitally concerned with and therefore partly responsible for the common utility or welfare of the realm which was the highest duty of the king to preserve; and finally that this concern and responsibility obligated them without question to contribute in accordance with their means sufficient aid that the king might maintain the 'estate of the realm' and the 'estate of the people.' " Cf. also May McKisack, *The Parliamentary Representation of the English Boroughs During the Middle Ages* (Oxford: Oxford University Press, 1932), pp. 128–29; G. L. Harriss, "Aids, Loans and Benevolences," esp. 5–7; and Brown, "Parliament, ca. 1377–1422," p. 125, pointing out that even the "right to assent" "was so new that the commons themselves still cautiously asked for it to be confirmed on several occasions."

81. The quotations here and following (with parenthetical line-references) are from the "Against the King's Taxes," ed. and trans. Aspin, *Anglo-Norman Political Songs*, pp. 105–115. There is analysis of the poem in Janet Coleman, *English Literature in History 1350–1400* (London: Hutchinson, 1981), pp. 79–84.

82. Hilton, *Bond Men Made Free*, pp. 160–64.

83. *CLR*, pp. 356 and 367. The disbursement mechanisms are discussed in L. C. Latham, "Collection of the Wages of the Knights of the Shire in the Fourteenth and Fifteenth Centuries," *English Historical Review* 48 (1933): 455–64; and, for the parallel and partially cognate problems about the payment of burgesses, see McKisack, *Parliamentary Representation of the English Boroughs*, pp. 82–99.

84. Cf. *CLR*, p. 366. Complete figures for all the Ricardian parliaments are supplied and analyzed in N. B. Lewis, "Re-election to Parliament in the Reign of Richard II," *English Historical Review* 48 (1933): 364–94.

85. Cf. Pearsall, *The Life of Geoffrey Chaucer*, p. 203. The county election procedures (those pertinent to the election of a knight of the shire like Chaucer) are discussed, e.g., in Richardson, "The Commons and Medieval Politics," 39–43, and in Brown, "Parliament, ca. 1377–1422," pp. 118–21; and on the burgess elections, see McKisack, *Parliamentary Representation of the English Boroughs*, pp. 24–43, and the discussion of persistent illegalities about the elections and attempts at their statutory reform in the fifteenth century, in K. N. Houghton, "Theory and Practice in Borough Elections to Parliament during the Later Fifteenth Century," *Bulletin of the Institute of Historical Research* 39 (1966): 130–40.

86. *Piers Plowman* 2.164, and see Crow and Olson, *CLR*, pp. 365–66 and n4, showing the evidence that lends "the list of mainpernors a fictitious appearance" in Chaucer's case and commenting, "returns of this period certainly include fictitious mainpernors in some counties." Richard was eventually criticized for abusing the sherival appointments, e.g., in the thirteenth and eighteenth of the deposition articles, in Given-Wilson, *Chronicles of the*

Revolution, pp. 176–77 and 178; see also the comments of Nigel Saul, *Richard II* (New Haven: Yale University Press, 1997), pp. 263, 369, and 383–84.

87. On Savage, see J. S. Roskell and L. S. Woodger, in *The House of Commons 1386–1421*, ed. Roskell (Stroud: Sutton, 1992), 4: 306–310, or Roskell's earlier *The Commons and their Speakers in English Parliaments 1376–1523* (Manchester: Manchester University Press, 1965), p. 362, where Chaucer's election is mentioned, as well as the fact that Savage was named an executor of the will of John Gower in 1408.

88. Trans. Given-Wilson, *Chronicles of the Revolution*, p. 178. The 1386 parliament sat from October 1 to November 28; Chaucer's customs successors were installed 1386 December 4 and 14. See *CLR*, pp. 366–67 and 268–69.

89. Barr, *The Piers Plowman Tradition*, p. 17. For discussion of the section of *Richard the Redeless* concerned with parliament, see Barr, "*Piers Plowman* and Poetic Tradition," *Yearbook of Langland Studies* 9 (1995): 47–49, or Frank Grady, "The Generation of 1399," in *The Letter of the Law: Legal Practice and Literary Production in Medieval England*, ed. Emily Steiner and Candace Barrington (Ithaca: Cornell University Press, 2002), pp. 223–26. Barr has elsewhere shown evidence to suggest that *Mum and the Sothsegger* may have been occasioned by the parliament of 1406, in "The Dates of *Richard the Redeless* and *Mum and the Sothsegger*," *Notes & Queries* 235 (1990): esp. 272–73, or at least that the poem's author was familiar with parliamentary affairs of that year, on which see Alan Rogers, "Henry IV, the Commons and Taxation," *Mediaeval Studies* 31 (1969): esp. 66–67.

90. *Richard the Redeless* 4.37 and 20–30.

91. *Mum and the Sothsegger* 1119–1121 and 1129.

92. *The Simonie* 480 and 496.

93. *Mum and the Sothsegger* 1134–1140 and *The Simonie* 499–501.

94. "Against the King's Taxes" 46–47.

95. *Richard the Redeless* 4.62–65, 83–90, and 53–54.

96. Pearsall, *The Life of Geoffrey Chaucer*, p. 204. On the Scrope–Grosvenor trial, see esp. Lee Patterson, *Chaucer and the Subject of History* (Madison: University of Wisconsin Press, 1991), pp. 180–94; and a contemporary Court of Chivalry trial, in which both parties were willing to die (and one did) for a like point of honor, is documented in John G. Bellamy, "Sir John de Annesley and the Chandos Inheritance," *Nottingham Medieval Studies* 10 (1966), 94–105.

97. The quotations are from *Parliament of Fowls* 491–495 and 501. For its date, a matter of considerable uncertainly but most likely between ca. 1373 and 1385, see Alistair J. Minnis, in *Oxford Guides to Chaucer: The Shorter Poems* (Oxford: Clarendon, 1995), pp. 256–61.

98. J. J. N. Palmer, "The Parliament of 1385 and the Constitutional Crisis of 1386," *Speculum* 46 (1971): 477–90; cf. Eberle, "The Question of Authority and the Man of Law's Tale," in *The Centre and its Compass: Studies in Medieval Literature in Honor of Professor John Leyerle*, ed. Robert A. Taylor, James F. Burke, Patricia J. Eberle, Ian Lancashire, and Brian S. Merrilees (Kalamazoo: Medieval Institute Publications, 1993), pp. 111–17.

99. Crow and Olson, *CLR*, p. 476. Another singularity about Chaucer's appointment was pointed out by Moore, "Studies in the Life-Records of Chaucer," 25–26: Chaucer was the only layperson to hold the office. A central works office, with a clerk and comptroller of its own, dated only from 1378, however: see Brown, Colvin, and Taylor, *The History of the King's Works: The Middle Ages*, 1:161–89.

100. The notion of production invoked here and throughout is fundamentally the complex, encompassing conception set out by Marx in the "Introduction" notebook of the *Grundrisse*, trans. Martin Nicholaus (Harmondsworth: Penguin, 1973), pp. 83–100, where he analyses production into component parts—production, distribution, exchange, and consumption—and asserts the components' subsumption within the general category:

> The conclusion we reach is not that production, distribution, exchange and consumption are identical, but that they all form the members of a totality, distinctions within a unity. Production predominates, not only over itself in the antithetical definition of production [i.e., p. 90: "The act of production is therefore in all its moments also an act of consumption"], but over the other moments as well. The process always returns to production to begin anew. That exchange and consumption cannot be predominant is self-evident. Likewise, distribution as distribution of products; while as distribution of the agents of production it is itself a moment of production. A definite production thus determines a definite consumption, distribution and exchange as well as *definite relations between these different moments.* (p. 99)

101. For the office, I rely on Brown, Colvin, and Taylor, *The History of the King's Works: The Middle Ages*, esp. 1: 189–201; also John H. Harvey, "The Medieval Office of Works," *Journal of the British Archaeological Association*, 3rd ser., 6 (1941): 20–87.

102. Sheila Lindenbaum, "The Smithfield Tournament of 1390," *Journal of Medieval and Renaissance Studies* 20 (1990): 9.

103. Saul, *Richard II*, pp. 351–52.

104. Lindenbaum, "The Smithfield Tournament," 19. The possibility that Chaucer's 1390 Smithfield tournament work experience may have had some relation to his writing of what became the *Knight's Tale* has been explored: see Stuart Robertson, "Elements of Realism in the *Knight's Tale*," *Journal of English and Germanic Philology* 14 (1915): 239 and 251–53, and Johnstone Parr, "The Date and Revision of Chaucer's *Knight's Tale*," *PMLA* 60 (1945): 317–24. A nearer event-analogue for the *Knight's Tale* than this 1390 Smithfield tournament may be the Court of Chivalry trial discussed in Bellamy, "Sir John de Annesley and the Chandos Inheritance," 94–105.

105. For the staff, see Brown, Colvin, and Taylor, *The History of the King's Works: The Middle Ages*, 1: 201–227, and 2:1045–1060.

106. Brown, Colvin, and Taylor, *The History of the King's Works: The Middle Ages*, 1:193.

107. Brown, Colvin, and Taylor, *The History of the King's Works: The Middle Ages*, 1:196 and 199.

108. Some of the documents to do with the robbery are collected in *CLR*, pp. 477–89; a significantly more complete collection is in Walford D. Selby, "The Robberies of Chaucer by Richard Brerelay and Others at Westminster, and at Hatcham, Surrey, on Tuesday, Sept. 6, 1390," in *Life-Records of Chaucer* 1, Chaucer Society Second Series 12 (London: Trübner, 1875).

109. For the Edwardian work on and around the St. George chapel, costing about £6,500, see Brown, Colvin, and Taylor, *The History of the King's Works: The Middle Ages*, 2: 872–75; for the work there during Chaucer's clerkship, costing a little more than £100, 2: 882–83 (and cf. Crow and Olson, *CLR*, pp. 471–72).

110. *The Legend of St. George* (*IMEV* 2592) headnote and 6–14, ed. Henry Noble MacCracken, *The Minor Poems of John Lydgate*, 2 vols., EETS es 107 and os 192 (London: Early English Text Society, 1911 and 1934), 1:145–54. Some useful information on the sociopolitical uses which the Garter cult of St. George served is collected in Jonathan Bengtson, "Saint George and the Formation of English Nationalism," *Journal of Medieval and Early Modern Studies* 27 (1997): 317 and 320–28.

111. On this problem, see Mervyn James, "English Politics and the Concept of Honour, 1485–1642" (1978), repr. in *Society, Politics and Culture: Studies in Early Modern England* (Cambridge: Cambridge University Press, 1986), pp. 308–415.

112. *To Henry V and the Knights of the Garter* (*IMEV* 3788 + 4251) 1 and 5–6, ed. Frederick J. Furnivall, in *Hoccleve's Works: The Minor Poems*, rev. edn., ed. Jerome Mitchell and A. I. Doyle, EETS es 61 and 73, in one vol. (London: Early English Text Society, 1970), pp. 41–43. These ballads' political context is discussed in Ruth Nissé, " 'Oure Fadres Olde and Modres': Gender, Heresy, and Hoccleve's Literary Politics," *Studies in the Age of Chaucer* 21 (1999): esp. 290–91 and n40.

113. Crow and Olson, *CLR*, p. 471.

114. *Mirour de l'omme* 25369–25370, ed. G. C. MacAulay, in *The Complete Works of John Gower*, 4 vols. (Oxford: Clarendon, 1899–1902), 1: 280.

115. Nightingale, "Capitalists, Crafts and Constitutional Change," esp. 8–16.

116. *CLR*, pp. 450–58: "de receptis et expensis circa operaciones regis apud Palacium Westmonasterii, Turrim Londinie, et alia diversa castra et maneria regis;" cf. pp. 404–08.

117. *CLR*, p. 408.

118. *CLR*, p. 407.

119. *CLR*, p. 403: "ad omnes illos quos in hac parte contrarios invenerit seu rebelles arestandos et capiendos et eos prisonis nostris mancipandos."

120. *CLR*, pp. 445–62.

121. Caroline M. Barron, "The Quarrel of Richard II with London 1392–7," in *The Reign of Richard II: Essays in Honour of May McKisack*, ed. F. R. H. Du Boulay and Barron (London: Athlone, 1971), pp. 173–201, and, on the

"blank charters," "The Tyranny of Richard II," *Bulletin of the Institute of Historical Research* 41 (1968): esp. 10–14.

122. Crow and Olson, *CLR*, p. 533. These later years of Chaucer's career in the public records are discussed in Sanderlin, "Chaucer and Ricardian Politics," 171–84.

123. Crow and Olson, *CLR*, p. 536.

124. On Maghfeld, see esp. Margery K. James, "A London Merchant of the Fourteenth Century," *Economic History Review*, 2nd ser., 8 (1956): 364–76; also Edith Rickert, "Extracts from a Fourteenth-Century Account Book," *Modern Philology* 24 (1926): 111–19 and 249–56. On the case of extortion, see *CLR*, pp. 504–06. For the forrestership, the evidence is collected in *CLR*, pp. 494–99, and discussed in Manly, "Three Recent Chaucer Studies," *Review of English Studies* 10 (1934): 258–62; on poaching, best is E. P. Thompson, *Whigs and Hunters: The Origin of the Black Act* (London: Allen Lane, 1975), though for a different view see Barbara A. Hanawalt, "Men's Games, King's Deer: Poaching in Medieval England," *Journal of Medieval and Renaissance Studies* 18 (1988): 175–93.

125. Crow and Olson, *CLR*, p. 548. See also Kuhl, "Chaucer and Westminster Abbey," *Journal of English and Germanic Philology* 45 (1946): 340–43; Pearsall, "Chaucer's Tomb: The Politics of Reburial," *Medium Aevum* 64 (1995): 52–56; and Saul, "Richard II and Westminster Abbey," in *The Cloister and the World: Essays in Medieval History in Honour of Barbara Harvey*, ed. John Blair and Brian Golding (Oxford: Clarendon, 1996), esp. pp. 210–12. The later history of the Chaucer tomb is also discussed in Joseph A. Dane, "Who is Buried in Chaucer's Tomb?—Prolegomena," *Huntington Library Quarterly* 57 (1994): 99–123.

Chapter 2   Writing

1. The fundamental analysis of this relation of culture to political economy is set out in summary terms in Marx's "Preface to a Contribution to the Critique of Political Economy," in Karl Marx and Frederick Engels, *Selected Works*, 3 vols. (Moscow: Progress Publishers, 1969), 1: 503–04:

> In the social production of their life, men enter into definite relations that are indispensable and independent of their will, relations of production which correspond to a definite stage of development of their material productive forces. The sum total of these relations of production constitutes the economic structure of society, the real foundation, on which rises a legal and political superstructure and to which correspond definite forms of social consciousness. The mode of production of material life conditions the social, the political and intellectual life process in general. . . . With the change of the economic foundation the entire immense superstructure is more or less rapidly transformed. In considering such transformations a distinction should always

be made between the material transformation of the economic conditions of production, which can be determined with the precision of natural science, and the legal, political, religious, aesthetic or philosophic—in short ideological forms in which men become conscious of this conflict and fight it out. Just as our opinion of an individual is not based on what he thinks of himself, so can we not judge of such a period of transformation by its own consciousness; on the contrary, this consciousness must be explained rather from the contradictions of material life, from the existing conflict between the social productive forces and the relations of production.

With the reaffirmations ("We make our history ourselves, but, in the first place, under very definite assumptions and conditions. Among these the economic ones are ultimately decisive") and self-critical apologies ("Marx and I are ourselves partly to blame for the fact that the younger people sometimes lay more stress on the economic side than is due to it") of Engels's 1890 "Letter to Joseph Bloch," in *Selected Works*, 3: 487–88:

> According to the materialist conception of history, the *ultimately* determining element in history is the production and reproduction of real life. More than this neither Marx nor I have ever asserted. Hence if somebody twists this into saying that the economic element is the *only* determining one, he transforms that proposition into a meaningless, abstract, senseless phrase. The economic situation is the basis, but the various elements of the superstructure—political forms of the class struggle and its results, to wit: constitutions established by the victorious class after a successful battle, etc., juridical forms, and even the reflexes of all these actual struggles in the brains of the participants, political, juristic, philosophical theories, religious views and their further development into systems of dogmas—also exercise their influence upon the course of the historical struggles and in many cases preponderate in determining their *form*.

In general, I rely on Raymond Williams's exegesis, "Base and Superstructure in Marxist Cultural Theory," *New Left Review* 82 (1973): 3–16.

The base-superstructure model has been criticized in the Marxist tradition, most notably perhaps in Louis Althusser's demonstration, in "Contradiction and Overdetermination: Notes for an Investigation," in *For Marx*, trans. Ben Brewster (1969; repr. London: Verso, 1996), esp. pp. 112–13, that, Engels's insistence to the contrary notwithstanding, "the lonely hour of the 'last instance' never comes." Still, even the most recent work with the concept of mediations of base and superstructure—e.g., Fredric Jameson, "The Brick and the Balloon: Architecture, Idealism and Land Speculation," *New Left Review* 228 (1998): esp. 26–27—corroborates the persistent utility of the basic Marxian analysis.

The specific concept of homology within this tradition here invoked— "one and the same structure manifesting itself on two different planes," the

NOTES 117

base of material production and the superstructure of culture-ideology—
comes from the work of Lucien Goldmann, e.g., "The Sociology of Literature: Status and Problems of Method," *International Social Science Journal* 19
(1967): 495–96 and 506, or "The Genetic-Structuralist Method in the History of Literature" (1964), repr. in *Towards a Sociology of the Novel*, 2nd edn.,
trans. Alan Sheridan (London:Tavistock, 1975), esp. pp. 159–63.The phrase
quoted above is from a pertinent section of the introduction in *Towards
a Sociology of the Novel*, pp. 7–11, at p. 8.There is useful brief discussion (as
there is also of much else besides), in Williams, *Marxism and Literature*
(Oxford: Oxford University Press, 1977), pp. 101–07.

2. This remark derives from a comment of A. C. Spearing, ed., *The Knight's Tale*
(Cambridge:Cambridge University Press, 1966), p. 23:"*The Knight's Tale* offers,
then, to its original aristocratic audience, an image of the noble life: an
image of human life as a noble pageant. It was not perhaps in every respect
the life that audience really lived,. . .but it was the life they aspired to live."

3. Chaucer's work in the genre is surveyed in W. A. Davenport, *Chaucer: Complaint and Narrative* (Cambridge: Brewer, 1988). I have been most influenced
by Julia Boffey, "The Reputation and Circulation of Chaucer's Lyrics in the
Fifteenth Century," *Chaucer Review* 28 (1993): 23–40, resting on the evidentiary basis set out in her earlier *Manuscripts of the English Courtly Love
Lyrics in the Later Middle Ages* (Cambridge: Brewer, 1985). For such poetry's
function, see Glending Olson, "Making and Poetry in the Age of Chaucer,"
Comparative Literature 31 (1979): 272–90, and "Toward a Poetics of the Late
Medieval Court Lyric," in *Vernacular Poetics in the Middle Ages*, ed. Lois Ebin
(Kalamazoo: Medieval Institute Publications, 1984), pp. 227–48. Otherwise,
in general I rely on Alistair J. Minnis, with V. J. Scattergood and J. J. Smith,
Oxford Guides to Chaucer: The Shorter Poems (Oxford: Clarendon, 1995).

4. Quotations in this paragraph are *Lady* 9, *Anel* 205 and 325–35.

5. Quotations in this paragraph are *Lady* 61–62; *Compl d'Am* 80, 74–75, and
78–79; *Bal Comp* 21 and 12–14; and *Pity* 2 and 33–34.

6. Quotations in this paragraph are *Lady* 31–32, *Anel* 222, *Pity* 77, *Compl d'Am*
11–12, *Ven* 6 and 15, *Anel* 258 and 284–86.

7. *As You Like It* 4.1. Cf. Richard Firth Green, *Poets and Princepleasers* (Toronto:
University of Toronto Press, 1980), p. 114.

8. This point is made in Patricia J. Eberle, "Commercial Language and the
Commercial Outlook in the *General Prologue*," *Chaucer Review* 18 (1983):
esp. 164–67; see also Lee Patterson, "Court Politics and the Invention of Literature: The Case of Sir John Clanvowe," in *Culture and History 1350–1600*,
ed. David Aers (New York: Harvester Wheatsheaf, 1992), pp. 24–26.

9. This memorial function is set in a material context, illuminatingly, by
Phillipa Hardman, "*The Book of the Duchess* as a Memorial Monument,"
Chaucer Review 28 (1994): 205–15.

10. Here (and throughout), the influence of Sheila Delany, "Politics and the
Paralysis of Poetic Imagination in *The Physician's Tale*," *Studies in the Age of
Chaucer* 3 (1981): 47–60, should be evident. What Delany demonstrates is
Chaucer's "virtually complete depoliticization of a political anecdote"

(47)—e.g., "the theme of class struggle is effaced" (51)—in the specific instance of the *Physician's Tale*, though in a way more generally applicable to Chaucer's writing: "To glorify rebellion—the original aim of the Virginius legend—is utterly alien to Chaucer's worldview: our poet is a prosperous, socially conservative, prudent courtier and civil servant, directly dependent for his living upon the good will of kings and dukes" (57), and (60)

> May we speculate about the *Physician's Tale* that the relevant social reality (insurrection) was simply too dangerous to write about for a courtier with everything to lose; or that it was not a topic appropriate to Chaucer's talent? Revolt is an absolute, not to be put in its place (like [the Wife of Bath,] an "uppity woman") with irony. It transcends rhetoric, or, as Leon Trotsky wrote of the Bolsheviks, 'They were adequate to the epoch and its tasks. Curses in plenty resounded in their direction, but irony would not stick to them—it had nothing to catch hold of.' One wonders if that is the real fear behind the multiple absences that constitute *The Physician's Tale*: that the tempestuous, ambitious bourgeoisie might after all prove adequate to the task. . . . We can hardly be surprised that the tradition of middle-class insurrection and republican rights evoked from Chaucer no energetic creative response.

11. Derek Albert Pearsall, *The Life of Geoffrey Chaucer* (Oxford: Blackwell, 1992), pp. 82–84 and 90–92.

12. Richard W. Kaeuper, *War, Justice, and Public Order: England and France in the Later Middle Ages* (Oxford: Clarendon, 1988), p. 6. For analysis of the demographic issues, see, e.g., M. M. Postan, *The Medieval Economy and Society: An Economic History of Britain in the Middle Ages* (London: Weidenfeld and Nicolson, 1972), pp. 27–39, or Alan R. H. Baker, "Changes in the Later Middle Ages," in *A New Historical Geography of England*, ed. H. C. Darby (Cambridge: Cambridge University Press, 1973), pp. 187–95. Population figures for the period are essayed in Josiah Cox Russell, *British Medieval Population* (Albuquerque: University of New Mexico Press, 1948), pp. 260–70, from whose paper, "Effects of Pestilence and Plague, 1315–1385," *Comparative Studies in Society and History* 8 (1966): 464–73, the fifty percent figure is taken. In *PardT* 661–701, of course, Chaucer himself makes some evocation of the plague's impact (at a distance, in Flanders), largely for dramatic-comic purpose; the passage has been taken "as evidence that as an artist Chaucer was indifferent to the tragedies that haunted England during his lifetime": see Peter G. Beidler, "The Plague and Chaucer's Pardoner," *Chaucer Review* 16 (1982): 257–69.

13. Göran Therborn, *The Ideology of Power and the Power of Ideology* (1980; repr. London: Verso, 1999), p. 45: "disarticulating uneven developments" are "any developments that tend to fracture the previous totality—from demographic trends affecting the relation between population and means of subsistence to the appearance of new and powerful neighbors;" cf. also p. 65. On forces and relations of production and their contradiction, the basic text

is probably Marx's "Preface to a Contribution to the Critique of Political Economy" (1859), in *Selected Works*, 1: 503–504: "From forms of development of the productive forces these relations turn into their fetters. Then begins an epoch of social revolution." Better known may be the specific application of this concept of the contradiction to the bourgeois-capitalist revolution earlier, in the "Communist Manifesto" (1848) (in *Selected Works*, 1: 113): "the means of production and of exchange, on whose foundation the bourgeoisie built itself up, were generated in feudal society. At a certain stage in the development of these means of production and of exchange, the conditions under which feudal society produced and exchanged, the feudal organization of agriculture and manufacturing industry, in one word, the feudal relations of property became no longer compatible with the already developed productive forces; they became so many fetters. They had to be burst asunder; they were burst asunder." The same notion was formulated as a generally applicable principle originally, it seems, in slightly different terms in Marx and Engels' unpublished notebook "Chapter I of *The German Ideology*" (1845–1846) (in *Selected Works*, 1:62): "All collisions in history have their origin, according to our view, in the contradiction between the productive forces and the form of intercourse. . . . The contradiction between the productive forces and the form of intercourse, which, as we saw, has occurred several times in history, without, however, endangering the basis, necessarily on each occasion burst out in a revolution." An important contribution of Althusser, in "Contradiction and Overdetermination," esp. pp. 99–101, was to emphasize the complexity of the contradiction, the "overdetermination" of this relationship between productive forces and relations of production by multiple, sometimes abstract and ideological variants, in actual historical events. "The concrete is the concrete because it is the concentration of many determinations," Marx himself wrote, in the *Grundrisse*, trans. Martin Nicholaus (Harmondsworth: Penguin, 1973), p. 101. Marx too was cautious about historical particularities, warning against elevation of 'my historical sketch of the genesis of capitalism in Western Europe [sc. in the 'So-Called Primitive Accumulation' chapter of the first volume of *Capital*] into an historico-philosophic theory of the general path every people is fated to tread, whatever the historical circumstance in which it finds itself,' in a letter published in 1877, in Marx and Engels, *Selected Correspondence* (Moscow: Foreign Languages Publishing House, n.d. [1955]), p. 379; Marx develops an example and then concludes: "Thus events strikingly analogous but taking place in different historical surroundings led to totally different results. By studying each of these forms of evolution separately and then comparing them one can easily find the clue to this phenomenon, but one will never arrive there by using as one's master key a general historico-philosophical theory, the supreme virtue of which consists in being super-historical."

14. Cf. Rodney Hilton, "Medieval Peasants: Any Lessons?" (1974), repr. in *Class Conflict and the Crisis of Feudalism*, 2nd edn. (London: Verso, 1990), pp. 44–47.

15. Ellen Meiksins Wood, *The Origin of Capitalism*, 2nd edn. (London: Verso, 2002), p. 82. There are instructive brief remarks on the economic utility of feudal-chivalric war—"war was possibly the most *rational* and *rapid* single mode of expansion of surplus extraction available for any given ruling class under feudalism" (p. 31)—in Perry Anderson, *Lineages of the Absolutist State* (London: NLB, 1974), pp. 31–33.

16. Patterson, *Chaucer and the Subject of History* (Madison: University of Wisconsin Press, 1991), p. 190; cf. also, above, pp. 8–11 and 106 n39.

17. Hilton, "Peasant Movements in England before 1381" (1949), repr. in *Class Conflict and the Crisis of Feudalism*, pp. 49–65, and "Popular Movements in England at the End of the Fourteenth Century" (1981), repr. in *Class Conflict and the Crisis of Feudalism*, pp. 79–91.

18. See Hilton, *Bond Men Made Free* (1973; repr. London: Routledge, 1988), esp. pp. 220–30, and "Social Concepts in the English Rising of 1381" (1975), repr. in *Class Conflict and the Crisis of Feudalism*, pp. 143–53.

19. "In tempore insurrectionis communium. . .uniusquisque nitebatur pro voto proprio regi ac abjicere penitus monarchiae jugum:" these recollections of Abbot John Whetehamstede are quoted from David R. Carlson, "Whetehamstede on Lollardy: Latin Styles and the Vernacular Cultures of Early Fifteenth-Century England," *Journal of English and Germanic Philology* 102 (2003): 23–24. The verses are from the "Dissipa Gentes," stanza 14 (unlineated), ed. Thomas Wright, *Political Poems and Songs Relating to English History Composed During the Period from the Accession of EDW. III. to that of RIC. III.*, Rolls Series 14, 2 vols. (London: Longman, 1859–1861), 1:235.

20. *English Historical Documents 1327–1485*, ed. A. R. Myers (New York: Oxford University Press, 1969), p. 993. Marx studied this statute and discusses it, in the "So-Called Primitive Accumulation" section of the first volume of *Capital* (in *Selected Works*, 2:122–23): "The spirit of the Statute of Laborers of 1349 and of its offshoots, comes out clearly in the fact, that indeed a maximum of wages is dictated by the State, but on no account a minimum," and that "the taking of higher wages was more severely punished than the giving them."

21. The verses are from "A Song of Freedom (1434)" (*IMEV* 849), ed. Rossell Hope Robbins, *Historical Poems of the XIVth and XVth Centuries* (New York: Columbia University Press, 1959), no. 22, p. 62. Cf. Hilton, *Bond Men Made Free*, pp. 151–55.

22. Hilton, *Bond Men Made Free*, pp. 160–64. The quoted verses are "Against the King's Taxes" 11–12, ed. and trans. Isabel S. T. Aspin, *Anglo-Norman Political Songs* (Oxford: Blackwell, 1953), pp. 105–115.

23. F. R. H. du Boulay, "The Historical Chaucer," in *Geoffrey Chaucer*, ed. Derek Brewer (Athens: Ohio University Press, 1975), p. 36; and cf. Derek Brewer, "Class Distinction in Chaucer," *Speculum* 43 (1968): 304–305. A different view of class-mobility has been argued by Paul Strohm, e.g., in "Chaucer's Audience," *Literature & History* 5 (1977): esp. 27–29, namely, that mobility yielded "a continued blurring of class lines" (39).

24. Cf. Eberle, "The Politics of Courtly Style at the Court of Richard II," in *The Spirit of the Court*, ed. Glyn S. Burgess and Robert A. Taylor (Cambridge: Brewer, 1985), esp. pp. 170–71.

25. Sheila Lindenbaum, "The Smithfield Tournament of 1390," *Journal of Medieval and Renaissance Studies* 20 (1990): 9.

26. That this is a distinctive and historically consequential contribution of Langland and Gower is the argument of Anne Middleton, "The Idea of Public Poetry in the Reign of Richard II," *Speculum* 53 (1978): 94–114. The analysis is extended to apply to some of Chaucer's pilgrims' performances in Middleton's "Chaucer's 'New Men' and the Good of Literature in the *Canterbury Tales*," in *Literature and Society: Selected Papers from the English Institute, 1978*, ed. Edward W. Said (Baltimore: Johns Hopkins University Press, 1980), pp. 15–56, where Middleton characterizes the *Canterbury Tales* as work of "the perpetually ingratiating entertainer Chaucer" (p. 47): "he must make us feel improved and vindicated, as well as entertained, *without manifesting any persuasive designs upon us*" (pp. 47–48 my emphasis).

27. Roland Barthes, *Mythologies*, trans. Annette Lavers (New York: Hill & Wang, 1972), esp. pp. 142–43. The fundamental analysis is in Marx and Engels, "Chapter I of *The German Ideology*," in *Selected Works*, 1: 24–26 and esp. 47–50, where, in the first place, they describe the generation of ideas from material processes of production ("The production of ideas, of conceptions, of consciousness is directly interwoven with the material activity and the material intercourse of men" [pp. 24–25]), insisting that (p. 25)

> We do not set out from what men say, imagine, conceive, nor from men as narrated, thought of, imagined, conceived, in order to arrive at men in the flesh. We set out from real, active men, and on the basis of their real life-process we demonstrate the development of the ideological reflexes and echoes of this life-process. The phantoms formed in the human brain are also, necessarily, sublimates of their material life-process, which is empirically verifiable and bound to material premises. Morality, religion, metaphysics, all the rest of ideology and their corresponding forms of consciousness, thus no longer retain the semblance of independence. They have no history, no development; but men, developing their material production and their material intercourse, alter, along with this their real existence, their thinking and the products of their thinking.

By consequence of this founding of "consciousness" in "material life-process," ideas can be class-specific and implicated in the class-struggle (in class-divided societies, ideas can only be class-specific and implicated in the class-struggle); in particular conditions (excepting "where speculation ends" and "there real positive science begins," "empty talk about consciousness ceases and real knowledge has to take its place" [p. 26]), class-notions are bound to be partial and so false; such partial, class-particular ideas are "ideology" in the specific sense (p. 47):

> The ideas of the ruling class are in every epoch the ruling ideas: i.e., the class which is the ruling *material* force of society, is at the same

time its ruling *intellectual* force. The class which has the means of material production at its disposal, has control at the same time over the means of mental production, so that, thereby, generally speaking, the ideas of those who lack the means of mental production are subject to it. The ruling ideas are nothing more than the ideal expression of the dominant material relationships, the dominant material relationships grasped as ideas; hence of the relationships which make the one class the ruling one, therefore, the ideas of its dominance, propagated by a ruling class's "active, conceptive ideologists, who make the perfecting of the illusion of the class about itself their chief source of livelihood" (p. 48).

The point is made more briefly later in the "Communist Manifesto" (*Selected Works*, 1:125): "What else does the history of ideas prove, than that intellectual production changes its character in proportion as material production is changed? The ruling ideas of each age have ever been the ideas of its ruling class."

Exorbitance of this Marxian concept of ideology, most often associated with Althusser's (influential but provisional and difficult) paper, "Ideology and Ideological State Apparatuses (Notes Towards an Investigation)," in *Lenin and Philosophy*, trans. Ben Brewster (New York: Monthly Review Press, 1971), esp. the concluding section "On Ideology," pp. 158–83—in which Althusser, though still repeatedly insisting on ideology's material implication (e.g., p. 166: "an ideology always exists in an apparatus, and its practice, or practices. This existence is material"), effectively equates "ideology" with "ideas" or "consciousness" generally—has had the negative consequence of tending to segregate ideology from class-struggle: all ideas and forms of consciousness, being reduced equally to ideology, are from this perspective all more or less indistinguishable. For example, Althusser's assertion here (p. 170), "there is no practice except by and in an ideology," leaves too little room or has too little use for scientific knowledge. These points were made (though not in response to Althusser's contributions, already) by Max Horkheimer, "A New Concept of Ideology?" (1930), in *Between Philosophy and Social Science: Selected Early Writings*, trans. G. Frederick Hunter, Matthew S. Kramer, and John Torpey (Cambridge: MIT Press, 1993), pp. 129–49.

28. Patterson, "Court Politics and the Invention of Literature," p. 13.

29. The quotations are *Mars* 186–87, *Lady* 38–39, *Mars* 213, and *Bal Comp* 13. Cf. Strohm, *Social Chaucer* (Cambridge: Harvard University Press, 1989), pp. 91–93.

30. The quotations are *Pity* 115–16, *BD* 1096–99 and 764–71.

31. The French poems are edited and translated in James I. Wimsatt, *Chaucer and the Poems of 'Ch'* (Cambridge: Brewer, 1982); and see Rossell Hope Robbins, "The Vintner's Son: French Wine in English Bottles," in *Eleanor of Aquitaine: Patron and Politician*, ed. William W. Kibler (Austin: University of Texas Press, 1976), pp. 147–72, and "Geoffroi Chaucier, Poète Français, Father of English Poetry," *Chaucer Review* 13 (1978): 93–115.

32. The comparative literature on present polyglot communities is surveyed in
Suzanne Romaine, *Bilingualism*, 2nd edn. (Oxford: Blackwell, 1995),
pp. 23–77; developments in Great Britain (including the history of the
Celtic elements) are discussed, in broad multinational context, in Ronald
Wardhaugh, *Languages in Competition: Dominance, Diversity, and Decline*
(Oxford: Blackwell, 1987), esp. pp. 64–96; more narrowly, on late fourteenth-
century England (properly perhaps, metropolitan England), see W. Rothwell,
"The Trilingual England of Geoffrey Chaucer," *Studies in the Age of Chaucer*
16 (1994): 45–67.

33. Cf. Pearsall, "The Alliterative Revival: Origins and Social Backgrounds," in
Middle English Alliterative Poetry and its Literary Background, ed. David A. Lawton
(Cambridge: Brewer, 1982), p. 47. For the notion that the alliterative poetry
represents "Chaucer's Other"—Ralph Hanna's phrase: "Alliterative Poetry,"
in *The Cambridge History of Medieval English Literature*, ed. David Wallace
(Cambridge: Cambridge University Press, 1999), p. 511—I depend on the
(circumspect) paired papers of Lawton: "The Unity of Middle English Alliterative Poetry," *Speculum* 58 (1983): 72–94, and "The Diversity of Middle
English Alliterative Poetry," *Leeds Studies in English* 20 (1989): 143–72; but
especially on John M. Bowers, "Piers Plowman and the Police: Notes
toward a History of the Wycliffite Langland," *Yearbook of Langland Studies* 6
(1992): 1–50; also, Pamela Gradon, "Langland and the Ideology of Dissent,"
Proceedings of the British Academy 66 (1980): 179–205, Lawton, "Lollardy and
the *Piers Plowman* Tradition," *Modern Language Review* 76 (1981): 780–93,
and Helen Barr, "*Piers Plowman* and Poetic Tradition," *Yearbook of Langland
Studies* 9 (1995): 39–64

34. Pearsall, *Old English and Middle English Poetry* (London: Routledge, 1977),
p. xii.

35. *Ven* 80.

36. Vincent J. DiMarco, in Benson, ed., *The Riverside Chaucer*, p. 993.
A. S. G. Edwards, "The Unity and Authenticity of *Anelida and Arcite*: The
Evidence of the Manuscripts," *Studies in Bibliography* 41 (1988): 177–88, shows
reason to doubt Chaucer's authorship of the *Anelida and Arcite*; still, even if
it is not Chaucer's writing, it can represent, in exaggerated form, a tendency
of Chaucer's authentic complaints. For an additional sort of formal-generic
elaboration characterizing the *Anelida*, see Strohm, *Social Chaucer*,
pp. 115–18; and on the matter of the artificiality in the fourteenth-century
English court poetry generally, see Patterson, "Court Politics and the Invention of Literature," pp. 14–16.

37. "Whan that I baar of your prison the keye,/ Kept I yow streite? Nay, god
to witnesse!": the triple roundel, beginning "Wel may I pleyne on yow, Lady
moneye" (*IMEV* 3889 + 1221 + 2640) 1.5–6 and 2.2 (etc.) and 17, in
Frederick J. Furnivall and Israel Gollancz, eds., *Hoccleve's Works: The Minor
Poems*, revised edn., ed. Jerome Mitchell and A. I. Doyle, EETS es 61 and
73, in one vol. (London: Early English Text Society, 1970), pp. 309–312.

38. The poem's envoy is discussed in Strohm, "Saving the Appearances:
Chaucer's Purse and the Fabrication of the Lancastrian Claim," in *Chaucer's*

England: Literature in Historical Perspective, ed. Barbara A. Hanawalt (Minneapolis: University of Minnesota Press, 1992), pp. 21–40, also in Strohm, *Hochon's Arrow: The Social Imagination of Fourteenth-Century Texts* (Princeton: Princeton University Press, 1992), pp. 75–94. On the Macedonians' problem, see Peter Green, *Alexander of Macedon*, rev. edn. (1974; repr. Berkeley: University of California Press, 1991), pp. 372–76.

39. The allusion is to Tariq Ali, "Literature and Market Realism," *New Left Review* 199 (1993): 140–45; cf. Wallace, *Chaucerian Polity* (Stanford: Stanford University Press, 1997), pp. 63–64 and 334: "Chaucer grasped the logic of state-sponsored patronage: that the poet taken up by the state would find his *makynge* shaped and constrained by the state's changing needs."

40. For *Troilus and Criseyde*, generally I rely on Barry A. Windeatt, *Oxford Guides to Chaucer: Troilus and Criseyde* (Oxford: Clarendon, 1992).

41. These are my translations of *Asclepius* 21 and Plotinus, *Enneads* 6.7.34; cf. Brian P. Copenhaver, *Hermetica* (Cambridge: Cambridge University Press, 1992), p. 79, and Plotinus, *The Enneads*, trans. Stephen MacKenna, ed. John Dillon (Harmondsworth: Penguin, 1991), p. 502.

42. The same terminology is used for describing mystical union in the pseudo-Dionysius, e.g., *The Divine Names* 4.3: "Divine love [*eros*] brings ecstasy, not allowing lovers [*erastai*] to belong to themselves, but only to the objects of their love [*erômenoi*]." [[*PG* III, col. 712a]]. These writings were in circulation in England in the fourteenth century, in the Latin translations of Robert Grosseteste, on which see Walter Berschin, *Greek Letters and the Latin Middle Ages*, trans. Jerold C. Frakes (Washington D. C.: Catholic University of America Press, 1988), pp. 249–55, and, for the sequel, Roberto Weiss, "The Study of Greek in England during the Fourteenth Century," *Rinascimento* 2 (1951): 209–39.

43. The Latin verses (probably twelfth-century) are quoted from Peter Dronke, *Medieval Latin and the Rise of European Love-Lyric*, 2nd edn., 2 vols. (Oxford: Clarendon, 1968), 2: 449.

44. *Cleanness* 697–708.

45. David Aers, *Chaucer, Langland and the Creative Imagination* (London: Routledge, 1980), pp. 145–46 and 159–60.

46. Herbert Marcuse, *The Aesthetic Dimension: Toward a Critique of Marxist Aesthetics*, trans. Herbert Marcuse and Erica Sherover (Boston: Beacon, 1978), pp. ix–xi. Marcuse himself describes this work as a product of the political despair that characterized his late years; on the other hand, Marcuse was already working with this notion of the value of the aesthetic in the 1937 paper, "The Affirmative Character of Culture," in *Negations: Essays in Critical Theory*, trans. Jeremy J. Shapiro (Boston: Beacon, 1968), e.g., pp. 98–100, where also the "aesthetic dimension" is already associated with "liberation"— particularly the liberation of erotic impulses that Marcuse developed most extensively in *Eros and Civilization*, 2nd edn. (Boston: Beacon, 1966), his critique and supercession of Freud's *Civilisation and its Discontents*, as well as in such late work as *An Essay on Liberation* (Boston: Beacon, 1969). Cf. too Walter Benjamin, "The Work of Art in the Age of Mechanical

Reproduction" (1936), in *Illuminations*, ed. Hannah Arendt, trans. Harry Zohn (New York: Schocken, 1969), p. 237: "One of the foremost tasks of art has always been the creation of a demand which could be fully satisfied only later." The influence of Ernst Bloch's (diffuse, inscrutable) work—summed up (sort of), e.g., in his late paper, "Ideas as Transformed Material in Human Minds, or Problems of an Ideological Superstructure (Cultural Heritage)" (1972), in *The Utopian Function of Art and Literature*, trans. Jack Zipes and Frank Mecklenburg (Cambridge: MIT Press, 1988), pp. 18–71—on Marcuse's aesthetics, or on the late Frankfurt School's turn to aesthetics generally, is not clear to me.

47. "Precisely because great literature presents the whole man in depth, the artist tends to justify or defy society rather than to be its passive chronicler": Leo Lowenthal, *Literature and the Image of Man: Sociological Studies of the European Drama and Novel, 1600–1900* (Boston: Beacon, 1957), p. viii. This work (with a dedication to Horkheimer) of Marcuse's Frankfurt School colleague is a salient practical work in pursuit of the literary-sociological possibility that Benjamin mentions to dismiss as the less interesting, "the *attitude* of a [literary] work to the relations of production." Lowenthal's investigations are based on claims that, within the work of literary art, the writer "presents an explicit or implicit picture of man's orientation to his society: privileges and responsibilities of classes; conceptions of work, love, and friendship, of religion, nature, and art" and so on, with the consequence that, "because of this representational quality, all literature, whether first or second rate, can be subjected to social analysis" (pp. vii and ix).

48. Benjamin, "The Author as Producer," in *Reflections*, trans. Edmund Jephcott (New York: Harcourt, 1978), p. 222. The most thoroughgoing contribution to developing the sociology of literary production adumbrated by Benjamin may have been the theoretical works of Pierre Macherey, esp. *A Theory of Literary Production* (1966), trans. Geoffrey Wall (London: Routledge, 1978), or, with Etienne Balibar, "On Literature as an Ideological Form" (1974), trans. McLeod, Whitehead, and Wordsworth, *Oxford Literary Review* 3 (1978): 4–12. Macherey would have been influenced by early writings of Goldmann, e.g., "Dialectical Materialism and Literary History" (1950), trans. Francis Mulhern, *New Left Review* 92 (1975): 39–51. There is instructive analysis of this theoretical work, geared to Chaucerians, in Stephen Knight, "Chaucer and the Sociology of Literature," *Studies in the Age of Chaucer* 2 (1980): 15–51; in practical literary-historical analysis, fundamental contributions are Norman N. Feltes, *Modes of Production of Victorian Novels* (Chicago: University of Chicago Press, 1986) and *Literary Capital and the Late Victorian Novel* (Madison: University of Wisconsin Press, 1993).

49. Macherey, *Theory of Literary Production*, pp. 41 and 67–68.

50. *Paradiso* 33.145, on which see John Leyerle, "The Rose-Wheel Design and Dante's *Paradiso*," *University of Toronto Quarterly* 46 (1977): esp. 301; the most pertinent of the fragments of Empedocles are edited and translated in G. S. Kirk and J. E. Raven, *The Presocratic Philosophers* (Cambridge: Cambridge University Press, 1957), pp. 327–31. The view of love in *Troilus*

and Criseyde espoused here derives from Leyerle, "The Heart and the Chain," in *The Learned and the Lewed: Studies in Chaucer and Medieval Literature*, ed. Larry D. Benson (Cambridge: Harvard University Press, 1974), pp. 113–45, and from Bonnie Wheeler, "Dante, Chaucer, and the Ending of *Troilus and Criseyde*," *Philological Quarterly* 61 (1982): 105–123; see also Peter Heidtmann, "Sex and Salvation in *Troilus and Criseyde*," *Chaucer Review* 2 (1968): 246–53.

51. The quotation is *Philosophiae consolatio* 2.m.8.13–15.

52. See, e.g., Hugh's *Quid vere diligendum sit* 1.1–1.3, ed. Roger Baron, *Hugues de Saint-Victor: Six opuscules spirituels* (Paris: Cerf, 1969); and also Bernard of Clairvaux, *De diligendo Deo*, esp. 8.24 and 15.39, ed. Jean Leclercq and H. M. Rochais, *S. Bernardi Opera*, vol. 3 (Rome: Editiones Cistercienses, 1963); and William of St. Thierry, *De natura et dignitate amoris* 1–7 and *De contemplando Deo* 6–8, both ed. Marie-Madeleine Davy, *Guillaume de Saint-Thierry: Deux traités de l'amour de Dieu* (Paris: Vrin, 1953). On the imbrication of this monastic culture and contemporary secular-aristocratic society, see Jean Leclercq, *Monks and Love in Twelfth-Century France* (Oxford: Clarendon, 1979), esp. pp. 8–26.

53. *The Two Ways* 812–13, ed. Scattergood, *The Works of Sir John Clanvowe* (Cambridge: Brewer, 1975); cf. also 28–35 and 422–44. There are useful remarks on this part of Clanvowe's writing in Lawton, "Chaucer's Two Ways: The Pilgrimage Frame of *The Canterbury Tales*," *Studies in the Age of Chaucer* 9 (1987): 38–40.

54. The quotations are Lucan, *Pharsalia* 9.1, 13–14, and 16–18, trans. Susan H. Braund, *Lucan: Civil War* (Oxford: Oxford University Press, 1992), p. 177.

55. On *Troilus and Criseyde*'s reference to current events, see Carleton Brown, "Another Contemporary Allusion in Chaucer's *Troilus*," *Modern Language Notes* 26 (1911): 208–11; John P. McCall and George Rudisill, "The Parliament of 1386 and Chaucer's Trojan Parliament," *Journal of English and Germanic Philology* 58 (1959): 276–88, and McCall, "The Trojan Scene in Chaucer's *Troilus*," *ELH* 29 (1962): 263–75.

56. Knight, *Geoffrey Chaucer* (Oxford: Blackwell, 1986), p. 46.

57. Patterson, *Chaucer and the Subject of History*, p. 107.

58. Strohm, *Social Chaucer*, pp. 129–30; cf. pp. 152–53.

59. There are suggestive remarks to this effect in Knight, *Geoffrey Chaucer*, pp. 16–23 and 4–5.

60. Knight, *Geoffrey Chaucer*, p. 63.

61. Aers, *Community, Gender, and Individual Identity* (London: Routledge, 1988), pp. 148–51.

62. The quotations are *LGW* F 420 and 426 (= G 408 and 416).

63. See esp. Pearsall, "Pre-Empting Closure in 'The Canterbury Tales': Old Endings, New Beginnings," in *Essays on Ricardian Literature in Honour of J. A. Burrow*, ed. Minnis, Charlotte C. Morse, and Thorlac Turville-Petre (Oxford: Clarendon, 1997), pp. 23–38.

64. In the verse letter to "Bukton" (*IMEV* 2262), evidently a friend though still not certainly identifiable, Chaucer refers to the *Wife of Bath's Tale*: "The Wyf

of Bathe I pray yow that ye rede / Of this matere that we have on honde," sc. the matter of "The sorwe and wo that is in mariage" (*Buk* 29–30 and 6, this last line quoting *WBT* 3); and there are substantive exact quotations from the *Wife of Bath's Tale* in the so-called "Moral Ballad" (*IMEV* 2264) of Henry Scogan (likewise a friend of Chaucer, evidently the recipient of the Chaucerian "Envoy to Scogan" [*IMEV* 3747]), written ca. 1400–1407, at lines 67–69 and 97–99 and 166–67, ed. Walter W. Skeat, *Chaucerian and Other Pieces* (Oxford: Oxford University Press, 1897), pp. 237–44. On Scogan, see further below, pp. 87–89.

65. Hoccleve mentions the Wife of Bath by name in the *Dialogue* 694 ("The Wyf of Bathe take I for auctrice" [ed. J. A. Burrow, *Thomas Hoccleve's Complaint and Dialogue*, EETS os 313 (Oxford: Early English Text Society, 1999), p. 67]), which Burrow has shown to date ca. 1419–1421: see "Thomas Hoccleve: Some Redatings," *Review of English Studies*, n. s. 46 (1995): 366–72. The parallels that lead Charles R. Blyth to assert that "at various points in his work, Hoccleve echoes the Pardoner, names the Wife of Bath, alludes to *The Book of the Duchess* and *The Legend of Good Women*, and (grotesquely) echoes a passage in the *Knight's Tale*," in *Thomas Hoccleve The Regiment of Princes*, METS (Kalamazoo: Medieval Institute Publications, 1999), p. 13, might in some cases admit more skeptical evaluation. For example, in evidence for Hoccleve's knowledge of Chaucer's Pardoner by the time Hoccleve wrote the *Regiment* ca. 1411, Blyth adduces the likenesses between *Regiment* 2425 "his tonge go so faste and yerne" and *CT* 6.398 (= *PardT* 398) "Myne handes and my tonge goon so yerne," and between *Regiment* 404 "He is a noble prechour at devys" and some conflation of *CT* 1.708 (in the *GP* description of the Pardoner) "He was in chirche a noble ecclesiaste" and *CT* 3.165 (in the Pardoner's interruption of the Wife of Bath) "Ye been a noble prechour in this cas." Similarly, Larry Scanlon's assertion, *Narrative, Authority, and Power: The Medieval Exemplum and the Chaucerian Tradition* (Cambridge: Cambridge University Press, 1994), p. 305 (cited by Blyth, p. 208), that *Regiment* 624–30 "explicitly recalls the *Pardoner's Tale*," may only be true in hindsight; otherwise, the stanza would appear to be what it says it is, another description of contemporary taverning-activity, drawn from Hoccleve's extensive self-documented experience, but not from the *Canterbury Tales*.

66. The discussion of the *Canterbury Tales* herein only develops points made by Patterson in two papers: "The 'Parson's Tale' and the Quitting of the 'Canterbury Tales,' " *Traditio* 34 (1978): 331–80, and " 'No Man his Reson Herde': Peasant Consciousness, Chaucer's Miller, and the Structure of the *Canterbury Tales*," *South Atlantic Quarterly* 86 (1987): 457–95, also in *Literary Practice and Social Change in Britain*, 1380–1530, ed. Patterson (Berkeley: University of California Press, 1990), pp. 113–55, some parts of which are treated further in *Chaucer and the Subject of History*. Otherwise, I have relied generally on Helen Cooper, *Oxford Guides to Chaucer: The Canterbury Tales* (Oxford: Oxford University Press, 1989).

67. The remarks that follow on representations of social relations in the *Canterbury Tales* derive from the paper of R. T. Lenaghan, "Chaucer's *General*

Prologue as History and Literature," *Comparative Studies in Society and History* 12 (1970): 73–82, concentrating on the one (chief) effect Chaucer's exclusions: in Chaucer's *General Prologue*, "there are certainly omissions from his roll [of pilgrims], but he does give good coverage to the middle segment of society" (73). Lenaghan shows that the governing category for Chaucer's representations of this "middle segment of society," on which he focuses, is economic: "the best way of establishing a pattern of organization is to infer it from Chaucer's practice and say the obvious: he presents his pilgrims by occupational labels, he is concerned with what men do. In the *General Prologue* as elsewhere, what men do falls largely into the category of economics" (74).

In emphasizing this preeminence of labor—when Lenaghan writes, for example, that Chaucer's "pilgrims are what they do, and what most of them do primarily is work" (79)—though there is no reference, Lenaghan is restating the basic Marxian anthropology, the notion that human beings (or humans' being) are (or is) produced, by humans themselves, in labor. "Labor" is "man's act of self-creation;" "The whole of what is called world history is nothing but the creation of man by human labor," as Marx put it already (though attributing the insight to Hegel) in the "Economic and Philosophical Manuscripts of 1844," in *Karl Marx Early Writings*, ed. and trans. T. B. Bottomore (New York: McGraw-Hill, 1963), pp. 166 and 213; and later, with Engels, in "Chapter I of *The German Ideology*" (*Selected Works*, 1:20): what humans "are, therefore, coincides with their production, both with *what* they produce and with *how* they produce."

In this perspective of economic activity that Lenaghan adduces, the "sources of livelihood" for the members of Chaucer's "middle segment" "fall into three large classes: land, the Church, and trade (understood to include everything not in the other two, manufacture, commerce, and services)" (74). Lenaghan shows that Chaucer's members of the church are variously implicated in landholding or varieties of trade—"Chaucer does not separate his churchmen into a special category. In other words, . . .clerical occupations are social and economic indicators in the same way as lay occupations" (78–79)—and that the economic activities of those in trade, be they lay or cleric, are dominated by a "rule of precarious individual interest"—"each of these pilgrims shares a common necessity to face the rigors of economic competition on his own" (76–78).

Additionally, Lenaghan establishes, "pilgrims deriving their livelihood from land fall into two Chaucerian subclasses: agents, who see to the operation and expansion of agricultural enterprises" or "the legal work of control and capital expansion," "and principals, the landholders" (75). The "differing kinds of agents work at different levels of removal from the land, but socially the important point is that they all work;" on the other hand, "the other class of pilgrims deriving their livelihood from land do not work, at least not directly for their own monetary gain" (76):

> The supporting wealth comes obviously from agricultural operations and less obviously from capital expansion, and it is earned by the agents who work for the landholders. The two groups are defined by

different activities: the agents get and the principals spend, the agents
work and the principals amuse themselves and render public service.
This is the central pattern of Chaucer's social structure. (76)

"Chaucer seems to hold with Fitzgerald rather than Hemingway: the
rich, at least the landed rich, are different from the rest" (80). In any case,
Lenaghan shows, this is the fundamental difference with which Chaucer
worked, "this difference between landed wealth and other wealth" (80), "his
basic distinction between landholders and the rest of society" (82). For the
Chaucer of the *General Prologue*, "there was a categorical distinction
between most men who struggled to live and a smaller group of landholders who were above the struggle" (80).

As Lenaghan also points out, landholders were not in fact "above the
struggle" quite as much as they might have wished to be; still, Chaucer
reproduces the basic class division and conflict within the *General Prologue*
in order again to advertise the well-being of the ruling-class: in Chaucer,
here again landholders' "social position" is made to look "far more secure. . .
and their style far more negligent of practical economics than the evidence
indicates" (82). In keeping with Chaucer's own real-world social position
(81–82), the purposes of "Chaucer's poetic narrative" are "practical charity,
orthodoxy, and social conservatism" (82). Also pertinent are the comments
on Chaucer's habitual, characteristic "omission of the victim," in Jill Mann,
Chaucer and Medieval Estates Satire (Cambridge: Cambridge University
Press, 1973), esp. pp. 190–91.

68. *Piers the Plowman's Crede* 420–42, in *Six Ecclesiastical Satires*, ed. James Dean,
METS (Kalamazoo: Medieval Institute Publications, 1991), p. 21.

69. There is much useful information on the situation of post-plague English
laborers of this sort in Robert Worth Frank, Jr, "The 'Hungry Gap,' Crop
Failure, and Famine: The Fourteenth-Century Agricultural Crisis and *Piers
Plowman*," *Yearbook of Langland Studies* 4 (1990): 87–104; see also Christopher Dyer, "Piers Plowman and Plowmen: A Historical Perspective," *Yearbook of Langland Studies* 8 (1994): 155–76, and, for the shock of Langland's
decision to use such a figure, Elizabeth D. Kirk, "Langland's Plowman and
the Recreation of Fourteenth-Century Religious Metaphor," *Yearbook of
Langland Studies* 2 (1988): 1–21.

70. Ellen Meiksins Wood, "Capitalism, Merchants and Bourgeois Revolution:
Reflections on the Brenner Debate and its Sequel," *International Review of
Social History* 41 (1996): 214 and 211.

71. On Chaucer's Plowman, see Gardiner Stillwell, "Chaucer's Plowman and
the Contemporary English Peasant," *English Literary History* 6 (1939):
285–90, who remarks "It is impossible to believe that, . . .in writing the
portrait, he was expressing his love of the laborer" (290): "the real plowman
of the time was revolting against everything Chaucer stood for" (285); cf.
also Strohm, *Social Chaucer*, pp. 173–74. Of course, the Plowman's silence
might be only a reflex of the incompletion of Chaucer's work: a tale might
eventually have been assigned him.

72. This point is made especially effectively in Strohm, *Social Chaucer*, pp. 67 and 172–74.

73. D. W. Robertson, Jr, *A Preface to Chaucer* (Princeton: Princeton University Press, 1962), p. 51: "To conclude, the medieval world was innocent of our profound concern for tension. . . .We project dynamic polarities on history as class struggles, balances of power, or as conflicts between economic realities and traditional ideals. . . .But the medieval world with its quiet hierarchies knew nothing of these things. Its aesthetic, at once a continuation of classical philosophy and a product of Christian teaching, developed artistic and literary styles consistent with a world without dynamically interacting polarities." Important critiques of these claims are in Patterson, "Historical Criticism and the Development of Chaucer Studies," in *Negotiating the Past* (Madison: University of Wisconsin Press, 1987), esp. pp. 31–37, and Aers, *Community, Gender, and Individual Identity*, pp. 6–12.

74. Strohm, *Social Chaucer*, p. 172.

75. Strohm, *Social Chaucer*, e.g., pp. xii and 181–82, uses this terminology. The best work on such utopian impulses in the *Canterbury Tales* may be the last two chapters in Aers, *Chaucer, Langland and the Creative Imagination*, pp. 143–95. In *Chaucerian Polity*, describing the Chaucer who wrote the *Canterbury Tales* as a figure "balancing allegiances to associational and hierarchical structures of authority in the attempt to establish a new form of authorial identity" (p. 216), Wallace is more pessimistic: the *General Prologue*'s proposition "that adults representing (almost) every profession, cultural level, age, and sexual orientation can come together under one roof, form themselves into a corporate unity and regulate their affairs without reference to external authority" is, "historically speaking," extraordinary, Wallace says (p. 65). "Chaucer's confidence in the possibility of constructing a functional associative polity (and a great work of fiction) from social elements that are so sharply diversified might seem to endorse a Durkheimian optimism concerning the social effects of the division of labor. Chaucer, I shall argue, tempers optimism with doubt" (p. 66), continuing

> The possibility of idealizing the *Prologue* as an associational form is, I shall argue, denied by Chaucer himself: the *Prologue* contains an extraordinary number of subgroups that operate within and against the unifying structure of the *felawschipe*; it also contains a number of extraordinary individuals (the Pardoner, the Wife) who remain unassimilable.

76. The allusion is to the "Communist Manifesto" (*Selected Works*, 1:112), where Marx and Engels are describing an effect of capitalism specifically: "The bourgeoisie, by the rapid improvement of all instruments of production, by the immensely facilitated means of communication, draws all, even the most barbarian nations into civilization. . . .It compels all nations, on pain of extinction, to adopt the bourgeois mode of production; it compels them to introduce what it calls civilization into their midst, i.e., to become bourgeois themselves. In one word, it creates a world after its own image." Elsewhere, they assert that the same result follows from class-dominance in any

mode of production, e.g., in the "Communist Manifesto" again (p. 123): "The selfish misconception that induces you to transform into eternal laws of nature and of reason, the social forms springing from your present mode of production and form of property—historical relations that rise and disappear in the progress of production—this misconception you share with every ruling class that has preceded you;" or in "Chapter I of *The German Ideology*" (*Selected Works*, 1:48): "Each new class which puts itself in the place of one ruling before it, is compelled, merely in order to carry through its aim, to represent its interest as the common interest of all the members of society, that is, expressed in ideal form: it has to give its ideas the form of universality, and represent them as the only rational, universally valid ones."

77. In *Chaucer and the Social Contest* (New York: Routledge, 1990), Peggy Knapp argues a case for "the insistent subversiveness of the *Canterbury Tales*" (p. 61), howbeit with some qualification: "This argument does not rest," she allows, "on the proposition that Chaucer was personally a rebel to the traditions and ideals of his time, or a visionary who saw possibilities for a non-feudal world and attempted to bring it into being, although he may have been either or both. . . .At the same time the fictional lives they live [sc. the Chaucerian characters in the *Canterbury Tales*] and Chaucer's narration of those lives may possess the power to transform social configurations as well as display them" (p. 9). Strohm's view, in *Social Chaucer*, esp. perhaps pp. xii-xiii, is somewhat more cautious:

> Chaucer certainly defines the boundaries of his texts in part by acts of exclusion. No nobleperson tells a tale on the way to Canterbury, and no peasant either. Yet I continue to be impressed more by what his text includes than by how much it omits: by the amount of conflictual matter to which it gives space and by its deep implication in urgent social contests of the time. Rather than viewing Chaucer's poetry as hegemonic and exclusionary, I associate myself with those critics who assert the possibility of unresolved contention, of a struggle between hegemony and counter-hegemony, of texts as places crowded with many voices representing many centers of social authority.

Stephen Knight too was inclined to see utopian or liberatory ambitions in Chaucer's representations of dissidence, though also making a point of their ultimate conservatism; e.g., *Geoffrey Chaucer*, pp. 82 and 132: "Chaucer will shape positions which are disruptive in political terms, his text will be to some extent a battleground for the forces of the period, and neither he nor many of his audience would approve of some of these forces. But they are to be created fictionally, with more power and with more daring than modern critics often can—or want to—see. . . .Those forces of disruption are nowhere more powerfully and more threateningly realized than in the consciously crafted opening sequence to this deeply historical poem, from the general prologue to Cook's tale." Nonetheless, in Knight's analysis, it turns out that "the forces of disruption are raised only to be rejected in that final sequence of increasingly overt conservatism, both secular and religious" at the end of the *Tales*, as the work "moves steadily towards a conservative and Christian stasis."

78. Morton W. Bloomfield, "Chaucer's Sense of History," *Journal of English and Germanic Philology* 51 (1952): 301–313, assembles evidence for Chaucer's "sense of cultural diversity," arguing that (by contrast with most of his contemporaries, at least) he "has a considerable sense of historic succession and cultural relativity" (305).

79. The flight of the Yeoman's Canon might be some kind of exception, though I do not understand it. The quotation is from Strohm, *Social Chaucer*, pp. 166–68; cf. also p. 157: "The pilgrimage continues, dealing with socially based dissensions as they arise, finding a way to submerge disputes in that realistic form of *coherentia* that seeks a common ground among otherwise incompatible interests. Even this limited assertion of *coherentia* must of course be seen as a considerable distortion of factional and schismatic actuality. Viewed as an ideologically constructed bridge between Chaucer and his predominantly *gentil* public, it must be acknowledged as a self-interested distortion as well, presenting a solution congenial to their own aims (maintenance of social order, but on terms receptive to previously excluded or underacknowledged ranks and groups) as a general solution for the good of all."

80. The quoted phrase is Lucan, *Pharsalia* 1.81, on which see Michael Lapidge, "Lucan's Imagery of Cosmic Dissolution," *Hermes* 107 (1979): 344–70. There is instructive discussion of the political contexts and import of the *Monk's Tale* in Wallace, *Chaucerian Polity*, pp. 299–336: "*De casibus* tragedy, which concerns the fall of great men, is a genre that few men wish to read, least of all a reigning monarch or other 'myghty man' at the peak of his powers" (p. 299).

81. Marcuse, "Repressive Tolerance," in Robert Paul Wolff, Barrington Moore, Jr, and Herbert Marcuse, *A Critique of Pure Tolerance*, 2nd edn. (Boston: Beacon, 1969), pp. 81–123. There are good pages on these strategies in the *Canterbury Tales*—by means of which, in order to "chastise anti-social impulses" (p. 152), differences are "repressed, contained, or surmounted" (p. 145)—in Strohm, *Social Chaucer*, esp. perhaps pp. 151–57; cf. also Strohm's earlier paper, "Form and Social Statement in *Confessio Amantis* and *The Canterbury Tales*," *Studies in the Age of Chaucer* 1 (1979): 30–34, claiming to find "tolerance, or even positive acceptance, of multiplicity" (40) in Chaucer's work.

82. Spearing, *The Knight's Tale*, p. 69.

83. Cf. Knight, *Geoffrey Chaucer*, pp. 86–90.

84. Delany, "Womanliness in the *Man of Law's Tale*," *Chaucer Review* 9 (1974): 70, concluding (71) that such "models of submission" as Chaucer's Man of Law's Constance "will remain the stuff of our literature as long as the social conflict exists which calls them into being." On the particular institutional basis of Chaucer's figure of authority, see Wallace, *Chaucerian Polity*, esp. p. 183.

85. The quotations are from Strohm, *Social Chaucer*, p. 69, and Alfred David, *The Strumpet Muse* (Bloomington: Indiana University Press, 1976), p. 92.

86. Cf. Knight, *Geoffrey Chaucer*, pp. 93 and 94: "Conflict without regret, animal-like fighting without the noble language of fraternity, these are by

implication a discredit to the lower classes (as they were in *The Parliament of Fowls*). They will next be developed as an overt weakness. The 'churles murmurynge' grew from a reference in the Knight's tale into a poetic riot in the Miller's response; now dissension among the 'churles' is developed into a savage and debilitating conflict, through the medium of the Miller's colleague on the ideal manor, his bitter enemy in disorderly reality, the Reeve." Then, "a further stage in lower class self-destruction appears to be the idea behind the Cook's tale. This unappealing servant of the bourgeoisie delights in the Reeve's vision of brutal chaos."

87. Strohm, *Social Chaucer*, p. 159.

88. Cf. Wallace, *Chaucerian Polity*, esp. p. 293.

89. Knight, *Geoffrey Chaucer*, p. 118.

90. Cf. Glenn Burger, "Kissing the Pardoner," *PMLA* 107 (1992): esp. 1145–48. Another image of reconciliation in the *Canterbury Tales* framework is discussed in Wallace, *Chaucerian Polity*, pp. 175–76.

91. In the pre-C versions only: the tearing itself was excised, though the rest of the *passus*'s criticisms of pardoning remained, as is argued by Frank, "The Pardon Scene in *Piers Plowman*," *Speculum* 26 (1951): esp. 319–24: "A dramatic passage was removed because it was confusing; it could be dropped completely only because the essential meaning of the scene is communicated without it" (322); with or without the tearing, "the scene simply tells man that he cannot buy salvation, he must do good to attain it" (327). For *Piers Plowman*, generally I rely on James Simpson, *Piers Plowman: An Introduction to the B-text* (London: Longman, 1990).

92. On the doctrinal situation of Chaucer's figure, see Patterson, "Chaucerian Confession: Penitential Literature and the Pardoner," *Medievalia et Humanistica* n.s. 7 (1976): 153–73, developed further in *Chaucer and the Subject of History*, pp. 367–421.

93. The chief passages in Langland's work dealing with these topics are analyzed in John A. Burrow, "The Action of Langland's Second Vision," *Essays in Criticism* 15 (1965): 247–68; cf. also, in broader context, Aers, *Chaucer, Langland and the Creative Imagination*, esp. pp. 13–23. On the pilgrimage framework of the *Canterbury Tales*, Knight, *Geoffrey Chaucer*, p. 69—suggesting that the London–Canterbury route of Chaucer's pilgrimage was an admonitory-allegorical reversal of the Canterbury–London route followed by a group of the 1381 revolutionaries: "the journey itself and its reversal of revolt into pilgrimage is a major overarching pattern of the text"—wrote:

> The world of *The Canterbury Tales* is the world of conflict that generated the Peasants' Revolt, and one of the major forces of the long poem is to realize the unrest and the quest for freedom and individual rights that were all central to this historically potent period. They were not represented with approval: Chaucer's own social position does not suggest that he would sympathize with revolution, and frequently there are signs that the forces of conflict are realized under strain and arouse inevitable constraint. Ultimately those forces are

neutralized in a number of ways. One of them is the overall plan, that contemporary conflict is being recreated within the model of a pilgrimage which is both a physical reversal of the peasants' march and also a cultural reversal of their secular and political concerns into an eventually dominant spiritual mode.

94. "Thorpe's Examination," ed. Anne Hudson, in *Two Wycliffite Texts*, EETS os 301 (Oxford: Early English Text Society, 1993), pp. 62–63. On Thorpe, see the instructive paper of Rita Copeland, "William Thorpe and his Lollard Community: Intellectual Labor and the Representation of Dissent," in *Bodies and Disciplines: Intersections of Literature and History in Fifteenth-Century England*, ed. Barbara A. Hanawalt and Wallace (Minneapolis: University of Minnesota Press, 1996), pp. 199–221, finding that (to quote Horkheimer, "The Authoritarian State" [written 1940 but unpublished], in *The Essential Frankfurt School Reader*, ed. Andrew Arato and Eike Gebhardt [New York: Urizen Books, 1978], pp. 98–99) "the revolutionary movement negatively reflects the situation which it is attacking," since "integration is the price which individuals and groups have to pay in order to flourish:" "Whatever seeks to exist under a state of domination runs the danger of reproducing it." See also Fiona Somerset, "Vernacular Argumentation in *The Testimony of William Thorpe*," *Mediaeval Studies* 58 (1996): 207–41, also in *Clerical Discourse and Lay Audience in Late Medieval England* (Cambridge: Cambridge University Press, 1998), pp. 179–215. Important information about Thorpe has more recently been published by Maureen Jurkowski, "The Arrest of William Thorpe in Shrewsbury and the Anti-Lollard Statute of 1406," *Historical Research* 75 (2002): 273–95.

95. "Thorpe's Examination," pp. 63–64; cf. Lawton, "Chaucer's Two Ways," 26–27, 33, and 36–38.

96. "Thorpe's Examination," p. 64.

97. Strohm, "Chaucer's Lollard Joke: History and the Textual Unconscious," *Studies in the Age of Chaucer* 17 (1995): 23–42—now also in *Theory and the Premodern Text* (Minneapolis: University of Minnesota Press, 2000), pp. 165–81—discusses other matters.

98. Lawton, "Chaucer's Two Ways," 12.

99. The quotations are *MilT* 3291 and 3276.

100. The quotations are *GP* 483, 518, 497, and *ParsT* 80 and 50–51, and Strohm, *Social Chaucer*, pp. 177 and 179. The various problems of understanding the *Parson's Tale*, including its authorship and its placement, are (conclusively) discussed in Lawton, "Chaucer's Two Ways," ending, 40: "It would not matter where fragment I [sc. *ParsT* + *Ret*] came in the 'order' of *The Canterbury Tales*; it would not distort our reading wherever it was placed; but it makes excellent sense as a closure sequence. It fulfills a formal expectation mirrored in *The Parson's Tale* itself: after the sin comes its remedy."

101. Pearsall, *John Lydgate (1371–1449): A Bio-bibliography* (Victoria: University of Victoria, 1997), nos. 13 and 13A, p. 59.

102. Cf. Strohm, "Chaucer's Audience," 30–31, and Wallace, *Chaucerian Polity*, pp. 349–56 and 365–70.

Chapter 3   Reception

1. To say so much is not to deny Chaucer active, subjective agency, in responding to the determinant circumstance. It is to say—to reflect my judgment—that, in Chaucer's case, agency is less consequential than determinant circumstance, for explaining both his writing itself and his writing's reception. To be dogmatic, however, would be an error: in other cases, or in the same case by light of other evidence, or by light of the same evidence weighed differently for different purposes, agency might be judged to be of greater moment. Marx wrote, "It is not the consciousness of men that determines their being, but, on the contrary, their social being that determines their consciousness" ("Preface to a Contribution to the Critique of Political Economy," in *Selected Works*, 3 vols. [Moscow: Progress Publishers, 1969], 1:503), and "Men make their own history, but they do not make it just as they please; they do not make it under circumstances chosen by themselves, but under circumstances directly encountered" ("The Eighteenth Brumaire of Louis Bonaparte," in *Selected Works*, 1:398)—a formulation confirmed by Engels's doctrinaire 1890 "Letter to Joseph Bloch" (in *Selected Works*, 3:487), "We make our history ourselves, but, in the first place, under very definite assumptions and conditions. Among these the economic ones are ultimately decisive." But Marx also wrote, "The materialist doctrine that men are products of circumstances and upbringing, and that, therefore, changed men are products of other circumstances and changed upbringing, forgets that it is men that change circumstances" ("Theses on Feuerbach III," in *Selected Works*, 1:13). Certainly, the tradition is not clear or univocal: Antonio Gramsci, for one, set considerable weight by possibilities for exercise of subjective agency, despite determinant material circumstance (esp. the Leninist voluntarism: see "The Revolution against *Capital*" [1917], in *Selections from Political Writings (1910–1920)*, ed. Quintin Hoare, trans. John Mathews [London: Lawrence and Wishart, 1977], pp. 34–37). Useful brief discussion of this agency—determinant circumstance problem is in Perry Anderson, *In the Tracks of Historical Materialism* (London: Verso, 1983), pp. 33–35; for greater detail, see the exegetical work of Martin Jay, *Marxism and Totality* (Berkeley: University of California Press, 1984); the most pertinent discussion for present purposes is that of Lee Patterson, *Chaucer and the Subject of History* (Madison: University of Wisconsin Press, 1991), esp. pp. 3–13.

2. Anne Hudson, "*Piers Plowman* and the Peasants' Revolt: A Problem Revisited," *Yearbook of Langland Studies* 8 (1994): 85–106; the evidence is reviewed also in Steven Justice, *Writing and Rebellion* (Berkeley: University of California Press, 1994), pp. 102–39.

3. Margaret Aston, "Lollardy and Sedition, 1381–1431" (1960), repr. in *Lollards and Reformers* (London: Hambledon, 1984), pp. 1–47, and, more

recently, "Corpus Christi and Corpus Regni: Heresy and the Peasants' Revolt," *Past & Present* 143 (1994): 3–47.

4. Hudson, "Lollardy: The English Heresy?," *Studies in Church History* 18 (1982): 261–83. On the language-politics, see now esp. Nicholas Watson, "The Politics of Middle English Writing," in *The Idea of the Vernacular*, ed. Jocelyn Wogan-Browne, Watson, Andrew Taylor, and Ruth Evans (University Park: Pennsylvania State University Press, 1999), pp. 331–52.

5. See, respectively, James Simpson, "The Constraints of Satire in 'Piers Plowman' and 'Mum and the Sothsegger,'" in *Langland, the Mystics and the Medieval English Religious Tradition*, ed. Helen Phillips (Cambridge: Brewer, 1990), pp. 11–30, and Watson, "Censorship and Cultural Change in Late-Medieval England: Vernacular Theology, the Oxford Translation Debate, and Arundel's Constitutions of 1409," *Speculum* 70 (1995): 822–64.

6. Paul Strohm, *Social Chaucer* (Cambridge: Harvard University Press, 1989), pp. 164–66; on the passage in question, see also Peter W. Travis, "Chaucer's Trivial Fox Chase and the Peasant's Revolt of 1381," *Journal of Medieval and Renaissance Studies* 18 (1988): 214–18. Another reference is alleged in J. Stephen Russell, "Is London Burning?: A Chaucerian Allusion to the Rising of 1381," *Chaucer Review* 30 (1995): 107–09.

7. The quotations are *Confessio amantis* prol.151–53 and "In Praise of Peace" (*IMEV* 2587) 2–4; cf. Strohm, "Form and Social Statement in *Confessio Amantis* and *The Canterbury Tales*," *Studies in the Age of Chaucer* 1 (1979): 26–30. On the *Visio Angliae*, see Andrew Galloway, "Gower in his Most Learned Role and the Peasants' Revolt of 1381," *Mediaevalia* 16 (1993): 329–47.

8. *Gawain* 35. David R. Carlson, "*Pearl's* Imperfections," *Studia Neophilologica* 63 (1991): 57–67, can be taken to represent an extreme (paranoid, even) estimate of the poet's capacities in this regard.

9. See esp. Watson, "The *Gawain*-Poet as a Vernacular Theologian," in *A Companion to the Gawain-Poet*, ed. Derek Brewer and Jonathan Gibson (Cambridge: Brewer, 1997), pp. 293–313.

10. See esp. Frank Grady, "*St. Erkenwald* and the Merciless Parliament," *Studies in the Age of Chaucer* 22 (2000): 179–211.

11. There are instructive remarks about the poet's disengagement in Charles Muscatine, *Poetry and Crisis in the Age of Chaucer* (Notre Dame: Notre Dame University Press, 1972), pp. 37–42.

12. Chaucer's lists include *LGW* G Prol. 255–66, 344, 405–20; *MLT* 46–89; *Ret* 1085–87; and *Adam*. For the reception-history, generally I rely on Seth Lerer, *Chaucer and His Readers* (Princeton: Princeton University Press, 1993), establishing how thoroughly interested, albeit variably interested, the construction of Chaucer was in its earliest phases; also of significance is John H. Fisher, *The Importance of Chaucer* (Carbondale: Southern Illinois University Press, 1992).

13. The *Siege of Thebes* prologue is edited and discussed in Bowers, *The Canterbury Tales: Fifteenth-Century Continuations and Additions*, METS (Kalamazoo: Medieval Institute Publications, 1992), pp. 11–22. A great deal of pertinent

information is assembled in Caroline F. E. Spurgeon, *Five Hundred Years of Chaucer Criticism and Allusion 1357–1900*, 3 vols. (1925; repr. New York: Russell & Russell, 1960), but Spurgeon's dates are often significantly wrong—though it has fewer citations, the presentation is much better in Derek S. Brewer, *Chaucer: The Critical Heritage*, 2 vols. (London: Routledge, 1978)—so for the Lydgate chronology I rely on Derek Pearsall, *John Lydgate (1371–1449): A Bio-bibliography* (Victoria: University of Victoria, 1997).

14. See above, pp. 54 and 127 n64.
15. For Clanvowe's quotations, see below, pp. 85–86.
16. I have been most influenced by the views of John H. Fisher, "Animadversions on the Text of Chaucer, 1988," *Speculum* 63 (1988): 779–93, and "A Language Policy for Lancastrian England," *PMLA* 107 (1992): 1168–80. The evidentiary fundamentals were laid out in John S. P. Tatlock, "The Canterbury Tales in 1400," *PMLA* 50 (1935): esp. 101–07, and, on relations between the Hengwrt and Ellesmere manuscripts and their relations to Chaucer's papers, 127–31 and 133–38; the soundest fundamental analysis on these latter points (as far as I am competent to judge) are the remarks of A. I. Doyle and M. B. Parkes, in "The Production of Copies of the *Canterbury Tales* and the *Confessio Amantis* in the Early Fifteenth Century," in *Medieval Scribes, Manuscripts & Libraries: Essays Presented to N. R. Ker*, ed. Parkes and Andrew G. Watson (London: Scolar, 1978), esp. pp. 185–92, and in their "Paleographical Introduction," in *The Canterbury Tales: A Facsimile and Transcription of the Hengwrt Manuscript, with Variants from the Ellesmere Manuscript*, ed. Paul G. Ruggiers (Norman: University of Oklahoma Press, 1979), esp. pp. xix–xxxiii.
17. Strohm, "Chaucer's Fifteenth-Century Audience and the Narrowing of the 'Chaucer Tradition,'" *Studies in the Age of Chaucer* 4 (1982): 5 and 18–22.
18. Cf. Lee Patterson, "Court Politics and the Invention of Literature: The Case of Sir John Clanvowe," in *Culture and History 1350–1600*, ed. David Aers (New York: Harvester Wheatsheaf, 1992), pp. 29–30.
19. For the Deschamps ballad, I cite the text from Brewer, *Chaucer: The Critical Heritage*, 1:40, and the translation of T. Atkinson Jenkins, "Deschamps' Ballade to Chaucer," *Modern Language Notes* 33 (1918): 270–71 (which article has a slightly differing text). The same text as is in Brewer (though with a different translation and notes) is also in James I. Wimsatt, *Chaucer and his French Contemporaries* (Toronto: University of Toronto Press, 1991), pp. 249–50.
20. This is the date derived by Alfred David, in *The Riverside Chaucer*, 3rd edn., ed. Larry D. Benson (Boston: Houghton Mifflin, 1987), p. 1104.
21. William Calin, *The French Tradition and the Literature of Medieval England* (Toronto: University of Toronto Press, 1994), p. 524 n27. On Chaucer and Deschamps otherwise, I rely on Wimsatt, *Chaucer and his French Contemporaries*, pp. 242–72.
22. These remarks draw on Ranajit Guha, "Dominance without Hegemony and its Historiography," *Subaltern Studies* 6 (1989): 210–309.
23. Ovid, *Met.* 4.121–24: "cruor emicat alte,/ Non aliter quam cum vitiato fistula plumbo/ Scinditur et tenui stridente foramine longas/ eiaculatur aquas atque ictibus aera rumpit."

24. Plato, *Apology* 24b; Xenophon, *Memorabilia* 1.1.1. Seneca's contribution to causing the revolt of Boudicca is alleged in the epitome of Dio Cassius (52.2.1).
25. Brewer, *Chaucer: The Critical Heritage*, 1:39, and Jenkins, "Deschamps' Ballade to Chaucer," 268.
26. Most recently discussed, with references to the earlier literature, in Wimsatt, *Chaucer and his French Contemporaries*, p. 340 n32.
27. Theodor W. Adorno, "Veblen's Attack on Culture," in *Prisms*, trans. Samuel Weber and Shierry Weber (Cambridge: MIT Press, 1981), p. 76.
28. The documentary evidence of Usk's life is reviewed in Gary W. Shawver, ed., *Thomas Usk: Testament of Love Based on the Edition of John F. Leyerle* (Toronto: University of Toronto Press, 2002), pp. 7–23; cf. Carlson, "Chaucer's Boethius and Thomas Usk's *Testament of Love*: Politics and Love in the Chaucerian Tradition," in *The Centre and its Compass: Studies in Medieval Literature in Honor of Professor John Leyerle*, ed. Robert A. Taylor, James F. Burke, Patricia J. Eberle, Ian Lancashire, and Brian S. Merrilees (Kalamazoo: Medieval Institute Publications, 1993), pp. 37–41; and Strohm, "Politics and Poetics: Usk and Chaucer in the 1380s," in *Literary Practice and Social Change in Britain, 1380–1530*, ed. Patterson (Berkeley: University of California Press, 1990), pp. 85–90, and "The Textual Vicissitudes of Usk's 'Appeal,' " in *Hochon's Arrow: The Social Imagination of Fourteenth-Century Texts* (Princeton: Princeton University Press, 1992), esp. pp. 145–53. Additional information is in May Newman Hallmundsson, "The Community of Law and Letters: Some Notes on Thomas Usk's Audience," *Viator* 9 (1978): 357–65, and Hallmundsson's suggestion, 362, of a possible Berkeley connection, is pursued in Lucy Lewis, "The Identity of Margaret in Thomas Usk's *Testament of Love*," *Medium Aevum* 68 (1999): 63–72. For quotations from the *Testament*, I have used Shawver, ed., *Thomas Usk: Testament of Love*, citing parenthetically by book, chapter, and line numbers; and from Usk's *Appeal*, R. W. Chambers and Marjorie Daunt, *A Book of London English 1384–1425* (Oxford: Clarendon, 1931), pp. 22–31, citing parenthetically by line number. The same text of the *Appeal*, with the same lineation, is reprinted in R. Allen Shoaf, ed., *Thomas Usk: The Testament of Love*, METS (Kalamazoo: Medieval Institute Publications, 1998), pp. 423–29.
29. Anne Middleton, "Thomas Usk's 'Perdurable Letters:' The *Testament of Love* from Script to Print," *Studies in Bibliography* 51 (1998): 69. Cf. Strohm, "Chaucer's Audience," *Literature & History* 5 (1977): esp. 31–33.
30. Galloway, "Private Selves and the Intellectual Marketplace in Late Fourteenth-Century England: The Case of the Two Usks," *New Literary History* 28 (1997): 302.
31. The Boethian elements of Usk's writing are treated more fully in Carlson, "Chaucer's Boethius and Thomas Usk's *Testament of Love*," pp. 41–46. See also Lewis, "The Identity of Margaret in Thomas Usk's *Testament of Love*," 66–67.
32. Strohm, "The Textual Vicissitudes of Usk's 'Appeal,' " p. 152.
33. Rodney Hilton, "Feudalism in Europe: Problems for Historical Materialists" (1984), repr. in *Class Conflict and the Crisis of Feudalism*, 2nd edn.

(London:Verso, 1990), p. 8. The analysis of Ruth Bird, *The Turbulent London of Richard II* (London: Longmans, 1949)—e.g., the summary statement at p. 30—is persistently clear about the class-conflictual implications of contemporary city politics; and there is clear, brief discussion of the place of urban economies within feudalism in Perry Anderson, *Passages From Antiquity to Feudalism* (London: NLB, 1974), pp. 150–51.

34. Northampton's political program and its background are discussed at length in Bird, *The Turbulent London of Richard II*, pp. 1–13, 30–43, and 63–85.

35. The information about Strode is reviewed, e.g., in Fisher, *John Gower: Moral Philosopher and Friend of Chaucer* (London: Methuen, 1965), pp. 61–62, though the most interesting information available is in the footnotes of Hallmundsson, "The Community of Law and Letters," 357–65. Cf. also Strohm, *Social Chaucer*, pp. 32 and 44.

36. Usk's use of *Troilus and Criseyde* is treated more fully in Carlson, "Chaucer's Boethius and Thomas Usk's *Testament of Love*," pp. 46–48 and 62–68.

37. See above, pp. 50–51.

38. Usk's use of Anselm was first detailed by George Sanderlin, "Usk's *Testament of Love* and St. Anselm," *Speculum* 17 (1942): 69–73; see now esp. Stephen Medcalf, "Transposition: Thomas Usk's *Testament of Love*," in *The Medieval Translator*, ed. Roger Ellis (Cambridge: Brewer, 1989), pp. 181–95, and "The World and Heart of Thomas Usk," in *Essays on Ricardian Literature in Honour of J. A. Burrow*, ed. Alistair J. Minnis, Charlotte C. Morse, and Thorlac Turville-Petre (Oxford: Clarendon, 1997), pp. 234–38.

39. This view of the text's transmission is argued in Middleton, "Thomas Usk's 'Perdurable Letters,' " 63–116.

40. The details of Usk's use of the work of other English writers have been well discussed: see esp. Medcalf, "The World and Heart of Thomas Usk," pp. 237–51; also Lewis, "Langland's Tree of Charity and Usk's Wexing Tree," *Notes & Queries* 240 (1995): 429–33; Joanna Summers, "Gower's *Vox Clamantis* and Usk's *Testament of Love*," *Medium Aevum* 68 (1999): 55–62; and Bowers, "Dating *Piers Plowman*: Testing the Testimony of Usk's *Testament*," *Yearbook of Langland Studies* 13 (1999): 65–100.

41. *Confessio amantis* 8.*2941-*57; on this passage and the date of the first recension, see Fisher, *John Gower*, pp. 26–34 and 116–27.

42. For the Chaucer-Gower relationship, I rely on the thorough discussion in Fisher, *John Gower*, pp. 204–302; there are also important comments in David, *The Strumpet Muse: Art and Morals in Chaucer's Poetry* (Bloomington: Indiana University Press, 1976), pp. 119–26.

43. The allusion is to Harold Bloom, *The Anxiety of Influence* (London: Oxford University Press, 1973).

44. Gardiner Stillwell, "John Gower and the Last Years of Edward III," *Studies in Philology* 45 (1948): 471.

45. The most thorough discussion is in Normand R. Cartier, "Le *Bleu chevalier* de Froissart et le *Livre de la duchesse* de Chaucer," *Romania* 88 (1967): 232–52; see also Wimsatt, "The *Dit dou bleu chevalier*: Froissart's Imitation of Chaucer," *Mediaeval Studies* 34 (1972): 388–400, and Susan Crane,

"Froissart's *Dit dou bleu chevalier* as a Source for Chaucer's *Book of the Duchess*," *Medium Aevum* 61 (1992): 59–74. On Froissart and Chaucer otherwise, I rely on Wimsatt, *Chaucer and his French Contemporaries*, pp. 174–209.

46. Chaucer's borrowings from contemporary French poets in the *Book of the Duchess* are presented compendiously in Barry A. Windeatt, *Chaucer's Dream Poetry: Sources and Analogues* (Cambridge: Brewer, 1982), pp. 167–68.

47. On Clanvowe's contributions, see Strohm, "Fourteenth- and Fifteenth-Century Writers as Readers of Chaucer," in *Genres, Themes, and Images in English Literature from the Fourteenth to the Fifteenth Century*, ed. Piero Boitani and Anna Torti (Tübingen: Gunter Narr Verlag, 1988), pp. 92–94, and *Social Chaucer*, pp. 78–82. I use the edition (sc. of *IMEV* 3361) in V. J. Scattergood, ed., *The Works of Sir John Clanvowe* (Cambridge: Brewer, 1975), pp. 35–53. The most thorough discussion of the authorship question remains Scattergood, "The Authorship of *The Boke of Cupide*," *Anglia* 82 (1964): 137–49.

48. See Siegrid Düll, Anthony Luttrell, and Maurice Keen, "Faithful Unto Death: The Tomb Slab of Sir William Neville and Sir John Clanvowe, Constantinople 1391," *Antiquaries Journal* 71 (1991): 174–90.

49. The use-value–exchange-value distinction invoked here and subsequently is discussed at length, especially by light of the consequences of the elaborations of exchange-value in capitalism and other monied economies, in the "Commodities" chapter of the first volume of *Capital* (Moscow: Foreign Languages Publishing House, 1954), pp. 35–83, most famously perhaps in the "The Fetishism of Commodities and the Secret Thereof" section, pp. 71–83, where Marx is developing his earlier discussion, in the *Grundrisse*, trans. Martin Nicholaus (Harmondsworth: Penguin, 1973), pp. 140–47. "At first sight, a commodity presented itself to us as a complex of two things—use-value and exchange-value," Marx wrote in the first volume of *Capital*, p. 41. "The utility of a thing"—"commodity" having been defined initially as "an object outside us, a thing that by its properties satisfies human wants of some sort or another" (p. 35)—"makes it a use-value. But this utility is not a thing of air. Being limited by the physical properties of the commodity, it has no existence apart from that commodity" (p. 36). But "when commodities are exchanged, their exchange-value manifests itself as something totally independent of their use-value" (p. 38): exchange-value "presents itself as a quantitative relation, as the proportion in which values in use of one sort are exchanged for those of another sort, a relation constantly changing with time and place" (p. 36):

> Commodities come into the world in the shape of use-values, articles, or goods, such as iron, linen, corn, etc. This is their plain, homely, bodily form. They are, however, commodities, only because they are something two-fold, both objects of utility, and, at the same time, depositories of value. They manifest themselves, therefore as commodities, or have the form of commodities, only in so far as they have two forms, a physical or natural form and a value-form. (p. 47)

50. John A. Burrow, "The Audience of Piers Plowman," *Anglia* 75 (1957): 377. That "all considerations of genius, of the subjectivity of the artist, of his

soul, are *on principle* uninteresting," because they are mystifications or evasions, is the extreme position, taken by Pierre Macherey, *A Theory of Literary Production*, trans. Geoffrey Wall (London: Routledge, 1978), pp. 67–68:

The various 'theories' of creation all ignore the process of making: they omit any account of production. One can create undiminished, so, paradoxically, creation is the release of what is already there; or, one is witness of a sudden apparition, and then creation is an irruption, an epiphany, a mystery. In both instances any possible explanation of the change has been done away with; in the former, nothing has happened; and in the latter what has happened is inexplicable. All speculation over man the creator is intended to eliminate a real knowledge: the 'creative process' is, precisely, not a process, a labour; it is a religious formula to be found on funeral monuments.

Macherey's work was published, in 1966, just before the more influential (less Leninist) papers of Roland Barthes and Michel Foucault making much the same assertion: Barthes's "The Death of the Author" (1968), in *Image, Music, Text*, ed. and trans. Stephen Heath (New York: Hill & Wang, 1977), pp. 142–48, and Foucault's "What is an Author?" (1969), in *The Essential Works of Foucault 1954–1984*, ed. Paul Rabinow, trans. Robert Hurley and others, 3 vols. (New York: The New Press, 1997–2000), 2:205–22; cf. also the still earlier contributions of Lucien Goldmann, insisting on the impersonal, social-collective 'authorship' of literary works, e. g., "Dialectical Materialism and Literary History" (1950), trans. Francis Mulhern, *New Left Review* 92 (1975): 39–44, or "The Genetic-Structuralist Method in the History of Literature" (1964), repr. in *Towards a Sociology of the Novel*, 2nd edn., trans. Alan Sheridan (London: Tavistock, 1975), pp. 156–59.

51. The loan is documented in *CLR*, p. 500. On Scogan otherwise, see R. T. Lenaghan, "Chaucer's *Envoy to Scogan*: The Uses of Literary Conventions," *Chaucer Review* 10 (1975): 46–47, esp. Hallmundsson, "Chaucer's Circle: Henry Scogan and his Friends," *Medievalia et Humanistica*, n s 10 (1981): 129–39, and also Strohm, "Fourteenth- and Fifteenth-Century Writers as Readers of Chaucer," pp. 94–96, though the comments and notes of Walter W. Skeat, in *Chaucerian and Other Pieces* (Oxford: Oxford University Press, 1897), pp. xli–xliii and 502–03, are still worth perusal, whence also, pp. 237–44, come the quotations herein from the text of the "Moral Ballad" (*IMEV* 2264), cited parenthetically by line numbers.

52. Cf. Strohm, *Social Chaucer*, pp. 76–78. Scogan's quotations (each extensive and unmistakably close) are "Moral Ballad" 67–69 = *WBT* 1121–22, "Moral Ballad" 97–99 = *WBT* 1131–32, and "Moral Ballad" 166–67 = *WBT* 1165–67. *Buk 29* is evidence for *in vita*, pre-*Canterbury Tales*, separate circulation of something of the Wife of Bath (see also above, pp. 54–55, 126–27 n64, and 68), and the rest of Scogan's citations may appear likewise to come from early Chaucerian writings, published during his lifetime. "Moral Ballad" 150 mentions the "Boece," to which Usk also had access c. 1385, and Scogan's remarks about historical figures, "Moral Ballad" 166–78,

might borrow phrasing from portions of what survives as the *Monk's Tale* in the *Canterbury Tales:* "Moral Ballad" 168–71 (on "Julius") > *MkT* 2671–76, "Moral Ballad" 174 (on Nero) > *MkT* 2463–64, "Moral Ballad" 175–76 (on Balthasar) > *MkT* 2186–88, and "Moral Ballad" 177–78 (on Antiochus) > *MkT* 2610–11 (the remark on "Tullius Hostilius," "Moral Ballad" 166–167, comes from *WBT* 1165–67, as noted above). The differing versions of the *Monk's Tale* and issues of priority amongst them are discussed in Donald K. Fry, "The Ending of the Monk's Tale," *Journal of English and Germanic Philology* 71 (1972): 357–63; the various arguments and evidence for the consequent possibility of a pre-*Canterbury Tales* version of the Chaucerian collection of tragedies were analyzed, dismissively, in Tatlock, *The Development and Chronology of Chaucer's Works* (1907; repr. Gloucester: Peter Smith, 1963), pp. 165–72.

53. Cf. Robert Epstein, "Chaucer's Scogan and Scogan's Chaucer," *Studies in Philology* 96 (1999): 20 n29. For information on the text of "Gentilesse" (*IMEV* 3348), I rely on George B. Pace and David, eds., *The Minor Poems Part One*, Variorum Edition of the Works of Geoffrey Chaucer 5 (Norman: University of Oklahoma Press, 1982), pp. 67–72.

54. The Shakespeare quotations are *1 Henry IV* 1.2, *1 Henry IV* 3.2, *2 Henry IV* 5.5, *Henry V* 5.2, and *Henry V* 1.1. Cf. Epstein, "Chaucer's Scogan and Scogan's Chaucer," 17–18.

55. Lenaghan, "Chaucer's Circle of Gentlemen and Clerks," *Chaucer Review* 18 (1983): 159.

56. *Piers Plowman* 10.24–25 and 28.

57. The intelligence comes from John Shirley, whose labors and contributions are most recently analyzed in Margaret Connolly, *John Shirley: Book Production and the Noble Household in Fifteenth-Century England* (Aldershot: Ashgate, 1998), though I have relied on the analysis in Lerer, *Chaucer and His Readers*, pp. 119–41. Hallmundsson, "Chaucer's Circle: Henry Scogan and his Friends," 129–30 and 134, points out that the Lewis John mentioned in Shirley's headnote eventually had extensive commercial dealings with the butler of the royal household, an office held by Chaucer's son Thomas, first in 1402 and then intermittently for the rest of his life, and held previously by John Payne, 1399–1402, who in that capacity had had dealings with Chaucer himself, near the end of the poet's life. Lerer's remark about the commodification of Chaucer comes in his contribution, "William Caxton," in *The Cambridge History of Medieval English Literature*, ed. David Wallace (Cambridge: Cambridge University Press, 1999), p. 734.

58. The point is well made in Lenaghan, "Chaucer's Circle of Gentlemen and Clerks," 156. In connection with this *House of Fame* passage, it may be noteworthy that the same conceit occurs in the *Noctes Atticae* (Praef. 4: "quoniam longinquis per hiemem noctibus in agro, sicuti dixi, terrae Atticae commentationes hasce ludere ac facere exorsi sumus") of Aulus Gellius—to whom Deschamps likened Chaucer (see above, p. 71)—this writer too being diurnally preoccupied with state-administrative service (e.g., 12.13.1: "Romae a consulibus iudex extra ordinem datus pronuntiare intra

Kalendas iussus;" or 14.2.1: "Quo primum tempore a praetoribus lectus in iudices sum, ut iudicia quae appellantur privata susciperem").

59. Speght's claim, in the 1602 edition of Chaucer's works, and the likelihood that it is true, are discussed in George B. Pace, "Speght's Chaucer and Ms. Gg.4.27," *Studies in Bibliography* 21 (1968): esp. 233–35.

60. Various documents detail the series of preferments that came to Chaucer by way of his connections with John of Gaunt and his family: see Martin M. Crow and Clair C. Olson, *Chaucer Life-Records* (Oxford: Clarendon, 1966), esp. pp. 271–75 and 525–34; see also above, pp. 6–7 and 35.

61. There is some further discussion of these issues in Carlson, "Chaucer, Humanism, and Printing: Conditions of Authorship in Fifteenth-Century England," *University of Toronto Quarterly* 64 (1995): 274–88, and "Morley's Translations from Roman Philosophers and English Courtier Literature," in *Triumphs of English: Henry Parker, Lord Morley, Translator to the Tudor Court*, ed. Marie Axton and James P. Carley (London: British Library, 2000), esp. pp. 131–37.

62. Richard Firth Green, *Poets and Princepleasers* (Toronto: University of Toronto Press, 1980), p. 211. The fundamental study remains Pearsall, *John Lydgate* (Charlottesville: University Press of Virginia, 1970).

63. The quotations here are: from the headnote to the "Mumming for the Mercers," in Cambridge, Trinity College, R.3.20, printed in Henry Noble MacCracken, *The Minor Poems of John Lydgate*, 2 vols., EETS es 107 and os 192 (London: Early English Text Society, 1911 and 1934), 2:695; and *Fall of Princes* 3.3865–71, ed. Henry Bergen, 4 vols., EETS es 121–24 (London: Early English Text Society, 1924–1927), 2:437. For the records of payment, see Pearsall, *John Lydgate (1371–1449): A Bio-bibliography*, p. 59, nos. 13 and 13A. It might be felt that more should be said herein about Lydgate's contributions. The matter is avoided, however, for two reasons (beyond the authorial indolence). First, Lydgate's literary relation to the Chaucerian legacy has been extensively discussed, for example, by Pearsall, "The English Chaucerians," in *Chaucer and Chaucerians: Critical Studies in Middle English Literature*, ed. D. S. Brewer (London: Nelson, 1966), pp. 203–22, and elsewhere, or A. C. Spearing, *Medieval to Renaissance in English Poetry* (Cambridge: Cambridge University Press, 1985), pp. 65–88. Second, and more pertinently, Lydgate's "Chaucerianism" is not innovatory. Instead, it is belated— none of his writing has been shown to antedate 1412—and repetitious, of the kinds of contributions to the tradition's development made earlier, already before ca. 1411, by Deschamps, Usk, the *Book of Cupid* poet, Scogan, Hoccleve, and so on. Nor does "Chaucerianism" seem an apt description of what Lydgate was doing, or was doing most distinctively: to describe the *Serpent of Division* (1422), for example—on which, see now Maura Nolan, "The Art of History Writing: Lydgate's *Serpent of Division*," *Speculum* 78 (2003): 99–127—as "Chaucerian" seems to me neither instructive nor accurate. Recently, Simpson, " 'Dysemol Daies and Fatal Houres:' Lydgate's *Destruction of Thebes* and Chaucer's *Knight's Tale*," in *The Long Fifteenth Century: Essays for Douglas Grey*, ed. Helen Cooper and Sally Mapstone

(Oxford: Clarendon, 1997), p. 21, has expressed his "disagreement with the following accounts of Lydgate (examples, in my view, of posterity's condescension): that he is 'medieval' and his humanism is only skin deep; and that he is overawed by Chaucer's presence." The seminal contributions may turn out to be Pearsall, "Lydgate as Innovator," *Modern Language Quarterly* 53 (1992): 5–22, and Patterson, "Making Identities in Fifteenth-Century England: Henry V and John Lydgate," in *New Historical Literary Study: Essays on Reproducing Texts, Representing History, ed. Jeffrey* N. Cox and Larry J. Reynolds (Princeton: Princeton University Press, 1993), pp. 69–107.

64. Cf. Ethan Knapp, "Eulogies and Usurpations: Hoccleve and Chaucer Revisited," *Studies in the Age of Chaucer* 21 (1999): 247–73. For Hoccleve's career and writings, generally I rely on Strohm, "Hoccleve, Lydgate and the Lancastrian Court," in *The Cambridge History of Medieval English Literature*, ed. Wallace, pp. 640–51 and 657–61; I have also been influenced by Bowers, "Hoccleve's Huntington Holographs: The First 'Collected Poems' in English," *Fifteenth-Century Studies* 15 (1989): 27–51, and "Hoccleve's Two Copies of *Lerne to Dye*: Implications for Textual Critics," *Papers of the Bibliographical Society of America* 83 (1989): 437–72.

65. Knapp, "Bureaucratic Identity and the Construction of the Self in Hoccleve's *Formulary* and *La male regle*," *Speculum* 74 (1999): 357–76; and cf. Malcolm Richardson, "Hoccleve in his Social Context," *Chaucer Review* 20 (1986): 313–22.

66. M. C. Seymour, *Selections from Hoccleve* (Oxford: Clarendon, 1981), p. xiii.

67. Pearsall, "Hoccleve's *Regement of Princes*: The Poetics of Royal Self-Representation," *Speculum* 69 (1994): 387–88.

68. On the *Letter*, see Patterson, " 'What is Me?': Self and Society in the Poetry of Thomas Hoccleve," *Studies in the Age of Chaucer* 23 (2001): 450–54.

69. The quotation is from the "Address to Sir John Oldcastle" (*IMEV* 3407) 319–20, ed. Frederick J. Furnivall, in *Hoccleve's Works: The Minor Poems*, rev. edn., ed. Jerome Mitchell and A. I. Doyle, EETS es 61 and 73, in one vol. (London: Early English Text Society, 1970), pp. 8–24.

70. In quoting Hoccleve's *Regiment* (giving the references parenthetically), I use the edition of Charles R. Blyth, *Thomas Hoccleve: The Regiment of Princes*, METS (Kalamazoo: Medieval Institute Publications, 1999).

71. Pearsall, "Hoccleve's *Regement of Princes*," 389. A different view of Hoccleve's advice is argued in Judith Ferster, *Fictions of Advice: The Literature and Politics of Counsel in Late Medieval England* (Philadelphia: University of Pennsylvania Press, 1996), pp. 137–59.

72. Cf. *Regiment* 281–385; the context of events in which these remarks of Hoccleve about John Badby were made is discussed in Peter McNiven, *Heresy and Politics in the Reign of Henry IV* (Woodbridge: Boydell, 1987), esp. pp. 199–219.

73. Cf. Larry Scanlon, "The King's Two Voices: Narrative and Power in Hoccleve's *Regement of Princes*," in *Literary Practice and Social Change in Britain*, ed. Patterson, esp. p. 231. Essential on the history of the genre's development is David Rundle, " 'Not So Much Praise as Precept:' Erasmus, Panegyric, and

the Renaissance Art of Teaching Princes," in *Pedagogy and Power: Rhetorics of Classical Learning*, ed. Yun Lee Too and Niall Livingstone (Cambridge: Cambridge University Press, 1998), pp. 148–69.

74. David Lawton, "Dullness and the Fifteenth Century," *ELH* 54 (1987): 761–99. Cf. Lenaghan, "Chaucer's Circle of Gentlemen and Clerks," 157–59.

75. On the manuscripts, see Seymour, "The Manuscripts of Hoccleve's *Regiment of Princes*," *Edinburgh Bibliographical Society Transactions* 4 (1974): 255–97; on the portrait, see esp. Alan T. Gaylord, "Portrait of a Poet," in *The Ellesmere Chaucer*, ed. Martin Stevens and Daniel Woodward (San Marino: Huntington Library, 1997), pp. 121–42; and on the copy of it reproduced herein (see frontispiece), see A. S. G. Edwards, "The Chaucer Portraits in the Harley and Rosenbach Manuscripts," *English Manuscript Studies* 4 (1993): 268–71.

76. Important contributions are Strohm, esp. perhaps "Chaucer's Fifteenth-Century Audience and the Narrowing of the 'Chaucer Tradition,'" pp. 15–22; also "Hoccleve, Lydgate and the Lancastrian Court," pp. 640–61, largely repeated in or from *England's Empty Throne: Usurpation and the Language of Legitimation, 1399–1422* (New Haven: Yale University Press, 1998), pp. 173–95, a book which also incorporates discussion of a number of the determinant conditions of the early Lancastrian writing.

77. There are important remarks on this development in Simpson, "Breaking the Vacuum: Ricardian and Henrician Ovidianism," *Journal of Medieval and Early Modern Studies* 29 (1999): 325–55, and in Lerer, *Courtly Letters in the Age of Henry VIII* (Cambridge: Cambridge University Press, 1997), esp. perhaps pp. 1–33.

BIBLIOGRAPHY

For quotations from Chaucer's writings is used Larry D. Benson, gen. ed., *The River-side Chaucer*, 3rd edn. (Boston: Houghton Mifflin, 1987), and the system of abbreviations for individual pieces given therein, p. 779; for John Gower's, G. C. MacAulay, ed., *The Complete Works of John Gower*, 4 vols. (Oxford: Clarendon, 1899–1902); for Langland's, the B-text except as indicated otherwise, A. V. C. Schmidt, ed., *The Vision of Piers Plowman*, 2nd edn. (London: Dent, 1995); and for the *Pearl*-poet, Malcom Andrew and Ronald Waldron, eds., *The Poems of the Pearl Manuscript* (London: Arnold, 1978). In citations of other Middle English poems—especially brief and obscure pieces, some often edited and reprinted, under varying titles—*IMEV* designations are supplied, for clarity's sake. For ancient authors, as for Shakespeare, only a standard *textus receptus*, widely available in numerous editions, is quoted, with references given by the standard systems of citation. In quotations of Middle English writings, orthography has generally been modernized (e.g., by use of "th" in place of thorn). In all quotations of editions of texts, editorial punctuation has sometimes been tacitly altered, by way of rectification or for fitting the quoted matter into context. Except where express credit is given otherwise, all the translations from original languages are authorial. The following abbreviations are used in endnotes and the bibliography:

CLR = *Chaucer Life-Records*. Ed. Martin M. Crow and Clair C. Olson, from materials compiled by John M. Manly and Edith Rickert, with the assistance of Lilian J. Redstone and others. Oxford: Clarendon, 1966.

EETS os *or* es = Early English Text Society original series *or* extra series.

IMEV = *Index of Middle English Verse*. Ed. Carleton Brown and Rossell Hope Robbins. New York: Index Society, 1943.

METS = TEAMS (The Consortium for the Teaching of the Middle Ages) Middle English Text Series.

Adorno, Theodor W. *Prisms*. Trans. Samuel Weber and Shierry Weber. Cambridge: MIT Press, 1981.

Aers, David. *Chaucer, Langland and the Creative Imagination*. London: Routledge, 1980.
———. *Community, Gender, and Individual Identity: English Writing 1360–1430*. London: Routledge, 1988.

Ali, Tariq. "Literature and Market Realism." *New Left Review* 199 (1993): 140–45.

Althusser, Louis. *For Marx*. Trans. Ben Brewster. 1969; repr. London: Verso, 1996.

Althusser, Louis. *Lenin and Philosophy and Other Essays.* Trans. Ben Brewster. New York: Monthly Review Press, 1971.

Anderson, Perry. *Lineages of the Absolutist State.* London: NLB, 1974.

————. *Passages From Antiquity to Feudalism.* London: NLB, 1974.

————. *In the Tracks of Historical Materialism.* London: Verso, 1983.

Andrew, Malcom, and Ronald Waldron, eds, *The Poems of the Pearl Manuscript.* York Medieval Texts Second Series. London: Arnold, 1978.

Aspin, Isabel S. T. *Anglo-Norman Political Songs.* Anglo-Norman Text Society 11. Oxford: Blackwell, 1953.

Aston, Margaret. "Lollardy and Sedition, 1381–1431" (1960). Repr. in *Lollards and Reformers: Images and Literacy in Late Medieval Religion.* London: Hambledon, 1984. Pp. 1–47.

————. "Corpus Christi and Corpus Regni: Heresy and the Peasants' Revolt." *Past & Present* 143 (1994): 3–47.

Baker, Alan R. H. "Changes in the Later Middle Ages." In *A New Historical Geography of England.* Ed. H. C. Darby. Cambridge: Cambridge University Press, 1973. Pp. 186–247.

Balibar, Etienne, and Pierre Macherey. "On Literature as an Ideological Form" (1974). Trans. McLeod, Whitehead, and Wordsworth. *Oxford Literary Review* 3 (1978): 4–12.

Baron, Roger, ed. and trans. *Hugues de Saint-Victor: Six opuscules spirituels.* Sources chrétiennes 155. Paris: Cerf, 1969.

Barr, Helen. "The Dates of *Richard the Redeless* and *Mum and the Sothsegger.*" *Notes & Queries* 235 (1990): 270–75.

————. "The Relationship of *Richard the Redeless* and *Mum and the Sothsegger*: Some New Evidence." *Yearbook of Langland Studies* 4 (1990): 105–33.

————, ed. *The Piers Plowman Tradition.* London: Dent, 1993.

————. "*Piers Plowman* and Poetic Tradition." *Yearbook of Langland Studies* 9 (1995): 39–64.

Barron, Caroline M. "The Tyranny of Richard II." *Bulletin of the Institute of Historical Research* 41 (1968): 1–18.

————. "The Quarrel of Richard II with London 1392–7." In *The Reign of Richard II: Essays in Honour of May McKisack.* Ed. F. R. H. Du Boulay and Barron. London: Athlone, 1971. Pp. 173–201.

Barthes, Roland. *Mythologies.* Trans. Annette Lavers. New York: Hill & Wang, 1972.

————. "The Death of the Author" (1968). In *Image, Music, Text.* Ed. and trans. Stephen Heath. New York: Hill & Wang, 1977. Pp. 142–48.

Baugh, Albert Croll. "Kirk's Life Records of Thomas Chaucer." *PMLA* 47 (1932): 461–515.

Beidler, Peter G. "The Plague and Chaucer's Pardoner." *Chaucer Review* 16 (1982): 257–69.

Bellamy, John G. "Sir John de Annesley and the Chandos Inheritance." *Nottingham Medieval Studies.* 10 (1966), 94–105.

Bengtson, Jonathan. "Saint George and the Formation of English Nationalism." *Journal of Medieval and Early Modern Studies* 27 (1997): 317–40.

Benjamin, Walter. *Illuminations*. Ed. Hannah Arendt. Trans. Harry Zohn. New York: Schocken, 1969.

———. *Reflections: Essays, Aphorisms, Autobiographical Writings*. Trans. Edmund Jephcott. New York: Harcourt, 1978.

Benson, Larry D., gen. ed. *The Riverside Chaucer*. 3rd edn. Boston: Houghton Mifflin, 1987.

Bergen, Henry, ed. *Lydgate's Fall of Princes*. 4 vols. EETS es 121–124. London: Early English Text Society, 1924–27.

Berschin, Walter. *Greek Letters and the Latin Middle Ages: From Jerome to Nicholas of Cusa*. Trans. Jerold C. Frakes. Rev. and expanded edn. Washington D. C.: Catholic University of America Press, 1988.

Bird, Ruth. *The Turbulent London of Richard II*. London: Longmans, 1949.

Bloch, Ernst. *The Utopian Function of Art and Literature: Selected Essays*. Trans. Jack Zipes and Frank Mecklenburg. Cambridge: MIT Press, 1988.

Bloom, Harold. *The Anxiety of Influence: A Theory of Poetry*. London: Oxford University Press, 1973.

Bloomfield, Morton W. "Chaucer's Sense of History." *Journal of English and Germanic Philology* 51 (1952): 301–313.

Blyth, Charles R., ed. *Thomas Hoccleve: The Regiment of Princes*. METS. Kalamazoo: Medieval Institute Publications, 1999.

Boffey, Julia. *Manuscripts of the English Courtly Love Lyrics in the Later Middle Ages*. Cambridge: Brewer, 1985.

———. "The Reputation and Circulation of Chaucer's Lyrics in the Fifteenth Century." *Chaucer Review* 28 (1993): 23–40.

Bowers, John M. "Hoccleve's Huntington Holographs: The First 'Collected Poems' in English." *Fifteenth-Century Studies* 15 (1989): 27–51.

———. "Hoccleve's Two Copies of *Lerne to Dye*: Implications for Textual Critics." *Papers of the Bibliographical Society of America* 83 (1989): 437–72.

———, ed. *The Canterbury Tales: Fifteenth-Century Continuations and Additions*. METS. Kalamazoo: Medieval Institute Publications, 1992.

———. "Piers Plowman and the Police: Notes toward a History of the Wycliffite Langland." *Yearbook of Langland Studies* 6 (1992): 1–50.

———. "*Pearl* in its Royal Setting: Ricardian Poetry Revisited." *Studies in the Age of Chaucer* 17 (1995): 111–55.

———. "Dating *Piers Plowman*: Testing the Testimony of Usk's *Testament*." *Yearbook of Langland Studies* 13 (1999): 65–100.

Brenner, Robert. "Agrarian Class Structure and Economic Development in Pre-Industrial Europe." *Past & Present* 70 (1976): 30–75.

———. "The Origins of Capitalist Development: A Critique of Neo-Smithian Marxism." *New Left Review* 104 (1977): 25–92.

———. "Agrarian Class Structure and Economic Development in Pre-Industrial Europe: The Agrarian Roots of European Capitalism." *Past & Present* 97 (1982): 16–113.

———. *Merchants and Revolution: Commercial Change, Political Conflict, and London's Overseas Traders, 1550–1653*. Princeton: Princeton University Press, 1993.

Brewer, Derek S. "Class Distinction in Chaucer." *Speculum* 43 (1968): 290–305.

Brewer, Derek S . *Chaucer: The Critical Heritage*. 2 vols. London: Routledge, 1978.

Brown, A. L. "Parliament, ca. 1377–1422." In *The English Parliament in the Middle Ages*. Ed. R. G. Davies and J. H. Denton. Philadelphia: University of Pennsylvania Press, 1981. Pp. 109–40.

Brown, Carleton. "Another Contemporary Allusion in Chaucer's *Troilus*." *Modern Language Notes* 26 (1911): 208–11.

———— and Rossell Hope Robbins, eds, *Index of Middle English Verse*. New York: Index Society, 1943.

Brown, R. Allen, H. M. Colvin, and A. J. Taylor. *The History of the King's Works: The Middle Ages*. 2 vols. London: HMSO, 1963.

Burger, Glenn. "Kissing the Pardoner." *PMLA* 107 (1992): 1143–56.

Burrow, John A. "The Audience of *Piers Plowman*." *Anglia* 75 (1957): 373–84.

————. "The Action of Langland's Second Vision." *Essays in Criticism* 15 (1965): 247–68.

————. "Thomas Hoccleve: Some Redatings." *Review of English Studies*, n.s. 46 (1995): 366–72.

————, ed. *Thomas Hoccleve's Complaint and Dialogue*. EETS os 313. Oxford: Early English Text Society, 1999.

Calin, William. *The French Tradition and the Literature of Medieval England*. Toronto: University of Toronto Press, 1994.

Carlson, David R. "*Pearl*'s Imperfections." *Studia Neophilologica* 63 (1991): 57–67.

————. "Thomas Hoccleve and the Chaucer Portrait." *Huntington Library Quarterly* 54 (1991): 283–300.

————. "Chaucer's Boethius and Thomas Usk's *Testament of Love*: Politics and Love in the Chaucerian Tradition." In *The Centre and its Compass: Studies in Medieval Literature in Honor of Professor John Leyerle*. Ed. Robert A. Taylor, James F. Burke, Patricia J. Eberle, Ian Lancashire, and Brian S. Merrilees. Kalamazoo: Medieval Institute Publications, 1993. Pp. 29–70.

————. "Chaucer, Humanism, and Printing: Conditions of Authorship in Fifteenth-Century England." *University of Toronto Quarterly* 64 (1995): 274–88.

————. "Morley's Translations from Roman Philosophers and English Courtier Literature." In *Triumphs of English: Henry Parker, Lord Morley, Translator to the Tudor Court*. Ed. Marie Axton and James P. Carley. London: British Library, 2000. Pp. 131–51.

————. "Whetehamstede on Lollardy: Latin Styles and the Vernacular Cultures of Early Fifteenth-Century England." *Journal of English and Germanic Philology* 102 (2003): 21–41.

————, ed. and A. G. Rigg, trans. *Richard Maidstone: Concordia (The Reconciliation of Richard II with London)*. METS. Kalamazoo: Medieval Institute Publications, 2003.

Cartier, Normand R. "Le *Bleu chevalier* de Froissart et le *Livre de la duchesse* de Chaucer." *Romania* 88 (1967): 232–52.

Carus-Wilson, Eleanora Mary. "Trends in the Export of English Woolens in the Fourteenth Century." *Economic History Review*, 2nd ser., 3 (1950): 162–79.

Chambers, R. W. and Marjorie Daunt. *A Book of London English 1384–1425*. Oxford: Clarendon, 1931.

Coleman, Janet. *English Literature in History 1350–1400: Medieval Readers and Writers.* London: Hutchinson, 1981.

Coleman, Olive. "The Collectors of Customs in London under Richard II." In *Studies in London History Presented to Philip Edmund Jones.* Ed. A. E. J. Hollaender and William Kellaway. London: Hodder and Stoughton, 1969. Pp. 181–94.

Connolly, Margaret. *John Shirley: Book Production and the Noble Household in Fifteenth-Century England.* Aldershot: Ashgate, 1998.

Cooper, Helen. *Oxford Guides to Chaucer: The Canterbury Tales.* Oxford: Oxford University Press, 1989.

Copeland, Rita. "William Thorpe and his Lollard Community: Intellectual Labor and the Representation of Dissent." In *Bodies and Disciplines: Intersections of Literature and History in Fifteenth-Century England.* Ed. Barbara A. Hanawalt and David Wallace. Minneapolis: University of Minnesota Press, 1996. Pp. 199–221.

Copenhaver, Brian P. *Hermetica: The Greek Corpus Hermeticum and the Latin Asclepius in a New English Translation with Notes and Introduction.* Cambridge: Cambridge University Press, 1992.

Crane, Susan. "Froissart's *Dit dou bleu chevalier* as a Source for Chaucer's *Book of the Duchess.*" *Medium Aevum* 61 (1992): 59–74.

———. "The Writing Lesson of 1381." In *Chaucer's England: Literature in Historical Context.* Ed. Barbara A. Hanawalt. Minneapolis: University of Minnesota Press, 1992. Pp. 201–21.

Cronin, H. S., ed., *Rogeri Dymmok Liber contra xii errores et hereses lollardorum.* London: Wyclif Society, 1922.

Crow, Martin M. and Clair C. Olson, eds, *Chaucer Life-Records.* From materials compiled by John M. Manly and Edith Rickert, with the assistance of Lilian J. Redstone and others. Oxford: Clarendon, 1966.

Crump, C. G. and C. Johnson. "The Powers of Justices of the Peace." *English Historical Review* 27 (1912): 226–38.

Dane, Joseph A. "Who is Buried in Chaucer's Tomb?—Prolegomena." *Huntington Library Quarterly* 57 (1994): 99–123.

Davenport, W. A. *Chaucer: Complaint and Narrative.* Chaucer Studies 14. Cambridge: Brewer, 1988.

David, Alfred. *The Strumpet Muse: Art and Morals in Chaucer's Poetry.* Bloomington: Indiana University Press, 1976.

Davy, Marie-Madeleine, ed. and trans. *Guillaume de Saint-Thierry: Deux traités de l'amour de Dieu.* Paris: Vrin, 1953.

Dean, James, ed., *Six Ecclesiastical Satires.* METS. Kalamazoo: Medieval Institute Publications, 1991.

———, ed., *Medieval English Political Writings.* METS. Kalamazoo: Medieval Institute Publications, 1996.

Delany, Sheila. "Womanliness in the *Man of Law's Tale.*" *Chaucer Review* 9 (1974): 63–72.

———. "Politics and the Paralysis of Poetic Imagination in *The Physician's Tale.*" *Studies in the Age of Chaucer* 3 (1981): 47–60.

Dobson, R. B. *The Peasants' Revolt of 1381.* London: MacMillan, 1970.

Doyle, A. I. and M. B. Parkes. "The Production of Copies of the *Canterbury Tales* and the *Confessio Amantis* in the Early Fifteenth Century." In *Medieval Scribes,*

Manuscripts & Libraries: Essays Presented to N. R. Ker. Ed. Parkes and Andrew G. Watson. London: Scolar, 1978. Pp. 163–210.

———. "Paleographical Introduction." In *The Canterbury Tales: A Facsimile and Transcription of the Hengwrt Manuscript, with Variants from the Ellesmere Manuscript.* Ed. Paul G. Ruggiers. Variorum Edition of the Works of Geoffrey Chaucer 1. Norman: University of Oklahoma Press, 1979. Pp. xix–xlix.

Dronke, Peter. *Medieval Latin and the Rise of European Love-Lyric.* 2nd edn. 2 vols. Oxford: Clarendon, 1968.

Du Boulay, F. R. H. "The Historical Chaucer." In *Geoffrey Chaucer,* ed. Derek Brewer. Athens: Ohio University Press, 1975. Pp. 33–57.

Düll, Siegrid, Anthony Luttrell, and Maurice Keen. "Faithful Unto Death: The Tomb Slab of Sir William Neville and Sir John Clanvowe, Constantinople 1391." *Antiquaries Journal* 71 (1991): 174–90.

Dyer, Christopher. "Piers Plowman and Plowmen: A Historical Perspective." *Yearbook of Langland Studies* 8 (1994): 155–76.

Eberle, Patricia J. "Commercial Language and the Commercial Outlook in the *General Prologue.*" *Chaucer Review* 18 (1983): 161–74.

———. "The Politics of Courtly Style at the Court of Richard II." In *The Spirit of the Court.* Ed. Glyn S. Burgess and Robert A. Taylor. Cambridge: Brewer, 1985. Pp. 168–78.

———. "The Question of Authority and the Man of Law's Tale." In *The Centre and its Compass: Studies in Medieval Literature in Honor of Professor John Leyerle.* Ed. Robert A. Taylor, James F. Burke, Patricia J. Eberle, Ian Lancashire, and Brian S. Merrilees. Kalamazoo: Medieval Institute Publications, 1993. Pp. 111–49.

Edwards, A. S. G. "The Unity and Authenticity of *Anelida and Arcite*: The Evidence of the Manuscripts." *Studies in Bibliography* 41 (1988): 177–88.

———. "The Chaucer Portraits in the Harley and Rosenbach Manuscripts." *English Manuscript Studies* 4 (1993): 268–71.

Embree, Dan. " 'Richard the Redeless' and 'Mum and the Sothsegger': A Case of Mistaken Identity." *Notes & Queries* 220 (1975): 4–12.

Epstein, Robert. "Chaucer's Scogan and Scogan's Chaucer." *Studies in Philology* 96 (1999): 1–21.

Feltes, Norman N. *Modes of Production of Victorian Novels.* Chicago: University of Chicago Press, 1986.

———. *Literary Capital and the Late Victorian Novel.* Madison: University of Wisconsin Press, 1993.

Ferster, Judith. *Fictions of Advice: The Literature and Politics of Counsel in Late Medieval England.* Philadelphia: University of Pennsylvania Press, 1996.

Finlayson, John. "*The Simonie*: Two Authors?" *Archiv für das Studium der neueren Sprachen und Literaturen* 226 (1989): 39–51.

Fisher, John H. *John Gower: Moral Philosopher and Friend of Chaucer.* London: Methuen, 1965.

———. "Animadversions on the Text of Chaucer, 1988." *Speculum* 63 (1988): 779–93.

———. "A Language Policy for Lancastrian England." *PMLA* 107 (1992): 1168–80.

————. *The Importance of Chaucer*. Carbondale: Southern Illinois University Press, 1992.

Foucault, Michel. *Discipline and Punish: The Birth of the Prison*. Trans. Alan Sheridan. 1977; repr. New York: Vintage, 1995.

————. *The History of Sexuality Volume 1: An Introduction*. Trans. Robert Hurley. 1978; repr. New York: Vintage, 1990.

————. *The Essential Works of Foucault 1954–1984*. Ed. Paul Rabinow. Trans. Robert Hurley and others. 3 vols. New York: The New Press, 1997–2000.

Fradenburg, Louise. "The Manciple's Servant Tongue: Politics and Poetry in *The Canterbury Tales*." *ELH* 52 (1985): 85–118.

Frank, Robert Worth, Jr "The Pardon Scene in *Piers Plowman*." *Speculum* 26 (1951): 317–31.

————. "The 'Hungry Gap,' Crop Failure, and Famine: The Fourteenth-Century Agricultural Crisis and *Piers Plowman*." *Yearbook of Langland Studies* 4 (1990): 87–104.

Fry, Donald K. "The Ending of the Monk's Tale." *Journal of English and Germanic Philology* 71 (1972): 355–68.

Furnivall, Frederick J. and Israel Gollancz, eds, *Hoccleve's Works: The Minor Poems*. Revised edn., ed. Jerome Mitchell and A. I. Doyle. EETS es 61 and 73 in one vol. London: Early English Text Society, 1970.

Galloway, Andrew. "Gower in his Most Learned Role and the Peasants' Revolt of 1381." *Mediaevalia* 16 (1993): 329–47.

————. "Private Selves and the Intellectual Marketplace in Late Fourteenth-Century England: The Case of the Two Usks." *New Literary History* 28 (1997): 291–318.

Galway, Margaret. "Geoffrey Chaucer, J. P. and M. P." *Modern Language Review* 36 (1941): 1–36.

Gaylord, Alan T. "Portrait of a Poet." In *The Ellesmere Chaucer: Essays in Interpretation*. Ed. Martin Stevens and Daniel Woodward. San Marino: Huntington Library, 1997. Pp. 121–42.

George, M. Dorothy. "Verses on the Exchequer in the Fifteenth Century." *English Historical Review* 36 (1921): 58–67.

Given-Wilson, Chris. "Wealth and Credit, Public and Private: The Earls of Arundel 1306–1397." *English Historical Review* 106 (1991): 1–26.

————. *Chronicles of the Revolution 1397–1400: The Reign of Richard II*. Manchester: Manchester University Press, 1993.

Goldmann, Lucien. "Dialectical Materialism and Literary History" (1950). Trans. Francis Mulhern. *New Left Review* 92 (1975): 39–51.

————. *Towards a Sociology of the Novel* (1964). 2nd edn. (1965). Trans. Alan Sheridan. London: Tavistock, 1975.

————. "The Sociology of Literature: Status and Problems of Method." *International Social Science Journal* 19 (1967): 493–516.

Gradon, Pamela. "Langland and the Ideology of Dissent." *Proceedings of the British Academy* 66 (1980): 179–205.

Grady, Frank. "*St Erkenwald* and the Merciless Parliament." *Studies in the Age of Chaucer* 22 (2000): 179–211.

Grady, Frank . "The Generation of 1399." In *The Letter of the Law: Legal Practice and Literary Production in Medieval England*. Ed. Emily Steiner and Candace Barrington. Ithaca: Cornell University Press, 2002. Pp. 202–29.

Gramsci, Antonio. *Selections from the Prison Notebooks*. Ed. and trans. Quintin Hoare and Geoffrey Norton-Smith. London: Wishart, 1971.

——— . *Selections from Political Writings (1910–1920)*. Ed. Quintin Hoare. Trans. John Mathews. London: Lawrence and Wishart, 1977.

Green, Peter. *Alexander of Macedon, 356–323 B.C.: A Historical Biography*. Rev. edn. 1974; repr. Berkeley: University of California Press, 1991.

Green, Richard Firth. *Poets and Princepleasers: Literature and the English Court in the Late Middle Ages*. Toronto: University of Toronto Press, 1980.

——— . "Arcite at Court." *English Language Notes* 18 (1981): 251–57.

——— . "Jack Philipot, John of Gaunt, and a Poem of 1380." *Speculum* 66 (1991): 330–41.

Guha, Ranajit. "Dominance without Hegemony and its Historiography." *Subaltern Studies* 6 (1989): 210–309.

Hallmundsson, May Newman. "The Community of Law and Letters: Some Notes on Thomas Usk's Audience." *Viator* 9 (1978): 357–65.

——— . "Chaucer's Circle: Henry Scogan and his Friends." *Medievalia et Humanistica*, n. s. 10 (1981): 129–39.

Hanawalt, Barbara A. "Men's Games, King's Deer: Poaching in Medieval England." *Journal of Medieval and Renaissance Studies* 18 (1988): 175–93.

——— , ed., *Chaucer's England: Literature in Historical Context*. Minneapolis: University of Minnesota Press, 1992.

Hanna, Ralph. "Alliterative Poetry." In *The Cambridge History of Medieval English Literature*. Ed. David Wallace. Cambridge: Cambridge University Press, 1999. Pp. 488–512.

Harding, Alan. "The Origins and Early History of the Keeper of the Peace." *Transactions of the Royal Historical Society*, 5th ser., 10 (1960), 85–109.

Hardman, Phillipa. "The *Book of the Duchess* as a Memorial Monument." *Chaucer Review* 28 (1994): 205–15.

Harriss, G. L. "Aids, Loans and Benevolences." *Historical Journal* 6 (1963): 1–19.

Harvey, John H. "The Medieval Office of Works." *Journal of the British Archaeological Association*, 3rd ser., 6 (1941): 20–87.

Heidtmann, Peter. "Sex and Salvation in *Troilus and Criseyde*." *Chaucer Review* 2 (1968): 246–53.

Hilton, Rodney. *Bond Men Made Free: Medieval Peasant Movements and the English Rising of 1381*. 1973; repr. London: Routledge, 1988.

——— . *Class Conflict and the Crisis of Feudalism*. 2nd edn. London: Verso, 1990.

Holmes, George. *The Good Parliament*. Oxford: Clarendon, 1975.

Horkheimer, Max. "A New Concept of Ideology?" (1930). In *Between Philosophy and Social Science: Selected Early Writings*. Trans. G. Frederick Hunter, Matthew S. Kramer, and John Torpey. Cambridge: MIT Press, 1993. Pp. 129–49.

——— . "The Authoritarian State" (wr. 1940, unpublished). In *The Essential Frankfurt School Reader*. Ed. Andrew Arato and Eike Gebhardt. New York: Urizen Books, 1978. Pp. 95–117.

Hornsby, Joseph Allen. *Chaucer and the Law*. Norman: Pilgrim Books, 1988.

————. "Was Chaucer Educated at the Inns of Court?" *Chaucer Review* 22 (1988): 255–68.

Houghton, K. N. "Theory and Practice in Borough Elections to Parliament during the Later Fifteenth Century." *Bulletin of the Institute of Historical Research* 39 (1966): 130–40.

Hoyt, Robert S. "Royal Taxation and the Growth of the Realm in Mediaeval England." *Speculum* 25 (1950): 36–48.

Hudson, Anne. "Lollardy: The English Heresy?" *Studies in Church History* 18 (1982): 261–83.

————, ed. "Thorpe's Examination." In *Two Wycliffite Texts*. EETS os 301. Oxford: Early English Text Society, 1993.

————. "*Piers Plowman* and the Peasants' Revolt: A Problem Revisited." *Yearbook of Langland Studies* 8 (1994): 85–106.

James, Margery K. "A London Merchant of the Fourteenth Century." *Economic History Review*, 2nd ser., 8 (1956): 364–76.

James, Mervyn. "English Politics and the Concept of Honour, 1485–1642" (1978). Repr. in *Society, Politics and Culture: Studies in Early Modern England*. Cambridge: Cambridge University Press, 1986. Pp. 308–415.

Jameson, Fredric. "The Brick and the Balloon: Architecture, Idealism and Land Speculation." *New Left Review* 228 (1998): 25–46.

Jay, Martin. *Marxism and Totality: The Adventures of a Concept from Lukács to Habermas*. Berkeley: University of California Press, 1984.

Jenkins, T. Atkinson. "Deschamps' Ballade to Chaucer." *Modern Language Notes* 33 (1918): 268–78.

Jurkowski, Maureen. "The Arrest of William Thorpe in Shrewsbury and the Anti-Lollard Statute of 1406." *Historical Research* 75 (2002): 273–95.

Justice, Steven. *Writing and Rebellion: England in 1381*. Berkeley: University of California Press, 1994.

Kaeuper, Richard W. *War, Justice, and Public Order: England and France in the Later Middle Ages*. Oxford: Clarendon, 1988.

Kemp, Barry John. *Ancient Egypt: Anatomy of a Civilization*. London: Routledge, 1989.

Kirk, Elizabeth D. "Langland's Plowman and the Recreation of Fourteenth-Century Religious Metaphor." *Yearbook of Langland Studies* 2 (1988): 1–21.

Kirk, G. S. and J. E. Raven. *The Presocratic Philosophers*. Cambridge: Cambridge University Press, 1957.

Knapp, Ethan. "Bureaucratic Identity and the Construction of the Self in Hoccleve's *Formulary* and *La male regle*." *Speculum* 74 (1999): 357–76.

————. "Eulogies and Usurpations: Hoccleve and Chaucer Revisited." *Studies in the Age of Chaucer* 21 (1999): 247–73.

Knapp, Peggy. *Chaucer and the Social Contest*. New York: Routledge, 1990.

Knight, Stephen. "Chaucer and the Sociology of Literature." *Studies in the Age of Chaucer* 2 (1980): 15–51.

————. *Geoffrey Chaucer*. Oxford: Blackwell, 1986.

Kuhl, Ernest P. "Chaucer and Aldgate." *PMLA* 39 (1924): 101–22.

Kuhl, Ernest P. "Chaucer and Westminster Abbey." *Journal of English and Germanic Philology* 45 (1946): 340–43.

———. "Chaucer the Patriot." *Philological Quarterly* 25 (1946): 277–80.

Lapidge, Michael. "Lucan's Imagery of Cosmic Dissolution." *Hermes* 107 (1979): 344–70.

Larson, Alfred. "The Payment of Fourteenth-Century English Envoys." *English Historical Review* 54 (1939): 403–14.

Latham, L. C. "Collection of the Wages of the Knights of the Shire in the Fourteenth and Fifteenth Centuries." *English Historical Review* 48 (1933): 455–64.

Lawton, David A. "Lollardy and the 'Piers Plowman' Tradition." *Modern Language Review* 76 (1981): 780–93.

———. "The Unity of Middle English Alliterative Poetry." *Speculum* 58 (1983): 72–94.

———. "Chaucer's Two Ways: The Pilgrimage Frame of *The Canterbury Tales*." *Studies in the Age of Chaucer* 9 (1987): 3–40.

———. "Dullness and the Fifteenth Century." *ELH* 54 (1987): 761–99.

———. "The Diversity of Middle English Alliterative Poetry." *Leeds Studies in English* 20 (1989): 143–72.

Leclercq, Jean. *Monks and Love in Twelfth-Century France*. Oxford: Clarendon, 1979.

Lenaghan, R. T. "Chaucer's *General Prologue* as History and Literature." *Comparative Studies in Society and History* 12 (1970): 73–82.

———. "Chaucer's *Envoy to Scogan*: The Uses of Literary Conventions." *Chaucer Review* 10 (1975): 46–61.

———. "Chaucer's Circle of Gentlemen and Clerks." *Chaucer Review* 18 (1983): 155–60.

Lerer, Seth. *Chaucer and His Readers: Imagining the Author in Late-Medieval England*. Princeton: Princeton University Press, 1993.

———. *Courtly Letters in the Age of Henry VIII: Literary Culture and the Arts of Deceit*. Cambridge: Cambridge University Press, 1997.

———. "William Caxton." In *The Cambridge History of Medieval English Literature*. Ed. David Wallace. Cambridge: Cambridge University Press, 1999. Pp. 720–38.

Lewis, Lucy. "Langland's Tree of Charity and Usk's Wexing Tree." *Notes & Queries* 240 (1995): 429–33.

———. "The Identity of Margaret in Thomas Usk's *Testament of Love*." *Medium Aevum* 68 (1999): 63–72.

Lewis, N. B. "Re-election to Parliament in the Reign of Richard II." *English Historical Review* 48 (1933): 364–94.

Leyerle, John. "The Heart and the Chain." In *The Learned and the Lewed: Studies in Chaucer and Medieval Literature*. Ed. Larry D. Benson. Cambridge: Harvard University Press, 1974. Pp. 113–45.

———. "The Rose-Wheel Design and Dante's *Paradiso*." *University of Toronto Quarterly* 46 (1977): 280–308.

Lindenbaum, Sheila. "The Smithfield Tournament of 1390." *Journal of Medieval and Renaissance Studies* 20 (1990): 1–20.

Loomis, Roger Sherman. *A Mirror of Chaucer's World*. Princeton: Princeton University Press, 1965.

Lowenthal, Leo. *Literature and the Image of Man: Sociological Studies of the European Drama and Novel, 1600–1900*. Boston: Beacon, 1957.

Lukács, Georg. *History and Class Consciousness: Studies in Marxist Dialectics*. 1967 edn. Trans. Rodney Livingstone. Cambridge: MIT Press, 1971.

MacAulay, G. C., ed. *The Complete Works of John Gower*. 4 vols. Oxford: Clarendon, 1899–1902.

McCall, John P. "The Trojan Scene in *Chaucer's Troilus*." *English Literary History* 29 (1962): 263–75.

——— and George Rudisill. "The Parliament of 1386 and Chaucer's Trojan Parliament." *Journal of English and Germanic Philology* 58 (1959): 276–88.

MacCracken, Henry Noble, ed. *The Minor Poems of John Lydgate*. 2 vols. EETS es 107 and os 192. London: Early English Text Society, 1911 and 1934.

McNiven, Peter. *Heresy and Politics in the Reign of Henry IV: The Burning of John Badby*. Woodbridge: Boydell, 1987.

Macherey, Pierre. *A Theory of Literary Production*. Trans. Geoffrey Wall. London: Routledge, 1978.

Manly, John Matthews. "Chaucer as Controller." *Modern Philology* 25 (1927): 123.

———. "Three Recent Chaucer Studies." *Review of English Studies* 10 (1934): 257–73.

Mann, Jill. *Chaucer and Medieval Estates Satire: The Literature of Social Classes and the General Prologue to the Canterbury Tales*. Cambridge: Cambridge University Press, 1973.

Mann, Michael. "State and Society, 1130–1815: An Analysis of English State Finances." *Political Power and Social Theory* 1 (1980): 165–208.

Marcuse, Herbert. *Eros and Civilization: A Philosophical Inquiry into Freud*. 2nd edn. Boston: Beacon, 1966.

———. *Negations: Essays in Critical Theory*. Trans. Jeremy J. Shapiro. Boston: Beacon, 1968.

———. *An Essay on Liberation*. Boston: Beacon, 1969.

———. "Repressive Tolerance." In Robert Paul Wolff, Barrington Moore, Jr, and Herbert Marcuse, *A Critique of Pure Tolerance*. 2nd edn. Boston: Beacon, 1969. Pp. 81–123.

———. *The Aesthetic Dimension: Toward a Critique of Marxist Aesthetics*. Trans. Herbert Marcuse and Erica Sherover. Boston: Beacon, 1978.

Marx, Karl. "Economic and Philosophical Manuscripts of 1844." In *Karl Marx Early Writings*. Ed. and trans. T. B. Bottomore. New York: McGraw-Hill, 1963. Pp. 61–219.

———. *Grundrisse: Foundations of the Critique of Political Economy (Rough Draft)*. Trans. Martin Nicholaus. Harmondsworth: Penguin, 1973.

———. *Capital Volume I: A Critical Analysis of Capitalist Production*. Moscow: Foreign Languages Publishing House, 1954.

——— and Frederick Engels. *Selected Correspondence*. Moscow: Foreign Languages Publishing House, n. d. [1955].

——— and ———. *Selected Works*. 3 vols. Moscow: Progress Publishers, 1969.

Matheson, Lister M. "Chaucer's Ancestry: Historical and Philological Re-Assessments." *Chaucer Review* 25 (1991): 171–89.

Medcalf, Stephen. "Transposition: Thomas Usk's *Testament of Love*." In *The Medieval Translator: The Theory and Practice of Translation in the Middle Ages.* Ed. Roger Ellis. Cambridge: Brewer, 1989. Pp. 181–95.

—— . "The World and Heart of Thomas Usk." In *Essays on Ricardian Literature in Honour of J. A. Burrow.* Ed. Alistair J. Minnis, Charlotte C. Morse, and Thorlac Turville-Petre. Oxford: Clarendon, 1997. Pp. 222–51.

Middleton, Anne. "The Idea of Public Poetry in the Reign of Richard II." *Speculum* 53 (1978): 94–114.

—— . "Chaucer's 'New Men' and the Good of Literature in the *Canterbury Tales*." In *Literature and Society: Selected Papers from the English Institute,* 1978. Ed. Edward W. Said. Baltimore: Johns Hopkins University Press, 1980. Pp. 15–56.

—— . "Thomas Usk's 'Perdurable Letters': The *Testament of Love* from Script to Print." *Studies in Bibliography* 51 (1998): 63–116.

Minnis, Alistair J., with V. J. Scattergood and J. J. Smith. *Oxford Guides to Chaucer: The Shorter Poems.* Oxford: Clarendon, 1995.

——, Charlotte C. Morse, and Thorlac Turville-Petre, eds, *Essays on Ricardian Literature in Honour of J. A. Burrow.* Oxford: Clarendon, 1997.

Moore, Samuel. "Studies in the Life-Records of Chaucer." *Anglia* 37 (1918): 1–26.

—— . "New Life-Records of Chaucer." *Modern Philology* 16 (1918): 49–52.

Morgan, D. A. L. "The House of Policy: The Political Role of the Late Plantagenet Household, 1422–1485." In *The English Court: From the Wars of the Roses to the Civil War.* Ed. David Starkey. London: Longman, 1987. Pp. 25–70.

Muscatine, Charles. *Poetry and Crisis in the Age of Chaucer.* Notre Dame: Notre Dame University Press, 1972.

Myers, A. R., ed. *English Historical Documents 1327–1485.* New York: Oxford University Press, 1969.

—— . "The Wealth of Richard Lyons." In *Essays in Medieval History Presented to Bertie Wilkinson.* Ed. T. A. Sandquist and M. R. Powicke. Toronto: University of Toronto Press, 1969. Pp. 301–329.

Nightingale, Pamela. "Capitalists, Crafts and Constitutional Change in Late Fourteenth-Century London." *Past & Present* 124 (1989): 3–35.

—— . "Knights and Merchants: Trade, Politics and the Gentry in Late Medieval England." *Past & Present* 169 (2000): 36–62.

Nissé, Ruth. " 'Oure Fadres Olde and Modres': Gender, Heresy, and Hoccleve's Literary Politics." *Studies in the Age of Chaucer* 21 (1999): 275–99.

Nolan, Maura. "The Art of History Writing: Lydgate's *Serpent of Division.*" *Speculum* 78 (2003): 99–127.

Olson, Glending. "Making and Poetry in the Age of Chaucer." *Comparative Literature* 31 (1979): 272–90.

—— . "Toward a Poetics of the Late Medieval Court Lyric." In *Vernacular Poetics in the Middle Ages.* Ed. Lois Ebin. Studies in Medieval Culture 16. Kalamazoo: Medieval Institute Publications, 1984. Pp. 227–48.

Ormrod, W. M. "The English Crown and the Customs, 1349–63." *Economic History Review,* 2nd ser., 40 (1987): 27–40.

—— . "The Peasants' Revolt and the Government of England." *Journal of British Studies* 29 (1990): 1–30.

Pace, George B. "Speght's Chaucer and Ms. Gg.4.27." *Studies in Bibliography* 21 (1968): 225–35.

———— and Alfred David, eds, *The Minor Poems Part One*. Variorum Edition of the Works of Geoffrey Chaucer 5. Norman: University of Oklahoma Press, 1982.

Palmer, J. J. N. "The Parliament of 1385 and the Constitutional Crisis of 1386." *Speculum* 46 (1971): 477–90.

Parr, Johnstone. "The Date and Revision of Chaucer's *Knight's Tale.*" *PMLA* 60 (1945): 307–24.

Patterson, Lee W. "Chaucerian Confession: Penitential Literature and the Pardoner." *Medievalia et Humanistica* n. s. 7 (1976): 153–73.

————. "The 'Parson's Tale' and the Quitting of the 'Canterbury Tales.' " *Traditio* 34 (1978): 331–80.

————. *Negotiating the Past: The Historical Understanding of Medieval Literature.* Madison: University of Wisconsin Press, 1987.

————. " 'No Man his Reson Herde:' Peasant Consciousness, Chaucer's Miller, and the Structure of the *Canterbury Tales.*" *South Atlantic Quarterly* 86 (1987): 457–95.

————, ed. *Literary Practice and Social Change in Britain, 1380–1530.* Berkeley: University of California Press, 1990.

————. *Chaucer and the Subject of History.* Madison: University of Wisconsin Press, 1991.

————. "Court Politics and the Invention of Literature: The Case of Sir John Clanvowe." *Culture and History 1350–1600.* Ed. David Aers. New York: Harvester Wheatsheaf, 1992. Pp. 7–41.

————. "Making Identities in Fifteenth-Century England: Henry V and John Lydgate." In *New Historical Literary Study: Essays on Reproducing Texts, Representing History.* Ed. Jeffrey N. Cox and Larry J. Reynolds. Princeton: Princeton University Press, 1993. Pp. 69–107.

————. " 'What is Me?': Self and Society in the Poetry of Thomas Hoccleve." *Studies in the Age of Chaucer* 23 (2001): 437–70.

Pearsall, Derek Albert. "The English Chaucerians." In *Chaucer and Chaucerians: Critical Studies in Middle English Literature.* Ed. D. S. Brewer. London: Nelson, 1966. Pp. 201–39.

————. *John Lydgate.* Charlottesville: University Press of Virginia, 1970.

————. *Old English and Middle English Poetry.* The Routledge History of English Poetry 1. London: Routledge, 1977.

————. "The Alliterative Revival: Origins and Social Backgrounds." In *Middle English Alliterative Poetry and its Literary Background.* Ed. David Lawton. Cambridge: Brewer, 1982. Pp. 34–53.

————. *The Life of Geoffrey Chaucer.* Oxford: Blackwell, 1992.

————. "Lydgate as Innovator." *Modern Language Quarterly* 53 (1992): 5–22.

————. "Hoccleve's *Regement of Princes*: The Poetics of Royal Self–Representation." *Speculum* 69 (1994): 386–410.

————. "Chaucer's Tomb: The Politics of Reburial." *Medium Aevum* 64 (1995): 51–73.

Pearsall, Derek Albert. "Pre-Empting Closure in 'The Canterbury Tales': Old End-
ings, New Beginnings." In *Essays on Ricardian Literature in Honour of J. A. Burrow*.
Ed. Alistair J. Minnis, Charlotte C. Morse, and Thorlac Turville-Petre. Oxford:
Clarendon, 1997. Pp. 23–38.

————. *John Lydgate (1371–1449): A Bio-bibliography*. English Literary Studies
Monograph Series 71. Victoria: University of Victoria, 1997.

Plotinus. *The Enneads*. Trans. Stephen MacKenna. Ed. John Dillon. Harmondsworth:
Penguin, 1991.

Postan, M. M. *The Medieval Economy and Society: An Economic History of Britain in the
Middle Ages*. London: Weidenfeld and Nicolson, 1972.

Power, Eileen. *The Wool Trade in English Medieval History Being the Ford Lectures*.
Oxford: Oxford University Press, 1941.

Putnam, Bertha Haven. "The Justices of Labourers in the Fourteenth Century."
English Historical Review 21 (1906): 517–38.

————. *The Enforcement of the Statutes of Labourers During the First Decade After the
Black Death*. Studies in History, Economics, and Public Law 32. New York:
Columbia University Press, 1908.

————. "The Transformation of the Keepers of the Peace into the Justices of the
Peace 1327–1380." *Transactions of the Royal Historical Society*, 4th ser., 12 (1929):
19–48.

————. *Proceedings before the Justices of the Peace in the Fourteenth and Fifteenth Centuries Edward III to Richard III*. Ames Foundation Series. London: Spottiswoode,
1938.

Richardson, H. G. "The Origins of Parliament." *Transactions of the Royal Historical
Society*, 4th ser., 11 (1928): 137–83.

————. "The Commons and Medieval Politics." *Transactions of the Royal Historical
Society*, 4th ser., 28 (1946): 21–45.

Richardson, H. G., and G. O. Sayles. *Parliaments and Great Councils in Medieval
England*. London: Stevens, 1961.

————. *The Governance of Mediaeval England from the Conquest to Magna Carta*.
Edinburgh: Edinburgh University Press, 1963.

Richardson, Malcolm. "Hoccleve in his Social Context." *Chaucer Review* 20 (1986):
313–22.

Rickert, Edith. "Was Chaucer a Student at the Inner Temple?" In *The Manly
Anniversary Studies in Language and Literature*. Chicago: University of Chicago
Press, 1923. Pp. 20–31.

————. "Extracts from a Fourteenth-Century Account Book." *Modern Philology*
24 (1926): 111–19 and 249–56.

Robbins, Rossell Hope. *Historical Poems of the XIVth and XVth Centuries*. New York:
Columbia University Press, 1959.

————. "The Vintner's Son: French Wine in English Bottles." In *Eleanor of
Aquitaine: Patron and Politician*. Ed. William W. Kibler. Austin: University of Texas
Press, 1976. Pp. 147–72.

————. "Geofroi Chaucier, Poète Français, Father of English Poetry." *Chaucer
Review* 13 (1978): 93–115.

Robertson, D. W., Jr. *A Preface to Chaucer*. Princeton: Princeton University Press, 1962.

Robertson, Stuart. "Elements of Realism in the *Knight's Tale*." *Journal of English and Germanic Philology* 14 (1915): 226–55.

Rogers, Alan. "Henry IV, the Commons and Taxation." *Mediaeval Studies* 31 (1969): 44–70.

Romaine, Suzanne. *Bilingualism*. 2nd edn. Oxford: Blackwell, 1995.

Roskell, John Smith. *The Commons and their Speakers in English Parliaments 1376–1523*. Manchester: Manchester University Press, 1965.

———, ed. *The House of Commons 1386–1421*. 4 vols. Stroud: Sutton, 1992.

Rothwell, W. "The Trilingual England of Geoffrey Chaucer." *Studies in the Age of Chaucer 16* (1994): 45–67.

Rundle, David. " 'Not So Much Praise as Precept': Erasmus, Panegyric, and the Renaissance Art of Teaching Princes." In *Pedagogy and Power: Rhetorics of Classical Learning*. Ed. Yun Lee Too and Niall Livingstone. Cambridge: Cambridge University Press, 1998. Pp. 148–69.

Russell, Josiah Cox. *British Medieval Population*. Albuquerque: University of New Mexico Press, 1948.

———. "Effects of Pestilence and Plague, 1315–1385." *Comparative Studies in Society and History* 8 (1966): 464–73.

Russell, J. Stephen. "Is London Burning?: A Chaucerian Allusion to the Rising of 1381." *Chaucer Review* 30 (1995): 107–09.

Ruud, Martin Bronn. *Thomas Chaucer*. Minneapolis: University of Minnesota Press, 1926.

Salter, Elizabeth. "*Piers Plowman* and 'The Simonie.' " *Archiv für das Studium der neueren Sprachen und Literaturen* 203 (1967): 241–54.

Sanderlin, George. "Usk's *Testament of Love* and St Anselm." *Speculum* 17 (1942): 69–73.

Sanderlin, S. "Chaucer and Ricardian Politics." *Chaucer Review* 22 (1988): 171–84.

Saul, Nigel. "Richard II and Westminster Abbey." In *The Cloister and the World: Essays in Medieval History in Honour of Barbara Harvey*. Ed. John Blair and Brian Golding. Oxford: Clarendon, 1996. Pp. 196–218.

———. *Richard II*. New Haven: Yale University Press, 1997.

Sayles, G. O. *The King's Parliament of England*. New York: Norton, 1974.

———. *The Functions of the Medieval Parliament of England*. London: Hambledon, 1988.

Scanlon, Larry. "The King's Two Voices: Narrative and Power in Hoccleve's *Regement of Princes*." In *Literary Practice and Social Change in Britain, 1380–1530*. Ed. Lee Patterson. Berkeley: University of California Press, 1990. Pp. 216–47.

———. *Narrative, Authority, and Power: The Medieval Exemplum and the Chaucerian Tradition*. Cambridge Studies in Medieval Literature 20. Cambridge: Cambridge University Press, 1994.

Scattergood, John. "The Authorship of *The Boke of Cupide*." *Anglia* 82 (1964): 137–49.

———, ed. *The Works of Sir John Clanvowe*. Cambridge: Brewer, 1975.

———. " 'Patience' and Authority." In *Essays on Ricardian Literature in Honour of J. A. Burrow*. Ed. Alistair J. Minnis, Charlotte C. Morse, and Thorlac Turville-Petre. Oxford: Clarendon, 1997. Pp. 295–315.

Schmidt, A. V. C., ed. William Langland, *The Vision of Piers Plowman: A Critical Edition of the B-Text based on Trinity College Cambridge MS B.15.17.* 2nd edn. London: Dent, 1995.

Scott, Florence R. "Chaucer and the Parliament of 1386." *Speculum* 18 (1943): 80–86.

Selby, Walford D. "The Robberies of Chaucer by Richard Brerelay and Others at Westminster, and at Hatcham, Surrey, on Tuesday, Sept. 6, 1390." In *Life-Records of Chaucer*, 1, Chaucer Society Second Series 12. London: Trübner, 1875.

Seymour, M. C. "The Manuscripts of Hoccleve's *Regiment of Princes*." *Edinburgh Bibliographical Society Transactions* 4 (1974): 255–97.

————. *Selections from Hoccleve*. Oxford: Clarendon, 1981.

Shawver, Gary W., ed. *Thomas Usk: Testament of Love Based on the Edition of John F. Leyerle*. Toronto Medieval Texts and Translations 13. Toronto: University of Toronto Press, 2002.

Sherborne, J. W. "The Costs of English Warfare with France in the Late Fourteenth Century." *Bulletin of the Institute of Historical Research* 50 (1977): 135–50.

Shoaf, R. Allen, ed., *Thomas Usk: The Testament of Love*. METS. Kalamazoo: Medieval Institute Publications, 1998.

Sillem, Rosamond. "Commissions of the Peace, 1380–1485." *Bulletin of the Institute of Historical Research* 10 (1932): 81–104.

Simpson, James. "The Constraints of Satire in 'Piers Plowman' and 'Mum and the Sothsegger.' " In *Langland, the Mystics and the Medieval English Religious Tradition*. Ed. Helen Phillips. Cambridge: Brewer, 1990a. Pp. 11–30.

————. *Piers Plowman: An Introduction to the B-text*. London: Longman, 1990b.

————. " 'Dysemol Daies and Fatal Houres': Lydgate's *Destruction of Thebes* and Chaucer's *Knight's Tale*." In *The Long Fifteenth Century: Essays for Douglas Grey*. Ed. Helen Cooper and Sally Mapstone. Oxford: Clarendon, 1997. Pp. 15–33.

————. "Breaking the Vacuum: Ricardian and Henrician Ovidianism." *Journal of Medieval and Early Modern Studies* 29 (1999): 325–55.

Skeat, Walter W. *Chaucerian and Other Pieces, Being a Supplement to the Complete Works of Geoffrey Chaucer (Oxford, in Six Volumes, 1894)*. Oxford: Oxford University Press, 1897.

Somerset, Fiona. "Vernacular Argumentation in *The Testimony of William Thorpe*." *Mediaeval Studies* 58 (1996): 207–41.

————. *Clerical Discourse and Lay Audience in Late Medieval England*. Cambridge Studies in Medieval Literature 37. Cambridge: Cambridge University Press, 1998.

Spearing, A. C., ed. *The Knight's Tale from the Canterbury Tales by Geoffrey Chaucer*. Cambridge: Cambridge University Press, 1966.

————. *Medieval to Renaissance in English Poetry*. Cambridge: Cambridge University Press, 1985.

Spurgeon, Caroline F. E. *Five Hundred Years of Chaucer Criticism and Allusion 1357–1900*. 3 vols. 1925; repr. New York: Russell & Russell, 1960.

Steel, Anthony Bedford. "English Government Finance, 1377–1413." *English Historical Review* 51 (1936): 29–51 and 577–97.

————. *The Receipt of the Exchequer, 1377–1485*. Cambridge: Cambridge University Press, 1954.

Stillwell, Gardiner. "Chaucer's Plowman and the Contemporary English Peasant." *English Literary History* 6 (1939): 285–90.

————. "John Gower and the Last Years of Edward III." *Studies in Philology* 45 (1948): 454–71.

Strohm, Paul. "Chaucer's Audience." *Literature & History* 5 (1977): 26–41.

————. "Form and Social Statement in *Confessio Amantis* and *The Canterbury Tales*." *Studies in the Age of Chaucer* 1 (1979): 17–40.

————. "Chaucer's Fifteenth-Century Audience and the Narrowing of the 'Chaucer Tradition.'" *Studies in the Age of Chaucer* 4 (1982): 3–32.

————. "Fourteenth- and Fifteenth-Century Writers as Readers of Chaucer." In *Genres, Themes, and Images in English Literature from the Fourteenth to the Fifteenth Century: The J. A. W. Bennett Memorial Lectures, Perugia, 1986.* Ed. Piero Boitani and Anna Torti. Tübingen: Narr, 1988. Pp. 90–104.

————. *Social Chaucer.* Cambridge: Harvard University Press, 1989.

————. "Politics and Poetics: Usk and Chaucer in the 1380s." In *Literary Practice and Social Change in Britain, 1380–1530.* Ed. Lee Patterson. Berkeley: University of California Press, 1990. Pp. 83–112.

————. *Hochon's Arrow: The Social Imagination of Fourteenth-Century Texts.* Princeton: Princeton University Press, 1992.

————. "Saving the Appearances: Chaucer's Purse and the Fabrication of the Lancastrian Claim." In *Chaucer's England: Literature in Historical Perspective.* Ed. Barbara A. Hanawalt. Minneapolis: University of Minnesota Press, 1992. Pp. 21–40.

————. "Chaucer's Lollard Joke: History and the Textual Unconscious." *Studies in the Age of Chaucer* 17 (1995): 23–42.

————. *England's Empty Throne: Usurpation and the Language of Legitimation, 1399–1422.* New Haven: Yale University Press, 1998.

————. "Hoccleve, Lydgate, and the Lancastrian Court." In *The Cambridge History of Medieval English Literature.* Ed. David Wallace. Cambridge: Cambridge University Press, 1999. Pp. 640–61.

————. *Theory and the Premodern Text.* Minneapolis: University of Minnesota Press, 2000.

Summers, Joanna. "Gower's *Vox Clamantis* and Usk's *Testament of Love*." *Medium Aevum* 68 (1999): 55–62.

Tatlock, John S. P. *The Development and Chronology of Chaucer's Works.* 1907; repr. Gloucester: Peter Smith, 1963.

————. "The *Canterbury Tales* in 1400." *PMLA* 50 (1935): 100–39.

Taylor, Robert A., James F. Burke, Patricia J. Eberle, Ian Lancashire, and Brian S. Merrilees, eds, *The Centre and its Compass: Studies in Medieval Literature in Honor of Professor John Leyerle.* Studies in Medieval Culture 33. Kalamazoo: Medieval Institute Publications, 1993.

Therborn, Göran. *The Ideology of Power and the Power of Ideology.* 1980; repr. London: Verso, 1999.

Thompson, Edward Maunde, ed., *Chronicon Angliae.* Rolls Series 64. London: Longman, 1874.

Thompson, E. P. *Whigs and Hunters: The Origin of the Black Act.* London: Allen Lane, 1975.

Thorpe, William. "Thorpe's Examination." Ed. Anne Hudson. In *Two Wycliffite Texts*. EETS os 301. Oxford: Oxford University Press, 1993.

Travis, Peter W. "Chaucer's Trivial Fox Chase and the Peasant's Revolt of 1381." *Journal of Medieval and Renaissance Studies* 18 (1988): 195–220.

Wallace, David. *Chaucerian Polity: Absolutist Lineages and Associational Forms in England and Italy*. Stanford: Stanford University Press, 1997.

————, ed. *The Cambridge History of Medieval English Literature*. Cambridge: Cambridge University Press, 1999.

Wardhaugh, Ronald. *Languages in Competition: Dominance, Diversity, and Decline*. Oxford: Blackwell, 1987.

Watson, Nicholas. "Censorship and Cultural Change in Late-Medieval England: Vernacular Theology, the Oxford Translation Debate, and Arundel's Constitutions of 1409." *Speculum* 70 (1995): 822–64.

————. "The *Gawain*-Poet as a Vernacular Theologian." In *A Companion to the Gawain-Poet*. Ed. Derek Brewer and Jonathan Gibson. Cambridge: Brewer, 1997. Pp. 293–313.

————. "The Politics of Middle English Writing." In *The Idea of the Vernacular: An Anthology of Middle English Literary Theory, 1280–1520*. Ed. Jocelyn Wogan-Browne, Nicholas Watson, Andrew Taylor, and Ruth Evans. University Park: Pennsylvania State University Press, 1999. Pp. 331–52.

Wawn, Andrew. "Truth-Telling and the Tradition of *Mum and the Sothsegger*." *Yearbook of English Studies* 13 (1983): 270–87.

Weiss, Roberto. "The Study of Greek in England during the Fourteenth Century." *Rinascimento* 2 (1951): 209–39.

Wheeler, Bonnie. "Dante, Chaucer, and the Ending of *Troilus and Criseyde*." *Philological Quarterly* 61 (1982): 105–23.

Williams, Raymond. "Base and Superstructure in Marxist Cultural Theory." *New Left Review* 82 (1973): 3–16.

————. *Marxism and Literature*. Oxford: Oxford University Press, 1977.

Wimsatt, James I. "The *Dit dou bleu chevalier*: Froissart's Imitation of Chaucer." *Mediaeval Studies* 34 (1972): 388–400.

————. *Chaucer and the Poems of "Ch" in University of Pennsylvania MS French 15*. Chaucer Studies 9. Cambridge: Brewer, 1982.

————. *Chaucer and his French Contemporaries: Natural Music in the Fourteenth Century*. Toronto: University of Toronto Press, 1991.

Windeatt, Barry A. *Chaucer's Dream Poetry: Sources and Analogues*. Chaucer Studies 7. Cambridge: Brewer, 1982.

————. *Oxford Guides to Chaucer: Troilus and Criseyde*. Oxford: Clarendon, 1992.

Wood, Ellen Meiksins. "Capitalism, Merchants and Bourgeois Revolution: Reflections on the Brenner Debate and its Sequel." *International Review of Social History* 41 (1996): 209–32.

————. *The Origin of Capitalism: A Longer View*. 2nd edn. London: Verso, 2002.

Wright, Thomas. *Political Poems and Songs Relating to English History Composed During the Period from the Accession of EDW. III to that of RIC. III*. Rolls Series 14. 2 vols. London: Longman, 1859–1861.

INDEX

LaVergne, TN USA
06 October 2009
159940LV00002B/4/P